BEATING
THE
BOOKS

BEATING THE BOOKS

WINNING ALWAYS
EXACTS A COST

MIKE SCOTT

NAVY
YARD
PRESS

979-8-9940099-0-1 Paperback
979-8-9940099-1-8 Hardcover
979-8-9940099-2-5 Laminate
979-8-9940099-3-2 eBook

This is a work of fiction. Names, characters, businesses, places, events, and incidents are either products of the author's imagination or are used fictitiously. Any resemblance to actual persons, living or dead, or to actual events is purely coincidental. Characters are fictionalized composites and are not based on any single individual. References to real companies, brands, or locations are used fictitiously and are not intended to imply sponsorship, endorsement, or affiliation.

Book design by Mark Karis

Published by Navy Yard Press

First edition, 2026

Printed on demand worldwide

Certain names, logos, and trademarks referenced in this book are the property of their respective owners and are used for descriptive purposes only.

FOR MY GIRLS. *Beware the illusions that only pretend to glow. Seek love, chase curiosity, and let wonder guide you always.*

CONTENTS

Prologue: Seventy-Eight Percent 1

1   Impact 6
2   Appetizer 15
3   Edge 23
4   The Oracle 30
5   First Hit 40
6   The Founder 49
7   Return on Investment 55
8   Perfect Cover 58
9   What You Can't Unsee 66
10 Unwrapped 70
11 Face of the Rebellion 77
12 Countdown 80
13 Invitation Only 94
14 Open Rate 99
15 The Executive 109
16 Capped 114
17 New Players 122
18 Screen Time 127
19 Crockpots 134

20	Fleeting Flame	139
21	Madness	150
22	Boat to Nowhere	157
23	Summer's Shadow	165
24	Missed Connections	174
25	Hard Eight	183
26	Final Housekeeping	195
27	The Stage	201
28	Aftermath	206
29	Bacchanal	214
30	Fear Premium	221
31	Workaround	230
32	Contagion	239
33	The Comfort of Maybe	243
34	Distance Without Danger	250
35	1:54	257
36	Peace	264
37	Nothing Left to Refresh	272
38	Containment	282
39	The Long Game	289
40	Presence	301
41	Weighted Coin	314
Acknowledgements		322
About the Author		326
Additional Resources		327

"Money often costs too much."
−RALPH WALDO EMERSON

PROLOGUE

SEVENTY-EIGHT PERCENT

TWENTY MONTHS OF MICRODOSING adrenaline had rewired his brain's Pavlovian response. When he first parked there on that simmering, listless June night, the faint buzzing from neon lights—or at least the ones whose innards hadn't fallen victim to time and neglect—soothed him, inviting him to take a rest from the stresses of everyday life.

But with each upward swipe of his right thumb, each tap of the inviting green icon, each pupil-dilating nanosecond awaiting the confirmation screen, the electric drone had evolved into an anthem of ecstasy—a psychological chorus of *cha-chings* that once marked booming businesses in the days of physical cash registers.

He used to tell himself it wasn't gambling. But this was different. Now he was all in. No hedge. No guarantees. Just blind faith and passive prayers.

At first glance, one wouldn't associate Cielo Verde with prosperity. A typical Mexican hole-in-the-wall restaurant, as colorful and flavorful as it was unprofitable, its endless chips and salsa mirrored the endless hours its first-generation American owners invested.

As he sat in the driver's seat, still tightly restrained to the Tesla's sleek leather, he couldn't help but wonder how the proprietors would feel if they knew he had made more while sitting in one of the fourteen spaces of their dimly lit parking lot than their restaurant had profited in the last two years combined.

To him, the nature of the business was irrelevant. A Mexican dive, a

Michelin-star Italian osteria, a drive-through fast-food behemoth—hell, even a chiropractor's office—it didn't matter. This address had only one thing of value. It was situated on the northeast side of Eastern Avenue NE, officially in the state of Maryland.

From the time his seat belt clicked in the driveway of his Washington, DC home to when he crossed under the brick arch that adorned the entryway to the parking lot, a mere six minutes passed. That six minutes had once transported him from the bureaucratic overregulation of the nation's capital to the lawless freedom of Maryland, the Free State, as if named precisely for this. Since November 2022, mobile sports betting had been live there.

For months, though, the trip had been an unnecessary, ritualistic pilgrimage. DC had unencumbered itself of the illegality that had necessitated this journey in the past, but old habits died hard, especially for those who wear superstition like armor.

Despite the familiarity of his surroundings, tonight was unlike any visit he had made before. Tonight, his heart beat like a war drum. He pulled back the sleeve of his faded Ohio State hoodie enough to expose the Apple Watch affixed to his left wrist. How many times had he made this exact movement, prompted by the siren song of guaranteed profit?

There had been no vibration to provoke this particular check-in, however. Instead, he pressed the watch's wheel, bringing the device to life, revealing a sea of endless apps.

Red with a heart. He tapped.

"Current Heart Rate: 107 BPM," it flatly told him, devoid of any emotion.

Numbers had become more commonplace to him than letters. Despite knowing he far exceeded his usual resting heart rate of fifty-two beats per minute, he found comfort in the knowledge that numbers once again were unassailably reliable.

He turned his attention to the Tesla's massive dashboard screen, twice the size of the iPad in his lap. It was twenty-four degrees outside, probably colder with the windchill.

Buzz.

His watch beckoned.

Dammit, didn't I turn them off?

Tonight was too important to be distracted.

He held the phone within view of his face. Access granted. He swiped down from the top. Funny how Apple changed Silent mode to Focus. That was exactly what he needed. It was time to focus.

Absent the impenetrable glass screen, the gradient green icon would be worn from the number of instances his index finger had touched that exact spot. He noticed, seemingly for the first time, that the design took the shape of a shield.

Defenders, he thought. *Clever. Assuage the fear of risk with an image of protection, of safety. Little did users know the only thing being protected were exorbitant profits.*

Sweat beaded above his temples. He glanced at his watch. "123 BPM." Climbing. Every sense felt heightened.

How twisted, he mused, *to feel most alive on death's doorstep.*

There was no need to search for what he needed. Kickoff was a mere forty-five minutes away. Celebrities and business executives mingled in suites a thousand miles south, down in New Orleans. Titans of industry reaping the benefits of their riches, buying proximity to the influencers of the age.

Every stadium outside the Caesars Superdome was dark tonight. The Super Bowl monopolized the imaginations of sports fans and cultural vultures alike.

The app featured a single event:

SUPER BOWL LXI
CLEVELAND BROWNS +350

He had done his homework. These were the best odds available.

The floorboard was all that sat between him and a hastily painted "#1" on the pavement below, his lucky parking spot. Yes, it was adjacent to the restaurant's overworked, untended dumpster. Sure, the paint was so faded that only a seasoned customer would even know there had once been a numbering system bringing order to this car kingdom. Of course, he knew luck was a fallacy, a figment of fiction to which numbers never bent. But this singular bet was too important. He had cast aside logic and was operating solely from emotion.

"$250,000," he typed in the Wager box next to the pre-populated dollar sign.

Red letters appeared above. He was expecting this.

"Max Wager: $224,999."

It was a higher limit than he had expected. He knew the Super Bowl was his chance to go big, but this was more leash than he had anticipated. Faceoff, those who wielded the shield, had allowed him to raise the stakes.

Were the gambling gods smiling upon him favorably, or were they gathering their bolts, preparing a final, fatal blow? It was impossible to know what it foretold.

His curiosity ran as deep as his conviction.

The once-hypnotic chorus of the neon's ancient transformers suddenly intensified to a deafening crackle, consuming his skull.

"To Win: $787,496.50," it read before he moved his thumb, glistening now, to its requisite position above the glowing screen.

He let gravity have its way. His thumb dropped. Eyes widened. The confirmation appeared.

And with that, he knew in five hours he would have $1,012,500 in his account...or nothing.

Satisfied with his action, like a coach who had called in the final play of the game, he closed his eyes, drew a breath, and whispered to no one in particular, "It's in Cleveland's hands now."

As he exhaled, his right hand slipped into the pouch sewn to the front of his hoodie. The cold metal offered relief from the stifling heat that had built inside the car, grounding yet terrifying. He gripped the handle and let his fingers migrate carefully to the barrel's tip.

There were no other cars in the lot. The restaurant was dark. He was alone on this odyssey. No one to cheer him on or pull him back.

He slid the gun deeper into the fabric, tucking it entirely out of sight. Almost without thinking, he did the math. Seventy-eight percent chance he'd reach for it again before the night was over.

1

IMPACT

CHASE DUPREE SLID OPEN THE BOTTOM FREEZER drawer like a poker player rechecking a losing hand, trying futilely to imbue hope into a hopeless situation. He felt equal parts pride and self-loathing that after all these years he still believed he could conjure a new outcome into existence despite the innate certitude that the odds were against him.

Cold air spilled out around his bare feet as he reached for the warped blue ice pack in the back, wedged next to a frostbitten bag of shrimp. The frozen compress fit right in—crusted over with faint white crystals, edges stiff after its repeated cycle of thawing and freezing.

He returned to the couch, placed the pack at the base of his neck, and winced. The incessant, aching pain gave way to the icy chill.

Trading one type of pain for another before the Sisyphean routine starts anew, Chase thought. He let the metaphor go. No energy for poetry.

Outside the window of his Navy Yard apartment, summer moved on without him. Nationals baseball fans, and an unsettling number of those insufferable visiting Phillies fans, streamed toward the stadium a few blocks away. Boats drifted under the Frederick Douglass Memorial Bridge, floating through the river's no-wake zone en route to the mighty Potomac. Horns blared as ever-shortening tempers met ever-more-congested streets. Inside, it was only him, the hum of an overworked air conditioner, and two shrieking little girls making a customized jungle gym out of the living room furniture.

Cecilia, five, better known as Cece, was balancing a stuffed giraffe on an impressively stable tower of magnetic tiles, while Savannah, three, was spinning in a trademark pink-princess tutu, light brown hair flying in all directions, confidently belting out a song she was making up in real time. She was somehow both horribly off-key and completely euphoric. Chase smiled.

He knew he should have been more present, should have been marveling at their creativity, filming a snippet for his wife to watch later, maybe even joining in the fun as an architect or songwriter himself, but his body had different plans. This was one of the bad days. He let himself sink back gradually. Every inch he descended brought a new signal of protest from his spine—tightness in the neck, heat across the traps, a firestorm beneath the shoulder blade.

"Dammit," Chase whispered, quiet enough to protect Cece's rapidly growing vocabulary, loud enough to register his frustration with the heavens.

Once he reached a tolerable position, he scrolled through Netflix until he landed on a sports documentary, one of those predictably feel-good chronicles where you knew before it started that the protagonist stared down defeat but overcame it in epic fashion in the end. Failure, grit, redemption, glory. Athletes at the peak of human performance, breaking records, beating the odds.

Muscle memory prompted his thumb to find the play button, but Chase wasn't really watching. His eyes might have been on the screen, but his mind was drifting, and like a projector flickering to life with an old family home movie, he was slipping backward in time to a different version of himself. Before marriage. Before the girls. Before this building even existed. Before the aching that never fully left.

* * *

It was nearly fifteen years earlier, the spring of 2011. Chase had been in the city less than four months.

Twenty-three, newly arrived in Washington, a fresh bachelor's degree and entry-level sales job to his name and giddy with that blend of awe and optimism unique to twenty-something transplants. Everything felt possible. The monuments, the ambition, the tactile sense of history and politics in the air, it all vibrated with promise and opportunity few cities around the globe could replicate.

He may have been crashing on a friend's couch in an apartment located in a rather seedy part of Chinatown, but who cared? He wouldn't have traded it for a mansion back in his home state of Ohio.

The frigid DC winter was reluctantly preparing to loosen its vise-like hold on the city, and on that day those who had braved the cold months were rewarded with a rare March reprieve. The sun gifted its warmth, and Chase seized the chance to properly explore his new stomping grounds for the first time.

After a day of sightseeing with some friends who had earned the distinction of "locals," having been in DC an entire nine months longer than Chase, someone suggested a nighttime bike ride around the monuments. Chase had brought precious little with him from the Midwest, but his beloved road bike was a necessity, and he was ecstatic to put it to use on the paths of the nation's capital.

They met at the Washington Monument as the sky turned various hues of pink and blue and the streetlights blinked awake. Without an agenda, they glided past the WWII Memorial and along the Reflecting Pool, before stopping at the base of the Lincoln Memorial for a requisite selfie. From there, they curved down toward the narrow paths of the Tidal Basin.

With the famed cherry blossom trees already in Stage Three, Chase knew these very footpaths would be unnavigable even by foot in a matter of weeks, and he had every intention of returning to play tourist when the peak bloom arrived.

The other three cyclists in the group had gone ahead, leaving Chase and his thoughts to bring up the rear. He coasted along as the others surged forward, their laughter fading into the distance. The Jefferson Memorial shone across the water, looking ghostly in the moonlight, its reflection below a twin apparition.

He felt that calm that came when the world reminded you how fortunate you were to be in it. He took it all in, hardly able to comprehend this was his new life, the awe of it all momentarily eclipsing everything else.

CRACK.

Instantaneous pain for a millisecond, before everything went black.

* * *

When he came to, Chase was lying on his side. Cold cement pressed against his cheek. A moment of uncertainty. His eyes haltingly came into focus on a bike, several feet away, crumpled in the shadows—damaged but functional, like him. *What the hell happened? How long have I been here?*

Gingerly, he began to take inventory. His head throbbed. Blood—or maybe tree sap—was smeared on his shoulder. He tried to sit up, but a pain in his lower neck roared to life, white-hot and unforgiving. He touched the top of his helmet and found it dented. He removed it with extra care, running his hands up and down each side of his face and through his hair. Dry. Intact. Seemingly no structural damage. Thank God.

As he blinked and became more aware of his surroundings, he first saw the railing, inches from where he was sitting, and a chilling realization, having nothing to do with the plummeting night temperatures, entered his mind.

I bounced off that railing. If it hadn't been there, my bike and I would be in that Tidal Basin, unconscious, sinking, he thought, muscles stiffening even more than they already had.

His gaze drifted back the direction from which he had been riding, and there, barely visible in the darkness between two streetlights, he saw the branch. Thick. Gnarled. Low-hanging. Camouflaged in a murky gloom. As he staggered to his feet and inched his way closer, his theory was confirmed as the light from his phone illuminated an oozing gash in the trunk's bark, as though the tree itself was the one bleeding. It too had been wounded in the unexpected exchange.

The most unnerving part wasn't the immediate pain or the disorientation that accompanied the likely concussion. It was the unmistakable feeling that something inside him had shifted. Something that wouldn't heal soon, if ever.

Over the years, the premonition proved correct. The pain would come and go like a stubborn debt collector, its presence ever threatening, mentally all-consuming. An innocuous movement—looking down at a text, a quick turn of the head backing out of a parking spot—could trigger an upper-body shutdown. First, a sharp twinge in the neck. Then a burning tightness across the back. Finally, all muscles from the shoulder blades north would be rendered useless, outside of their united ability to inflict intense pain.

At first, the spasms came once a year for a week at a time. *The price of a careless accident,* he would tell himself. Then they came twice a year. Then more. The recoveries grew longer. The time between episodes grew shorter. Doctors were baffled. "Soft tissue trauma," they said. "Muscle imbalances." "Rest." "Try yoga." "Buy an ergonomic chair."

Chase had tried it all—physical therapy, chiropractor, neurologist, natural anti-inflammatories, even acupuncture. Thankfully, insurance afforded him these medical luxuries. Some things dulled the edge. Nothing fixed it.

And since becoming a father, it started to feel like every time he lifted Savannah off the ground or bent to find Cece hiding under the bed, his body filed a complaint.

This most recent episode was bad, the worst yet. He was thirty-eight now. Most mornings, his neck felt like it belonged to someone forty years older. He couldn't remember the last time he'd woken up without stiffness or gone to bed without thirty minutes of targeted stretches, fearful tonight would yield another spasm and reset the recovery clock.

Healing required time, money, and the ability to commit to a plan, all things that were a luxury to him. Between fatherhood, a demanding job, marriage, errands, night after night of interrupted sleep, and the chronic stress it all brought, there simply wasn't enough margin left to truly recover. He got by with a patchwork of physical therapy exercises, ice packs, and over-the-counter ibuprofen while pretending everything was fine. But beneath the surface, the body had no room to breathe, and it exacerbated everything.

At least he had finally scheduled an MRI of his neck for next month, something he should have done ten years ago. But like everything, it had gotten pushed behind professional ambition, bills, diapers, and what always seemed to be more important deadlines.

The sound of Savannah's giggle brought Chase back to the present. She was at his feet, pulling on one of his socks, laughing more hysterically as it detached from his foot.

The documentary on the TV showed an athlete undergoing rehab, a tennis player Chase didn't recognize. For an instant, he allowed himself to entertain an alternate life, one in which he had chosen to leverage his high school state championship to play collegiate-level tennis, and where he had made a name for himself on the ATP Tour with access to the top doctors in the sports world.

He watched the therapist dig her elbow into the player's back like she was chiseling stone.

If only. If only there were room in the budget for the massages they'd all recommended. If only self-care weren't some luxury but a reliable part of life. Maybe then I could get this neck under control again.

Then came the voices.

"Daddy! We're hungry!"

He blinked.

Cece stood in front of him, hands on her hips and an absurdly serious expression plastered on her face, her eyes the color of a storm over open water, carrying an intensity beyond her years. Savannah peeked out from behind her, knowing she would undoubtedly benefit from her big sister's imploring.

"It's lunchtime!" Cece continued with resolve.

Chase grinned. "Mac and cheese?"

"And applesauce!" she shouted.

"Sam-wich!" Savannah added, holding up four fingers like she was placing a formal order.

He smiled. "Alright, alright." Standing up warily, he rolled the ice pack off his neck and set it aside. His short dark hair was still messy from the morning, tired hazel eyes blinking against the lingering ache. He had the kind of lean build former athletes carried into adulthood—strength that never fully disappeared, even if he hadn't trained like that in years.

A small jolt electrified his upper trap. It was mercifully short-lived but a staunch reminder of his psychological master nonetheless.

The girls didn't seem to notice, at least not this time. Chase had felt a pang of sadness the first time Cece yelled at Savannah, "Don't jump on Daddy! You'll hurt his neck!" Despite his best efforts, they were starting to see their father as someone with a chronic injury, one that they, in their young age, needed to avoid aggravating if they wanted to get the best version of their dad.

He made his way to the kitchen, pulling open cabinets and turning the stove knob with a practiced rhythm. Mac and cheese—the shells, not the long noodles. PB&Js with the crusts cut off. Apple and peach slices, if he was feeling ambitious.

The girls buzzed around the living room, arguing over whether jaguars could be queens. Chase distracted himself with the task at hand—boiling water, spreading peanut butter, prepping plates equitably.

He wanted to revel in this life he had built—the steady job, the beautiful wife, the two loving kids, and the apartment in a dream neighborhood.

But the truth was more nuanced. He felt a sense of being trapped. Of inertia in the wrong direction. Of time slipping away while his body slowly betrayed him. He didn't say it out loud—or even to himself, if he could help it—but the way this pain was affecting his life wasn't sustainable. Something had to change.

Later that night, after bedtime stories and the thirteenth "one more sip of water," Chase returned to the couch. The dishes were done. The apartment was in an unusual state of quiet.

He sank back into the familiar cushions once again and reached for his phone to see what from the outside world he had missed today. There was a string of texts on a thread including Tara, his wife who was traveling for work at the time, her college friend Julia Wexford, and Julia's husband Blaine.

Several years younger, Julia and Blaine had a single child of their own. In the pre-parenthood years, Chase had actually officiated their wedding. Amidst the demands of their current stage of life, they didn't see each other nearly enough.

It started with a text from Julia.

JULIA: You two free next Friday? There's a new place on 14th we want to take you. The food's supposed to be incredible.

Tara had already responded earlier.

TARA: Let me work our babysitter Rolodex! Tentatively count us in!

Par for the course. These days, Tara ran Chase's social life, on top of the otherwise impressive load she already carried. Wherever she told him to be, that was where he'd go. Honestly, he appreciated it. It saved him the effort of having to source his own occasional outings.

At the very bottom of the thread, Blaine chimed in.

BLAINE: Chase, I've been crushing it with a side hustle I know you're going to want to hear about...

Blaine had always walked a strange line—half methodical bureaucrat, half mad scientist. Whatever he was into now, Chase had no doubt it was mathematical...and probably bordering on the edges of legality.

Over many a drink with his buddy, Chase had confided that he wished he had the gumption to take on a side hustle, so admittedly he was curious to hear what Blaine was teasing so enticingly.

Chase added a like emoji to the message before reaching for the remote. The documentary had ended, and Netflix was serving up suggestions for his next mindless watch. None of them felt right.

He killed the TV and sat there, watching his own face stare back from the darkened screen, waiting for something, anything, to pull him out of the rut his life had become.

2

APPETIZER

"WAIT, is it the one right between Barcelona and Le Dip?" Tara called from the bathroom, mascara brush in hand.

"Yeah," Chase replied, struggling to button the front of his new linen shirt. "I think it's called Hot Fireplace or something."

"Hearth & Ember!" she playfully recited from the Google results on the screen. "You are such an old man!"

She set the phone on the bedside table and smoothed the front of her dress. "Do you realize this is the first time in months we won't have to ask for a kid's menu?"

Chase grinned. "I plan to order chicken tenders, just to keep the streak alive."

She rolled her eyes and grabbed her heels from the closet. "Remind me to Venmo the sitter later. She's going to be able to retire if we come home a minute after 10 p.m."

Chase, however, had stopped listening. Tara's dress—elegant, flattering, and snug in all the right places—had stolen his focus.

Her brunette hair fell around blue-green eyes, the small constellation of freckles across her nose giving her that blend of cute and stunning he'd never learned to look away from. Still as athletic as the day they met in college two decades ago, she carried the same confident beauty he'd first fallen for.

He gave her a once-over and dramatically raised his eyebrows. "I forgot what you look like when you aren't wearing oversized sweatshirts covered in yogurt."

"There's a reason we have two mini-yous, mister," she shot back, with a mischievous smile.

He smiled, savoring the flirty banter that used to be their norm before life got loud, fast, and full of tiny people who never stopped needing something.

"Uber's five minutes away," she said, grabbing her purse. "Let's go kiss our angelic demons goodnight and hit the town."

Twenty minutes later, after offering a quick thanks to the stranger who had ferried them across town, Chase and Tara stepped into the thick August night. The humidity hit like a wave, coaxing a slow trickle of sweat down Chase's back.

Hearth & Ember was nestled on the golden block of 14th Street, flanked by two of DC's culinary juggernauts. It was a gutsy location for a new restaurant, but Hearth & Ember didn't seem to care. It exuded charm: glowing pendant lights, a wood-fired scent that drifted onto the sidewalk, and an interior that felt hip without trying too hard—firelit corners, soft industrial lines, and enough brick to keep the Instagrammers happy.

It took them several minutes to weave through the sidewalk crowd, but once inside—and after asking whether the Wexfords had arrived— the hostess came to life like a windup toy, greeting them with an unexpected familiarity.

"You must be the Dupree party!" she chirped, beaming. "Right this way. Nora said you'd be joining them."

Chase glanced at Tara. "Who the hell is Nora?" he mouthed as the hostess turned to lead them toward the dining room.

"Owner's wife," Tara whispered back. "Julia met her at a playground. Their kids fought over a toy dump truck, and now the moms are basically soulmates. Classic."

Their table was a showstopper—window-side, slightly elevated, with a panoramic view of 14th Street's bustle. Inside, flickers of flame danced from the open hearth in the kitchen, while outside Washington buzzed with its usual self-importance—staffers walking like senators, consultants angling for contracts, everyone hoping to be seen.

Julia stood to hug them both, holding a nearly full cocktail in her hand. She absent-mindedly tucked a strand of dark curls behind her ear—a gesture so natural it felt woven into her charm.

"We already ordered you drinks," she said. "The waiter said they're on the house for the first two rounds. Nora's doing. We're spoiled tonight."

Blaine was already sipping his—something smoky in a heavy glass. Broad-shouldered and bulky, a former rugby player with blond hair cut tight to his head, he somehow always made even a tailored shirt look a size too small. His eyes lit up when he saw Chase.

"Glad you could make it," he said, clasping his shoulder like an old teammate. "You're gonna love this place."

Menus were passed around, but no one reached for them right away. Conversation bubbled up naturally, light and effortless, old friends easing into a night with no agenda. "To good food, good friends, and free drinks," they toasted and settled in.

"How's Cece liking the end of summer?" Julia asked.

"She's five going on fourteen," Tara said, affectionately annoyed. "Yesterday, she told me I was meaner than the ref at the Washington Spirit game."

"She said that?" Julia laughed. The candlelight caught her light complexion, casting a soft, luminescent warmth across her features.

"She's been watching sports with Chase nonstop," Tara said, nudging him. "And all I did, mind you, was tell her it was time for a bath."

"I'll bet she dominates kindergarten," Blaine said, smiling. "Quinn just learned to walk, and now she's trying to flush everything she can get her hands on, including one of my AirPods."

"Rite of passage," Chase said. "You have to lose at least one pair before you become a real parent."

Tara nodded toward Julia. "Have your parents been able to visit much? I know how excited they were to become grandparents."

"All the time," Julia said brightly. "They're obsessed. My mom shows up claiming she's there to help me out but really she just hogs Quinn the entire time while my dad actually pitches in and gives me a break."

Tara turned to Blaine. "What about your folks?"

Blaine's smile dimmed slightly. "My dad's been down a few times," he said. "Work's kept him busy."

That was it. No mention of a second grandmother. No elaboration. A smooth sidestep, like a door quietly closed before anyone thought to peek inside. Chase caught the flicker but filed it away like a puzzle piece still looking for its border.

Dinner arrived in waves, each dish more beautifully plated than the last: ember-blistered carrots with lemon-tahini and toasted sunflower seeds, grilled halloumi with ember-charred lemon and chili oil, ember-roasted chicken thighs glazed in fermented honey.

"They don't let you forget the 'ember' in Hearth & Ember, do they?" Chase joked to the table.

Even the side of sourdough had thick slices charred black at the edges, served with whipped butter and a pinch of sea salt so delicate it looked placed by tweezers.

Despite enjoying the night out, Chase, a numbers guy by nature, couldn't help but tally up the tab with each visit from their waiter.

"Twelve dollars," he whispered to Tara. "This is...bread. Really good bread. But like, bread."

"Capitalism, love. At least it's better than another night of mac and cheese."

Chase considered arguing the point but thought better of it.

Conversation drifted toward school logistics, a favorite topic of exhausted parents everywhere.

"Just wait. DC's universal pre-K is a financial game changer," Tara said. "It's like an instant promotion. After five-plus years of what felt like monthly pickpocketing between Cece and Savannah, we made our final daycare payment."

"That deserves champagne," Julia said.

"Oh, we celebrated," Chase said. "Briefly. Then we signed both girls up for before and aftercare programs and a bunch of extracurriculars and somehow ended up spending about half of what we thought was going to be newfound discretionary income."

"Truly inspiring how fast it disappears," Blaine added. "I ran projections through Quinn's college graduation. The spreadsheet formula finished loading, and I walked straight to the bar cart."

"I mean, of course we're grateful to have solid jobs and a good lifestyle," Tara said. "But if you'd told twenty-five-year-old me that two full-time incomes at a senior director and assistant-VP level wouldn't be enough to feel truly comfortable, even with two kids...I would've said you needed to learn how to budget better. But here we are, juggling three-thousand-dollar monthly daycare and forty-five-hundred-dollar monthly rent payments."

The waiter appeared with the check, timed so perfectly it could've been scripted.

Blaine swirled his drink idly, eyes fixed on the small cluster of bubbles trapped beneath the ice.

"You ever feel like you did everything right and still got shortchanged?" he said suddenly.

It was a question aimed at no one, and yet it hung over the table like steam from the hearth.

"I mean, I love my job. Mostly. Julia's crushing it at her firm. We're good, but lately I've started wondering if *good* is the ceiling."

Chase raised an eyebrow. "You're not about to pitch us on a timeshare, are you?"

Blaine cracked a smile. "No. Not that."

"Thank God," Tara muttered. "Because we sure don't have time for an annual 'free week' in Aruba."

Blaine leaned back and exhaled slowly. "I've been messing around with something. A side hustle, I guess you'd call it."

Julia's posture changed almost imperceptibly. She shifted her weight, took a sip, and didn't look at Blaine.

"Oh no," Tara said, catching the mood shift. "Is this crypto again?"

Blaine laughed. "No. No crypto, I swear. Although I *do* think it's the future, but that's a story for another time."

"Then what?" Chase asked. "You've been dangling this mystery for a week. I'll admit, the suspense has me intrigued."

Blaine looked around like someone about to reveal a magic trick. "It's called arbitrage."

Julia set down her glass a little too firmly.

"What is that?" Tara asked.

"It's when you take advantage of price differences between markets. Buy low, sell high, but simultaneously. No risk. It's exploiting inefficiencies. Imagine a vending machine sells Snickers for a buck. There's a guy a block away buying Snickers for a dollar and ten cents. Arbitrage is walking between the two, pocketing the difference. On repeat."

"You're arbitraging what? Stocks?" Chase asked.

"Nope. Sportsbooks."

Chase blinked. "Wait, gambling?"

"No," Blaine said quickly. "Not gambling. Betting, yes. But *riskless* betting."

Tara, eyes starting to glaze over at another one of Blaine's crazy moneymaking endeavors, tilted her head. "Is that a thing?"

"That's what I said!" Julia cut in. "When he first told me, I said it sounded made up."

"It's not," Blaine said a little too forcefully. "Picture this. Faceoff has the Commanders at +110 to win. Dynasty has the Cowboys at -105. Same game, different odds. You bet both sides. As long as the plus number is greater than the minus number, no matter who wins, you profit. It's math. Cold, beautiful math."

"Sounds...borderline illegal," Chase said.

"It's not. It's just under the radar. The books don't love it, obviously, but they value their proprietary oddsmaking algos more. It's completely legal."

Julia, appearing increasingly exasperated, swirled the last of her wine before tapping Tara's arm. "Come on," she said lightly. "Let the boys talk sports shop. I need another drink. Join me for a nightcap?"

As the women walked toward the bar, Blaine turned back to Chase, who was trying his best to play it cool, not wanting to sound like a mark if there was a catch.

"So you can make enough money to justify spending the limited free time we have these days?" Chase asked, chiding himself for sounding a bit too interested despite his best efforts.

"You want numbers?" Blaine said. "If I can get five hundred thousand in wagers down in a month—and I'm getting close—and the average arb is two and a half percent, that's twelve thousand five hundred in one month."

Chase stared. Betting half a million dollars in a month seemed as plausible as learning Mandarin overnight.

"How?" he gaped.

"With a few tools, you'd be shocked at how doable it is. There's a revolutionary app called LineSniper that makes it all possible. It scrapes every major book and flags arbs in real time. People are building personal empires with it. Seriously, look up the guy who made it. He's a Silicon Valley type. He and his engineer buddies started with five hundred dollars and built it into a multimillion-dollar operation."

"So *Revenge of the Nerds* to the extreme," Chase said.

Blaine grinned. "Exactly. Then you need PickTracker. Links all your books together and charts everything—profit, ROI, all visualized. Keeps you from having to track it by hand. It'd be impossible otherwise."

Chase nodded slowly. "And you have accounts at a bunch of sportsbooks?" he asked cautiously, fearing he sounded beyond naïve.

"You need at least two," Blaine explained. "But I'd recommend starting with the big ones in DC: Faceoff, Crowns, LionBet. Then expand. The more accounts, the more arb opportunities you'll get. This whole thing is volume. It's not about big wins, just stacking a ton of small, consistent ones. Make thousands a few bucks at a time."

Chase sipped what was left of his cocktail. He didn't say anything right away.

Across the room, he could see Tara and Julia leaning on the bar, laughing at something on Julia's phone. The hearth behind them cast dancing light on the shelves of firewood stacked floor to ceiling—staged but still strangely comforting. Real. Warm. But also dangerous.

Julia stole a glance in their direction—quick, almost casual, but not quite. There was a ripple beneath it. Unease. Something portentous.

He looked back toward Blaine. "I'm intrigued," Chase said at last. He didn't stand. He didn't walk away. Sometimes staying put was the first step forward.

3

EDGE

CHASE HELD THE MRI DISC with the caution of someone handling something far more important than it looked. It wasn't the plastic he feared. It was the contents. The images would reveal whether the structural problems he'd long suspected were in fact the true source of his worsening neck pain.

Capitol Hill was sleepy in that late-summer, August-recess kind of way—half the city out of town, the other half melting under the furnace-like sun. He trudged down Pennsylvania Avenue under a blue sky littered with clouds, humidity hanging like a damp towel around his shoulders. His walk took him past the familiar hum of Eastern Market, where only a few vendors had bothered to set up in the heat, and Barracks Row, where most restaurants still hadn't bothered to unlock their patio furniture, knowing full well only a masochist would sit outside on a day like this.

He'd made this walk at least two dozen times, but today his mind wandered. Was he overthinking it? He could still move, still lift the girls, still grind through work. The pain had become background noise, annoying but familiar. But the scan results would make it official, and official was harder to ignore.

No, you live in a state of constant fear, anxious every time your neck so much as twinges. You need to know what's going on.

District PT was past 13th Street SE on a block that practically defined gentrification—wedged between a dog-grooming boutique and a vegan bakery. It was the kind of unassuming storefront locals knew but first-timers missed. Chase reached for the handle, took a deep breath, and stepped inside.

Inside, it smelled like a well-kept gym—rubber mats, the chemical tang of cleaning supplies, and enough sweat to let you know they took rehab seriously. The space was industrial-chic—brick walls, steel beams, exposed ductwork overhead, and an open-concept floor plan that felt more like a CrossFit box than a clinic. The five therapists looked like they could still compete, and judging by the team logos on their water bottles, most of them had at one point. Chase half-expected someone to slap on a hype playlist and start powerlifting.

Miles, his PT, greeted him with the calm nod of someone who'd seen this kind of nervous energy a hundred times. He knew it was a big day. Chase handed over the disc, and before he could sit, Miles had it loaded.

"Okay, let's take a look," he said, thick dark eyebrows drawing together as he zoomed in and studied the screen. The quiet stretched. Seconds felt like minutes.

"C5–C6 and C6–C7 are both herniated," Miles finally said, tapping the monitor. "That's the textbook reason for your continued muscle locking and minimal range of motion."

Chase stared at the ghosted image of his own spine, queasiness settling in. It was like watching an X-ray of a crumbling cathedral—the arches intact, the foundations cracked. His body rendered not in flesh but in fault lines.

"So what now?" Chase asked, his voice thinner than expected.

Miles turned, calm but direct. "No surgery. Not yet. But you've got to step it up. Relentless consistency—mobility work, strength routines, postural overhaul. Deep-tissue massage, minimum twice a month. We're playing the long game here."

Chase nodded, even as he did the math. *Massages? $150 a pop, minimum. That's $300 a month. Not reimbursable. Not in the budget.*

"You okay?"

Chase deadpanned, "Yeah, I'm wondering how many organs I can sell and still function."

Miles didn't miss a beat. "You'd be surprised how much people pay for a kidney."

They spent the rest of the session on new exercises, including the forty-seventh different version of a chin tuck—something completely foreign before PT, now a begrudging part of his daily routine.

On the walk home, Chase tried to shake the conversation, but it followed him like a shadow. The weight of inevitability. That creeping sense that time was catching up. Gone were the days of state championships and star-athlete status. In real time, he was feeling the piercing of that once-impenetrable cloak of invincibility. For the first time, he felt foolishly, undeniably mortal.

That night, Chase was on the couch replaying the conversation. Tara had attentively listened to the MRI diagnosis recap, asking all the predictably right questions, saying all the appropriately comforting things before going to bed, Kindle in hand. Both girls were out cold, a rare gift. The apartment was unusually quiet.

His laptop sat open on his stomach. With nothing to do, curiosity seeped in. Tech and time were never a good mix.

He typed, "Arbitrage betting scam."

Blaine's pitch had been on his mind since dinner. Despite his stubborn skepticism, something Blaine said kept needling at him—risk-free profit built on market inefficiencies. Chase had spent enough time around data to know that inefficiency usually meant opportunity. Still, these were sportsbooks. At the end of the day, it was gambling. Wasn't it?

The search results were predictable: clickbait thumbnails, conspiracy-laced Reddit threads, and a few dusty blogs last updated in 2019.

He scrolled, skimmed, and almost closed the laptop and turned on Netflix.

Then a username on X caught his eye: ArbOracle.

He clicked.

"You're not a bettor. You're an operator. The line is inventory. Two books misprice, and you own the middle. Opportunities drop, and they're gone in seconds, maybe less. Move like code. Think like capital. Execute like your bankroll depends on it, because it does."

It was the kind of post that could've been written by a lunatic or a genius. Or both.

He scrolled some more. This guy was half cult leader, half finance bro. Every post was an enticement to join an elite club that was hellbent on one thing and one thing only: making money.

But it was the screenshots that hooked him. ArbOracle flaunted his own arb numbers. He was pulling in tens of thousands of dollars a month, and his roadmap was right there for anyone to steal. The life he teased was alarmingly intoxicating—a cocktail of freedom, money, and outlaw cleverness he could already taste.

Chase's phone buzzed, and he somehow knew who it would be. As if he had eyes on Chase, it was Blaine, right on cue.

BLAINE: Forgot to mention, don't sleep on the sign-up and referral bonuses. LineSniper, PickTracker, and the big books legal in DC. Should be $2,500 easy.

Below the text were five referral links. Chase stared at them like they were radioactive.

It felt sketchy, like a pyramid scheme with a good marketing team.

But again, curiosity trumped cynicism and kept propelling him forward.

He clicked the LineSniper link. The site was slick—dark theme, cobalt accents, pulsing data tiles. It looked less like a gambling site and more like a Bloomberg Terminal for degenerates.

There were testimonials on every page.

"Turned my stimulus check into a rent payment."

"Paid for my wedding in six months."

"Feels like I've been handed the cheat codes."

Gross, but also compelling. The sign-up bonus alone was $300 if you linked three sportsbook accounts.

PickTracker offered a similar look and feel. Slightly smaller bonus.

Then the books themselves, Crowns, Faceoff, LionBet, each offered deposit matches or risk-free bets, but only if you put real money in. Chase tallied it up.

He'd have to deposit $5,000 combined across the three. That was real money.

He leaned his head back and felt the familiar muscle tension. The dull pressure against his cervical spine was almost grounding. It gave him something to focus on that wasn't spinning numbers.

He remembered the massages. $3,600 a year. A completely unplanned-for expense. If he played this right, the sign-up bonuses alone would cover nine months of a potential road to relief.

Then another memory surfaced. Two years ago, he'd quietly pulled $3,000 from their vacation fund to cover an unexpected summer camp charge for Cece. He never told Tara, not to hide it but because it hadn't felt worth discussing. Problem solved. Fund restored within a month. No harm, no foul.

This felt similar. A short-term pivot for a long-term win. At least that was what he told himself.

He put his phone down, returned to his laptop, and shifted tabs. He needed to understand how this shadow industry came to be.

He dove into the legal history of sports betting. For decades, it had been confined to Nevada and a few grandfathered-in tribal areas. PASPA—the Professional and Amateur Sports Protection Act—had essentially outlawed betting nationwide since 1992. Then, in 2018, the Supreme Court overturned it in *Murphy v. NCAA*.

Since then? Chaos. States rushing to be first to market. Botched rollouts. Tax grabs. Lobbying blitzes. Even now, it was a legal patchwork. DC itself had only three licensed books, all very recent.

So how the hell had Blaine been doing this for months?

Chase thought back to dinner. Blaine had said something about how timing and location mattered. Certain books worked only in certain places. It had sounded like tech-speak at the time, but now it clicked. There were workarounds, apparently. Advantages to where you lived or where you traveled.

It made sense. It was real.

And if it was real, maybe the rest of it was too.

Tara's voice echoed from their conversation at the dinner table earlier. "Promise me you'll take care of yourself. We need you."

He believed her and appreciated the sentiment. She meant it. But belief and sentiment didn't cover the costs.

They were comfortable, but every dollar had a job. Rent. Groceries. Clothes. Activities for the girls. An occasional babysitter for a night out. House savings. Kids' 529 plans. Retirement. Emergency fund. The list went on. In trying to make money a source of security, they'd made it a straitjacket.

Chase gravitated back to his phone. Their down payment fund was in a shared high-yield account. Untouched. Sacred.

He opened the bank's app. The number stared back at him.

This isn't betrayal. He'd shifted money without telling Tara before. After all, it was his job to move the pieces. Besides, he'd be putting the money right back within a couple of months at most. The sign-up bonuses alone would generate a healthy profit. He was convinced. LineSniper and PickTracker weren't scams. They were software.

He'd track every dollar.

He moved the $5,000 to PayPal, startled by how easily his conscience stepped aside.

From there, he sent one-third to each of the sportsbooks. His email pinged with confirmations. His mind absorbed the digital reinforcements.

As soon as he linked his accounts, the LineSniper dashboard lit up. All he needed to do now was initiate his one-month free trial. No brainer. He provided the requisite personal information—far less than what he had already provided to Crowns, Faceoff, and LionBet—and, drawing from his favorite movie, set his username as "BetmanBegins," a nighttime crusader aspiring to Bruce Wayne–level wealth. It felt a little ridiculous, but it made him laugh. The data feed immediately flickered like a trading floor: market, odds, edge percentage.

It was late on a weeknight. Even so, an arb on a West Coast Giants versus Dodgers MLB game flashed green with a 3.2% edge. It was gone almost as soon as it appeared.

A tennis match for the following morning showed up. Total number of games over/under. Two books misaligned. A tiny edge. A window.

Chase didn't click.

He watched, overwhelmed but buzzing with excitement.

Another opportunity surfaced. Disappeared. Then another.

It felt like seeing the inside of a slot machine—gears whirring, reels clicking into place, the electric chirp of a payout frozen mid-burst. For the first time, the house edge was his.

The layout was clean. Unapologetically fast. There was no space for second-guessing. His brain synced to the rhythm of it—churning numbers, comparing values, honing a mental timer that ticked down like a fuse, its pace varying with the size of the edge. He realized these inefficiencies self-corrected based on the action other LineSniper users were pumping around the nation. A money glitch. A race against the clock.

A pop-up slid across the bottom of the screen. "Welcome, Chase. Let's find your edge."

He'd usually be asleep at this hour, but he'd never been more alert.

He wasn't sure if it was the thrill of discovery or the sting of a boundary quietly crossed, but the shift had happened.

He was in. There'd be no turning back now.

4

THE ORACLE

HIS KNEE BOUNCED UNDER THE DESK, a jittery metronome that had been running since before sunrise. Four monitors glowed in the dim upstairs office, each one a portal into a different part of his world: a LineSniper dashboard alive with shifting odds, his burgeoning social media empire, an offshore sportsbook site with its gray-market domain extension, and a Discord server where usernames he'd never met typed like lifelong friends.

In the chair sat Marco Gonzalez. On the screens, the persona that paid for it all, ArbOracle. He liked the separation. Marco could be tired, distracted, even worried. ArbOracle never was.

The air was a stale mix of long-cold black coffee and the faint, plasticky tang of a new mouse breaking in under his palm. Outside the half-open window, sprinklers hissed in measured arcs across perfect lawns. Somewhere downstairs, his five-year-old son, Mateo, was humming the ABCs while dragging a toy truck along the hardwood. The wheels clattered over the seams between planks in an irregular rhythm, enough to make Marco itch to fix it. He'd always been like that: notice the wobble, the uneven edge, the picture frame one degree off.

Then came a ping.

Not the bright chime of a new crypto deposit. Not the Discord tone that sometimes meant a new referral lead for him. This was the flat, almost apologetic ping of his email. The subject line read, "Account Limitation Notice."

His jet-black eyes skipped the pleasantries and landed on the only part that mattered. "Your account has been reviewed, and certain limits have been applied." The second one this week. Third, if he counted the offshore book that had quietly stopped matching his deposits. Limits were the beginning of the end—always a question of when, never if.

He slid the cursor to another monitor where a half-written post waited to be finished. Below it was a photo of his Corvette taken in golden-hour light. The cursor blinked like a dare.

Twenty-five thousand followers didn't want cracks in the armor. They wanted the dream. He typed the final line. "Clock in. Clock out. Clock me? I don't think so." He added a fire emoji and posted it.

The second monitor displayed a curated version of his life: him and Mateo in Aruba, linen shirts, sunburned cheeks, plastic cups of fruit punch—his with a quiet splash of rum—raised toward the camera. "Still working," the caption read. Wink emoji.

It was three months old. Tonight, he wore gray sweatpants and a hoodie with a faint gasoline smell from his time in the garage. The Corvette key fob was dead center on the desk, polished enough to mirror the bluish glow of the screens. He rolled it in his palm, felt the cold weight, then set it back exactly where it belonged.

The car wasn't simply a car. It was proof the money was real. Proof he'd outrun the grind everyone else seemed chained to. And it was a prop. Every so often, he'd park it at the perfect angle, snap a photo, and let the admiring replies roll in.

He scanned the office: monitors aligned to the millimeter, mouse pad perfectly parallel to the desk. A framed screenshot of his first $50,000 month hung slightly crooked. He stood, adjusted the corner until it was straight, and sat back down. Balance restored.

Motor oil still lived somewhere deep in his skin. Fifteen years of it—under his nails, in the seams of old work boots, etched into the calluses on his palms. He'd spent his twenties under the hoods of other people's cars, fixing their broken things while his own life drifted further from solvable. By the time Mateo was born, the math was ugly. Bills barely covered, credit-card debt that seemed to breed in the dark, winter mornings waiting at the bus stop with his toolbox balanced on his knees.

Then came LineSniper.

It was a buried post in a betting forum. Some self-styled Robin Hood out of Silicon Valley claimed he'd cracked the code and was here to "democratize" it. Marco didn't buy it. He'd seen enough "systems" to know most were garbage, but curiosity was its own kind of gravity. He tested it. One bet. Then another. The numbers added up. They kept adding up.

The first time he felt it, he was still at the shop, screen balanced on a rolling cart while he waited for a stubborn fuel pump to bleed out. A $37 win for doing nothing but placing two bets—safe no matter the outcome. It felt like a magic trick, like slipping his hand into a jacket he'd worn for years and finding a hidden pocket already stuffed with cash that wasn't his. He told himself it was luck. He told himself he'd stop if it stopped working. The profits didn't stop.

By the end of his fourth month, he'd made more than his job paid in half a year. By the sixth, he was in the manager's office, dropping his shop keys on the counter. His boss stared at them in shock. "You sure about this?"

Marco had nodded. His wife hadn't believed him until the first month his winnings covered not only the mortgage but the car payment and the groceries too.

A chime from the referral dashboard pulled him back. Another sign-up. Another revenue share. It wasn't the adrenaline of a big arb, but it was steadier. A staircase instead of a roller coaster.

Then another ping.

Different book this time, smaller, but one he'd been milking for weeks. The email was déjà vu. "Your account has been reviewed, and certain limits have been applied." He'd never received two limit notifications in a single day. The walls were closing in, and they'd picked up speed.

Marco switched to his tracker spreadsheet, fingers dragging absently through the short beard he tended to stroke whenever the numbers stopped lining up. Rows of accounts, each with its own status. Green meant active. Yellow meant limping. Red meant dead. Too much red lately.

His gaze drifted to the far-right column, unlabeled, where other people's names filled the cells. Friends. Cousins. A guy from middle school basketball. People he'd convinced to "partner" with him, lending their personal details to open fresh accounts. He told himself it was a win-win. They were partners, not pawns. They got a cut. He got to keep playing.

He clicked one of the names, "VIC – N." The notes read, "Paid 20% last month, asked about taxes, spouse nervous." He pinched the bridge of his nose. The spreadsheet was his lifeline and his indictment.

His phone buzzed. A text from Vic.

VIC: Got the check. We good for next month?

MARCO: Yeah. And I might have another one for you, if you're up for it.

The dots appeared. Disappeared. Appeared again.

VIC: As long as it's clean. My wife's been asking questions.

Marco's thumb hovered.

MARCO: Of course. Same as before. You'll be happy.

From the hallway came Mateo's footsteps, uneven and fast. The boy appeared in the doorway, clutching a blue folder.

"Dad, Mom said you need to sign this. It's for tomorrow."

Marco took it, scanning the form—emergency contacts, medical notes, a box asking if Mateo had allergies to peanuts, shellfish, bee stings. His own name looked strange in ink these days, like it belonged to another life.

"You ready for kindergarten, my dude?" he asked.

Mateo nodded, eyes bright. "They have a playground with two slides."

"Two slides," Marco said, adding his signature. "You'll be the king of both before recess is over."

The boy grinned, took the folder back with both hands, and strutted off down the hall. The footsteps shrank and disappeared. For a second, all Marco could hear was the soft purr of fans cooling the overworked monitors.

Top-rated district in the state. He'd done that. The down payment for the new house, the move this summer, the quiet street where kids still rode bikes into dusk. He had built a life for Mateo that would have sounded like a dream to Marco's younger self.

The spreadsheet was still on the screen when he looked back. It looked less like a ledger now and more like a map of a sinking ship, green for the decks still above water, red for the ones already gone.

He checked the time then jammed his AirPods in. He found the contact he wanted, "NATE – W."

Nate answered on the second ring. "Yo, what's good?"

"You got a minute?" Marco asked.

"For you? Always."

"I've got something that might interest you," Marco said lightly. "Simple. Clean. You made a couple hundred last time, right?"

Nate laughed. "My girl says it was sketchy as hell, but yeah. You paid on time. What's the catch?"

"No catch. Same structure. I handle everything. You get a cut. But I'd need a little more…verification this time."

A pause. "Like what?"

"The usual," Marco said. "DOB. Address. Maybe a scan of the front of your…" He didn't need to say more.

Another pause, longer this time. "I don't know, man."

Marco leaned back, eyes on the Corvette fob. "Look, I get it, but this is how grown-up money gets made now. If you're uncomfortable, no hard feelings. I've got other folks waiting."

"Percentage?" Nate asked reflexively.

"Twenty," Marco said.

"Twenty-five," Nate countered, "and you deal with the tax stuff if it comes up."

Marco swallowed. "Twenty-two, and I'll cover any taxes you owe on the 1099s you get issued."

Nate exhaled into the phone. Marco could picture him, pacing in socks, the way people did when their bodies tried to move them away from decisions their minds were still walking toward.

"Fine," Nate said, "text me what you need."

"Will do." Marco hung up and stared at the phone until the screen dimmed.

He set it down, rubbing his palms against his jeans. There it was again, that slick, invisible film he could never quite wash off. Every time he asked for someone's ID, it felt less like a partnership and more like picking pockets with their permission.

* * *

The Discord ping distracted him from the guilt before it could settle.

It was Aaron, founder and CEO of LineSniper. Username: LineKing.

LINEKING: Got a sec?

ARBORACLE: Always.

They traded two lines about a glitch in the morning feed and whether a certain regional book had started soft-limiting users. Then Aaron dropped what he'd come to say.

LINEKING: Been thinking about making a splash. Bigger than anything we've done. You'd be key to making it happen.

Marco leaned back. *Key.* He imagined the sound of it—metal on metal, unlocking a door he'd been standing in front of for two years.

LINEKING: Can't say more yet, but imagine bringing all these usernames to life. Not just DMs. Something real. Something live. Something epic.

Marco pictured a stage, lights hot on his face, a room full of people who'd once been mere avatars, cheering while a logo pulsed on a screen behind him. He imagined Aaron's hand clasping his on the way up the steps, a smile that said, "This is our moment."
Aaron added:

LINEKING: If you're game, I want you in the middle of it.

Marco typed back quickly:

ARBORACLE: I'm in.

ARBORACLE: Tell me where you need me.

LINEKING: You'll know soon. Keep the engine warm.

Marco sat for a long moment after the chat went quiet. "Keep the engine warm." He glanced at the key fob and felt a spark of ridiculous affection for an object that did exactly what it promised every time.
He toggled back to his DMs. The inbox was stacked. He answered a few, tossing encouragement like confetti, slipping in referral links. Engagement kept the machine running. If the books were going to tighten the noose on him personally, he'd build a different funnel, one he owned.
A new message appeared from an unfamiliar username: "BetmanBegins." Amusing.

BETMANBEGINS: Hey, I've been reading your posts. Trying to make sure I'm doing this right. Any advice for someone getting started?

Marco smirked. A rookie. The best kind. He cracked his knuckles and began typing—confident, warm, authoritative. The hook, the promise, the gentle steer toward the places where his codes lived.

> **ARBORACLE:** Welcome. First thing: it's real, but it's work. Start with the big books in your state, play small at first, read your confirmations twice, and keep records using PickTracker. Don't chase. Don't get cute. Shoot me your state, and I'll send you what you need. *You've got this.*

Send. Three dots appeared almost immediately.

> **BETMANBEGINS:** Thanks. I'm in DC, actually. Appreciate any pointers.

DC. Still pretty restricted but moving in the right direction. He copied over a clean list—books, links, a free-trial code for LineSniper tucked in with the rest. It didn't fully matter if this guy used them or had already signed up elsewhere. The ArbOracle brand would grow as he told others.

Marco didn't mention the limits. Not tonight. Confidence was a kind of currency too.

His wife's voice floated up the stairs. "Marco? You coming down? Mateo wants you to read the new dinosaur book."

"Two minutes!" he called back.

He glanced at the spreadsheet one last time. Green. Yellow. Red. He added a new row at the bottom for NATE – W and color-coded it a cautious yellow. He took a breath then stood and clicked off three of the four monitors. The room dimmed to a softer blue.

Before he left, he returned to his X tab and queued a post for the morning, something vague and aspirational, the kind of thing people retweeted into their own hopes.

"The future isn't waiting. It's underpriced. Be early."

He was surprised by how much he believed it. Then he scheduled it and slipped the key fob into his pocket, just to feel the weight.

At the top of the stairs, he listened to the smaller house noises, the sounds of a life he'd always wanted and ultimately manifested.

Downstairs, Mateo was already under the blanket on the couch, book open, hair still damp from the bath. "You said two minutes," the boy said, but he was smiling.

Marco sat, pulled the blanket over both their legs, and began to read. The dinosaur had plates down its back like roof shingles. It ate ferns and didn't care about odds.

When he finished, Mateo turned and looked at him with the grave seriousness only five-year-olds had. "Will they have ferns at my school?"

"They'll have everything," Marco said. "Two slides, remember?"

Mateo nodded, satisfied, and curled into his side. The boy's breath steadied. The house settled around them.

For a few minutes, it was quiet.

Later, after he'd carried Mateo upstairs and turned off the hallway light, Marco went back to the office and switched on only the smallest monitor. He opened his DMs. BetmanBegins had written back again— one more question:

BETMANBEGINS: Be honest, how nervous were you at the start?

Marco stared, surprised by the vulnerability of the sender and the flash of feeling it sparked. He thought of the bus stop winters, the grease under his nails, the first time a book told him he was winning too much, the first time he convinced a cousin to hand over their information and told himself it was "partnership." He thought of the Corvette and the kindergarten form, and the word Aaron had used, "key."

ARBORACLE: Nervous for sure. Fear's the tax on every good opportunity. Pay it and keep moving.

He added three final words:

ARBORACLE: You'll be fine.

He closed the window, sat back, and let his knee bounce until the rhythm matched the tiny fan inside the monitor. Tomorrow he'd push harder on referrals. He'd text Nate the list of documents. He'd DM the kid in DC a follow-up, maybe point him toward a beginner's guide he trusted. He'd wait for Aaron to say what "epic" meant and pretend he hadn't already imagined the stage lights.

Before shutting down, he set one more post to draft, a private note he might or might not ever publish.

"The game doesn't love you back, but it pays attention when you win."

He saved it and powered down. In the screen's reflection, he could see only a faint outline of his face and over his shoulder a small rectangle of hallway light. He walked toward it, passing the framed screenshot on the wall. In the dark, it looked like a window to a different life—a perfect month that could never be repeated, only chased.

5

FIRST HIT

TARA STEERED THE GIRLS toward the door, phone in one hand, a gift bag in the other, its tissue paper jutting out in bright, crumpled peaks. Cece darted ahead in pink sandals, brown-haired ponytail bouncing, while Savannah lagged behind, clutching her water bottle and counting, for the third time, the seven stuffed animals she insisted on bringing along.

"It's that playground with the *Wizard of Oz* theme in McLean," Tara called over her shoulder, needlessly reminding Chase of the location as she ushered the girls into the hallway. "Should be about three hours, maybe more if they have the bounce house."

The door clicked shut, and the apartment instantly felt bigger.

College GameDay—ESPN's rollicking live pregame show that turned Saturday mornings into a traveling carnival—hummed from the living room. Chase turned it up, letting the raucous roar from Columbus flood in from 500 miles away. Scarlet and gray flags rippled in the early morning sun, the stage perched beneath the iconic arch of the Horseshoe. At 103 years old, the stadium felt as timeless as it did weathered, a coliseum of Saturdays. Chase knew every curve of it, and even the pixelated image on his TV felt like a homecoming.

The camera found Lee Corso, not much younger than the stadium itself, smiling beneath his headset, eyes crinkled with the weight and joy of thirty-eight seasons.

"Final pick on GameDay, Coach," Rece Davis said, grinning into the camera. "We're back where it all started for you. Four hundred and thirty picks since you first donned Brutus Buckeye. Will you close the headgear chapter the same way you began it all those years ago?"

Corso grinned and gave a slow, toying shrug—ever the showman, a puppeteer holding the strings of the thousands behind him. He knew exactly what he was doing.

And what a game it would be. Columbus. Texas versus Ohio State. #1 against #2. For the first weekend of football, it didn't get any bigger.

Behind the set, a forest of fan-made signs swayed and bobbed—a *GameDay* tradition as old as Corso's headgear picks. Some were sharp jabs at Texas, "Horns Down Forever," others pure nonsense crafted for a fleeting second of national airtime. One neon poster, hoisted by a bearded guy in burnt-orange overalls, shouted, "RYAN DAY EATS CEREAL WITH A FORK." Another read simply, "TEXT BACK, MOM." In the center, a block-letter sign declared, "LESS COWBELL," with a bold X slashed through the Texas logo, as if the early-2000s *SNL* sketch had never ended. And over Rece's shoulder, a placard in Buckeye scarlet winked at gamblers watching from home. "Cover the Spread, Not Your Eyes."

Chase sat on the edge of the couch, tea warm between his hands, the crowd noise pulling at something deep inside him. He could almost feel the crush of the tailgate lot, smell the charcoal smoke, hear the drunken singalongs. He'd been born at Ohio State hospital. His first material possession had been a plush Buckeye football. This team wasn't merely part of his life—it was in his bloodstream.

The camera drifted past the sea of waving signs, lingering long enough on that gambler's nudge for Chase to catch it. The corner of his mouth twitched.

He'd planned to be there in person—his text thread with high school friends still sitting in his phone like a string of tickets that never got scanned—but life, logistics, and two young kids had pulled him in another direction. Now, instead of standing in that river of scarlet, he was here. Alone. And maybe the universe was giving him a sign that there was a different kind of game to play today.

His phone sat on the coffee table. ArbOracle's last message from the night before was emblazoned in his mind. "You'll be fine."

It had felt casual at the time. Now, in the sudden stillness left behind by Tara and the girls, it felt instructive.

He reached for the phone, the glass warm from a square of sunlight spilling through the window. Now all that was left was to cross the Rubicon.

LineSniper loaded instantly, and the feed hit him like the first step onto a crowded casino floor. College football's first full Saturday had unleashed a flood of numbers, and the matchups scrolled endlessly, each with its own set of twitching odds. Greens, whites, plus and minus signs flickered like they were alive. It was manic, mesmerizing—a digital whack-a-mole board, each edge appearing for an unknown stretch then retreating into the earth without warning.

At the very top: Alabama vs. Florida State, over/under 48.5. Faceoff had the under at -105. LionBet had the over at +115. Edge: 2.3%. He let the app auto-refresh several times. The numbers held. It looked stable. This would be his entry point.

He tapped the listing. The calculator popped up like a secret panel. $100 on the under at Faceoff, $90.81 on the over at LionBet. Guaranteed $4.43 profit, no matter what the scoreboard said at the end.

The moment of truth.

Faceoff first. His thumb hovered a beat longer than necessary, not hesitation about *whether* to do it but meticulous focus to avoid a rookie mistake. He found the game, entered $100 on the under, hit confirm. Bet locked.

Flip to LionBet. Too quickly. His thumb landed on the wrong icon—the calendar. "Dammit," he muttered, backing out. Second try, LionBet opened. Scroll, find the game, enter $90.81 on the over, confirm. Done.

He stared at both confirmation screens. It had worked. The numbers hadn't moved. The edge had remained fixed.

The realization was slow, almost physical. He'd locked in a profit.

The money wouldn't hit his account until the game ended, but that was irrelevant—the math was complete, the outcome predetermined. It was like having a check in his hand, already signed, while waiting for the bank to open.

"That's all it takes," he said under his breath. Not a question. A newfound truth.

He toggled on push notifications. It didn't feel like much in the moment, but it was the fuse. From now on, every time LineSniper found a new edge above the 2% threshold, his phone would buzz and his Apple Watch would vibrate—a subtle summons, a whisper in his ear, a hand discreetly sliding him a stack of bills. He told himself it was a convenience feature, a way to stay efficient. What he couldn't see yet was how quickly that watch would become a handcuff. Those pings would become the drumbeat of his day, each one pulling his eyes to the screen, promising another free dollar, until he stopped noticing whether he was the one chasing the bets, or if the bets were chasing him.

As soon as the alerts were enabled, his screen lit up, and his wrist tingled. He had barely finished savoring his inaugural arb.

This edge was bigger. 4.1%.

He pounced. $100 on Faceoff for the first leg. Confirmed. Flip to LionBet.

Wait, the number was wrong.

+115 had slipped to +105. In the space between two taps, the edge had completely vanished.

A thin spike of heat ran up his spine. Leaving that Faceoff bet exposed meant the guarantee was gone. This was no longer a neat, risk-free equation. It was a $100 coin flip in disguise. Blaine's words from dinner floated back, "It's just math," but the pitch sounded thinner now, like a balloon that had started to leak.

As panic began to swell, his mind flashed to a Reddit thread he had perused the night before.

"And if you ever get in a pinch, simply cash out," it had read.

That was it.

He flicked through the Faceoff screens, scanning for the option. Scrolls. Swipes. He passed Promotions, Deposit History, Past Bets. A rushing filled his head. Finally, he found it. On the Open Bets screen, the cash-out option appeared under his most recent blunder. Tap. Cash Out Confirmed.

The stake slid back into his balance, but the relief was muted, edged with unease. That had been seconds, and it was still almost too late.

Lesson learned. The moles didn't wait. The hammer had to fall fast or not at all.

He was spooked but not deterred. The fresh memory of a locked profit far outweighed the near disaster, and even that felt overstated after the cash-out reset.

Another buzz. Smaller edge. Clean execution. Enter stake. Tap. Confirm. Flip screens. Enter stake. Tap. Confirm. Smooth.

The rhythm built quickly, his assuredness and skill growing with every confirmation screen. Pings came in bursts—sometimes a few minutes apart, sometimes stacked so close together he barely had time to reset his fingers. Each one tapped his wrist, his hand moving toward the phone before his brain had even caught up. Bet. Confirm. Flip. Bet. Confirm.

With his thumb hovering over the LineSniper feed and his next kill, Chase's impulse to share suddenly surged. He swiped to Messages and opened his thread with Blaine.

CHASE: First arb in the books. Officially in the game.

The reply came in seconds, like Blaine had been waiting for this moment all along.

BLAINE: Yessss. My man.

Another bubble appeared immediately, the three dots bouncing like they were as excited as he was.

BLAINE: Welcome to the club. Membership dues are cheap, just a little bankroll and the good sense to let money make more money while everyone else is wasting their Saturday glued to the games.

Chase grinned.

BLAINE: No joke, you're about to change your life. Keep the pedal down and don't overthink it.

CHASE: Had a scare right after though. Line moved on me before I could get the second leg in. Thank God for cash out…

BLAINE: Preach. Don't sweat it if you get stuck on one side of a bet now and then and can't cash out. Think of it like running a grocery store. You're gonna have some spoiled product. Cost of doing business. Only difference here is that spoiled product still has a fifty percent chance of paying out. Those all even out in the long run.

A final text came in, pure Blaine:

BLAINE: Pro tip: celebrate every win, even if it's four dollars and forty-three cents. That's the sound of compounding, baby.

Chase closed out of the app, the grin still lingering. Blaine's energy was contagious, like a shot of something hot in his veins. He turned back to the feed, fingers already itching for the next hit.

During the lulls in LineSniper action, Chase worked the remote like a seasoned prison guard flicking through surveillance feeds—scanning for trouble, never lingering. The TV cycled through ESPN, ESPN2, Fox, CBS, BigTen Network, back to ESPN. He wasn't watching plays or highlights. He was watching the clocks. FAU vs. Maryland. Ball State vs. Purdue. Toledo vs. Kentucky. Games that would never matter to him otherwise now held pieces of his balance hostage. The closer to zero, the sooner the capital returned.

Another ping. Another clean arb. The motions were starting to happen without thought—swipe, tap, type, confirm, flip, repeat. He caught himself holding his breath without realizing it as if exhaling might make a line move. His grip on the phone was tighter than necessary.

A near-miss jolted him when a line moved as he was entering the second leg. His thumb hit cash-out so fast it surprised him. Another spike of relief when the funds returned.

He began cataloging patterns in his head. LionBet lagged on small-school underdogs. Faceoff had plenty of discrepancies on total score over/unders but moved nearly instantly to self-correct. Crowns was slow, sometimes comically so. He started adjusting his order of operations accordingly.

The pings kept coming, the whack-a-mole board flashing and dimming in no discernible order. He was a hunter in a field full of darting prey—some within reach, some gone before he could lift the rifle.

More games filled the Open Bet section of his accounts. More clocks to watch. He began flipping channels compulsively, spending seconds on each. The sound of the commentators became white noise, the crowd shots meaningless. Touchdowns, field goals, interceptions, none of it mattered. The sport had been stripped down to numbers on a screen and timers counting down to a balance refresh.

At some point, it dawned on him that he'd barely watched a snap of the Buckeyes game—the biggest matchup of the week, the one circled on his mental calendar since it was first announced as a blockbuster home-and-away series years ago. The TV had been on the whole time, but the moments he'd dreamed of seeing had been traded away for possession clocks in places like Muncie and Boca Raton.

He could feel a dryness in his mouth as he realized he hadn't had anything to eat or drink for as long as he'd been sitting there. The phone was warm in his hand now, a constant presence. His thumbs tingled slightly, not from fatigue but from sheer repetition.

The hours slid past unnoticed. The only markers were the growing list of pending bets and the subtle change in the light coming through the window. The clock was good at moving slow when you wanted it to move fast and fast when you wanted it to move slow. Today, it sprinted.

Suddenly, unexpectedly, the door swung open, letting in a blast of warmer hallway air and the noise of two small bodies.

"Daddy, Daddy! The playground had these swings that were—" Cece started.

"And I had mom push me backward!" Savannah interrupted.

He smiled, wondered how someone could push a swing backward, and casually slipped the phone into his pocket. The girls burst toward the refrigerator, already arguing about juice boxes.

Tara stepped in behind them, her eyes locking on him for a beat too long. "Did the Buckeyes already win a national championship? I thought this was the first week of the season," she said. "You seem amped."

He laughed lightly. "I'm trying out that thing Blaine was talking about."

She raised an eyebrow, skeptical. "How…is that going?" The pregnant pause betrayed her effort at matching his enthusiasm.

"It's really complex. You'd be bored before I finished the first sentence if I tried to explain it." He wished he had tempered his excitement before his girls had returned.

"Well, as long as you aren't *losing* money," she said. "Have some fun with it. Let me know what happens."

He nodded. "Of course."

The nod was reflexive, not binding. She didn't need the full picture. Not when the picture was still coming into focus for him.

When the apartment settled again, he synced to PickTracker. The number glowed on the screen: $289.53 projected return once the games ended.

Average edge: 5.8%. Nearly every dollar of the $5,000 he'd deposited was already on the field, $4,992 in motion. He was so invested in the moment that he didn't even realize he had deployed all his capital and couldn't place another bet until something finished.

"Holy shit," he whispered to himself. In one four-hour stretch, with a learning curve he was still mastering, with stakes that were intentionally low, he had nearly paid for his two monthly massages.

The thought came immediately: if $5,000 could do this, what could $15,000 do?

He opened his banking app, moved another $10,000 from the down payment fund to his PayPal account, and split it evenly between Faceoff, Crowns, and LionBet.

To him, it was scaling up a proven model. Expansion. Growth. The math was on his side.

The transfer confirmation email pinged. He thought it was a fresh arb.

No matter. Within seconds, another would present itself.

There were plenty of moles out there. And now, with more hammers in hand, he was ready to swing with a kind of reckless abandon that didn't care where the blows landed.

6

THE FOUNDER

AARON RAMSEY'S MORNINGS started with numbers. Not news headlines. Not social feeds. Numbers. And this Monday, he knew those numbers would be juicy.

Tall and gym-sculpted, he radiated a confidence that bordered on arrogance. His ash-brown hair was trimmed close, jaw taut, and a faint one-sided dimple surfaced only when he let himself smile. He looked every bit the founder who engineered his life, and his body, with intention.

The Scottsdale sun had barely cleared the jagged edge of Camelback Mountain, but his condo was already lit in gold—the same hue that drove his ambitions. He moved barefoot across the polished concrete floor, a mug of single-origin Ethiopian coffee in one hand, and woke the forty-nine-inch curved monitor that anchored his minimalist desk.

LineSniper's administrative dashboard came alive—a mosaic of colored tiles, each one a live heartbeat from somewhere in the country. The dev team had mocked up this Monday-morning "inventory" view exclusively for him: weekend engagement summaries, retention curves, trial conversions—patterns he liked to keep an eye on.

He scrolled through the weekend engagement logs, watching the same story play out line after line—fresh trial users logging marathon sessions, bouncing from market to market like kids set loose in an arcade.

One username caught his eye, "BetmanBegins."

Joined Friday. Over six hours on the platform Saturday. Chasing plays until close to midnight. Another three on Sunday. The clicks told the tale: not someone carefully hunting a single fat edge but a guy firing on anything that moved—college football, MLB, Premier League soccer—riding the high of having the tools in his hands for the first time.

Aaron smiled. The name had style. Clever. Cinematic. Like his own LineKing handle, another movie reference. His was a nod to *The Lion King*, but also to the idea that he ruled this particular jungle of lines and odds. This new user gave a rookie's wink to *Batman Begins*—part acknowledgment of his newness, part bold proclamation that this was the opening scene in his rise to hero status.

He clicked to open the full session replay, watching the ghost cursor move through the interface, the system flagging how BetmanBegins hovered over the Upgrade Now button twice without clicking. Barely forty-eight hours in, and he'd already been tempted by the deeper arsenal reserved for Platinum-Gold members willing to invest. Aaron knew what that meant. Every upgrade was more ammo for the user, and more cash flowing straight into his pocket.

Aaron had been watching users like this for years, ever since the first stranger sent him $49 through PayPal for access to a crude spreadsheet that scraped odds from a dozen sportsbooks.

He'd grown up a long way from the mountains outside his floor-to-ceiling windows—a bright kid in a faded Midwestern factory town where the math team practiced in a basement next to the janitor's closet. His dad worked double shifts at a local manufacturing plant until it closed. His mom pieced together hours as a bank teller and a weekend receptionist at a spa. Money was always short, but numbers were free.

It was a math teacher, Mrs. Cook, who spotted it first—the way Aaron could solve multi-step equations in his head before the chalk even hit the board. She pushed him toward math competitions, then computer programming, then summer programs at universities his parents had only seen in movies. By senior year, she was coaching him through the Stanford application. When the acceptance letter came, he became the first kid from his high school ever to go there. Full scholarship, nonetheless.

Thousands of miles from home, Stanford delivered exactly what he'd imagined—sun, ambition, and the kind of high-octane networking that could launch a career before graduation—but it also felt like another planet. The wealth, the ease, the quiet confidence of kids who'd spent summers abroad and drove cars worth more than his parents' house left him dizzy at first, a tourist in someone else's world. But he adapted fast, learning to speak the language, work the rooms, and turn that world into one he could navigate as easily as his own. He left with a degree in math and computer science the same summer the Supreme Court struck down the federal ban on sports betting. The market was opening. He just didn't know yet that it would be his market.

Instead, he landed in the soul-sucking purgatory of compliance technology at a mid-tier investment bank. A career advisor told him compliance tech was the smart route. It didn't take long for Aaron to realize he was wired for something other than days spent coding systems to make sure traders stayed inside regulatory guardrails, endless meetings where creativity went to die. The irony wasn't lost on him. He was building digital fences to stop others from gaming the market when every part of him wanted to climb over one and lend a hand to everyone behind him.

Nights were his own. Headphones on, terminal window glowing, writing code that turned the sportsbook's own slowness into money. He tapped his Stanford network like a resource map—classmates for design and coding, engineers to build a remote development team, a few well-placed alumni for seed capital. Investors were chasing the next big thing in mobile betting, and Aaron planned to make sure he was the one who struck pay dirt.

By the time the bank's fiscal year rolled over, he was making just enough from that crude odds-scraping spreadsheet to quit and focus full-time on turning the Excel doc into a company. The bank's loss was the birth of LineSniper.

He scaled it in stages: first a web app, then a sleeker interface, then an algorithm that learned user preferences and surfaced plays like a personal caddie. His engineers could ship code in their sleep and had no patience for meetings longer than fifteen minutes. Revenue climbed. The mailing list exploded. Affiliate deals started rolling in.

But even now, when the company was healthy, growing, and on a lot of radar screens, Aaron felt that familiar tension.

On one side: the pure capitalist in him—the hunter—the part that wanted a filthy, no-apologies payday, one fat wire transfer from an acquisition that would set him and his parents up for life.

On the other: the idealist. The guy who really did believe he was leveling the playing field. He kept screenshots of messages from users who'd paid off debt, left jobs they hated, or simply given their kids the Christmas they'd never had. "You've changed my life," one wrote. He wasn't immune to that. He liked knowing his work mattered, even if the ledger in his head always came back to money.

He sipped his coffee and moved down the dashboard, tagging trial users with high "conversion potential," his Monday ritual. Some he ignored. Others got a quick DM: a personal thanks from the founder, a tip about filtering for higher edges, a reminder about setting bankroll limits. Always friendly, always calibrated to keep them winning. Hook them for certain before the dopamine loop cooled.

A user in Kansas got one this morning. BetmanBegins didn't. Not yet. Aaron wanted to watch him a little longer.

The rest of the morning was meetings—a sprint review with the analytics team, a call with the marketing contractor about an aggressive September promo, a check-in with his attorney about a cease-and-desist letter they'd sent to a scraper site trying to steal LineSniper's feed. All the moving parts of a startup that was now less "scrappy" and more "well-oiled machine."

Not to mention, he set aside time every day to create content. YouTube videos. TikToks. Anything to show users and prospective users that he was more than simply founder and CEO. He was an active

LineSniper user, making money and sticking it to the books, right along with the rest of them.

But today, his mind kept drifting to an afternoon call—one that had nothing to do with code pushes or conversion funnels and everything to do with putting LineSniper on the industry's main stage.

At two o'clock sharp, he was on with the head of a Vegas event production company—all teeth and tanned skin on the other end of the Zoom feed. They'd been circling each other for weeks, tossing around the idea of an exclusive LineSniper Conference.

Not a conference in the conventional sense. This would be *the* gathering for serious arbers, the kind of people who spoke in edge percentages and could do implied probability math faster than they could text.

Panels with industry insiders. Closed-door sessions on advanced models. Real-time betting challenges projected onto thirty-foot screens. Even a lavish networking reception, highballs in hand, the Strip glittering in the background.

Aaron could see it. The social content would be insane, the FOMO off the charts. And once they got the whales in the room, others would beg to follow.

July 2026: less than a year to pull it off. Aggressive? Definitely. But in a space evolving at warp speed, moving slow wasn't only risky. It was fatal.

"This could be your South by Southwest," the CEO was saying, hands chopping the air for emphasis. "But for sports betting."

Aaron liked that a lot. This wasn't some vanity project—it was a growth engine. A brand moment. The kind of thing that could triple subscriptions in a quarter. And he had some ideas to ensure it would do just that.

After the call, he closed the laptop and leaned back in his chair. They'd made progress. He'd asked for a contract to be sent over. The conference was real now. This was the moment he'd been chasing, the chance to push LineSniper from a cult tool to a household name in the sports-betting world.

He wandered back to the dashboard for one last pass before calling it a day. New sign-ups were still rolling in, and the graphs were still pointing skyward. Every click, every upgrade, every extra hour spent on-platform meant more fuel for the rocket he'd built. He turned toward the Arizona horizon, already thinking about tomorrow's numbers. Aaron Ramsey had no intention of slowing down.

7

RETURN ON INVESTMENT

IT WAS EARLY OCTOBER, the kind of in-between stretch when the leaves still clung stubbornly to their branches but the air had started carrying that first crisp edge. Fall was coming. He could smell it on the walk over.

The Welcome Vestibule—as the brushed-gold sign on the glass door called it—was a lobby with a fancy title. But it did smell incredible, like walking into a dialed-down Yankee Candle Outlet. Warm, clean, layered—something green at the edges, something rich underneath. Subtle enough to feel sophisticated. Expensive, even.

Chase had never been a "spa guy." Robes, cucumber water, whispered voices—they had always seemed like something from the opposite end of the gender aisle. But here, surrounded by rich walnut paneling, deep leather chairs, an assortment of teas, gold-wrapped dark chocolates, and muted gray walls hung with black-and-white landscape photography, it didn't feel frivolous. It felt...calm.

He gave himself permission to sink into the cushions, shoulders loosening against the supple leather. No kids yelling. No email alerts. No ticking clock telling him to be somewhere else. He let the environment do its work and for the first time in months felt an unmistakable easing of the knots in his back, the absence of chaos reminding him how much chaos he normally lived in.

Yeah, he could get used to this. And it wasn't simply the indulgence. This was practical. Strategic. A critical step toward fixing the neck issues that had been dogging him for years. A reward, yes, but one with ROI.

The thought of ROI pulled him back to how he'd gotten here. He glanced around the so-called Tranquility Lounge, where he'd been ushered to wait for his "therapeutic practitioner," and pulled his phone from his pocket. For half a second, he expected a disapproving, whisper-voiced spa attendant to materialize and scold him. Instead, he thumbed to PickTracker and let September's profit number fill the screen.

$5,707.

Even now, weeks later, it gave him a little jolt. Sure, $2,500 of that was from sign-up bonuses, but the rest was pure arbs. Actual bets, actual edges, actual wins.

When his free LineSniper trial ended a few weeks earlier, he'd hesitated for all of thirty seconds before springing for the $1,500 annual subscription with a determined gulp, a year-long declaration that he was doing this for real. It was a commitment, a stake in the ground. Now it barely registered. In one month, he'd already covered a full year's worth of biweekly massages with change left over.

If anything, the number didn't merely make him proud—it made him restless. He was certain he could do better. September had been careful, calculated. Now he knew the ropes. If he could push more dollars into circulation, especially on weekends when football markets swung wildly, there was no reason he couldn't double this. Maybe triple it. Maybe more.

He leaned back, letting his eyes wander: the rippling water of a wall fountain, the soft guitar notes drifting through the air, the faint layered scent he still couldn't quite name. This was the picture he'd carried in his head back in August—a little more money, a little more breathing room, the means to take care of his body. And now he was living it.

The door opened, and a petite woman with an iPad stepped in. She glanced down. "Chase Dupree?"

He slid his phone back into his pocket, stood, and offered a polite smile toward the woman in the black spa uniform waiting to lead him back. His wrist buzzed. Reflex. *Why not make a couple extra bucks before going dark for an entire hour?*

"Give me a minute," he said, thumb already moving. Notification. Edge. Flip screen. Bet. Confirm. Flip. Bet. Confirm. Done. It took less time than it would to unwrap one of the chocolates on the table.

He pocketed the phone again. "Yes, that's me. It's nice to meet you," he said warmly, as he fell into step behind her toward the dim hallway lined with closed doors and flickering candles.

8

PERFECT COVER

BY MID-NOVEMBER, Chase was starting to wonder if even the sports-books wanted him to win. Everything was going his way. There had been some missteps, sure, but Blaine was right. The occasional botched arb almost always evened itself out. And the successful arbs individually packed together into a growing downhill snowball, gaining size and momentum with each green confirmation screen.

October had been his best month yet—a whopping **$11,321** in profit, a number he still checked twice a week in the Note he kept on his iPhone, and November was already shaping up to beat it. He could see the trend line, as steady and certain as the growing balance in his accounts.

He told himself nothing had changed. He was still the same guy— good dad, good husband, competent at work, bringing home the same steady paycheck. If anything, he was simply better resourced now.

No question about it, every single free minute—and *free time* was starting to cover territory it had no business covering, from bedtime stories to dinners with Tara—now went to arbing. But wasn't that the point of a side hustle? Using the margins of your day to widen the margins of your bank account?

He'd even gotten strategic about work travel, shifting several flights to late-night departures so he could be parked at DCA between 5 p.m. and 7 p.m., that magic window when NBA and NHL lineups dropped and the markets went haywire long enough to make him good money. Sitting at the gate, earbuds in, he was invisible. Efficient. A machine.

The machine was humming. And machines, he figured, didn't get tired.

* * *

The Tuesday before Thanksgiving, his phone buzzed with a text from Blaine.

BLAINE: Thanksgiving plans?

They'd been texting almost daily. Blaine had become the one person Chase could talk to about arbing without explanation or restraint, someone who understood the rush and matched his energy beat for beat. Lately, Chase found himself letting messages from his other friends sit unanswered, but Blaine's were different. They bookended his days with plenty in between.

CHASE: Driving to Indy to spend the holiday with Tara's side of the family.

BLAINE: The Hoosier State! How long?

CHASE: Four days.

BLAINE: Perfect. Download Dynasty. Also BetJungle, OddsBet, and some others I'll send. Indiana-only promos. You'll be rolling in it. Better start lining up excuses to sneak away now.

A list followed within seconds—the first three names familiar, the next four complete strangers. He downloaded them all before dinner. More books meant more opportunity. More opportunity meant more money.

That night, he shifted another chunk of their down payment fund across the digital divide. He'd stopped formally tracking the total, though somewhere in the back of his mind he knew it was north of $40,000, roughly half the fund. In his head, it wasn't spent. It was *deployed.* A different kind of savings account, one with a far better interest rate. And like any other investment, it wasn't something Tara needed to worry about. She was busy enough.

The next morning, they were up at the crack of dawn, hopeful they could beat the holiday traffic and hit I-70 before it clogged, a solid ten hours on the road, not counting the inevitable potty breaks. The Honda Pilot was packed to the ceiling, every nook crammed with some toy, book, or "necessity" the girls insisted they couldn't live without.

Cece and Savannah were barely buckled before the movie negotiations began.

"First hour of the drive, no screens," Tara reminded them, crammed between the two in the back at their continued insistence.

"Same rule for Daddy?" Cece asked, eyes narrowing.

Chase grinned and scrolled to his favorite SiriusXM station—Bon Jovi, the real rocker of New Jersey, no disrespect to The Boss. The first guitar riff from "Livin' on a Prayer" filled the car. Chase's favorite. Both girls groaned. So did Tara. He sang it every night, whether they wanted to hear it or not.

"Same rule applies to me, Cece, but driver picks the music for the first hour," Chase said in full dad mode, drumming the steering wheel. Truthfully, he'd have caved and queued up the Disney movie right then if it meant skipping an hour of screaming, pleading, and fruitless bargaining, but limits were important, he told himself.

The irony didn't cross his mind.

As they pulled out of the garage, the station flipped to "Bad Medicine." Jon's voice cut through the cabin, lyrics that spoke to having everything except the thing that actually mattered, about trying and failing to shake something toxic loose. Chase's grip on the wheel tightened for a beat. He knew the song was about love, but the sentiment landed closer to home than he cared to admit.

They hit the highway, Indiana-bound. Their Google Maps route was a ribbon of green. They'd beaten the traffic out of the DMV. If it held, they had 600 miles of smooth sailing ahead.

By late morning, notifications began to pop across the top of his phone—sweet little plus signs blinking like lures in dark water. State boundaries came and went, betting switches invisibly flipping on and off as they crossed each new jurisdiction. He couldn't help himself. There was money to be made, and the highway ahead was straight and empty. The car could practically drive itself.

Seventy miles an hour, left hand on the wheel, right thumb flicking across his screen, he placed wagers between exits, actively ignoring the "Don't Text and Drive" signs along the shoulder.

Tara sat in the back with the girls, silent. She didn't have to say anything. He could feel her watching.

It occurred to him briefly that she might be tallying something entirely different than profit. He pushed the thought aside. In a few weeks, she'd see the balance sheet and understand why he'd been so focused lately.

After more than ten hours in the car, Chase felt a surge of relief when they turned onto his brother-in-law and sister-in-law's street. Their community, Meridian-Kessler, had that old-neighborhood charm money couldn't fake—broad, tree-lined streets, deep front porches, and century-old homes that carried a lifetime's worth of stories in their walls. The air was crisp, carrying the faint smell of woodsmoke from a nearby fireplace. Dry leaves flitted across the driveway.

He killed the engine and stepped out into the amber wash of the November sunset, the brick and stone around them glowing as if the whole neighborhood had been polished for their arrival. TJ, Kristen, their two kids, and the family's overly friendly goldendoodle, Bella, spilled out the front door in a happy tangle of arms, voices, and paws. Genuine, overdue hugs followed before a burst of overlapping greetings as the four kids darted between adults and Bella wove frenetic circles around everyone's legs.

There was a round of small talk on the front steps. The words, "It's been too long" were traded more than once before Chase excused himself to "unpack." He hoped the Wi-Fi inside was a little more modern than the houses themselves. What he really unpacked once he got upstairs was his iPad and the Indiana-only books he'd loaded the night before. Prime arb hour was already ticking away, and he wasn't about to waste it.

* * *

Thanksgiving morning, he offered to take Bella for a long walk. "I'll help her burn some energy," he said. And he did, placing bets between fire hydrants and leaf piles along the way. He knew it would raise eyebrows. The Macy's Thanksgiving Day Parade was known by all to be one of Chase's favorite traditions, especially the moment when Santa Claus made his grand appearance to usher in the holiday season. And since becoming a dad, he'd felt an even deeper tug toward those holiday traditions.

They're five and three. They won't even remember, he'd reasoned with himself.

By the time the early dinner rolled around later that day, the house was full. TJ's brother—Chase's other brother-in-law—and his family had arrived, along with Chase's mother-in-law, Kat, and even a few faces from Kristen and TJ's circle of friends he didn't recognize. When it was all said and done, there were more than twenty people, each assigned to one of three tables like seating had been planned with the tight orchestration of a wedding reception. Chase registered immediately that it would make slipping away later a lot easier—more noise, more movement, more cover.

The spread was sumptuous and could have fed the group ten times over. Kristen and TJ had executed the day with precision—festive décor in warm autumn tones, candles flickering on the sideboard, and platters that seemed to appear at the exact moment anyone's plate had room for more. The courses arrived in perfect sequence, like trains pulling into a station exactly on schedule, each one greeted with a chorus of appreciative murmurs. From the golden-brown turkey to the pillowy mashed potatoes with a pool of melted butter, everything was meticulously planned, down to the last cranberry.

It struck Chase as quietly endearing, the kind of thoughtful touches that made it obvious Kristen and TJ cared about everyone being there and wanted the day to become a cherished family memory.

But despite his best efforts to create that memory, Chase couldn't block out the faint, muffled call of the Lions game drifting in from the living room. The soft intonation of the play-by-play threaded itself into the conversation at the table, tugging at him. He smiled, nodded at the right times, passed dishes as they came, but part of him was somewhere else entirely—itching to check a score, a line, an opportunity.

During the family chaos that ensued once the kids had been excused from their table, the bathroom became his office. No one questioned it. It was the perfect retreat. Long bathroom trips were what men did—though at one point late that night, when only the immediate family remained, TJ cracked, "Kristen's gravy not sitting right with you, Chase?" There was a ripple of nervous laughter.

Chase played along. "Hey, I'm making sure there's room for all the leftovers tomorrow." Better they laugh than pry.

The next day, they took the kids to the gymnasium at St. Michael's, where Kat had been an art teacher for nearly four decades. Over the years, she'd collected keys to about every door on campus, and now that access was paying off, giving the little ones a private place to wear themselves out on a particularly cold day.

Chase went along, begrudging and half-present. He distractedly called out encouragement from a chair along the court's sideline, until the sharp pierce of a whistle from right behind his head jolted him to attention. He turned, annoyed, to find Kat standing there with a whistle and a playful look. "One lap every time I catch you on that phone!" she teased. Irritation threatened to spill over. *Don't give them a reason to say you weren't yourself,* he warned himself.

Instead, he jogged a comically slow lap, played tag with the girls for a few minutes, then slipped away for another "bathroom break."

* * *

Saturday morning was cold and gray, but the air still carried anticipation. For Buckeye fans, this wasn't any other Saturday—it was The Game. Ohio State versus Michigan. The one that decided bragging rights for the next 365 days.

After breakfast, Chase and TJ bundled up and walked a few blocks to The Iron Stag, a local favorite with a massive rectangular bar dominating the center, booths and high-tops hugging the perimeter, and TVs covering nearly every inch of wall space. Today, nearly all of them were tuned to Ann Arbor, where kickoff was minutes away.

They ordered a bucket of beers and settled into a high-top with a perfect view of the main screen. But even as the Buckeyes started their march on the opening drive, Chase's eyes kept drifting down to his phone. Lines were shifting for the afternoon slate. Every time an edge notification popped up, it pulled at him. He'd glance up for a play or two, then thumbed back into his apps, placing arbs between third downs and timeouts.

By the fourth quarter, with the game tied and tension mounting, TJ leaned in. "Everything okay?" he asked, keeping his voice casual but his eyes fixed on Chase. "You've seemed a little…absent this trip."

It was one of the first times anyone had said it out loud. For a second, Chase felt something he hadn't in months: guilt—and the faint worry TJ might actually press the point. He slid the phone face-down on the table. "Yeah, all good," he said a little too defensively. "Sorry. Been dealing with some unexpected work stuff."

TJ nodded, letting it go. Chase forced himself to keep his hands off the phone for the rest of the quarter, riding the game out the way he used to—leaning forward on big plays, groaning on near-misses.

Ohio State won on a late field goal, a nail-biter that should have left him floating for days. But as the crowd roared and high-fives flew, Chase didn't feel it. Not really. For the second time that season, the euphoria that used to carry him after a big Buckeye win wasn't there.

* * *

The drive back home that afternoon was quieter. Tara's frustration showed in the way she folded her arms, in how her gaze stayed fixed on the passing scenery. So he made a point to avoid betting while behind the wheel. But the itch was still there. Every fill-up, potty break, and snack stop became an arb-filled lightning round, and he made sure to add a few extra pull-offs for good measure. "Better safe than sorry," he told her at their fifth stop. Her look said she knew the truth he wasn't going to say.

The day after they returned to DC, on the last day of the month, Chase sat at the kitchen table, phone perched in front of him, his profit Note glowing like a scoreboard. The number next to November read **$16,243**. Another record and a jaw-dropping milestone. His side hustle had surpassed the monthly income from his nine-to-five job. He set the phone down and leaned back, shaking his head in utter disbelief.

Somewhere in the back of his mind, a place he was getting better at ignoring, he wondered how long streaks like this could last.

He pushed back from the table and started toward the bedroom, ready to call it a night. But as he was pulling back the covers, a buzz jolted his wrist. To his mind, it was like a factory whistle at dawn, sharp and unrelenting, summoning workers to the line whether they wanted to be there or not. He turned, almost without thinking, and slipped back out to the living room to avoid waking Tara, already swiping before he'd even settled onto the couch.

9

WHAT YOU CAN'T UNSEE

THE MONDAY AFTER THANKSGIVING always felt like a hard gear shift, but this one slid in with a hollow calm. The apartment was remarkably back in order—suitcases unpacked, weekly groceries neatly lining the refrigerator shelves, the girls' coats once again hanging on the proper hook inside the front door. Tara had been up late last night, hours after they returned from Indianapolis. Maybe she'd been antsy after the long car ride. Maybe she'd been avoiding Chase. Either way, she'd thrown herself into tidying the apartment as they approached the final and busiest month of the year. Yet something about this morning's stillness and order unsettled her.

She stood at the kitchen counter, rinsing grapes under a slow stream of water, prepping school lunches. Savannah's voice floated in from the living room, lilting and certain. "Mommy, will you read me bedtime stories tonight after school?"

That was new.

For years, bedtime stories had been Chase's thing. The girls piled on either side of him on the couch or in bed, his voice carrying them into whatever imaginary world they chose that night. She'd been the understudy, stepping in if he was running late from work or stuck on a call. But lately, it was as if the casting had been quietly reversed without anyone telling her.

She shook the water from her hands, listening for Chase's response, expecting a firm objection, his usual mock outrage whenever the girls asked for anyone but him to take the coveted bedtime story role. But it didn't come. A moment later, she heard the muted scrape of a chair leg against the floor in the other room. Chase appeared seconds later, eyes locked on his phone, mumbling, "I need to get to work. Love you all. Have a good day." And he was out the door without a second glance.

Emotion swelled in her chest—tears not yet heavy enough to fall, but waiting, queued for the moment they'd be called upon. And she knew that moment was coming soon.

That evening, she found him at his desk, laptop open, face lit by its pale glow. The sound of the girls giggling in their bedroom carried across the apartment, competing with the faint murmur of the TV in the living room. Chase didn't look up when she walked in.

"You eating with us?" she asked from the doorway.

"Yeah," he said, still typing. "Give me two minutes."

Two minutes had become his favorite unit of time lately. Two minutes to finish an email. Two minutes to wrap up "one more thing." Two minutes to the point where they'd start eating without him, the plates already cooling on the table. It had become so constant that Savannah, all of three years old, now parroted him, chirping, "Two more minutes, Mama!" as her own stalling tactic.

When he finally arrived to dinner, Chase laughed at something on his phone, an abrupt guffaw that startled both girls mid-bite. Tara smiled reflexively, waiting for the explanation, but he only shook his head. "Group chat," he said, quickly darkening the screen with a click before setting it face-up beside his plate, biding time before the next tempting message, another that would prove more absorbing than the conversation in front of him.

Later, as she was cleaning up, her phone buzzed on the counter. Julia's name lit the screen.

JULIA: Weird question—do you know if something's going on with Chase? Blaine's been glued to his phone. Like, constantly. Every time I sneak a glance, it's a message from Chase. They're texting all the time.

Tara frowned. The low thrum of unease she'd been harboring suddenly sharpened into something with edges. She typed, "Not sure. Why? You think something's up?" But she deleted it.

This warranted more than a text. With the girls asleep, she stepped onto the patio, a prickle of nerves creeping in, though she wasn't entirely sure why. She pressed the Call button under Julia's name. The cold night air nipped at her cheeks as she waited, the neighborhood silent below.

Julia picked up on the third ring. "Hey, sorry for the random text. It's just... Blaine's been different lately. On his phone nonstop. Up late. Gets weird if I ask about it. I know he and Chase have always talked, but lately it's been a lot."

Tara leaned against the railing. "Yeah," she said slowly, "I've noticed a few changes too."

Julia sighed into the receiver. "I'm probably overreacting. Maybe it's some sports thing. I don't know. But at Thanksgiving Blaine barely looked up from that damn phone. I felt like I was eating with a stranger. My mom was *not* happy. She pulled me aside before the trip home. She's worried he's not pulling his weight with Quinn. And she was pretty offended he barely said a word to her the entire trip."

Tara pictured Chase at the Thanksgiving table, half listening to the conversation, half absorbed in compulsively checking his phone beneath it. She'd told herself he was decompressing, that work had been stressful lately. But hearing Julia describe Blaine the same way made that excuse feel flimsy.

"You're not imagining it, Julia. Chase is basically a carbon copy of what you described with Blaine, maybe not as far gone but definitely not himself."

As Julia kept talking, Tara's mind drifted, unbidden, to a dim hospital waiting room years ago. Beige walls, the pungent smell of antiseptic, a Styrofoam cup cooling in her hands. She'd stared at a single cracked tile in the floor for so long it had imprinted itself in her mind, the kind of detail you never remember unless it's tied to something you'd rather forget.

She blinked the memory away before Julia could notice the silence. "Maybe we should keep an eye on it," she said.

"That's exactly what I was thinking," Julia replied. "But listen, if he's the same at Christmas as he was at Thanksgiving, I'm saying something. I can't pretend I don't see it."

Tara's chest tightened. She dreaded the thought of a conversation with Chase that would land like an accusation. It felt too soon for that, but she didn't tell Julia she was wrong. "Okay," she said instead, "let's see how the next few weeks go."

Tara instinctively weighed her options. *If I push too hard, he'll shut down. If I say nothing, it might get worse.* She'd seen him testy before. Lately, though, his patience felt thinner. Chase had always been slow to snap, the type to let small annoyances roll past. Now he bristled over nothing—a misplaced spoon in the dishwasher, a question about his day, or worst of all any hint that she thought he wasn't fully present. The shift had been subtle at first, but it was becoming impossible to miss. And once she'd seen it, she couldn't keep pretending it wasn't there.

When she hung up and walked back inside, the apartment was still. She paused in the doorway, taking in the scene.

Chase was on the couch, the girls tucked into bed hours ago, his feet propped on the ottoman. The TV screen glowed against his glasses—the ones he only wore when his eyes were tired from hours in front of a screen—reflecting rapid flickers of color.

The phone buzzed twice in his lap. Without looking away from the TV, he picked it up instantly, thumbs moving fast, mouth curling in the faintest smile.

Tara eased into the couch beside him, saying nothing, unnoticed. She watched the glow of the phone dance across his face, illuminating a small, private world.

And for the first time, she wondered if she was on the cusp of losing someone again to the pull of something dark and relentless.

10

UNWRAPPED

CHASE HAD GROWN ACCUSTOMED to the velocity. He could toss $750 on one side of a bet without hesitation. Have $30,000 in play by lunch on a football Saturday. In the beginning, a bet like that would have made his palms sweat, if he could stomach it at all. Now, it felt almost small. Profits that once felt monumental now rolled in without so much as a second thought.

But in the last week, something had shifted. The profits weren't accelerating. The slope of the graph was still rising, but the climb felt... slower. And to Chase, slower was unacceptable.

He fired off a text to Blaine.

CHASE: Feels like I'm leaving money on the table. We know this arb window won't last forever. Need to max it out. Need another edge.

BLAINE: Haven't mentioned it yet, but I've been live arbing for two months. Frenetic, but I'm sold. Crazy numbers if you've got the nerve.

CHASE: Live arbing?

BLAINE: Yup. LineSniper premium. Gives you access to arbs during games. Pregame lines are kiddie pool. Live is the ocean. Massive edges. Total game changer.

Blaine's quick rundown was all it took—odds shifting in real time, lines dancing and strobing before, during, and after every play. It was faster. Riskier. And, according to Blaine, a gold mine for those with the reflexes to pounce.

That night, Chase dropped another $1,500 for LineSniper's live module. Within minutes, it felt like he'd swallowed the red pill. Doors he hadn't known existed now flying open. His screen became a blur: markets opening and closing mid-play, a rebound line jumping two points after an early substitution, a money line flipping favorites after a fumble.

The first live arb hit like a chemical reaction. Why hadn't he done this sooner? Pregame arbing suddenly felt like betting on the weather. It also meant more time on his phone, each edge another minute he'd never get back.

* * *

Work emails had finally slowed to a trickle, the one true hiatus of the calendar year. The last gifts had been handed off to teachers, and the obligatory cookie-tin deliveries had been made to local friends. For once, there were no deadlines, no stacked calendars, no grinding weight of midlife adulting pressing down. A few days to breathe.

They packed the trusty car once more and pointed it toward the Midwest, bound for their second trip there in a month.

The Duprees rolled into Columbus the day before Christmas Eve, pulling into the sprawling apartment complex Louise, Chase's mom, had called home for more than five years. It was the kind of place where the quality was undermined by uniformity, identical beige buildings lined in perfect rows, each front door indistinguishable from the next. Even after years of visits, Chase still crept along at five miles per hour, racking his brain to remember which barracks-like section was hers.

He finally spotted it, helpfully marked by the inflatable Santa waving from her balcony—a new addition for the girls. As they rolled into the nearest guest parking spot, Louise stood waiting outside their door, practically bouncing like a puppy that hadn't seen its owner in weeks, long black hair cascading over a bright holiday scarf. Hugs came first, her perpetual deep tan standing in warm, vivid contrast to her fair-skinned son.

Cece and Savannah squealed as Bebe, their nickname for Grandma, handed each of them a reindeer cake pop the moment they climbed out of the car.

"Nice, Mom. You just earned yourself bedtime duty. Have fun with that sugar crash," Chase said with a grin. There was something undeniably endearing about watching grandparents spoiling their grandkids, even if it blew up the fragile routines children and their exhausted parents depended on.

As they unloaded the car, Chase noticed the community lawn had become a dull patchwork of brown grass. It looked like a reverse canvas, muddy, awaiting a cleanse from the first snow. Inside, Louise's apartment was warm in every sense. It was akin to stepping into a Hallmark movie—tasteful, not kitsch: two full-sized trees adorned from star to skirt, framed photos of the girls on Santa's lap, cozy red blankets draped over pristine white couches, and a rotating menu of homemade cookies. She'd been a stay-at-home mom when Chase was growing up, and she still had a knack for making every visit feel like an exhale.

Settling into the familiar armchair, Chase replayed the internal dialogue that had consumed much of the car ride.

He could tell he was on thin ice with Tara. Her patience had frayed, her glances colder, her silences heavier. For the next few days, he resolved to be the best version of himself. He owed his family that much. He'd get his bets in before dawn, then another round after dark, once the house was asleep. The phone would stay silent during the day.

And for a while, it worked.

Christmas Eve and Christmas Day passed in a warm, golden blur. There was Christmas Eve Mass at St. Brigid and a candlelit Holy Dinner—the long-standing Slovak tradition where the rituals outshone the food, but togetherness was the most cherished part of all. A lazy morning of gifts and giggles, the girls in stunned awe that Santa had found them all the way in Ohio. Board games, sugar cookies slathered with frosting, *A Charlie Brown Christmas* for the fifth time in two days, and *Christmas Vacation* for the adults at night. Tara looked lighter, quicker to laugh, quicker to lean over and kiss Chase's cheek. Chase felt a quiet pride in himself, proof that he could balance it all—family, work, and the hunt for edges.

But that glimpse of balance was only a mirage. The morning after Christmas, Chase volunteered to make a grocery run. Just a quick trip for eggs, bread, and a few things Louise needed for a snowman s'more project with the girls. The store was a three-minute drive. It should take forty-five minutes, tops.

His initial intent had been genuine—a helpful trip for his mom. Two days of restraint, however, had created a dangerous buildup, pressure behind a dam that couldn't hold. All those NBA Christmas Day games abandoned, all that profit left on the table. He had targets to hit if December was going to break another record. As soon as he cut the engine in the parking lot, his darker impulse took over. And once inside, the hours bled together under the buzz of fluorescent lights, the sweet smell of the bakery hanging in the air—holiday rolls, cookies, bread—tempting everyone but him. His eyes stayed locked on odds, not groceries. By the time he swiped his card at the register, even he was shocked at how much time had vanished.

Three and a half hours later, he returned...without the bread. He blamed the store itself—aisles laid out like a maze, shelf labels so tiny you'd need a magnifying glass, self-checkout lines moving at a molasses state of confusion, retirees shuffling like extras in a bad comedy.

The women of the house weren't buying it. Tara's lips pressed into a flat line. Louise didn't say anything, but he caught the hint of concern before she turned back to the counter.

Though Chase would never admit it, their concern was justified.

* * *

The next afternoon, Cece wanted to try the fake snow science kit Bebe had given her, a gift born of Ohio's increasingly snowless Christmases. Chase was assigned chaperone duties. He and Cece bundled up, Chase wishing it were like her first Christmas, when seven inches of real snow had fallen unexpectedly overnight, a scene off a postcard. They headed for the access road behind the building. It wasn't a street so much as a glorified alley for residents to get to and from their garages.

Cece howled with giddy laughter as she mixed the mystery powder from bag one with the secret ingredients of bag two, conjuring a personal one-square-foot winter wonderland.

Chase sat on the curb, knees bent, phone in hand, lining up a live arb on a Knicks player's three-pointer over/under total. One more click.

A horn blast. Screeching tires.

He jumped to his feet, heart pounding. A gray Kia Telluride was twenty feet away, barely out of its garage, the driver's hand still on the wheel, eyes wide. Cece stood frozen, a mitten half-raised like a miniature traffic cop commanding the car to halt.

Before Chase could react, Tara burst out the back door, eyes ablaze, her fury fixed squarely on him.

"What in the HELL is on that goddamn phone that's more important than your child?"

Her voice cut through the cold air, raw and shaking. She grabbed Cece without looking at him and stormed inside.

Shit. She'd been watching from the window the whole time, keeping tabs after yesterday's poorly explained disappearance.

He stayed there a moment, the sound of his blood still coursing through his ears, breath clouding in front of him.

His girl was safe, thank God. He'd only looked down for a minute. The street was barely used. Cece had played back there countless times in her five years of visiting Bebe. This wasn't his fault.

The rest of the day was uncomfortable, thick with the kind of tension that crackled in the air like static before a storm.

74

Later that night, after the girls were asleep, Louise suggested a movie. Chase was fine with that. He knew a conversation with Tara was coming, and this diversion bought him time to brace for it. *If people don't have anything nice to say, silence them with a movie,* he thought, twisting the old adage to fit his circumstances.

The cinematic interlude also gave him a chance to mindlessly place live arbs on the late-night NBA games.

To this day, he couldn't say what the movie was about—some Ryan Gosling (or was it Ryan Reynolds?) rom-com with an ending as predictable as an arb profit.

As the credits rolled, Louise, who lived alone, couldn't help herself. She finally had company, and the questions came rapid-fire. "Did you have any idea he was going to come back for her? How much do you think a night costs at that resort where they met? Haven't I seen his mother in something before? She's famous, isn't she?"

Chase didn't have the energy to feign interest.

"It really wasn't that great, Mom. Can we not do this?"

She studied him. At first, frustration, but her maternal instincts won out. Her expression softened. "Are you okay, honey?"

"I'm fine. It's *my* free time. I work hard. I parent. If I want to make money instead of watching some dumb movie, that's my choice."

He could see the confusion register on her face. Tara's eyebrows rose ever so slightly at the admission of how he had been spending his time. He immediately regretted the snap. He'd been so disciplined about taking the criticisms in stride these last four months. Even to his own ears, this sounded defensive. But he didn't take it back.

When it came time to return to DC, Chase hated the heaviness in the air, a stark contrast to their joyous arrival, but there was nothing he could do to reverse it now.

"Take care of yourself, Chase," Louise said as he wedged the last piece of luggage into the car-turned–three-dimensional puzzle. There was a sadness in her voice, the kind he now recognized that came from a parent who could only ever be as happy as their unhappiest child.

Why couldn't anyone see that he was finally making his own happiness, taking action for the first time in years? He knew money alone wouldn't buy contentment, but it was giving him control. He was using it to fund direct action, investments in his health that were already paying physical dividends. And beyond that, he was staring at tens of thousands of dollars more than he'd ever imagined when this began. Think of what he could provide for his family, and for himself, with those resources.

New Year's resolutions had always mattered to Chase. And now, he resolved to carve out time in the coming days to map exactly how he'd use his winnings. Surely, when Tara and the others saw the tangible results his efforts had produced, they would understand. They'd invariably support his unrelenting drive, no different from an entrepreneur in the early days of building a company. Short-term sacrifice. Long-term security.

The drive home evoked an eerie sense of déjà vu. Same highways. Same characters. Same prophetic messages from SiriusXM.

Tara stared out the passenger window, saying nothing. Another Bon Jovi track played faintly through the speakers. The title alone, "Rich Man Living in a Poor Man's House," felt pointed, and the song's story of a husband overlooking the wealth that existed right in front of him hit harder than Chase cared to admit.

He kept his eyes on the road, the lyrics curling through his head, reshaping into a message that he couldn't decide was comforting or condemning.

One thing he knew with certainty: 2025 wasn't ending the way he'd envisioned.

11

FACE OF THE REBELLION

MARCO LEANED AGAINST THE IRON RAILING of a balcony in Lisbon, the December morning air cool enough to sting his cheeks. Down below, the tiled streets shimmered with holiday lights, golden strands looped between buildings. Behind him, Mateo announced, to no one in particular, that tonight he was going to try pistachio gelato. His wife was calling for him to come inside, but Marco ignored them both. The angle was too perfect.

He raised his phone, framing the selfie with influencer instinct: pastel facades, cobblestones, a cathedral spire cutting into the sky. It was a much-needed pause from the endless stream of beaches and palm trees he'd been pumping into his feed. This was why they were here. Europe was different. Europe was cultured. Europe diversified the dream life he was selling and gave it an air of sophistication beyond sun-drenched leisure. The post would write itself. "Trading turquoise seas for centuries of history. Same freedom, new backdrop."

As the faux shutter clicked, his phone buzzed. A new message. A name lit the screen, one that sent a jolt through him every time. Aaron Ramsey.

Marco still couldn't quite believe it. The shift had come in late fall—casual on the surface, seismic underneath. LineKing had sent a Discord message, offhandedly suggesting they dispense with aliases and speak as Aaron and Marco. Efficiency, on paper. In reality, it was an invitation. A seat at the table. A partnership advancing. And with it a new deal: his referral cut doubled—half of every dollar his recruits paid, locked in for as long as they stayed on the platform. Every user he funneled into LineSniper was now a permanent annuity. His own private pension, paid in green checks. Marco had never felt closer to the inner circle. Hell, he *was* the inner circle now.

Marco looked at the time.

10:00 a.m. local.

That meant it was 2:00 a.m. in Phoenix. It seemed like Aaron never slept.

> **AARON:** Big news, man. LineSniper LIVE is locked with the venue. Invites go out Jan. 1 to the top 350 users. You're the face. Need a welcome video from you to embed in the email. Can get a production guy to you when you're back in the States.

He reread it three times, ego swelling with each pass. "You're the face."

It made sense, of course. Even Aaron knew it. LineSniper was his company, sure, but Marco—ArbOracle—was the one who'd built the mythology. He was the one people screenshotted, quoted, memed, cursed, prayed to. If LineSniper LIVE was going to land like thunder, it needed his voice guiding the storm.

Aaron had pulled back the curtain on a Vegas gathering weeks ago, and Marco hadn't hesitated. He hadn't even bothered to check his calendar. Whatever was on it could move.

The rollout plan sounded razor-sharp, as Marco knew it would. An email on New Year's Day. Three hundred and fifty golden tickets dropped into the inboxes of the top users of 2025. Exclusive, cryptic, impossible to ignore. Click open, and there he'd be, inviting them in for the ride of a lifetime. Not a PDF. Not a banner ad. A face. A presence. Proof that the underground had gone prime time.

He could already see it. "If you're watching this, it's because you've proven you can see the angles others miss. LineSniper LIVE is where we sharpen those edges together."

MARCO: Hell yeah! Count me in. Tell me what you need and when.

A pause. The gray dots bubbled, disappeared, then returned.

AARON: Good. Plenty more to discuss. We'll talk by phone.

Whatever Aaron had to say, Marco was already in. His moment had arrived.

12

COUNTDOWN

THE APARTMENT HAD SETTLED into that familiar, deflating state of transition that always followed Christmas. The stacks of holiday cards had been unceremoniously tossed in the recycling bin, the Santa dishtowels swapped with plain ones, the half-burned gingerbread candles tucked back into their box in the storage unit. And yet a few remnants lingered stubbornly. The tree still stood by the window, proud but weary, its needles sagging beneath the strain of decades' worth of ornaments, its lights glowing defiantly against the gray afternoon beyond the glass.

Chase sat alone in the quiet, the apartment matching his mood. Melancholy. The holiday was over, the shimmer of the season gone, the tensions from Ohio still raw, and the new year hadn't yet begun. Tara had barely spoken to him since the near-disaster with Cece, and now she'd taken the girls to the mall for returns, no small endeavor, leaving him to the silence.

And so he did what had become a recent habit when the stillness pressed too hard and distraction felt easier than facing ugly truths. He turned to the numbers. His trusted refuge. His apps never scolded, never demanded, never rolled their eyes. They simply shone back at him with certainty. They were the one place he still felt in control, the one place that had yet to fail in sparking a trace of joy.

He unlocked his phone, opened PickTracker, and with a lazy swipe pulled up his monthly totals.

As the page loaded, Chase rubbed his temples—part fatigue, part disbelief. He'd already checked it twice, but the number refused to change. **$20,454.**

That was December's haul, and he still had two days left. Added to the prior three months, his running tally since Labor Day weekend came to $53,725. By the time the clock struck midnight and 2025 disappeared, he'd be above $54,000.

He leaned back in his chair, the squeak of the cheap IKEA frame unnervingly loud without the usual clatter of family life around him.

Fifty-four thousand dollars.

He'd set out hoping to scrape together $300 a month, a modest supplement for massages twice a month. Before he won that first arb, he'd even harbored aspirations of making enough for a new Nationals quarter-zip, maybe a golf round here or there. Nothing more extravagant than that. Instead, he had averaged more than $13,500 a month. In four months, he'd brought in over a third of his annual salary.

The absurdity of it made him shake his head, still stunned by the cheat code he'd stumbled onto, like he'd unlocked God mode in real life and no one else had noticed. This wasn't a side hustle anymore. It was something else entirely, something that had swallowed every fragment of time not claimed by work or fatherhood, and even stolen minutes that belonged to those categories too.

And for what?

That was the question gnawing at him lately.

Arbitrage wasn't an adrenaline-fueled hobby anymore: the nervous sweats, the pounding heart when he pressed Confirm. Now it was about systems. Precision. Volume. If he was going to keep this pace and justify the sacrifices, it needed a framework. Something that made sense not only to him but to Tara.

The thoughts had been swirling in his head for weeks. Now he finally had time to organize them. He pulled a yellow legal pad from under a stack of dusty books and cleared his desk. At the top he scrawled, "Arb Profit Plan—2026 and Beyond."

Like a man drafting the budget for a kingdom, he divided it into percentages. A blueprint. A ledger with a conscience. A home for every dollar. He'd divvy up the profit at the end of each month accordingly. Taxes: First things first. No one dodged the IRS. He earmarked a conservative 25% off the top, leaving him 75% to allocate.

10%–FAMILY SAVINGS: Practicality demanded it. Their joint savings account had inched along for years, chasing elusive goals—a hefty down payment, an early retirement, a cushion for emergencies. Now he could accelerate it, quietly bolstering their foundation without touching their salaries.

10%–COLLEGE FUNDS: Cece and Savannah. That was non-negotiable. Every win, every bleary-eyed midnight session glued to odds feeds would be, in some small way, laying bricks for their future. He pictured Cece at a library desk, Savannah bustling across some leafy campus quad, both of them buoyed by his secret ledger.

10%–FUNDOWMENT: His private joke. A personal endowment where the principal stayed untouchable, spinning off a perpetual 4% "payout" each year. A hedge against the future, a nod to permanence in a life that lately felt exceedingly volatile.

20%–FUN ACCOUNT (CHASE): He felt a thrill as he wrote it. Golf and ski trips. Concert tickets. Lavish dinners with friends or family. Whatever struck his fancy. His allowance. His justification. His reason to keep grinding.

25%–BIG BUCKETS: The experiences that could change the family's current trajectory. The memories he and Tara might recount in rocking chairs someday. The trips Cece and Savannah would still talk about when he was gone.

Within this category, he'd create buckets, funding them one at a time, like a genie granting wishes. His handwriting tightened as he carved out dreams.

- **$15,000–COUPLES TRIP TO ITALY:** Tara's birthright, never realized. She was a citizen, yet they had never gone together. He imagined the two of them wandering cobbled alleys in Florence, sipping Chianti in Tuscan hills, Venice at sunset.

- **$15,000–DISNEY WORLD:** Not the budget version, but a blowout. A week on property, deluxe resort, multiple parks, front-of-line wristbands, VIP tours, both sets of grandparents in tow. The kind of trip that would etch itself into Cece and Savannah's childhoods like pure magic.

- **$10,000–TROPICAL FAMILY VACATION:** Sand, surf, turquoise water. He could see the girls building castles on some distant beach.

- **$10,000–FAMILY SKI TRIP:** Matching ski jackets, hot cocoa breaks, Tara glowing by a fire. Chase had started skiing when he was three. It was time to introduce his girls to the family tradition.

- **$7,500–BIRTHDAY WEEKENDS:** He planned to let his girls, Tara included, have access to $2,500 to plan a long weekend trip for their respective birthdays. Acelas to New York. Five-story putt-putt courses in Myrtle Beach. Bottomless tastings at the World of Coca-Cola in Atlanta. If they could dream it, they'd be there.

Chase set the pen down, perfectly parallel to the pad that now held his unspoken hopes. He flexed his fingers, realizing how tightly he'd been gripping it as he scribbled.

He studied the page, admiring his work. A roadmap. A call to action.

Evidence that all the hours had a purpose. That the grind added up to something bigger than numbers on a screen.

The future was accounted for. The percentages were his 2026 North Star. But 2025's profits still sat in a savings account, waiting for direction. He flipped the page. Of the $54,000 he'd already made, after the 25% to Uncle Sam, more than $40,000 remained. The pen went back to work.

- **$4,500–MASSAGES:** Accounted for what he'd already spent these past four months, and fully funded bimonthly sessions through 2026.

He smiled at the absurdity of budgeting for massages alongside Italy. But that was the point, wasn't it? To make the small luxuries count as much as the big dreams.

- **$1,000–SPECIAL PAYMENT:** He had a plan he was about to put in motion, and it involved setting aside a nominal piece of his earnings. An investment in his future ability to grow profits further.

- **$20,000–BOAT CLUB MEMBERSHIP:** Tara and Chase had always joked about retiring to a waterfront community. Chase reminded her they already lived in one, even if they'd only watched the boats from shore all these years. Now, a big surprise for the family. Enough for at least three summers on the water, learning the ropes, making memories.

And for himself?

- **$10,000–THE 2026 WINTER OLYMPICS:** Northeast Italy. Hockey, alpine skiing, speed skating. His buddy in London had been tempting him to go for the last two decades. This would finally be his time to say yes. A pilgrimage, financed by odds.

He sprinkled the remaining $4,500 between the college funds, fun account, and big-bucket trips, just to get things started.

Chase sat back, surveying the architecture of it all. For the first time since he started the arb path, he felt clarity, not simply about the numbers but about the why.

His underlying rule for all of it was simple. Arb profits were for experiences, never material things. Stuff wore out, went out of style, got shoved into closets. Experiences etched themselves into memory, became part of a family's story. If he was sacrificing what little time he had to pursue this, the winnings had to buy moments that mattered.

Of course, it all hinged on one thing. The profits had to keep coming. For the time being they did, faster than he ever could have imagined, and he batted away any doubt like an enemy at the gate.

Now came the hard part, selling Tara.

For months, as he grasped the full potential of arbitrage, Chase had been weighing how to approach Tara. He settled on going big on New Year's Eve. If the faucet was still flowing by then, he'd know it was the real deal.

Several weeks prior, he had locked in their preferred babysitter. Madison conveniently lived right down the hall. The girls loved her. She loved them. He had her scheduled to arrive at nine the following night.

He'd also called in a favor from a friend in the restaurant industry, a buddy who still owed him after Chase had hosted a sizable client dinner at one of his friend's fledgling locations. And his friend delivered. The payoff: a reservation at La Grande Boucherie, the new crown jewel of DC dining, with cathedral ceilings, gilded mirrors, and an inaugural New Year's Eve soirée that was the buzz among Washingtonians.

It promised to be an extravagant evening—a ten-course prix fixe menu, champagne towers, a live twenty-two-piece band, indoor pyrotechnics—the whole glittering package.

He hadn't told Tara yet. That had always been the point, and the gravity of it all felt even greater now with the tension mounting between them.

When she returned from the mall with the girls and directed them straight to their seats for lunch, he finally sprang the news.

"Hey," he said with a mischievous grin. "You might need to head back to the mall for yourself. We've got plans tomorrow night."

She raised an eyebrow, worn out from fending off the gift-return crowds while corralling two wild toddlers.

She waved him off. "Plans? Chase, it's New Year's Eve. Our plan is frozen pizza, Ryan Seacrest, and bed by 10:30."

"Bold," Chase said. "A full hour later than last year."

She rolled her eyes, but he caught the trace of a smile she tried to hide.

"Not this year." He grinned. "I got Madison. She'll be here at nine. And we...have a reservation at La Grande Boucherie."

"Wait, what? You were able to get us into Boucherie? For New Year's?"

Her eyes lit up, but Chase caught something else flicker there too, a shadow of curiosity. How had he pulled this off? And why? She didn't ask, but he felt the unspoken question linger.

"Private table. Champagne at midnight, probably plenty before then too. You and me. We deserve it. We need it."

Tara blinked, the corners of her mouth twitching despite herself. "Who are you, and what have you done with my husband?"

She snatched the keys, and with a wink borrowed from their flirty, pre-parenting days, gushed, "Back to the mall. This new husband better be ready for a wife who's going to turn heads tomorrow night."

A current ripped through him. Maybe 2025 wouldn't end so badly after all.

* * *

Madison knocked at nine sharp, as reliable as ever. She breezed in with a smile, dropping her bag by the door and kicking off her house slippers. The girls squealed with delight when they saw her enter.

"How was the commute?" Chase joked.

"Nearly tripped on that loose carpet square outside apartment 310. Perilous on the roads these days," Madison quipped back.

Chase chuckled. Madison had always been quick-witted.

"Chase! You look so dapper!"

He was sporting a tailored midnight-green suit, the shade so deep it almost looked black, paired with a crisp white shirt and slim black tie—bold but controlled, every detail deliberate.

"Don't sound so surprised," he said with a grin. Turning his attention to the bedroom, he called out, "Tara, you ready?"

"Three minutes! Call the Uber!"

"On it!"

Chase turned back to Madison. She was younger than them, finishing her master's at American University, the type of babysitter every parent prayed for—smart, trustworthy, beloved by the kids, and always right on time. They traded small talk about her classes and their respective holiday trips.

As Madison was lamenting her delayed flight back from Kansas City earlier that week, the bedroom door opened.

Tara stepped out, and Chase's response evaporated in his throat.

Her off-the-shoulder dress fit so perfectly it was hard to believe it had come from the mall and not a tailor. Gold sequins shimmered. Her collarbones and shoulders gleamed under the light, slim sleeves hugging her arms before skimming further at the wrist. It was short, unapologetically so, drawing the eye to her long, toned legs, the cut leaving no doubt she knew exactly the effect she was having. Her lips were painted red. Her hair, pulled high into a sleek ponytail, only sharpened the line of her cheekbones, giving her a look of magnetic, almost dangerous elegance. Confidence moved with her. The sight made his chest jackhammer. She wasn't simply his wife tonight. She was the kind of woman who stopped conversations. And for one dizzying moment, Chase couldn't believe she was walking out with him.

A shiver went through him involuntarily.

Madison, oblivious, bent to pick up her bag. "You two look incredible. Have fun and happy New Year!"

The girls chorused from the living room, Cece waving a stuffed animal like a flag, Savannah clutching her blanket. "Bye, Mommy! Bye, Daddy!"

"Happy New Year, little loves," Tara said, her voice warm, eyes re-locking on Chase's.

He swallowed, fumbling for composure as he gave the girls one last hug and kiss and ushered her toward the door. They stepped into the hallway, hand in hand, the elevator already humming its way up to meet them. The city awaited.

* * *

La Grande Boucherie was a scene. The air hummed with overlapping laughter, clinking glasses and cutlery, the band reverberating through the cavernous room. The scent of seared filet mingled with truffle and champagne, sharp enough to make Chase's stomach growl despite himself. Camera flashes popped as national news anchors posed with their spouses near the entrance, the black-and-gold step-and-repeat ensuring that, for all of history, the restaurant's brand would linger in the background of family albums belonging to the city's power elite. Recognizable members of Congress leaned over cocktails in the corners, trading gossip disguised as small talk. Women shimmered in sequins and silk, men in tuxedos and tailored suits—a modern-day Gatsby tableau.

Chase forced himself not to gape. They had made it. This was the room everyone fought to get into. And for all the spectacle—DC's powerful and beautiful crammed into one golden space—he didn't think anyone there held a candle to Tara.

A hostess intercepted them at the door, her black dress as tailored as the smile she offered when she asked for their name. "Dupree, party of two," Chase heard himself say, and she lit up like she'd been waiting for them all evening. As they followed her down the red carpet, Chase caught the subtle turn of heads in their wake—men stealing second looks, women appraising Tara's dress with something between envy and awe.

He swelled with pride, walking taller at her side. Another hostess took over with seamless choreography. For a fleeting moment, they stood in the spotlight, flashes popping as a photographer positioned them shoulder to shoulder. "A stunning couple," he said, grinning behind the camera before sending them on their way. The next hostess greeted them as though they were royalty, telling them it was a pleasure to have them at La Grande Boucherie tonight, before leading them up the grand staircase. At the top, a private table waited on the balcony, overlooking the swirl of bodies and lights below, as if the party itself had been staged for them.

As the hostess poured champagne and slipped away, Tara crossed her legs beneath the table, letting her hand come to rest on Chase's thigh. Not the casual touch of a spouse at dinner—it lingered a little higher than usual, a little firmer, enough to make sure he understood. Her eyes stayed fixed on the glittering room below, but the message was unmistakable. She liked how this night was going.

"Okay," she whispered, leaning close, her hand still warm on his leg. "You've officially impressed me. Now tell me what's going on."

As the chaos of the room swirled around them, Chase swallowed. The noise fell away. The moment had come.

His palms felt slick against the stem of his glass. He studied her face for any sign of skepticism, terrified she'd laugh before he got the words out.

"I called in a favor to get us here because I wanted tonight to feel special, the right backdrop for something life-altering."

Her brows lifted, eyes staying locked on his. "Life-altering, huh? Now you've really got my attention."

Chase started with the basics: the dinner at Hearth & Ember, Blaine's pitch, the MRI results, Miles's massage recommendation, the $300 goal, the first arb. How it felt like a money glitch every time it worked. He spoke carefully, gauging her reaction. Tara's eyes narrowed at first, but when he laid the number on the table—$54,624 projected by the end of tonight—she actually gasped.

"You've made how much?"

"Over fifty-four grand. In four months."

She sat back, stunned. "That's… Chase, that's a lot of money. And you think you can keep it going?"

He nodded, reached into his jacket, and pulled out a thick, crisp envelope. He slid it across the table.

"What's this?"

"Your arb wife payment. I know I've been a little absent lately, getting the hang of this. It hasn't been fair. I want you to feel like a partner in it. A thousand bucks. Cash. Yours. No rules. Whatever you want."

She opened it, revealing a neat stack of hundreds.

Tara blushed, shaking her head. "You're ridiculous." But the smile lingered, and she slipped the envelope into her clutch with care, as if afraid it might vanish if she looked away.

Chase pressed on: the boat club membership with initiation fee already paid, his trainings scheduled for spring. The buckets, the Olympics—with her blessing—of course, the percentages, the Italy trip, the Disney blowout, the vacations, the birthday weekends.

"I know this won't last forever, but I think we can ride it hard while it lasts."

"Oh my God, Chase!" Tara was dazzled. Her lips parted, her eyes wide. She couldn't remember the last time she'd seen this much fire in him, the last time she'd felt this drawn to her husband.

It was absurd. Unbelievable. "We're going to be a boating family? Chase, you can't even tie a decent knot. This is insane." She shook her head, then added with a knowing grin, "And I suppose Declan already knows you're finally caving on the Olympics thing? He's been pestering you for decades."

Chase smiled and gave a small nod. She knew him too well.

Her voice carried disbelief, but the kind laced with amazement, not scorn. Against her will, excitement crept in, the kind that had her picturing it all. But even as the vision of what could be swept her up, a voice inside reminded her of the last four months—the missed dinners, the irritability, the glow of his phone from the other side of the bed each night, the extra burden she'd had to shoulder.

She placed her hand over his. "I love how you're planning to use this for the family. I really do. But if this is going to work, we need balance. Guardrails. I need my husband, not the bookmaker version of him. Can you promise me that?"

Chase nodded, relief and gratitude mixing. "So what do you want?"

"Weekly checks. I'll give you space to do your betting, but every Sunday we'll sit down and agree on what you're doing with the girls, what you're handling at home. And every week we assess if you've held up your end. Deal?"

"Deal."

She smiled, squeezing his hand. "Okay then, let's enjoy tonight."

After dinner, absorbed back into the crowd below, they felt euphoric, their heads deliciously heavy from hours of endless drinks, their bodies sweat-kissed and glowing from the dance floor's heat.

And then, without warning, the band struck their final note—a screech of silence that dropped like a blade. For half a beat, the room held its breath. Then the massive screens overhead blazed to life, the Times Square ball burning against the night sky, seconds slipping away. The crowd swelled to meet it, voices rising, glasses hoisted high, the entire room tipping into crescendo as the countdown began.

"Ten... nine... eight..."

Chase and Tara turned to each other, the noise a tidal wave around them, eyes locked, lips parted, the countdown pulling them toward a kiss that felt less like tradition and more like inevitability.

"Three... two... one!"

The room erupted. Corks popped, confetti cannons burst, the band struck the triumphant first chords of "Auld Lang Syne." They kissed, long, certain, and hungry, while the world roared around them.

The money was flowing, Tara was his again, and Chase felt untouchable, as if nothing could break this streak.

By the time they successfully hailed an Uber, it was well after one. They stumbled back into the apartment, cheeks flushed, Tara's heels dangling from her fingers. Madison slipped out with a knowing smile and a wave. Chase tipped her generously, thumbing the Venmo payment before the night's blur made him forget. Tara padded across the apartment to peek into the girls' room—both fast asleep—then withdrew to their bedroom.

When Chase followed a few minutes later, he froze in the doorway.

Tara was waiting at the foot of the bed. The gold sequined dress was gone, puddled somewhere on the floor. In its place was black lingerie he'd never seen before and would never forget—minimal fabric, mercilessly cut, lace scant. The soft spill of bathroom light caught her at an angle, tracing every contour of a body forged by discipline and honed into the kind of perfection that invited lust like magnetism. There was no need for imagination. Desire, insatiable and absolute, took its place. If he'd thought she was sexy at dinner, she was goddess-like now, brazen and devastating.

His reaction was nearly instantaneous. Tara's eyes flicked down then back up with a wicked grin. "Well, someone approves."

Her eyes locked on his. "Come here." It wasn't a request. It was a summons.

He obeyed.

Tara seized him the moment he was close enough, crushing her mouth to his with a hunger that nearly knocked him off his feet. This wasn't gentle or measured. This was possession. She devoured him with an intoxication, fingers clutching, like she couldn't get enough of the man who had just revealed himself as something more than a husband.

She pushed him backward, sending him sprawling onto the mattress, and climbed on top like a predator claiming its kill.

"I can't believe you've been hiding this from me," she hissed, her hips pressed flush against his. "Fifty-four thousand dollars."

She moved against him with a wild urgency, every shift of her body claiming him as wholly hers, until the room itself seemed to tilt, the night spilling over into something unrestrained.

Chase grabbed her waist, meeting her tempo, lost in the relentless rhythm of it. The taste of salt and wine clung to her skin, rich and elemental, as if the whole night had distilled into her body.

He realized with a jolt that the same rush that had carried him through every arb was alive here now but multiplied, magnified, set aflame.

Their rhythm quickened, frantic, both of them chasing the edge.

"Don't you dare stop," Tara gasped, her voice breaking.

She felt his body surging toward the point of no return. The raw, undeniable rush of control lit a fierce satisfaction. She was driving this surrender, commanding this moment.

Midnight had already passed, but this was their real countdown, ending in fireworks only they could feel.

The anticipation that had built throughout the night spilled over all at once. They came undone together, desperate to hold the bond even as their bodies shuddered with release.

For months he'd been hiding in shadows, making excuses, chasing bets. Tonight, there were no shadows. He'd won. And Tara was the proof.

She collapsed against him, skin hot and slick, her chest heaving in aftershocks before her breath slowly began to steady.

Chase wrapped his arms around her, staring at the ceiling, heart still thundering.

No hesitation, no restraint. Just the passion of two people who had once fallen hard for each other and rediscovered a fire that had never truly gone out.

And though some part of both of them knew it couldn't last forever, tonight it didn't matter. Tonight, the world felt golden.

13

INVITATION ONLY

THE FIRST SOUND CHASE HEARD was the sizzle of batter hitting a hot skillet. A faint sweetness hung in the air—vanilla, butter, maple—and for a moment he thought he was still dreaming. His head was heavy, his body loose in the way it only ever felt after too many drinks and too little sleep. He blinked himself upright, rubbed the crust from his eyes, and shuffled barefoot to the bedroom door.

The living room was bright with that peculiar winter light—low, honeyed, cutting sharp angles across the floorboards. The TV was already humming with cartoons, Cece curled on the couch in a fleece blanket, Savannah perched beside her with one of her dolls dangling in her lap. The girls were sticky-faced, syrup smudged across their cheeks.

Tara stood in front of the stove, hair knotted in a messy bun, an oversized Miami University sweatshirt slipping off one shoulder as she flipped pancakes. She turned as she sensed him enter, smiling at him over her shoulder with the kind of grin that was both casual and conspiratorial. Then she gave him a quick, deliberate wink, enough to tell him that last night hadn't been a dream.

"Daddy! Happy New Year!" Cece shouted, not looking away from the TV.

"Hi, Daddy!" Savannah echoed, her eyes also still fixed on the screen.

Chase crouched down between them, kissed the tops of their heads, and grinned. "So, did you two party animals stay up all night without us?"

Cece puffed out her chest. "I was up really, really late! Savannah fell asleep eating her crackers at the table!"

Chase laughed, and Savannah, without looking up, muttered a small, "Nu-uh." That only made Cece giggle harder. A quiet warmth swelled in his chest. For this. For them. For the way the night had ended and the way the morning had begun.

The apartment felt whole in a way he hadn't realized he had been missing.

Chase drifted toward the kitchen, the smells pulling him in. Tara slid another pancake onto the stack and set the spatula down long enough to lean in for a quick kiss. Her lips brushed his, light but lingering, the kind of kiss that said she remembered last night as vividly as he did.

"You look rough," she teased, handing him a tall glass of ice water with two ibuprofen already waiting on the counter. "Can't keep up with me anymore, old man?"

Chase grinned, downing the pills and the water. "You single-handedly kept those bartenders employed. I should've tipped them extra for hazard pay."

Tara laughed, shaking her head. "Oh please. They should be tipping *me* for keeping the place lively."

Chase nodded at the stack. "Any chance this batch has my name on it?"

Tara tipped her head toward the living room. "You'll have to take that up with the pancake monsters. If they leave you any scraps, you're in luck."

From the couch came a giggle, Cece clearly listening in.

Chase leaned on the counter, rolling his shoulders loose. "I need to rally. Big day of bowl games today."

"I hate that Daddy has to work on a holiday," Tara said, mock-pouting as she plated another pancake. "But I get it. Big promises to keep. Better strike while the iron's hot."

He reached for her hand across the counter. "That's the plan."

She held his gaze, the playfulness softening into something steadier.

"Don't lose sight of us while you're doing it, okay?"

Chase squeezed her hand once, a silent promise.

Then his wrist buzzed. An edge this early? Instinctively, he glanced down, expecting the first arb of the day. But the notification wasn't from a sportsbook.

It was an email from LineSniper.

He slipped his phone off the counter and opened it.

The subject read, "Exclusive Invitation: LineSniper LIVE — Las Vegas, July 14–16."

The email was slick, more polished than anything he'd seen from them before. At the top, the word "exclusive" shimmered in bold font, followed by a line explaining the invite was extended only to LineSniper's top users as a reward for their loyalty. The dates leapt off the screen: mid-July, perfectly timed to the All-Star break, the slowest betting days of the year. They'd turned a dead zone into an opportunity to gather the faithful without anyone losing a dollar of action. Brilliant.

Halfway down the email was a video thumbnail, a black box with the LineSniper logo etched in sharp white. Chase tapped.

Music hit immediately: a low, pulsing bass, cinematic, dangerous.

The first shot was a sweeping drone view of the Las Vegas Strip, neon lights dotting the desert sky. Then a cut to the Aria's glass facade, glinting like a jewel.

The camera snapped to a figure in shadow. He stepped into frame, ArbOracle. Dressed in black, voice steady, he carried himself with the certainty of someone who had already glimpsed the future. Half Steve Jobs unveiling the next iPhone, half Jordan Belfort selling the dream of limitless upside. Hard to tell if he was a showman or a visionary. Either way, Chase believed. He was leading his flock toward major profits.

"You've been finding edges. Sniping lines. Now it's time to connect the sharpest minds in the game."

Quick cuts: rooms filled with glowing laptops, bettors watching screens side by side, hands slapping shoulders in celebration. A conference stage, blurred but grand.

"LineSniper LIVE isn't another meetup. It's the gathering of those who see angles where everyone else sees noise. A chance to learn, share, build. With sessions designed to sharpen your craft, maximize your profits, and keep you up to speed on the industry's latest trends."

The video spliced him against shots of sports—slow-motion basketball dunks, pitchers mid-throw, football collisions—then cut back to his face.

"Vegas. July 14th. Be there. Don't just play the game. Redefine it."

The screen faded to black, and the words flashed in stark white. "LINESNIPER LIVE — ARE YOU READY TO GO ALL IN?"

Chase exhaled slowly, thumb hovering over the screen. It was slick. It was dramatic. It was validation. He wasn't merely winning. He was being told he belonged among the arbing elite.

Before he could even process, his phone buzzed again. A text from Blaine.

BLAINE: You get the email?!?

BLAINE: This is it, man. BIG league!

Chase looked from the phone back to the kitchen. Tara had moved on to dishes, putting the flour-strewn kitchen back into working order, humming absently, never missing a beat, forever-focused on the family over herself.

"Babe," he called out, unable to hold it in, "you're not gonna believe this."

Tara wiped her hands on a dish towel and came around the counter, curiosity written across her face. Chase angled the phone so she could see. Together they watched the video from the beginning—the neon Strip, the Aria's glass towers, ArbOracle emerging with the polished confidence of a man unveiling revelation, the kind of presence that drew people in and refused to let them look away.

When the screen finally faded to black, Tara let out a low whistle.

"Wow. That's...actually really impressive." She looked at him, eyebrows raised. "I had no idea it had this kind of gravitas behind it."

Chase beamed. "Right? It's next level."

She nodded, still smiling, though a note of caution crept in. "I thought this whole thing was virtual. Apps and alerts. What do you really get out of flying across the country for a conference?"

The question lingered longer than he expected.

Chase opened his mouth, then closed it again, still staring at the bold text on his screen. "ARE YOU READY TO GO ALL IN?"

His phone buzzed again—Blaine, blowing it up with more exclamation points.

BLAINE: You're killing me. Tell me you got this! You going?!?

Chase felt the grin spread before he even realized it. Whatever Tara's reservations, this was too big, too exciting to temper.

CHASE: Huuuuge! I'm all in! Vegas, here we come!

14

OPEN RATE

AARON OPENED HIS EYES to a ceiling that wasn't his. Black-painted steel, old joists shouldering decades of other people's lives. Brick that carried the city's cold in its pores. On the chair was a jacket he didn't remember hanging. On the concrete floor was everything else, from his black cashmere sweater to his wingtip shoes. As he registered the total absence, he felt the silky sheets smooth against his skin. The loft was staged to look careless, the kind of disorder only the wealthy can afford.

He turned his head and took stock of the woman next to him. Blonde hair—the shade marketers try to brand as California gold or sunrise wheat—spilled across the pillow. The rest of her looked curated, fragments revealed like a painting studied in pieces: the elegant line of a shoulder, the soft curve of a hip, one perfect breast exposed to the morning. She didn't look asleep so much as displayed, the kind of body you woke beside only after earning your way into the gallery.

A quick mental inventory followed. *Where am I? Who is that? What did I promise?* The answers came as he preferred. New York City, someone gorgeous, nothing binding.

Flashes from the night before came flooding back: strobing lights and bass rattling the penthouse windows fifty stories above Times Square. Looking down on the madness from behind glass, the crowd below pressed together like livestock corralled for spectacle, while he raised a glass of champagne, safe in the heat and height of real privilege. A streak of blonde hair, pearly teeth, the countdown and ball drop, confetti like static in the air. Lips pressing against his, laughter spilling in the back of an Uber to Tribeca, fumbling with keys, mouths magnetized.

He sat up, the loft's air calibrated to sixty-five degrees, as he liked it, every inch of bare skin was wakened by the chill, a reminder of the control he'd built. Rising, his feet touched the cool concrete, and the mirror returned his exposed form in full, every detail on display. He allowed himself a moment of private self-regard. The trainer was paying off—nine months of early lifts and intervals, paired with meticulous macronutrient tracking. Lines now edged his abdomen that hadn't been there before. Superficial, maybe. But from last night's demonstration, there was at least one person in Manhattan who'd appreciated the investment more than he did.

Aaron pulled on black designer briefs that cost more than his entire high school wardrobe. The absurdity wasn't lost on him; neither was the evidence that they worked.

He hadn't set an alarm. The phone on the bedside table glowed 8:58 a.m. when he glanced at it. His body knew. He didn't need a chime or vibration to tell him when it was time to watch LineSniper LIVE take flight. He'd been training for mornings like this for years, the anticipation wired deeper than sleep.

He ambled into the kitchen and leaned on an island the color of old slate. At 9:04 a.m., he unlocked the dashboard with a glance. The LineSniper LIVE campaign had gone out at nine sharp, Eastern Standard Time, exactly as designed. The numbers were already moving, rolling in like a tide he'd scheduled.

Open rate: 23.2% at two minutes
Click-through: 22.9%
RSVPs confirmed: 75
Aria room block: 35% claimed

Unbelievable. A near-perfect conversion rate, four minutes in. The kind of numbers marketing textbooks claimed to be impossible.

He texted the event director in Vegas.

AARON: Room inventory watch? I want tranche two queued the second we cross 60%.

DIRECTOR: These numbers are wild, Aaron. We're ready though. Aria has another 75 they can release.

AARON: Prep ops doc for CEO panel contingency—security routing, comms plan, strict mod protocols, no surprises.

DIRECTOR: You expecting fireworks?

AARON: It's Vegas. Fireworks are the product.

On the RSVP stream, names and handles stacked one after another, clean as chips across a felt table.

SharpeShooter. SureThingSarah. Edgehog42. BetmanBegins. He smiled at that one, the cinematic rookie he'd watched hover over "Upgrade" for days before finally pulling the trigger in December, as Aaron knew he would. The kid had walked to the cliff's edge and jumped. They always did.

He pinged engineering in Tempe.

AARON: Any strain on RSVP database? Spinning up a VIP flag so concierge can spot them on arrival.

ENGINEERING: All green. Already live with a "VIP_ROUTE" tag. You can flag whales as needed.

AARON: Tag users who booked a room before RSVP. They've already told us who they are.

His thumb moved on instinct, the heat map flaring: New Jersey, New York, Connecticut, Virginia, Ohio, Indiana—the East Coast and

Midwest lighting first, legal markets staking their claim.

He pictured the Aria block vanishing like inventory in a flash sale. Then the ballroom, packed to capacity, standing room only. The screens glowing. The murmur before the first session. And on the final day, CEOs of the national sportsbooks onstage across from the very people who'd been taught how to beat them. The image thrilled him far beyond its PR value. Predator and prey under the same lights, each mistaking the role they were playing.

He refreshed the numbers, drinking them the way other people drank coffee.

Open: 47.5%

CTR: 44.9%

RSVPs: 105

Aria: 48%

Having seen Ohio light up the heat map, his thoughts drifted to the Midwest—the factory town where the math team practiced beside a janitor's closet, a father who had worked steel until steel stopped paying, a mother who worked two jobs and wore kindness over exhaustion like a uniform. Mrs. Cook, all chalk and patience, who pointed him at Stanford and told him to stop apologizing for being fast. He'd carried that speed to Palo Alto and translated it into status. Status became leverage. Leverage became a product that turned other people's slowness into his margin.

This would be the year it all paid off, and the exit options for LineSniper presented themselves like items on a tasting menu.

Private equity was the obvious, clean choice, a number with commas that meant freedom. His investors liked that story. His parents would understand it.

User ownership, a spin on employee ownership, was democratic and brandable, a story his flock would fund, even if it wasn't quite as lucrative as following the suits on Wall Street.

A national sportsbook was the counterintuitive play, but he sat on the cleanest behavioral dataset in the market—exact users who could anchor lifetime value if you learned to build for them instead of against them. His arb community wasn't casual bettors chasing promos, but rather addicts who hated the word and loved the feeling. You could grow a market two ways: widen the funnel or deepen the well. He had a blueprint for the second.

For now though, he needed to get them in the room. Let the atmosphere do half the work. Let the spectacle say what no deck ever could. The first step was to start a conversation.

He opened his contacts and scrolled through a subset that actually mattered—expensive ones, earned one by one. Dynasty: intro secured via a Stanford donor who collected founders like watches. LionBet: the carcass of a content deal but left behind access to the company's chief. Crowns: a law-firm partner with courtroom eyebrows and casino connections.

And then there was Ainsley Caldwell, the one he had coveted most. Faceoff's top post. The name courtesy of a man who collected private emails and traded them for future favors.

Emboldened by the morning's numbers, he sensed the momentum of a fresh year, the kind of clean slate that made opportunity feel predestined. The air itself seemed to whisper forward. He typed out the message with conviction, knowing exactly what he wanted to say and how he wanted to say it.

Subject: Invitation to Join LineSniper LIVE CEO Forum

Dear Ainsley,

Happy New Year. I'm Aaron Ramsey, Founder and CEO of LineSniper. This morning, we sent our 350 most engaged users an exclusive invitation to LineSniper LIVE, a first-of-its-kind gathering in Las Vegas, July 14–16, 2026.

As I write this, I'm watching the data in real time: more than 65% of recipients who opened the email have already registered within the first twenty minutes. These are fanatically loyal users and among the most active on your platform.

On July 16, the event's final day, I'm convening a session designed to draw national attention: leaders of the country's largest books on stage before an audience that takes pride in beating them. Strict moderation, no theatrics, just an honest conversation about where the industry is headed.

My intent isn't to hurt mobile sports betting. It's to expand it, to bring more players into the ecosystem and keep them longer. Our data offers a behavioral blueprint that I believe would be invaluable to your algorithms.

I hope you will consider joining the CEO forum. As you know, the market is shifting quickly. My goal is to lead that change rather than react to it, and while some might see us as natural adversaries, I believe the strongest moves are made in unlikely alliances.

I look forward to your thoughts.

Respectfully,

Aaron Ramsey

Founder & CEO, LineSniper

He sent it at 9:19 a.m. The click itself was its own narcotic. The void could have it for an hour, a day. He was already on to the next move.

Behind him, the sound of bare feet on concrete. The unnamed blonde appeared in the doorway, unhurried, utterly unconcerned with covering herself. Hair tousled, fresh from sleep and somehow flawless, she leaned against the frame and gave him the kind of smile reserved for mornings when nothing urgent had to be decided.

Aaron let his eyes linger. Awake, she was even more striking, beauty that seemed inexplicably both genetic and designed, the kind of body born with an inheritance and then perfected by knowing exactly how to use it. For a moment, he felt pride more than desire. Affirmation that his life now drew this caliber of company without effort.

She tilted her head, amused, and finally broke the silence. "You coming back," she asked, "or marrying that phone?"

Instinct made him glance at the screen. Willpower made him put it face-down. "The phone and I are in a committed relationship," he said, pausing, "but it's open."

She feigned offense. "Is that supposed to be charming?"

"It's supposed to be honest."

"Honesty's hot," she said, turning and leading him back toward the California king. "Show me."

He slid back into the bed, a man who knew how to be present when presence was the most efficient thing to be. The city seeped through the glass. Below, a horn screamed its impatience. Farther away, a siren remarked on someone else's morning. He allowed himself exactly the amount of attention this moment deserved and no more. People called that cold. He called it calibration.

In an instant, her staccato breaths gave way to a long, satisfied exhale. "Now that was honest."

She stretched across the sheets, content to let the morning idle, then rolled to her side and reached for her phone.

He stayed there, eyes on the brick, and thought about a night nearly a decade earlier when a bouncer at a club not far from here had glanced at his ID, then at his shoes, and said "not tonight" with a politeness that burned the skin. It hadn't been unfamiliar, but the reservoir of resentment had deepened.

Spite had paid for his first term at Stanford in a currency nobody else recognized. Spite kept paying. He didn't worship it, but he respected how resourceful it could be when other fuels ran low.

He reached for the phone again, because restraint was never part of the job description, especially not while the numbers were still climbing.

The dashboard told the story: open rates, click-throughs, RSVPs, room reservations—every metric well above target. Early-bird West Coasters were starting to stir, pushing the curve higher. He scrolled past the RSVP stream to the map and let himself have the moment, little dots becoming arterial lines, arterial lines converging on a strip of desert that had agreed to house his idea. Outside the app, his messages stacked in neat succession: the second tranche of Aria rooms had been quietly released; marketing flagged an unexpected bump in press interest; ArbOracle had checked in, seeking the kind of validation Aaron knew how to dole out in rationed doses. He skimmed, replied where it mattered, and let the rest feed the momentum.

Crossing the room to the window, New York humming below, he relished being the kind of person who could move between desert clarity and city chaos without losing his balance.

He checked his sent mail and reread the note to Ainsley. He liked the cadence. No reply yet, which was right. People at her level didn't reward enthusiasm with speed. They rewarded results with access. He was good at both, and he didn't need her answer to know it would eventually be yes. His life had been built on the premise that inevitability could be willed into existence.

Pleased and feeling supremely in control, Aaron gave the phone a rare reprieve, setting it down on a slab of blackened steel masquerading as furniture.

He drifted back to the kitchen, caffeine calling. It wasn't only the coffee though. It was ritual, discipline rehearsed in the mundane so it came natural in the moments that mattered. The espresso machine hissed, steam sketching shapes into the air that vanished before they meant anything. He carried two matte-black ceramic cups back to the bed, each one small, dense, warm against his fingers, and handed one to his morning visitor. She accepted it with a practiced thank-you, her posture the easy grace of someone who had been thanked often.

She'd pulled on an oversized sweatshirt of his, the kind that swallowed her shoulders but left her legs bare. Somehow the look was more tantalizing than the night before, more inviting, and he better understood how he'd let himself fall under her spell. Despite having had her several times already, the sight made him stir again, proof that some assets appreciated with use.

"You seem busy already. Big day?" she asked.

"Bigger year," he said.

"Seems like you're pretty important. Are you?"

The line was rehearsed, designed for men who craved approval. The question an invitation to flaunt.

He responded casually, "I build the rooms people don't realize they need until they're inside."

"Is that a yes?"

Her smile said she was enjoying the exchange as much as he was.

"It's a useful answer."

The grin widened. She was unaccustomed to men who saw through her game.

"So, Aaron-who-makes-rooms-happen," she said, stretching into a spill of sunlight from the window, "this is your year, huh?"

He glanced at the chair with his jacket, the concrete with his shirt. He thought about the numbers, the desert, the email in the void. The stage that lived in his head at a level of detail that would make an architect ask for the plans. A factory town. A Stanford dorm. A compliance-tech job that felt like auditing walls he'd never climb. And the long, thankless persistence it took to win in public because you practiced in private in the quiet hours nobody else bothered to claim.

"Yeah," he said. "It's my year."

Aaron knew what was coming. He'd written the room, and the room always showed up.

The nameless companion swung her legs off the bed, tugged his sweatshirt lower, and slid back into the impossibly tight pants from the night before. "I should get going," she said. "Mind if I keep the sweatshirt as a memento?"

It had been a gift from a prior girlfriend, lasting about as long as an edge on LineSniper.

"All yours."

She grinned. "I'll keep an eye out for this big year of yours. Aaron, was it?"

"That's right. Aaron Ramsey."

He never bothered to ask hers.

15

THE EXECUTIVE

THE WALL STREET JOURNAL was spread across the marble counter, its front page straining to invent urgency on a morning when the world wanted none. Markets had been closed for days, politicians were on vacation, CEOs still recovering from rooftop parties and private dinners. Only the most obsessive of subscribers, or the most ambitious, would be reading on New Year's Day at all.

Central Park lay beneath her, hushed and skeletal. Beyond it, the city's towers climbed skyward—Billionaire's Row stabbing the clouds, Midtown's glass glinting even in winter's weak light. The contrast made the park look almost innocent, the skyline anything but.

Here, forty-three floors above the park, light already burned. 15 Central Park West's crown jewel penthouse glowed with a deliberate, lived-in order: French press steaming, pen set neatly beside notepad, year-end reports from her policy team waiting at the corner. This was not the chaos of celebration's aftermath. This was command.

Ainsley Caldwell crossed the kitchen barefoot, a cashmere wrap draped carelessly over her shoulders. Her blonde hair was cropped in the crisp executive style of someone who ran an empire. In her late fifties, her features carried an elegant severity, every angle communicating an authority that belied her petite frame.

To the outside world, she was the chief executive officer of Faceoff, the woman who had steered the company to dominance in the years since mobile betting was legalized in the U.S. To herself, mornings like this were evidence of something simpler: discipline rewarded. She scanned the headlines with quick, predatory eyes—trained long ago to notice not what was written but what was missing. As she suspected, nothing of note. Newsmakers weren't interested in making news, and journalists weren't interested in reporting it, a tacit détente in a cycle that carried trillions on its back.

The apartment was quiet, the kind of silence money bought in Manhattan. It was a silence she had once longed for and then come to defend. She had traded noise—the clatter of family dinners, a boy's laughter—for mornings like this. Most days she told herself she didn't miss it. Most days, she believed it.

By 9:20 a.m., after she'd finished editing the first draft of what would become Faceoff's annual report, her phone buzzed. Strange. She had turned off work notifications. This was something else—her personal email.

The subject read, "Invitation to Join LineSniper LIVE CEO Forum."

Ever-prepared, she rarely felt curiosity catch her off guard. She tapped it open.

Aaron Ramsey. Founder and CEO of LineSniper. She knew the name well. Her team had been briefing her on the fledgling upstart, now a thriving movement, for several years.

She skimmed once then read again more deliberately, savoring the audacity. An exclusive event in Las Vegas. Three hundred and fifty of his "most engaged" users—sixty-five percent signed up within twenty minutes. And on the final day, a CEO forum: the leaders of the country's biggest books, paraded before an audience that prided itself on beating them.

Ainsley smiled thinly. Not many people had this email address. The fact that he had found it meant something. Competence, boldness. She respected both. She'd built her career on finding doors others assumed were locked and walking straight through.

She stepped to the window, her preferred place to think. As her gaze moved across the park, she traced the path that had brought her here: boarding schools that prized endurance as much as excellence, an Ivy League education where intelligence and charm learned to work in tandem, and Kellogg School, where she discovered that numbers, wielded precisely, carried more power than words. Consulting had honed her edges, placing her in boardrooms where she was often the only woman—and always the one who had done the work. And then the leap to Faceoff, entrusted to her in the seminal moment the U.S. cracked open mobile sports betting.

Every rung had been a test. Every room, a reminder that brilliance wasn't enough. She had learned to be relentless, to wield charisma like a scalpel, to win allies even as she quietly crushed opponents. It was why she now stood here, atop the industry, while so many others had burned out or been forgotten.

She lifted the phone again, reread the email. Aaron's message carried the confidence of someone who knew his value—and was unafraid to place it directly in front of her. He wasn't begging entry; he was extending an invitation. To the outside world, Faceoff and LineSniper were adversaries. But she could see the truth beneath it: two visionaries, circling the same frontier from different angles. The only question was whether those angles would converge into partnership or continue colliding in rivalry.

She had known about LineSniper from the start. What began as a fringe curiosity, obsessives combing for mismatched odds, had become a movement. Arbitrage. Arbing. Whatever they called it, the phenomenon had scale now.

At first, she'd dismissed it as a sideshow for math wonks. But the data told another story. These users weren't dabblers. They were hooked, absolutely addicted to the grind. Arbitrage required volume, and the LineSniper faithful supplied it in droves.

On paper, Faceoff was actually profiting from the rebellion. Arbitrage required two sides of a bet, and on Faceoff's side those wagers were losing 50.6% of the time. Users thought they were bleeding the house. In reality, they were bleeding Faceoff's rivals, while Faceoff claimed its share. Ainsley's house was winning.

But the risk was real. If that win rate slipped, even briefly, the movement could turn profits into losses. Her job was to protect against the cracks most susceptible to spreading.

Her thoughts sharpened. Arbitrage survived for one reason: the books refused to coordinate. Each guarded its line-making algorithms like crown jewels, a proprietary edge. Pride stronger than logic. If the books ever aligned, they could suffocate arbitrage overnight. That stubborn pride was the moat the arbers depended on.

But the numbers were the easy part. Sentiment was harder.

Beyond the math, there was a more dangerous force, a more pressing concern: the culture forming around arbitrage, raw and emotional, harder to contain.

She pulled up a deck her policy team had compiled. Screenshots of Reddit threads and Discord servers. Anger, swelling louder each week.

"They don't cap the addicts who lose their life savings, only the winners who figure it out."

"The monopoly is real."

"The fix is in."

Thousands of upvotes. Hundreds of furious comments. The beginnings of an insurgency.

Her jaw tightened. She'd seen this movie before: mortgage collapses, pharma pricing scandals, bank fees turned political lightning rods. Outrage was volatile and could harden into regulation overnight. Sports betting was young, fragile. A scandal mishandled could turn governors, attorneys general, entire committees against them.

Faceoff had played it smarter than rivals—limiting less aggressively, keeping a veneer of fairness. But even that hadn't silenced the chorus.

Her eyes returned to Aaron's email. "Our data offers a behavioral blueprint I believe would be invaluable to your algorithms."

He had no idea how right he was.

If she acquired LineSniper, she wouldn't merely defuse a threat. She would seize the high ground: data on the most active, most compulsive users in the industry. These weren't casual bettors. They were men and a few women who sat for hours, clicking like day traders chasing blips on a screen. Conditioned to profit. Hooked on motion.

With the data, she could map behavior, anticipate every move. And when she chose, she could starve them. Tighten limits, cut off their edge. Once they'd tasted daily wins, the absence would gnaw. They would chase regular bets, reckless bets, desperate to recreate the hit. And the house would reclaim the advantage.

Elegant. Ruthless. A masterstroke hidden in plain sight.

She'd learned long ago that power didn't come from striking first but from striking at the exact right moment. Aaron had made the first move. The question was when she would make hers. Responding immediately would be amateurish. Power resided in restraint. Silence could be louder than speech.

Three days. That was the move. Long enough to remind him of the gulf between them, brief enough to demonstrate respect.

Her calendar was already being held for July 16. Las Vegas. Aaron could have his event, his eager disciples packed into a conference hall, convinced they were there to watch him. She already saw the scene more clearly than he did: her entrance, her presence, the shift in air when the audience realized the house was no longer the villain on the defensive, but the master of the game itself.

Las Vegas would be his stage. But it would be her performance.

16

CAPPED

CHASE'S BLOOD RAN COLD.

The wager box on Crowns lit up in angry red: "Wager exceeds limit."

He blinked and entered his usual wager again. Same result.

He toggled over to LionBet. Red.

Dynasty. Red.

Back to Crowns, hoping it had been a glitch. No, the scarlet warning still glared at him like a stoplight holding him hostage for its own amusement.

It wasn't a one-off. It wasn't a mistake.

They'd cut the engine mid-flight.

A week ago, he'd been pushing five hundred, seven hundred, even a thousand dollars a side without a second thought. Now? He was limited to as low as ten bucks in some instances. Ten. A lunch order. A rounding error.

His thumb moved faster, toggling from one book to another, as though he could outmaneuver the system if he just stayed in motion. But each refresh slapped him with the same verdict. "Wager exceeds limit." Over and over.

Faceoff, mercifully, still let him through for a few hundred, but it felt fragile. Temporary. Like a window about to slam shut.

It was January 7. Last week he'd been riding high, piling it on through New Year's games. He'd made more in the past week than all of October combined. Now the books had reset the table, and they'd reset it against him.

The panic came quick, tight in his chest. Arbitrage wasn't about hitting one big score. It was about volume. Constant churn. Hundreds of bets stacked each day, edges compounding. The more money in play, the more the machine printed. But cut the stakes and the math collapsed. Ten dollars at a time wasn't arbitrage. It was a joke.

He stared at the number and felt embarrassed. Last week, he'd told Tara she was officially his partner in this. He'd shown her the profits and sold her on the promise. She had looked at him differently then, with admiration, like finally he'd found the thing that could change their future.

And now he was capped out like a kid with the smallest allowance in the class.

What will I say if she asks? That it was over just after it had started? That the sure thing had fizzled in four months?

His face burned at the thought.

He tossed the phone onto the counter, let it skid against the granite, then snatched it back up again. No, he couldn't let it end here. He still had plays to fire, edges to capture.

Another toggle, another attempt. Ten bucks. Red letters.

The absurdity of it only made the dread sharper. He wasn't a predator anymore. He wasn't even a participant. He was a punchline.

The silence of the apartment pressed in. Tara was at work. The girls were at school. It was him and the suffocating realization that the gears had locked up.

He ran the math again in his head, almost desperately. Thousand-dollar days reduced to tens. A crushing diminishment.

Icarus came to mind. He'd believed he could fly higher, further, without consequence. Now he was falling, wings singed, the ground rushing up fast.

It was unworkable. The model was dead.

And the humiliation was worse than the loss.

He thought of Tara, the way she had nodded when he'd explained that volume was everything, that the more he could stake, the more abundant the returns. She'd even teased him about sounding like Warren Buffett, compounding his way to wealth. She'd agreed to let him keep doing this. She'd volunteered to take on more. She'd trusted him.

Now the compounding was gone. The inevitability gone. Her trust at risk of vanishing too.

He thought of how she'd lit up at the promised Disney trip, how he could see she'd already started half-planning it in her head—now sitting unfunded, unlikely to happen at all.

It felt like failure. Naked, undeniable failure.

And for the first time since this all began, he wasn't sure if he had the words to explain it away.

The thought left him hollow, staring at the wall as if an answer might appear there.

A buzz. Right on cue, because somehow he always was in these pivotal moments of Chase's arb journey. Blaine's name lit up the screen.

BLAINE: You getting hit with these massive limits?!

Chase's stomach tightened. He typed quickly.

CHASE: Yeah. Crowns. LionBet. Dynasty. All capped. Big time.

BLAINE: This isn't chance, dude!

BLAINE: It's coordinated!

BLAINE: It's collusion!

CHASE: Yeah, man. Feels like they're targeting us.

BLAINE: Exactly!

BLAINE: They let losers torch their bank accounts all day long!

BLAINE: But the second we win, the second we actually beat them…

BLAINE: They kill us! How is this shit even legal?!

CHASE: It's unreal. Can't believe they're allowed to get away with this.

BLAINE: Allowed?!

BLAINE: They own the game!

BLAINE: Who the fuck is going to stop them?!

BLAINE: No rules! No appeals!

BLAINE: Can you imagine any other company in America shutting down a competitor the moment they started to lose market share?

BLAINE: It's un-American! Anti-capitalist! Somebody has to stop them!

Chase slammed his phone down on the counter, heat rising in his chest. Blaine was right. It was rigged, a setup, the house changing the rules the moment they started to lose.

Chase tried to work. He really did. The laptop sat open, a spreadsheet filled with donor data idling in front of him, but the numbers blurred. His other screen, his real screen, was where the action was. Odds feeds. Lines that used to mean easy money.

He opened PickTracker and watched the day's numbers refresh. His balance nudged upward, not by hundreds, not even by tens. By cents. $6.53.

That was what he was on pace for today. Jesus. He stared at it, the number mocking him from the dashboard. An hour's grind already, toggling, refreshing, splitting scraps between accounts, for the price of a drive-thru sandwich, no fries.

Not worth the time. Not worth anything.

His head was buzzing with frustration. He pushed back from the desk and wandered to the bathroom, locking the door behind him.

A hint of shame hit as he caught his reflection in the mirror. Middle of the workday, hiding in the bathroom like a teenager. Not something to be proud of. But the frustration was stronger, the knot cinched too tight. Maybe he could cut through the din, reset. A quick release. A high that didn't come from a confirmation screen. A few minutes and maybe he could focus again.

His mind drifted, welcoming the familiar rhythm, hand moving on muscle memory. For a few seconds, the tension subsided, the stress of the day slipping away—until the phone buzzed against the counter. Once. Twice. A volley of pings, stacked like gunfire.

Edges.

His stomach dropped.

He glanced over, mid-act, the notifications lighting up: names of NBA benchwarmers and backup forwards he'd never even heard of. Props he needed to hit now or not at all. He'd been wired to believe each second cost him money, and his body still reacted that way—even now when today's reality was mere cents. Pathetic scraps dangled like bait, and he lunged for them like gold all the same.

He forced an untimely, quick finish, the act stripped of anything but urgency. The second it was over he was reaching, frantic, for the phone.

His feed was a blur of names and numbers. Over 7.5 rebounds. Under 1.5 threes. Random journeymen who might as well have been created by AI. His thumbs fired, splitting stakes by the tens, not the hundreds, bouncing between books, scrambling to salvage scraps.

Half-naked, breathless, sweating over bets that wouldn't feed the parking meter.

When it was done, he flipped back to PickTracker, eyes darting to the new daily projection. $9.47. Not even twice what he'd had that morning.

This was what he'd been reduced to, and still he couldn't stop.

* * *

Chase slipped into character the moment Tara and the girls walked through the door.

He was already in the kitchen, sleeves rolled up, chopping vegetables with an energy that bordered on theatrical. He asked about her day before she could ask about his. He set the table, poured her a glass of wine, even coaxed the girls into helping rinse lettuce for the salad.

It was over the top, but Tara didn't see it that way. To her, it looked like follow-through. She'd asked him to be more present, to make this feel like a shared effort instead of him disappearing behind a screen, and here he was—helpful, engaged, a partner. She smiled across the counter, that easy smile she wore when she let her guard down. She believed the compromise was working.

After dinner, he handled bedtime with saintly patience. He read extra pages from Cece's new chapter book, pretended Savannah vanished every time she covered her face, then carried them each to bed with a tenderness that hid the pressure lodged in his chest. On his way into the girls' room, Tara kissed him on the cheek.

She didn't suspect a thing.

When the apartment finally went still, Chase slipped out to the patio. The January air nipped at his face, cold enough to strip away the warmth he'd been faking all evening. He'd converted the space into a four-season outpost, adding a heater and stacking enough blankets to make a ski lodge jealous. More nights than not, he ended up out here, the streetlights of Navy Yard below him and the bridge arching across the Anacostia in the distance, his only company while he thought.

He dropped into the chair, the weight of the limits pressing down. After a day that had stripped him raw, one question kept circling back. *How am I going to tell her?*

A week ago, he'd looked her in the eye and promised this was the start of something real. That he'd found the angle, the edge that could change things for their family. She'd believed him. Trusted him.

Now it felt like a mirage.

The red letters replayed in his head. "Wager exceeds limit." Each one hammered the point home. What he'd sold her was already gone. She'd agreed to carry more of the family load so he could chase something that had dried up overnight.

He buried his face in his hands. Fool. Reckless. Worse, a liar. The phone buzzed on the table beside him.

Reliably, right on cue.

BLAINE: You free tomorrow morning?

Chase straightened. The tone was different—measured, steady. No exclamations, no jagged bursts. Just a simple question, as if Blaine had smoothed himself back into control. Chase noticed it immediately.

CHASE: Yeah, after school drop-off. What's up?

A pause. Then Blaine's reply, crisp and decisive.

BLAINE: Let's get breakfast. Pete's. 9 a.m.

There was no room for feedback.

BLAINE: I've been digging.

BLAINE: Found a workaround.

Chase leaned forward. His anticipation spiked, every nerve braced for what came next.

CHASE: Workaround?

The three dots blinked. Vanished. Blinked again. Each hesitation dragged for what felt like minutes.

BLAINE: New players. And they're going to make us more money than ever.

The screen glowed in his hand, far brighter than the city lights beyond the patio rail.

17

NEW PLAYERS

THE SMELL HIT HIM before the sign did—bacon crisping on a flat-top, the kind of scent that rounds a corner first and takes your hand. Chase turned onto 2nd Street SE and felt his shoulders loosen. Pete's sat in the narrow band of morning light like a time capsule: a faded blue awning stretched above the doorway, a neon green "Open" sign buzzing faintly, and giant stock photos of pancakes and omelets plastered across the front windows. A bell tattled on every entrance, revealing a counter that had seen more gossip than the Hill press room.

There was a legendary corner stool at the far end, the unofficial throne of a former Speaker of the House who'd strolled in daily before sunrise for years, his Secret Service detail sweeping the place before he ordered breakfast. Everyone who ate at Pete's knew the rule: leave the Speaker alone, offer nothing more than a head nod on his way in and out. The stool was empty now, but the myth still warmed the vinyl.

Blaine was already in the last booth, back to the wall, a study in composure. No caps, no exclamation points. Shaved, tailored suit, crisp open-collar shirt, eyes steady—pure business. On the table were two waters beading condensation, a laminated menu with bent corners, salt and pepper, and an array of condiment bottles.

"Morning," Blaine said calmly. Hard to believe this was the same man who'd been firing off frenetic texts less than twenty-four hours ago.

Chase slid in opposite, the old wood groaning under his weight.

A server in a faded white polo dropped two sets of silverware, each wrapped in a napkin, with a practiced clink.

"What'll it be, gents?" he asked, so practiced it sounded dismissive.

"Eggs and bacon. Coffee. Black," Blaine led.

"#2. Scrambled. Home fries. Wheat bread. Butter on the side," Chase fired off.

An approving look of recognition from the server. A regular.

"It'll be right up," he offered brightly, already pivoting toward the kitchen.

Small talk came first—school drop-off, the DMV traffic grind, the cold that almost made you long for August's swampy hundred-degree haze.

But Chase's patience had a half-life. He leaned in. "Quite the cliffhanger last night. So what'd you find? Is there a way around these limits?"

Blaine leaned back like an artist at a gallery opening, savoring the pause before unveiling his masterpiece. "Gamified sportsbooks." His eyes twinkled, like he'd shared the secret to life.

Chase had a fleeting concern for Blaine's sanity. "What?"

"Think Chuck E. Cheese or your favorite beachside arcade," Blaine explained. "You buy tokens, play the games, win tickets. The tickets trade in for prizes. Now imagine those tokens could be used to place bets instead of racking up Skee-Ball scores. And at the end of the night, you don't walk out with a stuffed animal—you walk out with cash."

Chase's head tilted. Maybe Blaine really had lost his mind. "Tokens?"

"I don't care if they call them coins, shells, or gummy bears. They still cash out in green bills."

"The app is called Atlantis," he continued, lingering on the name as if it could sell the vision on its own. "It's all officially dressed up as a sweepstakes, but the money's real. I placed my first bets yesterday and made a withdrawal last night. Money hit my bank account this morning."

The plates hit the table with a heavy diner thud, piles of eggs steaming between them. Blaine didn't even look down.

"Between Faceoff and Atlantis alone, you could spend all day exploiting inefficiencies. The volume is limitless." Blaine was clearly pleased with himself.

"The lines are so out of step with these gamified sportsbooks because their feed lags the big shops. It's an all-you-can-eat arbitrage buffet. There are a couple of others nipping at their heels, but Atlantis is the gold standard right now."

"Sweepstakes," Chase repeated, still struggling to keep up.

"It's the Wild West, man. No sheriff, no fences. You can strike gold or get robbed. Unlike the big sportsbooks, it's barely regulated, if at all. The folks in charge are the same ones who've been babysitting Publishers Clearing House since the fifties. Way out of their league. Atlantis knows it, and they're pushing hard for growth. New users are their currency, and they're throwing serious cash to get them."

Chase felt like he was listening to the Willy Wonka of sports betting and had just been offered a golden ticket.

"They're so desperate for users that they've created mind-blowing promos. Right now, Atlantis will 5x your deposit if you agree to a 10x playthrough. Put in five hundred dollars, they give you an extra *twenty-five hundred dollars* on top. You can't touch the deposit match until you've wagered five thousand with them. That's supposed to lock in a normal bettor for weeks. For us? We churn that in a *day*."

Chase had to admit it sounded compelling.

Blaine grinned like a game show host about to reveal there was more. "And here's the kicker. You can load your account with a credit card, unlike the big books. Drop in a thousand, Chase Bank kicks Chase Dupree twenty bucks. Two percent cash back. Play through, cash out, pay off the card, and do it again. That's an easy grand a month in rewards cash for doing the thing you were already doing. It's like laundering drug money through a car wash but totally above board...for now."

Blaine was electrified, practically vibrating in his seat.

"There has to be a catch," Chase finally managed to cut in.

Blaine nodded like a teacher pleased by the prompt. "Catches? Please. It's background noise compared to the opportunity," he said, waving it off. "I already told you. The people 'regulating' this stuff are clueless. Could the big books push for change if they think these guys are siphoning too much action? Sure. But that's a state-by-state slog that takes months, maybe years."

A seriousness descended suddenly.

"You *could* wake up to new rules or a platform that suddenly 'temporarily disables withdrawals' while they 'enhance security protocols.' Your bank might decide coin purchases look like cash advances and tack on fees. KYC could freeze your account if the selfie robot decides your Tuesday face doesn't match your driver's license. And the doomsday scenario? You've got fifty grand parked in Atlantis, they go belly-up, and poof—it's gone. No recourse, no regulator, no safety net."

Chase exhaled. "So the house is even wobblier."

"The house is brand new," Blaine said. "They're still painting the trim while we're hauling furniture inside. But if tens of thousands are guaranteed, I'll risk moving in."

Blaine finally took a breath, and the background noise rushed to the forefront: forks scraping plates, the register dinging, feet shuffling at the counter. For the first time all morning, Chase had room to process.

"Who's behind Atlantis?" Chase asked after a long silence.

"A guy out of Austin," Blaine said, leaning in, reverence in his tone. "His name's Mason Rushmore. Still a student at Dartmouth when he built an algorithm that picked bets for him. He was crushing the books until they limited him. He put everything into building Atlantis, and at twenty-one, with the venture money pouring in, he dropped out and never looked back. The VCs loved him because he wasn't some boilerplate founder with a pitch—he was channeling his fury into a platform designed to shake the old guard. They were betting that, harnessed right, that kind of fire could power something formidable.

"A founder with a grudge and a name that sounds like a legend rising," Chase said. "Beautiful."

"Beautiful and useful," Blaine said. "Because grudges pay, at least for a while."

Chase drifted to the memory of last night's patio—cold air, blankets, the red letters drilling into him. Yesterday's profit was so small it had been insulting, and it had gnawed at something primal. He couldn't live in the no-profit world. Not after his promises to Tara. Not now.

"Send me the referral code. I'm signing up now."

18

SCREEN TIME

THE STEAM CLIMBED IN SHEETS, ghostly and slow, wrapping the cedar walls until the room felt more like a cloud than a chamber. The place was meant for healing, for rinsing the city from the skin—an enforced solitude to soften the body and still the mind.

The little timer on the wall said 5:58 a.m. It was February 1. Above him, several floors up, the apartment was still dark. Tara and the girls bundled in their own pockets of warmth.

Chase sat alone on the top bench, every breath drawing in heat so thick it seared his throat like a shot of liquor. His chest rose and fell. Sweat slicked his shoulders and ran rivers down his back. The hiss of the vent was the only sound.

Chase had always thought of it as a sanctuary, but this morning his sanctuary carried its own intrusion: the glowing rectangle in his hand.

Sweat was proof the room was doing its work, yet it blurred the one thing his mind refused to release. The screen fogged, a blur of light behind water. He swiped once, twice, each attempt leaving only streaks. He wiped the glass with his forearm, but the victory dissolved instantly. New droplets traced the grooves of his fingerprints, as if the body itself were trying to reclaim him, to remind him this was a place for surrender, not control.

He cursed and stood, towel cinched at his waist, pushing through the fogged door. The timer still glared: seven minutes left. The locker room air hit like liberation—cool tile, faint chlorine, the low mechanical hush of the indoor pool beyond. He sat down on the bench, sweat still coursing down his skin in beads. He blotted the phone with a towel, and at last the screen unlocked.

He'd woken before sunrise for this, January's final tally. He couldn't wait. PickTracker had greeted him with a static banner instead, a blunt message. "Down for temporary maintenance."

Irritated, he'd paced the apartment, checked twice more, then descended to the steam room to kill minutes, to sit in solitude until the system came back online.

Now, towel-dried glass in hand, the wheel finally spun. He knew it was going to be his best month yet, but when the total finally appeared, he quietly gasped.

$41,237 in a month.

It was impossible to deny now. Blaine's discovery was a stroke of genius. Atlantis not only provided an endless supply of mismatched odds with Faceoff, but its deposit multiplier was like a faucet no one had bothered to shut off, and Chase was pulling in $1,500 a day by catching the overflow.

The figure burned in his mind, too large to keep to himself. He opened his messages.

CHASE: You up?

CHASE: Just tallied January.

CHASE: I swear you're not ready for this.

It took only a matter of seconds for the reply to roll in.

BLAINE: I'm up now after that volley of texts. Had me thinking the arbs were starting extra early today.

BLAINE: So…what's the haul?

CHASE: Cleared $41k in January!

CHASE: You're a genius, man. None of this happens without you.

BLAINE: Damn right! I told you Atlantis was the cheat code.

The back-and-forth with Blaine left him self-satisfied. His best month yet, and his mentor all but knighted him for it. He placed the phone on the bench, leaned back, and let the approval settle in.

Then the mirror caught his eye.

For years, Chase had been an athlete, the kind of guy who took pride in the curve of his shoulder, the taper of his waistline, the visible payoff of consistent hours logged in the gym. Even after the accident, even with the neck, he'd kept himself sharp. But the man staring back now was the worst version he'd seen. Definition gone in the chest, shoulders rounded, arms softer. His midsection turned into something he didn't recognize. The scale had crept to an all-time high. To anyone else, nothing obvious. But here, stripped down and sweating, the flaws screamed at him.

And it wasn't only his body. January had been full of these small trades, each one easy to justify in the moment.

A little reshaping of Outlook calendar blocks here, a moved meeting there, and suddenly his afternoons were free for opportunity.

An offer to make some returns on Tara's behalf at the mall, idling on a food court bench as West Coast edges lit up.

Night after night, Tara curled on the couch once the girls were down. "Want to watch a show?" she'd ask.

"Five minutes," he'd promise. Forty-five later, he was still at his desk, face lit by NHL props, couch abandoned.

He told himself the boxes were checked. School drop-offs. Donor calls. Groceries in full supply. If the essentials were covered, what was the harm in stealing a few minutes for profit?

He did have one twinge of guilt. A micro-crack. There'd been the choir showcase. Cece had practiced for weeks, spinning in the kitchen, belting her lines with the confidence only a five-year-old could carry. It was circled on the calendar, a family event.

Chase had promised he'd meet there after a quick work call. But an edge dump hit, and five minutes of arbing bled into twenty. By the time he jogged up the school steps, the room was already echoing with applause. He caught Cece's bow, not the song.

Tara squeezed his hand in the hallway, smiling for Cece's sake. "Got caught up?"

"Work," he'd said. "I'm sorry."

Both were true. One more than the other. She didn't press, but he suspected she knew.

Suddenly, a ripple fired through the back of his skull, jolting him back to the present. Dammit. Another one. The headaches—sharper, more frequent—nagged at him without explanation.

He exhaled, long and steady, averting his eyes from what he'd become, and forced the reflection into context. Who cared if his body had slipped a little? This was short-term sacrifice. A temporary trade. Riches first, repairs later. He knew it all could vanish as suddenly as it appeared. The only move was to take everything he could, while he still could. He could make peace with the toll later. When it closed, he'd fix himself. Until then, he wasn't about to step away from free money.

* * *

Chase still felt loose from the morning steam, his muscles slack in a way Miles would approve of. He figured he'd lead with that, a little victory lap before the session even began.

Miles met him at the table, his calm half-smile offering the same quiet encouragement as always. A former college soccer player, he still carried a lithe frame, trim joggers emphasizing calves so honed they looked carved.

"Range of motion looks better," Miles said, guiding Chase's arm overhead. "Thoracic mobility's coming along."

For a moment, Chase let himself feel proud. He'd been steady with PT for months, equally consistent with the massages Miles had prescribed. He'd stuck to the system, and the results showed.

Then Miles's fingers found the muscles at the base of his neck, and the brief pride evaporated.

His expression tightened. "Traps are really tight," he murmured. His thumb pressed against the small knot of muscle behind Chase's head. "Suboccipitals are completely locked too. How long are you sitting during the day?"

Chase gave a vague shrug. "I'm working a lot lately."

Miles nodded, jotting a mental note. "About how many hours a day, would you say?"

Chase deflected. "The neck feels better, but I've been getting these headaches. Worse as the day goes on. They're pretty rough."

Miles's hands stilled. "That lines up with cervicogenic headaches. You're stacking too many triggers—bad posture, stress, old neck issues. The pain's your body telling you the system isn't right."

Chase nodded, already halfway out of the conversation, thinking about the 5 p.m. tranche LineSniper would inevitably be pushing out.

Miles exhaled through his nose, and Chase recognized it as concern unspoken. "Progress in one lane doesn't prevent a pile-up in another, Chase. Set timers. Take walks. Do breathing work. Stretch. If you don't manage the balance, those headaches will only get worse."

Chase forced a grin. "I hear you. I'll do it. You haven't steered me wrong yet."

But even as he said it, he was already calculating whether he'd make it back in time to catch the next line move.

That night, stretched out on the carpet beside Savannah's bed, guarding against closet monsters she swore were there, Chase pulled up Google. "How to see screen time on iPhone?"

A second later, his thumb flicked through Settings. Miles's question had stuck. He found it: *Screen Time.* The purple hourglass icon—time rendered in pixels.

Blue bars rose like skyscrapers. His daily average was 11h 12m.

Pickups: 421. Spikes between 4 p.m. and 6 p.m., and again from 8 p.m. to 10 p.m., the hours he'd have sworn belonged to his daughters, to Tara, to himself.

It was an extra workweek, hidden in plain sight.

Top apps: LineSniper, Faceoff, Atlantis, Outlook, ESPN, Podcasts, Maps, YouTube, Notes. His entire ledger glowing back at him.

For a moment, he stared, aghast. Then the rationalizations came in a rush. Podcasts count. Maps count. Even directions while driving added hours. But he knew the bluff, those podcasts and short drives couldn't possibly stack to numbers this high.

He'd expected arbing to chew up hours. He hadn't grasped how completely it consumed them.

The graph wasn't accusatory. It just kept the receipts.

His phone offered a solution, labeled Downtime, glowing below the damning data. A built-in chance to self-limit. But limits were the last thing he wanted these days.

He slid the toggle just to see. Not today. Cancel. Maybe tomorrow.

Later, the apartment hushed, Chase stood at the sink, scrubbing a pot crusted with mac and cheese, the phone resting upright against the soap dispenser, screen angled for the next alert. The steady rush of water filled the silence, louder than any conversation he'd had with his wife in days.

Tara eased out of the girls' room, careful not to wake them, making her way toward the kitchen. She leaned against the counter, exhaling. "Phew. Both down before nine. That's a win for Mom and Dad."

Chase didn't answer. His eyes kept straying to the phone, hands working the brush in tight circles.

Tara watched him a beat, unable to shake the familiar ache she'd felt creeping back these past weeks—the unsettling sense of him being there, but not really there. She said, "You feel...far again."

He looked up, more annoyed than inquisitive. "Far?"

"You're here, but you're somewhere else. Clipped answers. Irritable. And with the girls, whether you see it or not, little things are slipping by. You're a great dad, Chase, but these are moments you'll want back."

Chase stiffened, the inventory already queued: "I'm doing the school runs. Laundry. Dishes. Bedtimes. My job. Groceries are stocked. Bills are paid. What more do you want? I'm doing it all." The snap back was more defensive than he intended.

Tara flinched. "Someday they'll stop asking for you, Chase."

She pulled out a chair and sat, watching him at the sink. "On New Year's, you promised me more presence." She shook her head lightly. "I don't want a checklist. I want you, not the version lost to your phone."

"I'm doing exactly what I said I would!" His volume spiked, frustration spilling. "I'm holding up my responsibility to this family. You said you wanted more freedom, more memories for us. That's what I'm working for."

Tara's lips parted as if to answer, but she closed them again. The hurt flickered across her face, silent, heavier than words.

19

CROCKPOTS

THE DRIVEWAY OVERFLOWED WITH SUVs, bumper to bumper. It was an unseasonably warm February afternoon, Super Bowl Sunday, and the yard showed it—balls abandoned in the grass, scooters tipped along the curb. From inside came the shrieks of kids, loud enough to rattle the storm door.

Chase, Tara, and the girls entered the fray, balancing coats and a bowl of guac. As they walked inside, the warmth of crockpots and the comfort of familiar voices greeted them.

Coats slung over the banister, piles of Legos like landmines underfoot, kids weaving between legs. A sectional couch sagged under a tangle of neighbors and old friends, the kind of sprawl only a cul-de-sac could hold. Chase couldn't help but chuckle, knowing the scene in the basement would be worse, a thundering free-for-all of sugar and Nerf darts.

As he slipped off his shoes, the unmistakable boom of their host, Javier, echoed from the foyer.

Javier stepped into view in his usual uniform—khakis and a navy quarter-zip emblazoned with a country club logo. A little soft around the middle after years of work and parenting, he wore it without a trace of self-consciousness. His smile took his whole face with it, eyes crinkling, cheeks lifting, the kind of welcome that dissolved any tension the moment you saw it.

"Dupree!" He slammed a cold beer into Chase's hand before he'd even had a chance to take his coat off. "Godfather privileges guarantee delivery upon entry."

Chase grinned. "Always been the best part of the job."

They'd been fraternity brothers in college, a bond that had turned into real brotherhood over twenty years. From crashing on Javier's couch when he first moved to DC to having five kids between them in nearly as many years, their lives had moved in parallel.

They made their way to the kitchen, a lineup of crockpots steaming in unison. Queso, buffalo chicken dip, meatballs, and in the middle Javier's famed Skyline chili, an edible tribute to his beloved Cincinnati Bengals.

Javier's wife, Leslie, appeared with the deftness of someone who hosted often, exchanging hugs, always an eye on the kids, quick to referee when needed.

"Did you see?" she nudged Tara. "The house across the street went up for sale. Massive backyard with swing set. There's even a playroom off the kitchen where you can toss all the toys and close the door. Great neighbors too, I'm told. It's practically made for you."

Javier groaned, and a handful of friends in earshot perked up, knowing what was coming next.

Chase raised his beer, on cue, and announced in a theatrical voice, "I've said it before. The only way I'm leaving our Navy Yard apartment is in a body bag."

Laughter rolled across the room, easy and familiar.

"Keep it up, and I can have that arranged," Tara quipped with a smile, though after their recent argument, Chase alone knew the line wasn't all good humor.

"Hey, you've always said the one place you'd want to live more than this cul-de-sac is a water community, and I just made that happen."

Javier and Leslie leaned in, intrigued by one of the few surprises left between such close friends.

"That's right. We joined a boat club. Official members. Come summer, the Duprees will be cruising the Potomac."

Javier whistled. "Ordering life jackets now. You captain, and I'll stock the cooler."

Chase grinned. "If this Skyline chili tastes as good as it looks, you'll have earned it."

Leslie leaned toward Tara. "Would those two even notice if their wives and kids didn't show?"

Tara laughed, shaking her head, "Not until the cooler ran out."

The crowd drifted to the living room as the kickoff neared: Buffalo Bills vs. Detroit Lions. Neither team had ever hoisted the Lombardi, which meant by night's end one fan base would taste euphoria and the other sink deeper into despair.

Someone read off the prop bets—national anthem length, coin toss, the color of Gatorade dumped on the winning coach—soliciting responses from the room.

A neighbor Chase had yet to meet was making his case for green Gatorade. Javier declared it an un-American choice.

Blaine appeared, annoyingly but predictably in a Cleveland Browns jersey—a diehard with no issue repping his team even when they weren't anywhere near the field.

Unprompted, he rattled off historic anthem averages. Then the stupidity of coin-flip props, citing the house's vig, known to most as the "house edge." Even the impact of wind shear on punting props.

The room chuckled awkwardly, eager to move on. Blaine's eyes stayed locked, wired with calculation.

By the second quarter, Blaine had migrated to a corner outlet, phone tethered to a charger, shoulders huddled. He wasn't watching the game at all; it only existed on the small screen in his hand, reduced to a stream of opposing bets, always collapsing toward the same singular, winning outcome.

Chase had found reasons to discreetly duck out twice already—first with a bathroom excuse, later under the pretense of checking on the kids to fire off a live total and catch a mismatched player TD line. Each time he told himself it was quick, contained. Nothing like Blaine.

A friend clapped Chase on the shoulder. "I hear you're heading to Milan for the Olympics? That's awesome! How'd you swing that?"

Sensing Tara on his arm, Chase replied quickly, "Can't wait. Super lucky that Tara gave me the green light. My mom's driving in to help with the kids too."

Another voice from the couch carried toward Tara. "I'm impressed you're letting him jet off that long in the middle of the school year."

Tara smiled, no hesitation. "It's always been a dream of his. I'm glad he's going. He deserves it." She said it like she once believed it, but it felt more hollow to Chase than it had over a month ago.

From the other side of the couch, a neighbor chimed in, "Do yourself a favor in Milan. Gelateria della Musica. You'll think you died and went to heaven."

Chase beamed, tucking it away. "Thanks. I plan to pack on a few gelato pounds while I'm there."

When the halftime show hit, the basement erupted—kids shrieking, leaping off couches, singing along to a Latin pop anthem they knew from car radios and YouTube. Adults upstairs traded smiles, grateful for a breather, that it wasn't their turn on basement duty. For a few minutes, the house was pure noise and delight, the kind of chaos that felt like memories being made.

As the act wrapped, someone joked about their total score under ticket being toast after such a high-scoring first half. Blaine scoffed loud enough to still the room. "That's what casuals do, donate to the books. Why waste money guessing when you can print it risk-free?" His tone carried more pity than mockery. People shifted uncomfortably, embarrassed for the guy. Leslie shot Julia a look that asked if this was normal. Julia only shrugged, eyes fixed on her plate of nachos, doing her best to dodge the secondhand humiliation.

Tara caught the exchange from across the room, the unease evident. Blaine, once the center of conversations, had become someone people skirted around. Tara watched Julia shrug, weary but unsurprised, and felt a chill of recognition run through her. Chase wasn't there yet, she told herself. He still laughed at the right moments, still carried the surface of normal. But the line between them felt thinner than she wanted to admit.

By the fourth quarter, the party thinned. Kids sprawled across couches, chili remnants were scooped into Tupperware, paper plates spilled from the trash can.

Blaine hadn't moved, still anchored to his makeshift corner office, eyes welded to the screen as though the game's outcome depended on it.

Chase slid onto the back deck, embracing the chill that had descended with the sinking sun, bistro lights twinkling overhead. Javier joined him, still laughing at the risqué beer commercial that had the room rolling.

His tone shifted. "Hey, what's up with Blaine?"

Chase kept his eyes on the sprawling darkness beyond the yard, careful with his words. "He's been betting a lot lately, living on his phone. Whole thing's gotten…pretty consuming for him."

It was true. Every word. And yet plenty was left unsaid.

Javier shook his head, clicking his tongue in disapproval. "A real shame. The guy's got a good thing going with Julia, and she seems beyond frustrated. Hope he doesn't mess it up."

Chase only nodded.

He told himself that his response had been fair. Blaine was on another level—lost in mania, blind to the room. Chase still laughed at the right beats, still had balance. He wasn't Blaine. Not yet.

20

FLEETING FLAME

"LET ME HELP YOU WITH THAT, SIR."

The flight attendant's smile looked painted, deliberate as a brush-stroke. She lifted his carry-on before he could protest, sliding it neatly into the overhead. Chase had barely stepped into the cabin and already felt the difference. This was not survival travel. This was indulgence. It was his first time in first class, and he let himself drink it in.

A flute of champagne appeared before his seatbelt clicked. Crisp, cold, absurdly unnecessary—exactly what he wanted it to be. The leather seat stretched wide, then reclined until it threatened to become a bed. A lie-flat seat. Uninterrupted sleep across the Atlantic, a luxury he'd once only read about in travel blogs.

He ran a hand over the armrest controls like they were instruments on a private jet. This was his splurge. His reward. Every dollar of it traced back to the edges he'd played. Arbitrage had bought him this. Not his salary. Not Tara's paycheck. Him. His system. His discipline. His adaptability. He'd made this happen.

His phone buzzed. Tara had sent a video.

Cece and Savannah appeared on screen, pajama-clad, hair tangled post-bath. "We love you, Daddy!" Cece shouted too close to the camera.

"Bring gelato!" Savannah chimed in before falling out of frame in giggles. He replayed it twice, grinning, warmth in his chest that no luxury seat could match. A perfect send-off.

Funny thing about parenting—you could spend a whole day desperate for ten minutes of silence, then miss them unimaginably the instant you got it.

The cabin door sealed with a hydraulic sigh. Then came the voice through the overhead speakers. "Ladies and gentlemen, the main cabin door is now closed, and we are preparing for departure. Please switch all devices into airplane mode."

As Chase's thumb hovered over the plane-shaped toggle, his phone buzzed. Not another video, a LineSniper notification. An edge. Odds off by just enough to matter. He pounced.

Another notification rolled in. Then another. Fingers moving quick as code, he hammered through apps, firing off wagers as though he could stack a week's worth of profit in the next five minutes. The jurisdictional cliff of online betting approached, six days offline looming like a prison sentence.

He closed the privacy door beside him and let the cocoon shield him from the others in the cabin. His seatmates sipped pre-flight drinks, settled into novels, vanished behind eye masks. His world shrank to a six-inch screen.

"Cabin crew, prepare for takeoff."

The engines swelled then roared, a deep-bellied rumble that rattled the cabin walls. Runway lights smeared into white as the plane gathered speed, the weight of it straining toward flight. His screen still blazed, stubborn against the announcement. When he should have been savoring the money he'd made, he was consumed with worry over the money he might miss.

The nose lifted. Wheels left the ground. He jammed in the final side of a bet right as the plane pierced the low-hanging clouds. The cabin shuddered, and his screen flashed "Bet Placed" a split-second before the signal cut.

He dropped the phone onto the console, pulled the blanket across his lap, and reclined the seat into its improbable flatness. Champagne within reach, the hush of the cabin wrapped around him, everything here was built for comfort. And yet, as the plane tilted toward the night sky, he was restless, surprised at how little joy there was in shutting it all down.

With no direct flight between DC and Milan, Chase connected in Paris. He saw none of the city, only another lounge with another bowl of almonds and another board of flight numbers rolling over like tides. On the last leg, the sky broke open to reveal the Alps like a rumor someone finally confirmed. A small, involuntary awe rose.

After the long layover, Milan arrived as evening—sleek and cool, winter lights strung in sensible lines, taxis queued like beads on a rosary.

Waiting for him past the customs line, like a familiar chapter pulled from an old book, was Declan with his easy grin and grounded energy.

They had been two years apart in their fraternity—Chase the pledge educator, Declan the pledge—bonding not through hierarchy but over the organization's long history and fabled lore. What started as guidance had become friendship, the kind that held through years, cities, and countries.

"Chase Dupree! In the flesh at the Olympics," Declan said, pulling him into a hug.

He looked unchanged—tall and thin, all elbows and angles, dark hair forever a little unruly, clear-framed glasses giving him the air of a Silicon Valley philosopher. And that grin: huge, white, wildly sincere. Pure Declan.

"Finally, two decades in the making. After this week, you're never going to forgive yourself that it's taken this long."

"All credit to your persistence," Chase said. "Consider this your legacy."

Declan had the lived-in look of someone unburdened by urgency. He'd been one of the first hires at a tech company now big enough to be a noun, his career carrying him across continents until his calendar looked like a time zone map. After years of that churn—and the now-lucrative stock options that came with it—he announced, without apology, a professional gap year. Eleven months in, he wore the identity effortlessly.

The last time they'd seen each other in person was when Declan lived in LA. He'd selflessly driven down to Oceanside, north of San Diego, no short commute, to meet Chase while he was stuck at a conference. Not long after, Declan found a man who captured his imagination, a fitness obsessive and consultant with the kind of job that allowed him to live anywhere in the world. After several months together, they chose London, packed up, and hadn't looked back.

Whether it was his newfound European proximity or the luxury of spare time, Declan had done it all for this trip—the tickets, the lodging, the schedule—down to details Chase wouldn't have thought to consider. Chase's only jobs were booking his flights and firing off Venmos for his share. It suited him fine. Declan had the knack and past expertise, and Chase was content, maybe even relieved, to just be along for the ride.

"I landed this morning," Declan said. "Already have us checked in. Let's get your bags to the room."

"Where are we staying?"

"Second thoughts about trusting me with the details? Still as OCD as ever?"

"Not at all. I simply want to hear you sell it like a tour guide."

Declan grinned. "After all those pledge lessons you made me sit through, it's about time I got to do the planning. Navigli. You can walk everywhere. And the restaurants are so good, the food will ruin you for the rest of your life."

"Love it," Chase said. "Let's go get ruined."

The quips came easy, like they were still solving the world's problems over greasy pizza on High Street. One line set up the next, and the rhythm clicked back like no time had passed.

They boarded the train from Malpensa, the city unfurling outside the window in shifting frames. Scooters arranged in haphazard logic. Stone arches ribbed like vertebrae. A cathedral spire piercing the dusk. Chase pressed his forehead to the glass, struck by the whiplash of it. Here, the skyline carried centuries, not seasons.

They barely let the bags hit the floor before heading out again, both eager to trade the room's four walls for the city waiting beyond. As they stepped onto the street, Milan opened in strata, like the cross-section of a fossil.

With every corner they turned, it was impossible not to feel the contrast. Back home, Navy Yard was a dense thicket of new high-rises, glass towers younger than his daughters, the neighborhood still smelling of fresh concrete. Here, streets were older than America. The most historic corners of Washington suddenly felt like newcomers beside these narrow lanes. Even the graffiti seemed older, weathered into permanence. This was something else entirely—enduring, rooted, a reminder that life could stretch beyond the rush of what was new and trendy into something lasting.

They moved through the urban center, two faces in a jubilant crowd, swept along by a current bigger than either of them. The Olympic Village was a stone's throw away, with clusters of fans in every color and crest—Norwegian knitted caps, Canadian parka hoods, Japanese scarves—drifted past like tributaries feeding into one great river of celebration. Flags draped over shoulders like capes. Voices braided into a kind of international song: dozens of languages blending all at once.

"This is my favorite thing about host cities at night," Declan mused. "Nations fight like mortal enemies, but for two weeks we remember we're one human family."

Chase nudged him with a grin. "I can't tell if those are wise words from a man on his sixth Olympics or if you've become a philosopher in your old age."

The air smelled like pasta and melted chocolate. Cafés, buzzing and glowing, served aperitivos. They walked with no map, no agenda, following where the city wanted to take them.

Declan pointed suddenly across the street. "There's one of the pubs I've heard about," he called excitedly, already weaving through the crowd. He ducked inside before Chase could answer, motioning for him to follow before disappearing into the warmth beyond.

Out of reflex, Chase's hand twitched toward his pocket. Muscle memory: his fingers itched to check lines, edges, scores. It was the tell he couldn't hide, evidence that no matter how far he traveled, the habit traveled with him. But this time he resisted, pleased with himself, and followed Declan inside.

* * *

The next morning, light crept through the shutters of their Navigli flat. Chase's suitcase lay open, neatly displayed as if it had been staged for inspection. Shirts folded, sweatshirts stacked, every hat slotted neatly, each piece owning its square of the puzzle. Every last article was red, white, or blue.

Declan gave an exaggerated gasp and laughed. "Dude, even your underwear and socks look like Uncle Sam's standard issue. You already send an annual Fourth of July card. We get it. You love America."

Chase laughed. "What can I say? Patriotism's a year-round job."

Declan shook his head, amused. "Somewhere Betsy Ross is looking down, proud as hell and maybe a little concerned."

They spent the four days that followed in a rhythm that belonged entirely to the Olympics.

In the cavernous hockey arena, their seats were close enough to hear the slash of blades and the bodies hit the glass like exclamation points. The ice itself shone under the floodlights, a mirror fractured by every turn of a skate. Chase wore his voice thin cheering for the U.S. against Finland, swept up in the din of the crowd, drums pounding from one section, chants rolling from another. The atmosphere demanded participation, and their effort paid off with a 4–2 win for the Stars and Stripes. They were through to Saturday's final.

At figure skating, they watched in reverent silence, the crowd collectively holding its breath as steel carved the ice with impossible precision. Sequins caught the spotlights and threw shards of color into the rafters, as if the skaters were pulling light down to skate with them.

Speed skating brought them back to noise and adrenaline. The oval track magnified sound, the roar of the crowd swelling as racers whipped around turns with physics-defying grace. Chase picked a favorite in each heat—always American—and cheered like a man unburdened.

At night, Milan transformed into a lantern-lit festival. Trattorias overflowed with spectators in national colors, turning the district into a moving patchwork quilt. They traded stories with Canadians over espresso and limoncello, listened attentively to a couple from Oslo who explained curling with the patience of science teachers, laughed with a Brazilian family who'd somehow adopted ski jumping as their sport of choice, clinked glasses with Kiwis celebrating a snowboarding medal. Declan seemed to know how to summon people into conversation, and Chase followed his lead, awed at how quickly the world shrank around a table.

* * *

The tickets for the United States versus Canada—Olympic gold on the line—were outrageous, but Chase hardly blinked. What was the point of making all this money if not to seize moments like this?

The arena was a cauldron, chants of "U-S-A" and "Ca-na-da" crashing against each other like waves. Team Canada struck first, a goal in the second period that brought half the building to its feet. Chase pounded a fist into his thigh, throat raw from yelling, but when the U.S. evened the score minutes later, he was right there with thousands of others screaming himself even hoarser.

It stayed tied, 1–1, into the final minute. The puck slid along the boards in the Canadian zone, sticks clattering, tension drawn taut, thirty thousand leaning forward, waiting for history to render its verdict. A pass cycled back to the blue line. Everyone—Americans and Canadians alike—braced for another setup down low. Instead, the defenseman wound up and unleashed a shot.

The puck blazed through the air. The red light burst alive. The horn screamed.

Goal.

For a heartbeat, a collective inhale—and then the rink detonated. Chase was airborne, hugging Declan, high-fiving neighboring revelers.

Every muscle fired at once, celebration confined to a single seat. As the podium was being set, he realized he hadn't been this invested in the outcome of a game for months. It was joy without calculation, unburdened and whole.

As the anthem began, the U.S. team gathered at center ice. Their eyes visibly glistened as they belted the words, gold medals heavy and bright around their necks. They weren't playing for money. They were playing for pride, for legacy. And in that moment, Chase envied them, the purity of it, the permanence. He felt his own face wet, tears sliding down before he realized they were there.

They carried the game with them into the night, bodies still vibrating from the roar of thirty thousand people erupting at once. Every time they crossed paths with another American flag, a fresh round of "U-S-A!" chants rippled between strangers who felt like teammates. The city had become one sprawling victory lap.

"There's only one logical conclusion to a night like this," Declan declared, stopping as the realization struck him. "Gelato."

He spotted a corner shop packed with locals—always the best sign—and tugged Chase toward it before he could answer. Behind its glass guard, pastel tubs gleamed. The case was a row of color fields: pistachio that looked like the inside of an old church, blood orange like a fox's coat against snow, mango that glowed like bottled sunlight. Declan went straight for mango. Chase, less adventurous, went with the safe choice, chocolate.

They carried their cups outside, where the night opened above them—clear, cloudless, almost unnervingly still after the roars of the day. A single heat lamp glowed over the tables, pulling them into its orbit. They sat, spoons in hand, racing the melt with every sugary bite.

Chase blurted, "Today's been crazy. I actually felt it again, the love for sports. I've let that slip lately. Along with a lot of other things, if I'm being totally honest."

Declan's eyes held Chase's, steady and patient, inviting the full story. What came out next was like water bursting through a dam. He told Declan everything—the MRI results, the massages, the dinner with Blaine that had cracked the door open, the insane money flowing in since, his hellbent effort to keep his day-to-day obligations in check.

"I keep telling myself it's temporary, that it's smart, that it's not gambling if the math checks out. Hell, I wouldn't even be here if it weren't for arbing," he said.

He admitted the conflict with Tara, the missed moments with the girls, the small lies compounding as fast as the profits. Even the rationalizations—how they'd only started sounding like rationalizations since he'd been in Italy without a phone, twitching for it like a junkie. He confessed the fear too, that the moment his plane touched down in the States, he'd start right back up again.

"I don't know how to stop," he concluded.

By the time he finished, his gelato was soup, his spoon sunk in the middle like a white flag.

When Declan finally spoke, his voice was level. "So what are you really chasing, the money or the feeling?"

Chase stared at the swirl left in his cup.

"It's both," he admitted. "The feeling...absolutely. Growing up, winning was second nature. This makes me feel like I'm winning again. And it's not the money itself, not really. It's what it lets me be. A boater. An Olympic spectator. The husband who can still surprise and impress his wife. The dad who can give his kids Disney."

Declan leaned back, watching him without judgment. "You've got Tara. Two little girls who adore you. A solid job. You're a husband. A dad. A provider. A good person. Sounds like you've already got the identities you care about. Maybe you're just scared they don't feel like enough?"

Chase looked down.

Declan let the silence sit before continuing, his tone quiet, almost reflective. "This isn't only you, Chase. It's what people do. They get the win, they buy the thing, they feel the high, and then it fades. So they go looking for the next one. Temporary has a way of colonizing everything. Psychologists call it hedonic adaptation. I think of it as the treadmill.

No matter how fast you run, the horizon doesn't get closer."

"You make it sound inevitable. So what's the move? Accept it?" Chase asked.

Declan leaned back, eyes on the dark canal. When he spoke, it was with the clarity of someone who had already lived the question. "It's not acceptance. It's redefinition. Decide what enough is—and let it be enough."

Chase's gaze fixated on Declan, the kid who used to look up to him, who once needed his approval. Now here they were, roles inverted. Chase realized he was no longer the guide. He was the one being guided.

* * *

The last day had arrived, and for the closing ceremony they traded Milan for Verona, a final pilgrimage before the flame went dark.

The train to Verona hummed through the flat expanse of Lombardy, a quick blur of villages and vineyards. Declan dozed against the window, his head bobbing in rhythm with the tracks, but Chase stayed awake. His body was tired, yet his mind was alive, running through the prior night's conversation. "Decide what enough is, and let it be enough." The words looped with the steady click of the rails, as if the train itself were carrying the thought forward.

By the time they stepped onto the platform an hour and ten minutes later, the march toward the stadium had the softness of a farewell disguised as a parade. Crowds still funneled in unity, but the energy had shifted—slower steps, conversations that drifted more than surged. Vendors held out scarves and pins with a touch more urgency, their calls carrying the plea of a last chance. It had the feel of the last day of camp: reticent goodbyes, everyone trying to stretch a moment they knew was about to end.

Inside the amphitheater, however, the air was charged. Spotlights swept across aged stone, washing it in myriad colors. Athletes processed past, tired but radiant, the closing song of a fortnight that had consumed the world.

When the announcement came, the formal declaration that the Games were closed, he felt a small, private pang, the particular ache that comes when something long-awaited finally ends, when anticipation dissolves and the extraordinary slips into memory. For six days, his head had been clear. His neck hadn't hurt. He'd slept like a person who had lived each day fulfilled.

But now, a familiar weight returned. The Games were over, closed with a single truth, unspoken but absolute. His freedom had been fleeting. His trip had been a reprieve, not a cure. He knew himself well enough to know what he'd do when the wheels touched down on American soil.

A gust of cold threaded the stands, and he shivered. Declan glanced over, smiling, dancing lights mirrored in his glasses, the easy restraint of a man who knew not to interrupt an internal moment.

The flame began to dim, and the stadium fell into a hush. The torch burned small, then smaller, until the final flicker gave way and sighed into nothing. Extinguished. Darkness, then an eruption of fireworks overhead.

Tomorrow, the horizon would be waiting.

21

MADNESS

THEY TOUCHED DOWN WITH A JOLT, the pilot braking hard as the Dulles terminal slid into view. He barely registered the view outside. Declan's words still echoed, but Chase had been waiting for this moment with childlike impatience.

Before the plane even made contact with the runway, he deactivated Airplane Mode and opened LineSniper. Edges populated instantly. He toggled to Faceoff and for a half-second feared a lag in geolocation. But there it was. "Location Verified." Every sportsbook account lit up, alive again. He was home. Money to be made. Lost time to claw back.

Off the plane, the customs line inched forward, a serpentine of backpacks and carry-ons. Chase kept his eyes down, locking in a handful of plays before the line advanced.

"Next."

He stepped forward blindly, still thumbing wagers, settling back into rhythm: odds, percentages, certainty.

"Passport please. And I'll need your attention," a customs agent barked, breaking his concentration.

"Trying to get back to work. The American way, right?" Chase tossed his passport onto the counter, blinking as the words registered, startled by the brazenness in his own tone toward a federal agent.

Outside baggage claim, he summoned an Uber. The driver greeted him with family-like enthusiasm, stopping just short of a hug. He hoisted

Chase's suitcase into the trunk, confirmed their seatbelts were fastened, and eased them onto the toll road toward DC. Out the window, sunset bled across the horizon, but Chase's eyes stayed fixed on the screen. He checked the spreads on college hoops, eyed an NHL line for his hometown Capitals, watched a prop swing half a point between two books.

The eager driver tried conversation once then gave up and turned up the radio when Chase offered nothing back.

By the time the Uber stopped outside his Navy Yard apartment, Chase was already tallying the day's profit in his head with the ease of a seasoned banker.

Upstairs, Tara and the girls would be waiting, Cece likely stationed at the door, Savannah whispering "SHH!" Both would be ready to erupt with a scream as if he'd been gone a year instead of six days. He pictured Tara and his mom behind them—expectant, exhausted—waiting for the childcare relief it was his job to deliver.

The reunion could wait. He lingered outside the front door. Another alert flashed—an arb, small but simple. He tapped it in, double-checked the stakes, hit confirm. Another popped. Then another.

He stepped inside the lobby, but even then he didn't head for the elevator. He stopped short, back pressed to the cool marble wall, thumbs flying. Bets stacked on bets, the entryway around him a blur of comings and goings. He told himself it would only take a minute, that he needed to finish this one sequence before going upstairs.

The elevator doors opened, a young couple stepping out. Chase didn't move. He let the doors close again while he chased down one last line. Upstairs, his family was waiting. He'd be there soon. But not yet.

* * *

The call overtook his screen mid-bet.

Mom.

The name filled the display, a green and red door at the bottom daring him to choose. What could she possibly want? She'd only flown back to Ohio four days ago and had FaceTimed the girls every night since—deep in grandmother withdrawal. She knew they'd be asleep this time of night.

He sighed. Accepted.

"I'm sorry to drop this on you right after you got back," Louise said. Her voice carried that weighty tone that always meant bad news was coming. "It's Paul. Cousin Paul passed away."

Chase blinked. *Paul?* It took a moment to place the name. He could picture a guy at some family reunion fifteen, maybe twenty years ago—thick gold chain, slicked-back hair, carrying himself like a small-time mob boss—and little else.

"Oh." He kept his tone flat, respectful enough. "I didn't realize he'd been sick."

"He wasn't. It was sudden. The funeral's this weekend. I'd really like you to come with me."

Chase's first thought wasn't grief or logistics. It was geography. Was Paul being buried in Ohio—where he'd grown up and where betting was live—or in Florida, where he'd moved years ago and where Chase's apps would be as useless as bricks?

"Where's the funeral?" he asked.

"Florida," Louise said.

Instantly, he dismissed the idea. No way. It wasn't the girls' weekend plans, that he'd just gotten back from Italy, or even the last-minute travel. It was that Florida meant dead air, no bets, no edges. He couldn't imagine anything worse than losing a weekend of betting to sit through eulogies in Miami.

"I'm sorry, Mom. There's no way," he said, raking a hand through his hair. "The girls have activities all weekend, and I was just gone for a week. It wouldn't be fair to Tara."

A sigh on the line. "I understand. It just would've meant a lot."

"Yeah." He swallowed, his mind already drifting to the blinking edges vanishing the longer he stayed connected. "I really am sorry."

* * *

The end of the month meant ritual.

March 1—fittingly, a Sunday. While others filed into pews—a weekly pilgrimage Chase himself had all but abandoned—he sat at his kitchen table at dawn, ready to update his sacred monthly profit Note. This was his service. The quiet of the apartment, the stillness of the hour, gave it the air of worship.

February: **$28,942**.

He stared at the number. Almost twenty-nine grand, but less than January. His first step backward.

He drummed his fingers against the table, jaw tight. It didn't matter that he'd been overseas, that a week had gone by without a single wager. Regression was regression. Arbitrage was supposed to be a machine, a stairway that only climbed higher.

He typed the figure into his running ledger, the black text glaring back at him. Beneath January's bolded $41,237, February looked small, diminished.

March would fix it. Had to fix it.

* * *

From his perch on the seventh floor—the building's modest summit—Chase's office claimed a corner of glass that looked down on Connecticut Avenue. Directly below, the street was a patchwork of eras stitched together without reason: a Potbelly Sandwich pressed against a stone church, a cannabis shop beside a Thai restaurant, a low-slung car wash throwing off steam beyond. But high above it all, the view stretched farther—across the blooming branches of Rock Creek Park, the sprawling embassy complexes, the radio towers that broadcast the news of the nation. His corner office looked like a mark of arrival, though Chase knew it was more accident of floor plan than proof he'd reached the peak.

The first half of March had already blurred together in a fever of bets, his obsession climbing with the calendar. He'd been like a man possessed, clawing for every edge, hellbent on proving January hadn't been the ceiling, but rather a baseline.

And today promised money. March Madness was slated to tip off at 12:10 p.m. EST. He lamented being stuck in the office, wishing he'd managed an excuse to work from home, free to devote himself to the live action arbers dreamed about.

So he'd make the best of it.

At 1 p.m., he trudged to the main conference room named for a donor long gone. The division's senior leadership team was gathered, and Chase had been invited to provide unit-specific feedback on the campaign strategy already projected on the wall when he arrived.

Anticipating that the invite had been a courtesy at best, he half-hid his phone beneath a notepad, flicking through live edges while the room debated prospect lists.

"Chase?" The vice president's voice cut sharp. "What's your read on this pipeline?"

He blinked, caught mid-bet. "Sorry, say that again? I was taking notes."

An eyebrow arched at the end of the table, but the meeting rolled on. Sweat pricked at his temple. Chase slid his phone into his pocket, chastened. He'd dodged a bullet. For the next twenty minutes, he kept the phone sheathed. The irony wasn't lost on him. He'd clawed through a career to reach this table, only to risk it all under that very table chasing lines.

"Thanks for coming, everyone," the VP said in closing, though Chase was already out the door, headed back to his office. He closed his door, opened his iPad, and activated Multiview mode. Four games streamed at once, his desk monitor displayed LineSniper larger than life, and his phone became a personal betting kiosk. Bets fired off in sequence, odds shifting with every possession, discrepancies everywhere as the books scrambled to keep up.

Sitting there in his private office—tailored suit, crisp white shirt, red power tie, hair slicked back—he felt like Gordon Gekko, profit not a question but a guarantee.

A knock at the door. His assistant stepped in, eyes flicking nervously toward the sports-fueled setup on his desk.

"How did the call with David Rosenthal go?"

Shit. He'd seen the five-minute warning flash across his laptop, minimized it, then lost the thread chasing a lucrative middle. The biggest donor to his unit—missed. Major mistake.

"Fine," Chase said quickly. "I'll follow up with him early next week on a couple items."

She nodded, unconvinced, and slipped back out.

Chase leaned back, rubbing his temples. He'd think of something. Maybe send a new pullover as a gift, some gesture to smooth it over. He'd worry about it later.

As the clock ticked toward five, his calendar stared back with an appointment he didn't remember adding. "Work Dinner, 6:00 p.m." It was from his personal calendar, the one Tara could see. He frowned. *Did I put that there? Must have, in the heat of some scramble.* At first, he almost deleted it.

If Tara asked, the entry supplied a ready excuse. He'd already told her. Might as well take advantage. She'd be planning to get the girls, handle dinner, manage bedtime. No harm.

The office emptied, lights dimmed, but Chase stayed. Alone, blinds drawn, screens glowing. His corner office became a war room. Every possession another chance to push toward surpassing January's peak.

His wife thought he was out shaking hands, cutting steaks, pitching vision. Instead, he was chasing lines, his calendar the perfect cover.

* * *

Birthday cards were on the counter, stacked against two wrapped presents, "Daddy" scrawled inside a heart in the uneven handwriting of a five-year-old.

It was April 1. His birthday.

For years, Tara had insisted on being the first up that morning—hanging the family birthday banner, preparing his favorite breakfast spread, conducting the girls in chorus as he emerged from the bedroom.

If he ever stirred early, she'd scold him for spoiling it.

When she undoubtedly protested this year, he would tell her he hadn't meant to steal her thunder—he just couldn't sleep. It was true enough. But the real reason was less innocent. More important than silly birthday traditions, it was the first of the month. A new tradition had taken hold.

He headed for the patio, fleece blanket slung around him, a winter chill reminding the early birds that spring had yet to wrestle back full control.

He opened PickTracker and swiped to the monthly totals.

March: **$33,714.**

His birthday balloon, burst before sunrise. Higher than February, sure, but still well short of January. He tapped it into his Note, each keystroke a muted thud. Nearly thirty-four grand in profit, and he was furious that the machine seemed to be leveling out, that the stairway had stopped climbing, abandoned mid-construction as if the builders had walked off to another site.

The patio door swung open behind him. Tara stepped out, hair pulled back, sweatshirt draped over her shoulders.

"Hey, birthday boy," she said. "Up at five, huh? Didn't think thirty-nine made you so old you couldn't fall back asleep after getting up to pee."

She was perfect, everything he could ever want in a wife. And yet the number burned in his mind, overshadowing what stood right in front of him.

"Looks like you need warming up." She came and sat in his lap, nuzzling up against him.

Chase tried to put on the smile she wanted, tried to wrap his arms around her and savor it.

"Yeah, it's chilly out here. I was just heading inside," he said, shifting her gently off his lap and rising.

Tara let him go, her smile faltering as he slipped back into the apartment. "Happy birthday to you," she murmured, though he was already out of earshot.

22

BOAT TO NOWHERE

YARDS MARINA WAS LESS than a ten-minute walk from their apartment—if not for corralling the two feral animals they called children. The double stroller served a different purpose today, one side carrying a cooler, the other stuffed with life jackets.

As they split between the towering Department of Transportation buildings and slipped down a brick-laden alley that harkened back to older times, the Anacostia came into view—a billion diamonds shifting in rhythmic morning unison. Despite the short commute, Chase still felt like they'd traveled miles. Maybe that was the point of it, this boat club membership—escape without really having to leave.

For over a decade, Chase had stood along the same boardwalk, watching fiberglass hulls carve lines into the water, sunlight flashing off decks like polished coins. He'd wonder who those people were. What kind of lives let them traverse the river like minority owners of an exclusive club?

Now, standing with his family at the top of the dock, he felt a subtle, private satisfaction. Somewhere, someone was watching them—Tara with a tote bag slung over her shoulder, the girls orbiting like satellites in matching nautical outfits—and wondering the same thing. The Duprees had become the people he used to puzzle over. Boating people.

Since leaving the apartment, Cece and Savannah had been chanting, "RIP IT, CAPTAIN! RIP IT, CAPTAIN!" Their little voices reverberated as if they were leading a parade. Chase smiled despite himself. The refrain was his doing—three words that transformed the mechanical act of pushing the throttle into something with flair, into a family signature. He'd stolen it from the Blue Angels after watching a late-night documentary on the famed fliers. He'd been struck by the lead pilot's clipped command—"Rip it!"—issued a second before the jets broke formation and split in impossible directions. The first time he took the girls on the water, he'd explained with pretend solemnity that this was what real pilots and captains said before going fast. His daughters had embraced it with gleeful obedience.

They stood near the Freedom Boat Club gate, waiting for their guests—Javier, Leslie, and their three additional zoo animals. Chase's eyes went to the shimmering water, his mind drifting, as it did too often these days, back to his ledger.

April had closed at **$24,622**, nine thousand less than March, nearly seventeen thousand below his January high-water mark. Like a TV analyst, he broke down the factors. Atlantis had pulled the deposit multiplier in early April, cutting off his most lucrative stream. NCAA basketball was finished. The NBA and NHL had funneled into the narrow bottleneck of playoffs—fewer games, fewer bets. Baseball was there, but baseball was a grind, slow and consistent, rarely yielding excitement. The doldrums of summer were ahead, notoriously unprofitable. If he'd have any shot at eye-popping profits again, it wouldn't be until September and the start of football season, with its promise of volume and mismatched lines. But even then, the ceiling would be lower without Atlantis's free cash. January's pinnacle was likely gone, a reality he was still struggling to accept.

He squeezed the railing with his free hand. This wasn't the time. A dull headache, his near-constant companion, pressed from the base of his skull—a reminder of the two ibuprofen he'd swallowed at the sink before they left, still taking their sweet time to kick in. Near-daily use seemed to stretch the gap between ingestion and relief, a few more minutes with each passing day.

"Earth to Chase." Tara's voice snapped him back. She was in the process of slathering sunscreen on Cece and Savannah.

He turned, pasted on a grin. "I was visualizing today's voyage."

"You nervous?" she asked, raising an eyebrow.

He widened his eyes in mock offense. "Me? I practically have gills now."

She let out a laugh. "Right. Is that why you paced our living room last night practicing docking an invisible boat?"

"Those were highly realistic simulations. Besides, I'm a walking encyclopedia of captain wisdom these days." He tapped his temple. "Red, right, return. I know those buoys by name out there."

In truth, his stomach buzzed with the same cocktail of nerves and anticipation he'd felt the first time he slid chips across a blackjack table, or clicked Confirm on a four-figure bet.

Lord knew he'd done the work. An eight-hour safety course online, two more hours on Zoom with a seasoned captain drilling him on rules of the road and right of way. Then a final two hours on the water with that same captain barking commands and judging every maneuver. And even then, when the instructor slapped him on the back and said, "You handled her better than most their first time out. Keys are yours, Captain Dupree. Go enjoy yourself," Chase balked. He wanted another session, wanted certainty. That was the OCD streak in him, the part that hated leaving risks unmitigated.

The captain had laughed. "The best are the ones who respect the water to the point they never feel ready. Happy to set up another session, kid."

Only after that extra training did he finally take Tara and the girls out. Once, twice, a third time. Each trip a little smoother than the last, confidence growing with repetitions.

Today was different though. Not only family but, for the first time, guests. Friends on board meant a pressure he couldn't explain, the responsibility of souls entrusted to his hand on the throttle. He tried to frame it as pride—*look at me, the suburban kid turned Navy Yard dad,* *captaining a $75,000 boat on the Potomac, finally with witnesses,* but the pride was braided with fear.

A shout carried down the boardwalk. Javier and Leslie were making their way toward them, kids in tow.

"Captain Dupree!" Javier boomed. "Sorry we're late. We came from swim lessons. Wanted to be brushed up in case you flip us out there."

"Thanks for the vote of confidence, asshole," Chase retorted.

The dockhand swung the gate open, and they crossed the threshold separating the public from the mariners. At the bottom of the ramp floated the NauticStar 223 Chase had reserved for them.

He guided everyone aboard with the delight of a new homeowner welcoming friends for the first time. The boat was in pristine condition. While everyone jockeyed for seats, Chase ran through his checklist: flares and registration accounted for, radio check successful, Simrad screen displaying depth and speed, kids secured in life jackets, the adults' stowed under the bow seats. He lowered the single 150-horsepower engine and turned the key. The response came back deep and steady. The sharp scent of fuel mingled with brine and sunscreen, the olfactory cocktail of summer on the river. They were ready to go.

Within minutes, the lines were untied, the fenders lifted. A gentle shove freed them from the wall, and the throttle clicked into motion. The kids squealed from the open bow, snacks—the true draw of these boat rides—attacked with fury. Bags of Pirate's Booty ripped open. Juice boxes speared by sword-like straws. Gummy bears traded like baseball cards.

Nationals Park appeared off their starboard side as they cleared the marina, its steel skeleton quiet but expectant. The ballpark scoreboard sat like a watchtower against the morning sky, the concourses dormant for now. But the boardwalk was already stirring—fans in Mets blue lining up for brunch, joggers weaving around strollers, vendors rolling coolers toward the park for the afternoon game. Chase felt the distinct long-weekend hum of a Memorial Day crowd as the river opened and his hands eased on the wheel.

"Oldest kid picks the first song," he announced. Lily, his goddaughter, beamed.

"Can you play the song from Titanic, Uncle Chase?" Lily asked, with the complete innocence of a seven-year-old.

Chase's face went white. Javier, Leslie, and Tara doubled over in laughter behind them.

"She watched it at a sleepover. Don't blame us!" Javier managed between fits of laughter.

They idled through the long no-wake zone, gliding beneath the colossal Frederick Douglass Bridge—the most expensive infrastructure project in DC's history—and past the developing Buzzard Point neighborhood before the stately War College emerged on the point of Fort McNair. As they reached the buoy that marked the end of the Anacostia's no-wake zone, Cece and Savannah, on cue, threw their arms skyward.

"RIP IT, CAPTAIN!"

Chase flipped his hat backward, lest it become a tribute to the depths. His head stayed on a swivel as they entered the most treacherous stretch of river—the confluence of the Anacostia, the Washington Channel, and the Potomac. Seeing no congestion, he pushed the throttle gently forward, felt the bow rise, and then stabilize as they reached plane.

He swung them north toward Georgetown, relishing the surge of power as he directed the three-thousand-pound vessel like an aquatic conductor. He set his course and glanced at the Simrad. Twenty-seven miles per hour. He could take her faster, but this was his preferred limit, fast enough to feel alive without losing control.

Javier whooped from the bow, fist-pumping like a Jersey Shore extra decades past his prime. Leslie snapped pictures of the kids, a mass of windswept hair. Tara smiled, frantically corralling trash before it blew overboard. This was the image Chase had envisioned.

Then a shift in the air, a roar overhead. A shadow grew, blotting the sun for a heartbeat. They were directly below the final descent into DCA, jets dipping so low it felt as though the wheels might skim the water.

The NauticStar chewed through the water as familiar sights appeared from a novel angle: the Washington Monument, its stone subtly shifting color a third of the way up. The Lincoln Memorial, its ring of state names visible to those who knew where to look. The Kennedy Center, hovering over the river as though they might pull alongside and walk in for a show.

Georgetown's waterfront appeared with sudden energy: massive yachts already lined the wall, bikinis stretched across the decks in a see-and-be-seen hotspot. Onshore, umbrellas flared open, buskers tuned guitars, tourists leaned on the rail, waving at them as they floated by.

He turned them south again, arcing past historic Old Town Alexandria, several tall ships on display, crowds straining to get a view from land. Chase steered them closer, eyes widening as necks tilted skyward, the masts seeming to stretch forever.

The river widened again, and Chase let loose. They breezed past National Harbor, the Ferris Wheel bright against the sky, the last sign of a bustling city before the shoreline grew hushed and green, vibrant now in more natural ways. A bald eagle cut across the distance, wings sharp as blades. Javier pointed, yelling, "Eagle! Eagle!"

They turned a bend. "Mount Vernon up ahead on your right," Chase called out.

The estate rose on its bluff, red roof and white columns commanding the river. They slowed to take in its majesty.

Javier came back to the helm and stood beside him. "It's wild," he said, "raising our kids with all this history right in our backyard."

Chase thought about his girls, sticky with juice boxes, chanting, "RIP IT!" They were growing up in a city where their local news was national news for the rest of the country.

Chase nodded. "Pretty remarkable. We've done alright, haven't we?"

A buzz on his wrist. Then four more in rapid succession.

He recognized it instantly, even under the motor's steady vibration. LineSniper. A quick glance showed a slew of middles—an easy couple hundred in two minutes if he played it right. He scanned the water and found a large yacht crossing ahead, throwing up a heavy wake. Perfect cover. He pulled the throttle back. "Let's let this one pass."

The boat rocked gently. Everyone braced. Chase slipped his phone from his pocket, his attention diverted.

With his eyes down, the wake broadsided them harder than expected, jerking the boat sideways. He snapped his head up, jolted the wheel, overcorrected. The kids shrieked, oblivious. Javier grabbed the back of Chase's seat to balance himself, nearly hitting the deck. "Whoa, Captain! Keep her steady!"

From the stern, Tara's eyes cut to his hand, to the phone, then back to the horizon. He caught that look, a warning, feeling like a kid caught cheating on a test, the guilt immediate, the denial automatic. For half a breath, he thought about owning it, admitting he'd let his eyes slip, but the instinct passed as quickly as the wake.

"These yachts are always trying to swamp the little guys!" Chase declared.

They looped back north, the sun climbing, the cooler lighter, everyone pleasantly worn. By the time they reached the Anacostia, all the kids were asleep, strewn across the seats in a tangle of limbs and life jackets. Chase guided the boat into its slip, whispering "neutral is your friend" like a prayer. The fenders kissed the dock with a soft bump as the dockhand caught the bow line and looped it around a cleat with practiced ease.

"Well done, Captain," Javier said, clapping him on the shoulder. "Looks like we didn't need those swim lessons after all!"

Everyone laughed, gathered their bags, and made plans to do it again.

They ascended the dock ramp, adults lugging the day's remnants, kids deciding if their boat naps were enough to stave off afternoon meltdowns.

Chase paused at the gate and glanced back at the NauticStar rocking in its slip. Even tethered, the boat looked eager, alive, as if it might lunge forward the instant the ropes were loosed.

He rubbed the back of his head where the ache had returned, felt the ibuprofen rattling in his pocket, and decided he could make it home without another round. Then he followed his family toward the neighborhood noise. The spell was broken; back on land, they were just another family in busy Yards Park.

Maybe that was the thing about boats. They gave you the temporary feeling of going somewhere, even when you ended up right back where you started.

23

SUMMER'S SHADOW

THE CLOSER THEY GOT TO THE LAKE, the more Route 2 felt like memory—flat farmland giving way to water, the bridge over Sandusky Bay materializing ahead. Chase knew to look right, where the skyline of Cedar Point rose. As a kid, he'd lived for those rides—the gut-drop of Millennium Force, the rush of Magnum. Last summer, taking his own daughters for the first time, he'd been surprised by the difference. Where thrill once lived, there was only a nervous fear he hadn't expected. Now it was the girls in the back seat squealing about Pop and Gram, and for them the summer tradition held all the promise of youth.

The annual migration was written into the Dupree family DNA, and the girls could sense the impending arrival. A series of questions came flying from the back seat as they drew closer, one tumbling over the other in dizzying succession. Would Pop be at the house already? Would Gram have popsicles waiting? Could they go swimming the minute they arrived? Would the golf cart be charged and ready? Tara fielded the barrage with practiced patience, turning in her seat to negotiate with Cece while Savannah kicked her legs like she might propel them there faster.

By the time they pulled into his dad's driveway, the air heavy with the smell of cut grass, Chase felt the compression of time—past and present overlapping, coexisting.

Chase hadn't even cut the ignition before Cece cried out, "They're waiting for us!" She unbuckled her car seat—a fun new milestone—and bolted up the walk to the porch, Savannah close behind after some assistance from Tara.

Scott—tall, still broad-shouldered, carrying executive presence even in retirement—swept them into his arms, laughing. The strength was still there but not quite what it had been. Chase caught the faint stiffness in his father's movement, the trace of effort behind the embrace that once would have been effortless.

Kathleen, known as Gram to the girls, was beside him, arms open for Tara then for Chase. She had always threaded her role with intentional grace, never pretending to replace Louise, never angling for the spotlight, never slipping into caricature. She knew what she wasn't, and more importantly, what she could be. By the time Chase was finishing high school, she had proven herself dependable. Two decades later, she was family, plain and simple.

"How was the drive? Your dad and I will get the bags. Make yourselves at home. And shoes off inside please."

Kathleen was the only one who could out-OCD Chase. He nodded obediently.

Inside, photos of the grandkids dotted the mantel, while lemon cleaner and a lake-scented candle battled for dominance in the air. The girls tore through the rooms as if they'd never been there before.

Chase made his way to the pantry, stocked, as he knew it would be, with all the indulgences he so diligently avoided at home: M&Ms, family-sized bags of Ruffles, Cheez-Its. The lake was his perpetual cheat week.

They settled into the guest rooms on autopilot, while Kathleen whipped up dinner in the kitchen.

Chase hovered over Cece's suitcase as he unpacked it, realizing he hadn't checked his phone since leaving DC more than eight hours ago. There'd be plenty of time for LineSniper this week. He had a plan brewing, one he was convinced would lift profits while cutting the hours he spent glued to his phone. Tomorrow would prove whether the research paid off.

The next morning, Chase was up before the house had stirred. He eased the golf cart out of the garage and onto the street, its tires humming against the pavement as he steered toward the Catawba Island Club, CIC to its members. The seven-minute ride was a ceremony of summer, the morning chill pressing against his skin, sharp and refreshing. The cart crested the final hill, and Lake Erie spread out before him, sudden and immense.

He always marveled at how the lake revealed itself—all at once, unannounced—a stark contrast to the ocean, whose salt disclosed it miles inland. Here the water seemed to materialize without warning, a surprise every time. By the time he reached the dock, the world felt pared down to its essentials: the bite of the breeze, the creak of moored boats, the day still unformed before him.

He checked out a paddleboard from the rack. The dock was empty at that hour—no attendant in sight, only a couple of summer interns on the yacht bows, hosing away the mayfly hatch from the night before. The club ran on the honor system in the mornings, and Scott's member number—30338—was etched in Chase's memory after years of summers like this.

He paddled steadily, muscles remembering, skimming out of the narrow channel into open water. The lake was glass at that hour, a fine mist hovering above it. The Davis-Besse nuclear plant stood like a sentry in the distance, its lines sharp even twenty miles away. Out there, with no sound but the dip of the paddle, his thoughts surfaced.

May had been his weakest month since November.

$19,196.

Still more than his monthly salary, still impressive if you said it aloud, but a cliff compared to January's high. And his third straight monthly slide.

Arbing was safe. Controlled. But it had a ceiling, and he'd hit it.

He sat, letting the paddle rest across the board, drifting as the horizon brightened. The rising sun burned off the chill, its warmth settling across his shoulders and chest, merging with the heat already in his arms from the workout.

The forums buzzed with stories of bettors riding mispriced lines to riches, doubling or quintupling what arbs could ever yield. And he'd read them all. They called it SV+, Skewed Value Plus. On LineSniper, every edge came from one book being out of step with the rest. Nine sportsbooks lined up on one number, and one hung something different. Arbitrage meant betting both of those sides—steady as hitting singles, piling up runs one base at a time. SV+ was the opposite: you swung only at the outlier, betting solely the lonely number, aiming for home runs. Riskier, more volatile, but with a payoff that could be substantially bigger.

The decision crystallized. This week, here, he would test it. Between boat rides and ice cream cones, while everyone else lived summer, he'd swing for the fences.

Beyond the island's point, a fishing boat cut hard across the bay. Even from far off, Chase could see the urgency in its wake, driving hard for open water. The first ones out always hauled the biggest catch. This would be no different. He'd be at the forefront of SV+, chasing the kind of gains others would be too slow to claim.

* * *

The following days blurred into long-held traditions.

Afternoons at the CIC pool, girls counting down the fifteen-minute rest periods, Savannah debuting her so-called "cannonball" that looked suspiciously like a regular jump. Chase's skin still surrendered to burn despite copious sunscreen, a summer inevitability he never quite learned to avoid. Tara stretched in a lounge chair, head tilted back, shoulders softening in ways they never did in DC.

A trip to Toft's, where the scoops towered a mile high for Midwest prices. Savannah and Cece's chocolate chip cookie dough dripping down their cone far faster than they could eat it.

Fireflies speckled the backyard like magic, golf cart rides grew so frequent Chase feared they'd leave grooves in the path, and movie nights under cozy blankets.

A boat day, Scott at the helm of his forty-foot Regal, every bit the veteran captain. Chase enjoyed being a passenger after months of carrying the responsibility of the wheel himself. He felt a newfound respect for all the years his dad had chauffeured family and friends across these waters. They skimmed toward Middle Bass, circled the revelry of Put-in-Bay, sped by Perry's Monument, and raced to the Marblehead Lighthouse for an annual picture.

Seltzer in hand, Chase chatted with Kathleen and Tara on the back of the boat, the girls perched in their laps, asking when they'd see dolphins.

But, unknown to all, his bankroll was bleeding. SV+ bets kept missing, outcomes bending against him again and again, improbabilities accumulating. By Tuesday, he was down several thousand. By Wednesday, as they jetted across the lake, it was worse.

He glanced down. Another notification: a moneyline soccer bet lost. No hedge. $500 gone as if he'd set it on fire.

Thursday afternoon called for a Walmart run. Paper towels, more chips and berries, sunscreen—a mundane errand of summer. Scott offered to drive. Chase climbed into the truck beside him, grateful for a break from the chaos. They rode in silence for a stretch, the road winding along the lake.

"I heard mention of a Vegas trip next month?" Scott offered.

"It's a sports thing with my friend Blaine. A few days on the Strip," Chase replied, cautious.

"Well, I hope you stay out of trouble."

More silence.

"Everything good with you and Tara?" His tone was casual, but the question landed heavy.

"Yeah," Chase said quickly, "Just one of those stages. Young kids, demanding jobs. You remember those years. We're fine."

Scott nodded, jaw set. "Good. Good." A pause. Then, quieter: "Marriage matters more than you realize when you're in the thick of it. Don't forget to invest in it."

Chase turned and caught the glint of moisture in his father's eye.

The old wound of his life with Louise—two people who drifted until the tether finally snapped, despite best efforts—was still raw under the scar. Scott had rebuilt with Kathleen, nearly two decades strong now, but the family fracture lingered like phantom pain.

Chase swallowed hard. "I know. Don't worry about me, Dad. I promise we're good."

The low twang of a country song filled the void, leaving both men tangled in ghosts.

* * *

That evening, the whole family dressed for dinner at the club—one of the few reliable occasions for a family photo. After managing a single shot with everyone smiling, eyes open, on the fastidiously manicured lawn, they headed for the main clubhouse. Cece clutched Chase's hand as they walked the hallway lined with framed portraits of club officers through the decades. Halfway down, she let out a squeal.

"Pop!"

There he was. Vice Commodore, whites pressed crisp, smile dignified. Cece's excitement was uncontainable, her voice ringing down the corridor as she insisted on taking a photo with Pop and his wall-mounted picture.

Chase stared, an emptiness opening inside him. Respect. Stability. Legacy. He had no portrait on any wall. No evidence that what he was building even existed outside of his phone. His life was invisible, written in disappearing ink.

They were seated at the prime table, next to the window, overlooking the lawn where they had posed, the lake glittering beyond, glowing orange as the sun sank.

The club's owner—a fixture for fifty years, as present now as when he inherited the place from his father—swooped in and set a small flag in front of Scott. A perk of leadership, a signal to the room: this table meant something.

As the wine flowed and the girls colored, Chase laughed along, doing his best to ignore each buzz, scolding himself for lacking the discipline to silence it for even one dinner.

* * *

The day's sun had tired the girls, and the evening's wine had tired the adults. Within thirty minutes of parking the golf cart in the garage, and removing shoes, of course, everyone was asleep. Everyone except Chase.

He slid open the glass door and stepped onto the back patio, the fire pit spinning flames in an endless loop against the dark. Moonlight spread across the golf course's second fairway. A rabbit nosed around the edge of a sand trap twenty yards out, pausing, ears high. It looked fragile against the wide-open course, one mistake away from being swallowed whole. Chase watched it for a moment, then unlocked his iPad.

The Lakers and Timberwolves filled the screen, streaming through his ESPN app. He had a single prop: Jamaal Turner under 2.5 threes. A thousand dollars riding on it. He was surprised Faceoff had allowed such a steep wager on a player prop, but the books got lenient in the playoffs, enticing players to swap volume for stakes.

With three minutes left, Turner had a single three. Chase's shoulders loosened. Finally—one going his way.

Then…a corner three. One minute to play. Tie game.

The next sixty seconds was a comedy of errors, neither team managing a single point.

Overtime.

One minute in, Turner made another. The over hit.

A thousand gone. It pushed him past an ugly threshold. Down more than ten grand on this new system in a single week.

He stood, rage boiling, and kicked a chair hard enough to topple it. Then he punched the air, fists useless against fate, muttering furiously to himself. *How does this keep happening? It's mathematically impossible. Keeps happening again and again, the worst-case sneaking in through the cracks nearly every damn time.*

He lumbered to bed, a headache drilling behind his eyes. In the dark, he popped an ibuprofen, dry swallowing. He hoped sleep might dull the sting. It never came.

By dawn, the decision was made. No more SV+. He wasn't built for this volatility. This damn system was eating him alive.

Back to arbing. Safe, mechanical, controlled. Smaller profits, maybe, but solid ground.

At breakfast the next morning, Kathleen appeared with a conspiratorial smile.

"We've booked something for you two," she announced, eyes locked on Chase and Tara. "A night on Kelleys Island. Bed and breakfast. We'll keep the girls."

Tara's eyes went wide. "Are you serious?"

Scott grinned, pleased with her enthusiasm. "You deserve it. Go enjoy."

Tara reached across the table and squeezed Chase's hand, her joy radiating, while he struggled to summon gratitude in his sleep-deprived state. He forced a smile, telling himself maybe a night of peace and quiet would do him some good.

A few hours later, the ferry churned across the bay, carrying them to an island that felt removed from the stresses of the mainland. Tara leaned against the railing, hair lifting in the wind, her eyes alight in a way Chase hadn't seen in months.

They ate at a waterside restaurant, the sunset turning the sky into a pink-and-red lava lamp. Candlelight reflected in Tara's glass of wine as she laughed, touched his arm. Her laughter carried across the table, warm and easy, the kind of sound that once lit him up.

Chase tried—he really did. They talked about the girls. Reminisced about trips to the lake before kids. But his thumb twitched for the phone. He had too much ground to claw back from the week's devastation, one arb at a time.

Later, back at the B&B, Tara slipped into the bedroom. Chase flopped onto the couch, lines glowing, edges filling the LineSniper feed.

Behind the closed door, Tara studied herself in the full-length mirror, a wine-fueled confidence rising as she held her own gaze.

The cropped sweatshirt rode high, each sway of fabric flashing a forbidden curve. Below, arctic-white boy shorts clung snug and low to her hips, brazenly cheeky. It reminded her of another version of herself, from the carefree days of their youth. The contrast was deliberate: cozy yet provocative. Casual but undeniably sexy. She liked the way it looked on her, the quiet power of knowing she still could. And tonight, she wanted Chase to forget everything but her.

She opened the door and crossed the room slowly. "Hey," she whispered, wrapping her arms around him from behind, lips grazing his neck.

Chase's eyes never left the phone, fingers flying over bets. "Hey, be in soon."

She froze. The hurt was immediate, raw. For a moment, she lingered, hoping he'd look up. He didn't.

Without a word, she retreated, closing the bedroom door softly.

She slipped into bed alone, the mattress cool against her skin.

She'd come back to the B&B ready for him, charged by the same spark that had carried her boldly on New Year's Eve. She stared at the ceiling, frustration building hotter by the second. Her mind raced to those early hours of 2026, the way he'd pulled her in close, the raw urgency of it, the way she'd felt. The memory stirred her body awake, even as the other half of the bed lay cold.

"Fine," she whispered to herself, a note of defiance in her voice.

Her hand slipped beneath the blanket, moving with a quick, restless urgency. She shut her eyes and let the memory of him take over, her breathing growing unsteady. The room filled with small, muffled sounds as she chased what he should have given her, ecstasy temporarily replacing the loneliness.

By the time the wave crested, Chase was still out there, bathed in the sterile glow of his phone. He hadn't heard. He didn't know.

Outside, the lake was still under the moon. Inside, two lives ran parallel, no longer converging—separated only by a wall, yet impossibly far apart.

24

MISSED CONNECTIONS

CHASE'S STOMACH TILTED as he stepped onto the Woodley Park escalator, his hand snapping to the rail instinctively. Two hundred and four feet of metal teeth descended into the earth, the third longest in the WMATA metro system, a chute that looked and felt more like an enclosed water slide than public infrastructure. Looking down too long invited vertigo. He kept his eyes forward and let the motion carry him. At the bottom, he pulled up the card in his virtual wallet. One tap, a green light, the fare gate split open.

The platform was crowded, the usual rush-hour mix of backpacks and briefcases, but not claustrophobic. To Chase, the press of bodies barely registered. He'd endured Nationals playoff crowds and the tourist stampedes of cherry blossom season. This felt routine, almost civilized. Everyone had their heads bent at the same angle, necks tilted in obedient prayer to palm-sized screens. He decided to join the congregation.

Sliding into the Red Line car three minutes later, he spotted the last open seat and took it, a small win in a day short on them. The train lurched forward with its familiar metallic groan, shuddering as it rumbled down the track toward Dupont Circle. Next to the doors, posters promised advanced degrees, hawked local theater shows, even pitched a dermatology trial for psoriasis.

He stared at his reflection superimposed on the train's glass—thirty-nine, creases sneaking across his forehead, dark crescents under his eyes.

Not sleep debt so much as the interest paid on small compromises. July's heat only deepened the impression.

The Fourth, his favorite holiday, had come and gone, as fleeting as the burst of a firework fading into smoke.

He thought back on the prior week, replaying it like a highlight reel. The Barracks Row parade: a jumble of flags and strollers, a drum line rattling the sidewalk, Cece and Savannah hauling home tote bags sagging with candy, DC's mayor herself stooping down to press a fistful into their hands.

Later, they piled onto a boat with two other families—six parents and six kids packed into every corner—Chase at the helm once again, and joined a patriotic armada on the river, fiberglass hulls flying flags as they glided past the stadium while a Nationals day game let out. A passing breeze off the water briefly numbing the heat that had baked the city all afternoon.

By nightfall, the Mall had become a sea of picnic blankets and sparklers, anticipation tightening with every minute. At 9:09 p.m. sharp, the first shell launched, blossoms of fire unfolding over the Washington Monument like time-lapse flowers, cannon blasts from the Capitol concert booming behind them. Mere minutes after the finale, both girls were out cold in the stroller, heads tilted at mirrored angles as Chase, Tara, and their neighbors threaded into the dispersing crowd, each family peeling off in separate directions.

And still Chase wasn't ready to let it end. He rode the elevator to their fourteenth-story roof as he always did. The horizon burned in 360 degrees—neighborhoods and backyard pyros, suburban shows and renegade mortars stretching into Virginia and Maryland—all of it streaking skyward at once in a kind of collective rebellion against gravity. Even at his ripe old age, the magic never wore off. It was still his favorite night of the year.

Four days later, the glow of the Fourth already felt remote, the photos like artifacts from another life. He scrolled through them—kids, parade, fireworks—killing minutes until the next stop. Then muscle memory took over. Notes app. There it was again, line after line of numbers that could be read as brag or confession depending on who was looking. June's tally stared at him.

June: **$16,940**.

A week into July, he was still tormenting himself, still opening it, still cursing the ten grand he'd torched at the lake with that stupid SV+ detour. A respectable number to anyone else. But all he saw was the phantom version, June: $27,000.

Idiot. He knew better.

He tacked on a line beneath it, a reminder to his future self to avoid his past stupidity.

"SV+ at lake: -$10,000. Don't be cute."

The train screeched to a halt at the next stop. Behind him, a tourist asked if they'd passed Judiciary Square yet. People shuffled on and off. The doors closed and it lunged forward again.

A buzz on his phone. Julia.

Not unusual. She popped up every so often, sometimes with a joke about Blaine's "two wives" (her and Chase's text thread), sometimes rolling her eyes at his latest harebrained hack, sometimes simply to say, "Tell your kids to stop growing so fast in those photos. You're making me feel ancient." She'd once told him she could map his and Blaine's exchanges by sound alone, *ding ding ding* in rapid fire from his phone when the two of them were working some angle, Blaine refusing to ever turn off notifications in case a line moved in his favor.

But this time it had been weeks, maybe more, since she'd sent anything. He opened her message with no idea what waited on the other side.

JULIA: He didn't show up for daycare pickup. Again.

Chase felt his jaw lock. He knew Blaine had been falling short in recent months. There'd been a few cryptic but clearly bitter texts from Julia to Tara. But this was the most direct she'd been, frustration pouring straight through the screen.

CHASE: Today?

JULIA: Yes. Last week too. You have no idea how hard this is on me. I'm going to snap, Chase.

Something in the cadence of her texts—short, flat, no emojis—made him sit straighter.

CHASE: I didn't realize it was that bad.

A delay, five seconds that stretched into twelve. Another buzz.

JULIA: Bad? He walked out DURING dinner last week. Just…left. Who does that?

The train lights stuttered. The car bounced over a track joint. In the overhead panel, the route map blinked red dots as they moved from station to station.

CHASE: Jesus. I'm sorry, Julia.

JULIA: He was still betting at 2 a.m. last night. I woke up at 6 and found him passed out on the couch, phone in hand. I had a meeting at 8. Did drop off. Was late to work. Guess which one of us looked unreliable? Guess who couldn't care less?

He swallowed.

CHASE: You've talked to him about this, right?

JULIA: Over and over. He shrugs it off. Tells me I don't get it. That it's "work."

JULIA: Laundry's piling up. Yard's a jungle. Bedtime's all on me. I'm doing EVERYTHING.

He pictured Quinn, watching the door at daycare while the clock moved toward closing. The image landed hard, a weight in his gut. At least he wasn't Blaine, the one leaving his kid stranded.

CHASE: That's really not fair.

JULIA: No shit it's not fair.

JULIA: I can't do this anymore. If he doesn't change, I'm done.

A longer pause, then the one that snapped the reason for this tirade into a focus:

JULIA: You're with him in Vegas next week. Please say something. I don't know if it will help, but please. I'm desperate.

He stared at the gray floor, at the flecks in the composite that looked like confetti embedded in stone and felt a flicker of shame at how quickly his mind reached for comparison, reassuring himself he was still functional.

He typed.

CHASE: Of course, Julia. I'll say something to him.

The train lumbered into Farragut North. The doors flung open to a platform bristling with activity. People poured in. He didn't move, watching the text bubbles portend whatever was coming next.

JULIA: He listens to you more than anyone.

JULIA: Sometimes I think you two just enable each other, but…he still listens.

He read "enable" and felt an inward wince. He read "listens to you" and felt taller. Both could be true. His brain moved, as it often did, toward the narrative that let him keep moving.

CHASE: I get it. I'll talk to him in Vegas. You have my word.

The recorded voice announced the next stop. People shifted in anticipation, tugging bags into their laps and straightening to stand. His phone buzzed once more.

JULIA: Please. At pickup, the teacher gave me that "your husband dropped the ball again" look. I can't keep being the only adult in this house.

He imagined Julia, professional and composed, eyes that could be mistaken for stern when she was just tired. He imagined Quinn asking innocent questions where the subtext was heavier than the grammar could carry. He imagined Blaine—not imaginary at all—lost at 2 a.m. in a bath of blue light and the dopamine drip of markets that never slept.

The doors slid open at Metro Center with a clack. "Transfer to Blue, Orange, Silver," the speaker chirped cheerfully. Chase didn't hear it, absorbed in the weight of Julia's texts.

The crowd surged. Chase looked up. The doors chimed a warning and inched toward each other. He lunged, and the rubber seals kissed an inch from his outstretched hand. The train began to move.

"Dammit!" The outburst was louder than he meant, earning a few side-eyes.

He watched the platform slide away, the signage strobing to blur. Tara had asked him to grab dinner from Whole Foods on his way back—rotisserie chicken, bagged salad, the suburban cheat code for a home-cooked meal—and now he was late.

He texted Tara:

CHASE: Running a bit behind. Missed connection.

Then, almost in the same muscle movement, he wrote back to Julia:

CHASE: I'll talk to him the first chance I get. I won't let it slide.

He couldn't believe Blaine had strayed this far. He'd always been eccentric but never irresponsible. He'd have to tell Tara. She'd be worried about Julia. And it might have the added benefit of seeding enough concern that his own transgressions looked minor stacked against Blaine's.

He pictured how the confrontation might go in Vegas—noise and neon, the two of them on a casino carpet that looked like a coral reef under a blacklight.

He'd say it straight. "You're making money but losing your family." Missed pickups. Missed meals. Missed bedtimes. He could sell that because he believed it. And also because believing it made him the responsible one.

The phone buzzed again. Julia wasn't done.

JULIA: He keeps his ringer on for those dumb alerts. But when I call? "Didn't hear it." I want to throw his phone in the river.

Chase smiled despite himself, a momentary beat of the old banter.

CHASE: If you throw his phone in the river, he'll dive in after it and then blame you for water damage.

A pause. Then:

JULIA: I need *someone* to care more about our daughter than about -110 vs. +112.

He didn't have a joke for that one.

CHASE: I hear you. I'm really sorry everything's fallen on you.

She didn't respond. Maybe she'd said all there was to say. Maybe she was wrangling bath time. Maybe she'd put her phone face down on the counter, reminding herself that life existed beyond the glass rectangle.

When the train pulled into Gallery Place, he got off and backtracked, bearing the deserved humiliation of a fifteen-year resident who'd missed his stop.

He texted Tara a second update, tossed in a dumb joke about being held hostage by WMATA, then finally put the phone away for real.

On the Green Line, the car felt brighter, newer, less sad. Even the ads above the seats were cheerier. His reflection looked better here too, and he wondered how much of a person was just the angle you looked at them from.

At the Navy Yard stop, he pushed through the turnstiles and jogged the two blocks to Whole Foods, grabbing what was needed. The elevator in their lobby was slow, so he took the stairs two at a time, each step sending a stab of pain through the back of his head.

Tara was at the kitchen island when he came in, typing on her laptop with one hand and sorting the girls' art with the other, a talent unique to parents. The AC pushed cool air across the room in a steady, relieving sheet.

"Sorry," he said, setting the bag down, breath half-caught. "For once, this one's on me, not Metro."

Tara gave him the look you give a person you've lived with long enough to have replaced words with body language. "What'd you grab for dinner?"

"Salad and chicken, acquired." He lifted the container in a small, faux victory.

"And Ben & Jerry's, penance for my sins," he whispered, low enough only Tara could hear. He lifted the cardboard pint out of the bag, keeping it beneath the counter, out of the girls' eyesight. Despite her continued frustration with him since the lake, she responded with delighted eyes.

She slid the laptop aside. "Girls, wash hands!" she called, which in their house meant to run water over the general area and make a wet mess.

Chase set his phone face down on the counter, a prop to make him look the part he was about to play. He turned to Tara and let a note of performance into his voice, the kind he told himself was necessary—a way to deliver the message with enough voltage to be believed.

"You're not going to believe the text exchange I had with Julia," he said, opening the chicken. "Blaine is completely off the rails."

Tara's hands paused above the plates. She looked up, eyes narrowing. "Oh yeah?" she said as if she were reserving judgment until the rest came out.

He recounted what Julia had revealed—the daycare, the dinner, the couch at 6 a.m. Tara looked mortified.

"That's terrible. Poor Julia and Quinn," she said, shaken.

Chase nodded, matching the concern on her face. He wasn't a villain. He was looking out for his friend, ready to say what needed to be said in Vegas. And if he also used that conversation to build a case for himself—that he wasn't Blaine, that his family was steady, that this side hustle was manageable—well, he could hold two truths at once.

The AC hummed. The girls banged forks against plates. He carved the chicken in clean, decisive strokes, as if clarity were something you could slice and serve.

25

HARD EIGHT

SOMEWHERE HIGH ABOVE NEVADA, Blaine swirled the plastic cup and pressed another bourbon to his lips. His fourth—or maybe fifth—and Chase wondered if the only chance to catch him clear-headed had already slipped by.

"You're hydrating, right? Maybe mix in a water every now and then," Chase said.

Blaine let out a laugh that tumbled into a hiccup, sloppy and loud enough for half the cabin to turn. "Bourbon is just Kentucky water."

The seatbelt sign chimed. The plane banked over a patchwork of brown and red before the grid of Las Vegas revealed itself—straight streets, cul-de-sacs, and a strip of glass shimmering at the center.

"City of second chances," Blaine said, already slurring the edges. "Third, fourth, whatever."

Chase stared past him at the Strip, its hotels propped like movie sets against the desert. He thought of Julia's last text, sent as he was en route to the airport.

JULIA: Please don't let him go off the rails.

He'd typed back:

CHASE: I've got him.

He believed it when he sent it, except Blaine had started pouring alcohol into himself the second they cleared cloud cover. He told himself he'd have Blaine under control, but watching the bourbon disappear felt like watching a leash unravel in real time.

The wheels hit the runway and chirped. The landing was bumpy and the cabin applauded as if the pilot had done them a personal favor. Blaine raised his empty cup in a toast to no one and grinned.

"Time to mint money," he said.

"Or not bleed it," Chase said. "Let's start there."

In the terminal, their driver was waiting with a placard and, to Blaine's delight, addressed him as "Mr. Wexford." As he escorted them outside with professional neutrality, the desert heat hit like someone opened an oven door in his face.

Bags loaded, the black sedan merged into a river of taxis and rideshares all funneling toward the same promise. In the distance, the ARIA towers curved like glass blades, built to make the rest of the Strip look obsolete.

Fifteen minutes later, they pulled beneath the modern temple. "Sky Suites arrival," the driver said, ushering them not to the crowded valet but to a quieter portico with a discreet door. The cool air inside felt expensive. A woman in a charcoal dress glided over, introduced herself by first name only, and handed them sleek keys as if she were surrendering state secrets. "We've taken the liberty of arranging in-suite check-in, gentlemen."

They rode a private elevator up—no jingles, no lobby cacophony, only a whispering machine. The doors opened onto a hallway that funneled them into a suite so sprawling it felt improbable they'd have it to themselves.

Chase stood inside and let the scale rearrange his brain. Two-story windows, a Strip panorama that made the city look like a blinking motherboard. The sofa could have seated a baseball team. Four massive televisions lined the walls. The bar was stocked and backlit. A bowl of strawberries rested beside a chilled bottle of something gold-capped and celebratory. He thought of his apartment in DC. This place could have swallowed it twice over.

Blaine whistled. "This," he said, arms flung wide at the view, "is what edges buy."

Weeks ago, Blaine had waved Chase off when he asked about the hotel, saying he'd "take care of it" and that he wouldn't owe more than a couple hundred a night, nothing crazy. Blaine knew how to work the Vegas off-season, how to squeeze comps from his top-tier LionBet status and the incalculable pile of points he'd banked along the way. But Chase hadn't imagined this. Not two stories of glass and marble. Not a suite that made his DC apartment feel like student housing. This wasn't a room—it was a flex.

A man in a tailored vest appeared with practiced quiet. "Welcome, Mr. Wexford, Mr. Dupree. I'm Rafi. I'll be your butler during your stay." He said "butler" without irony. "May I unpack for you? Turndown service is at your discretion. If you need anything, the tablet controls will connect to me directly."

Mid-strut, Blaine flopped onto the sectional. "Unpack the bourbon," he said then laughed at his own line. He was already glassy-eyed, the rush of arrival turning his bloodstream into the noisy lobby they had bypassed.

Chase caught Rafi's eye. "He had a long flight," he said, embarrassed to be the adult in the room.

Rafi's gaze wandered, not unkindly, to Blaine's swaying smile and back. "We're here to help, sir," he said to Chase, voice pitched so it felt private. "We've seen this story before."

Not judgment, exactly. More the worn insight of someone who knew that different stories often collapse into the same ending.

Blaine didn't notice. He kicked off his shoes and strolled to the glass, forehead nearly touching it, as if he could drink the view like another bourbon. "We made it," he said. "Vegas, baby." He turned, shrugging off his button-down so it hung halfway, like he couldn't decide if he was dressing or undressing. "Where first? Pool? Bar? Casino? Why not all of them?"

"Pool," Chase replied. "Cold water might do you good."

"Cold water?" Blaine snorted. "That's for athletes and A.A. meetings." But he was already headed for the water.

The Sky Pool wasn't the chaos of the main deck. It was exclusive luxury—limestone underfoot, immaculate palms, shade that felt curated. A handful of women in bikinis lounged across the sun chairs, sunglasses tipped, inviting the very gaze they knew every man was already sneaking their way. Their laughter drifted over the water, intentional yet careless.

Blaine stopped mid-stride, took it in like he'd stumbled onto a buffet. "If this is the appetizer, ARIA better have a hell of an entrée waiting." Chase couldn't tell if he meant the pool itself or the women draped around it. Either way, the ambiguity made it worse.

Blaine tiptoed in with performative caution, then plunged with a full-body splash. Chase sat on the edge, calves in the pool, forearms on his knees, watching Blaine float on his back as if nothing in the world could touch him.

A dirty blonde in a red bikini adjusted her straps, eyes locking with Chase's for a beat longer than polite—a dare more than a look. It jolted through him, an invitation he knew better than to accept but wouldn't easily forget. For months, numbers had been his drug; now, in the slow days of sports, with no lines to chase, temptation was finding other ways in.

Another of the women brushed by him into the pool, glancing at Blaine floating in the water. "Your buddy's drunk."

"He's just a nervous flier," Chase said. The excuse came out too smoothly, a reflex. Only then did he see it—he wasn't defending Blaine, he was defending the life they both shared. If Blaine was in freefall, then maybe he wasn't far behind.

"Happy hour," Blaine called, spraying droplets as he clambered out, shaking himself off like a Labrador. "Let's get dolled up."

Chase watched him vanish toward the suite, loud and dripping, and wondered if he'd just seen the last trace of the Blaine that Julia had wanted to save.

* * *

ALIBI sat like a jewel box tucked off the ARIA casino floor—a dark room lit by hundreds of points that looked like hovering stars. A hostess slid open a velvet rope, and they stepped into a sponsored dream: high tables, low couches, a DJ who seemed to be scoring a movie no one could see. At the entrance, a tidy table of badges: first names in clean sans serif, LineSniper handles beneath in italics as if they were stage names.

Chase pinned his to his lapel. "Chase," it read. Under it, the alter ego he had only ever typed. "BetmanBegins."

The name flushed him with self-consciousness then—absurdly— with pride.

Beneath Blaine's badge, a handle that made two guys in polos elbow and nod. "DCLimitSmasher."

Recognition rippled through the room—not the warmth of friendship, but the inventory-taking of a market. He watched the moves—the quick glance down to the handle, the fraction of a second spent remembering who you were online, the recalibration of tone.

At the bar, the back wall glowed amber. Chase, subliminally conditioned after a day with Blaine, ordered a bourbon on the rocks— one, not four. Enough to blend in, not enough to follow his friend off the cliff. The bartender nodded and set it down on a napkin stamped with the bar's insignia.

"BetmanBegins?" a voice to his right said, interested and faintly amused. "Not bad. Too many in here sound like failed startups. Yours sounds like a franchise."

Chase turned and knew instantly who it was. Aaron Ramsey in the flesh—slim-cut navy suit that was more fashion week than boardroom, no tie, sneakers chosen to be noticed. Handsome in a way that suggested focus more than genes.

"You don't need a badge," Chase said, managing a smile. "Half the room would trade their bankroll to shake your hand."

Aaron's grin carried both charm and calculation, as if he'd heard a line like that before and still appreciated the delivery.

His eyes flicked to the badge. "Always liked that handle. Origin story in a name. Implies you're still in Act One."

"I'm laying the groundwork to rake it in with the sequels," Chase said.

"Money makes the world go round," Aaron said, lifting his highball. "Why not get your share?" He clinked Chase's glass lightly. "How are we treating you so far?"

"Overwhelming," Chase admitted. "I've never felt so important while doing absolutely nothing."

Aaron shook his head. "You're not doing nothing, Chase. You're here. That's the whole point. You made it inside the room. Most people will never even get close." He lifted his glass once more, a showman's grin breaking through. "And trust me, the next two days won't feel like standing still. We've packed it wall to wall. And we're saving something unforgettable for the end. Don't miss."

Chase raised his glass back. "I'll be there. If this year's taught me anything, it's that when LineSniper points, I follow."

"You came with Wexford, right? DCLimitSmasher." Aaron asked, like a file clicking open in his head. "Where is he? I want to say hi."

Wow. The man came in knowing his people. Impressive, almost unnerving. "Somewhere between the bar and a bad idea," Chase replied.

Aaron chuckled. "That narrows it down."

"I'll let you enjoy," he said, setting down his glass. "Let me know if you find a better handle than yours out there." A light comment that left Chase beaming. Then he was gone, sliding into another circle, the space he left collapsing neatly in his wake.

Across the room, Chase recognized a figure in a cream blazer—Marco, the ArbOracle. He could have sworn he recognized the guy he was talking to. It hit him. Mason Rushmore.

Chase's phone buzzed.

JULIA: Did you talk to him yet?

He typed, erased, typed again.

CHASE: Not yet. He started drinking on the plane. Didn't feel like the right time.

He hit send and felt like he was lying, even though it was true.

Blaine reappeared by his side, cheeks flushed, eyes bright in a way that set off a small alarm in the back of Chase's head.

"You ready to see me work a table?" Blaine said, rocking on his heels.

"Depends. Which direction?"

"Does it even matter if they keep bringing the drinks?" Blaine cackled.

* * *

The craps table didn't look dangerous. That's the trick. Green felt, polished rail, dice that topple like two happy kids in a bouncy house. It gathered a crowd, a magnet for anyone who craved triumph one roll, catastrophe the next.

Blaine bullied into a spot at the rail beside a man with a gold watch and slicked-back hair, drawing a visible eye roll from a serious player who clearly hated sharing space with someone so intoxicated.

"Five thousand," Blaine said aloud with the calm of someone ordering a steak, laying the stack of hundreds on the felt. The dealer spread and counted them then pushed out stacks of chips that slapped with a seductive click.

Chase had never been a gambler in the traditional sense. Arbitrage was math that happened to live in the gambling world. Watching Blaine's hands deftly drop chips throughout the table felt foreign but captivating, finally feeling his own inhibitions loosen after a few welcome-reception drinks. For a beat, Chase envied his friend's ability to draw a crowd and handle the attention with such confidence.

Blaine was the shooter, the man designated to throw the dice, the fate of the entire table in his hands. Bystanders collectively leaned forward. "Blow on 'em for luck," someone shouted. Blaine obliged, relishing the moment, the star of the casino floor.

He threw. The dice skittered, kissed the back wall, swayed on their edges, landed with a dull thud. Six. The table cheered, high-fives to newfound teammates.

Chips clattered around the oval. Chase watched Blaine take his entire stack and move it to the center of the table. Gasps on either side, frantic looks exchanged. The woman to his right shook his arm, leaning close to utter something of grave concern, inaudible to Chase. Blaine brushed her off. The man next to Chase said, "That guy is crazy."

"What just happened?" Chase asked.

"Put his entire stack, looks like five thousand dollars, on a hard eight."

"Meaning?" Chase prompted.

"That dude needs both dice to land on four before he rolls a seven or hits an eight by any other combo," the man replied with a macabre fascination at what was playing out before him.

"And if he doesn't get two fours, he loses it all?" Chase felt a ripple tear through his stomach.

"Yep. But if it hits, he pockets forty-five grand."

Chase didn't need further consultation to know the odds of that happening were low. He looked back at Blaine, a bourbon-ginger in one hand, two dice in the other, sloppy grin plastered above. He was the ringleader now, his crowd primed for the next act.

Letting the drama build, he held the dice high, milking the moment. His hands dropped, dice flew, repeated their dance down the table. Chase felt the invisible hand of the room tug at him, an ancient human impulse to belong to the story unfolding in front of you. The first landed. Four. The second continued, seemingly weightless, before abruptly coming to a rest. Three. Total of seven.

The table groaned, losers all around. Money had disappeared, but the sounds were strangely polite. All eyes turned to Blaine.

"Easy come, easy go. It's only money. You can't take it with you." He shoved back from the table, scooped up the two bourbons the waitress had set down, and stumbled toward the Sky Suite's private elevator.

Chase stared after him, praying those bourbons were the most expensive drinks Blaine would ever buy, knowing deep down they wouldn't be.

* * *

Even the blackout shades couldn't hold back the Vegas sun. By early morning, its rays threaded through the tiniest seams, lulling Chase awake with slow persistence. He rubbed the jet lag and a mild hangover from his eyes, shuffled into the living room, and found Blaine sprawled fully clothed across the sectional, shoes still on, head tilted back in a snore. Chase shook him gently until he stirred.

"Hair of the dog," Blaine croaked, already pointing toward the minibar. Chase cracked a beer and handed it over, the can hissing like an alarm clock, convincing himself he was doing his friend a much-needed favor rather than enabling the start of a second straight day of debauchery.

They showered, dressed, and ate the generous spread Rafi had left on the counter, his presence felt only in absence, like a ghost moving through their space.

Downstairs, the main conference ballroom loomed. An LED screen covered the wall, large speakers hanging high. The opening-session countdown clock rolled down from ten seconds, and the room cheered as if it were a person who'd done something to earn it.

Aaron appeared, seemingly from thin air, sparks raining down from behind him. "Fellow arbers, welcome to LineSniper LIVE!" His voice bellowed, bouncing off the walls, reverberating.

The lights dropped, and for a split-second, the room was shrouded in total darkness. Then a video illuminated the screens, opening with Aaron's voice over a montage of streaming edge feeds and fast-cut highlights. "It started as a crack in the market. A flaw they thought no one would notice. A way to turn their own system against them." The beat thumped harder, images stacking—phone balances climbing, red-to-green flips, lines shifting in bursts. "They told you it wasn't possible. That *they* always win. That's the lie."

A cut to ArbOracle, hood up, his voice steady and magnetic. "We're not here to play their game. We're here to change lives."

The music swelled. The cuts quickened—arbers roaring at cashouts, clocks hitting zero, neon streaks of the Strip spliced with fireworks, champagne corks firing into the dark.

Back to Aaron, eyes locked on camera. "This room is the rebellion. Modern-day Robin Hoods taking back what's ours."

Then the faces came, rapid-fire: men and women, LineSniper users, one after another, staring into the camera, shouting in succession. They merged into a single chant that shook the ballroom walls.

"We own the edge."

The artistry was undeniable. It felt like a rallying cry. Despite his skepticism that LineSniper faithful were a "team," Chase felt something stir, an urge to do battle with those around him, even if the opponent was undefined.

From the back, a voice pierced the hush that followed the video's end. "Fuck the books!" Others picked it up, first in scattered echoes, then in rhythm, until the whole ballroom shook with the chant. "Fuck the books. Fuck the books."

Chase was taken aback by the vitriol, but the current was irresistible. Before he knew it, his own voice had joined the chorus. The chant layered and rose into a roar, the ballroom walls trembling with it. The opponent had been defined.

A spotlight found Aaron again, his smile edged with guarded approval as he reclaimed the room. LineSniper LIVE was underway. He said all the right things, commending the team for putting together one hell of a show in a city where everything was a show and expectations were high.

By 4 p.m., Chase had attended sessions as varied as "Maximizing Arbs in a Limits World" and "Grow the Movement: Referrals = Cash." There was even "Avoid the Taxman," its title promising outlaw secrets. But the session delivered by a former IRS lawyer contained nothing but compliance tips. Chase knew everyone in the room was pretending not to have heard what he'd said—inconvenient facts for those who wanted to skirt every part of the system.

Leaving the last session, he spotted a kid in a shirt that read, "LINE

SNIPING IS A HUMAN RIGHT." Chase laughed, but he knew it wasn't a joke.

That night, Chase ended up in a booth at one of ARIA's restaurants, the kind of spot that smelled of soft leather and fresh-baked bread baskets. He'd followed a handful of guys he'd met during the day—guys with handles like ParlayPrince, HedgeYouLose, and SureShotSam, but who were really Kevin, Nick, and Sam.

Since he'd started arbing nearly a year earlier, Chase had always seen it as an act of isolation, the discipline of numbers, the focus of a lone operator. But here, at this table, there was something unexpected. The conversation pinged from war stories of one-sided losses to friendly arguments over college football. Laughter rose over cocktails like it belonged in a college dining hall. It wasn't especially profound, but it was shared.

He caught himself smiling more than he expected. He felt fully accepted, surrounded by those who understood the rush of a big edge, the thrill of a four-figure profit staring back at you at the end of a football Saturday. They spoke the same language, finished half-formed thoughts, traded stories no outsider would ever understand. It was kinship, raw and a little ridiculous, but kinship all the same.

After dinner, his new friends retired to their rooms for the night, all amped for tomorrow's grand finale. Chase realized he still hadn't heard from Blaine, who'd slipped out before the tax session to "call Julia" and never returned. A sober moment with him remained elusive. Vegas kept moving the target.

Chase suspected he knew where he'd have the best chance of finding his friend. He strolled onto the casino floor, sweeping the rows of table games and slots. Surprisingly, Blaine, who loved a flourish, was tucked away in a corner, not at a table, not with a crowd. He was perched on a stool at a dollar slot, drunk enough to mistake the machine's sparkling flashes for sunlight.

Chase watched his hands—tap, pull, tap, pull—the movements of a man going through the motions. It was a sight both mesmerizing and haunting.

"Hey," Chase said, leaning on the back of the stool. "You want to head up? Big day tomorrow."

Blaine didn't take his eyes off the screen. "Soon," he said with the tone of someone who had no such intention.

26

FINAL HOUSEKEEPING

BY MORNING, the entire conference had distilled to one final session, reduced in the program to two plain words: "Final Housekeeping." Only the bold font hinted it might matter at all. On paper, it sounded like nothing more than closing announcements and thank-yous. But Aaron Ramsey had been dropping the same line for two days, his voice low and deliberate each time. "Don't miss it."

And no one was bailing.

The breakfast tables at Salt & Ivy brimmed with food and speculation. The restaurant sat off ARIA's casino floor, a glass-walled space meant to feel airy but still humming with the resort's perpetual energy. Every chair was filled with guests donning LineSniper badges, lanyards twisted and knotted after two days of hard wear. The smell of butter and espresso clung to the air, competing with the tang of vodka and tomato juice. Plates of brioche French toast, omelets spilling cheese, and towers of Bloody Marys loaded with bacon skewers and pickled vegetables crowded the tables, barely touched, conversation overrunning appetite.

Kevin, Nick, and Sam sat at a table with Chase and Blaine, leaning over mugs of black coffee and sweating orange juice glasses, trading guesses with the kind of urgency usually reserved for live odds.

"A rebrand," Nick said. "LineSniper rolling out a whole new look. Bet on it."

"Celebrity cameo," Sam countered. "Shaq, Drake, someone big."

Kevin stabbed his fork in the air at Chase. "Or maybe they comp everyone a stack of free play. I could see Aaron wanting to end on a high note."

Speculation wasn't confined to their table—snatches of theories floated from every direction. One man swore it was an IPO announcement. Someone near the window cracked a joke about free Teslas for everyone in attendance. Chase clocked how strange it all looked—grown adults whispering over pancakes like kids trying to guess what was under the Christmas tree.

Blaine stirred his Bloody Mary like it was a prescription. He hadn't said much all morning, but when he did, it was sharp. "You don't stage security like this for logos or giveaways."

Chase frowned. "Security?"

Blaine shrugged. "Guy in the casino last night told me he saw metal detectors going up. Whole new ballroom we haven't been in yet."

Chase was more impressed Blaine had managed to process the words of another human last night than by the intel itself.

The new scoop landed. Even Sam froze mid-bite. "Why the hell would they need that?"

The table fell quiet, each man chewing on the same thought. Whatever "Final Housekeeping" was, it wasn't housekeeping.

Their phones all buzzed in unison. A push notification from the conference app lit up their screens. "Seating opens in fifteen minutes. Don't be late."

They didn't linger. Bills hit their table, then the ones around them. Chairs scraped. The rumor mill followed them out into the corridor, chatter folding into the stream of badges moving toward the unknown.

The funnel began at the edge of the convention floor: stanchions, velvet rope, and a pair of metal detector arches. Blaine's source had been legit. Guards in black polos moved briskly, wands buzzing, eyes scanning. Attendees traded looks—nervousness laced with intrigue—but no one resisted. Phones and wallets clinked into trays and badges beeped in succession, the procession oddly reminiscent of boarding a plane. Each flashed the same message in clean font. "VERIFIED—FINAL."

Inside, the new venue revealed itself: a steep amphitheater, no banquet rounds, no clustered chairs. All eyes forward. The stage was stripped to essentials—five minimalist armchairs and a low table next to each, crystal glasses and tumblers etched with the ARIA logo, all perched just so, branding deliberately facing the crowd. Above it all, the LineSniper infinity glyph looped slowly across the LED wall, benign as wallpaper. The venue had been transformed beyond recognition from the bland ballrooms they'd sat in all week.

Chase and Blaine found seats halfway down, dead center. The room hummed—not rowdy but not calm either. The air carried a waiting-room buzz, everyone pretending calm while bracing for what came next.

Once the final row had been filled, all seats fully accounted for, latecomers left standing in the back, the house lights dimmed.

Aaron emerged from the shadows so smoothly it looked as if he were stepping out of the LED wall itself. He wore a matte-black bomber jacket cut close at the shoulders, slim charcoal trousers cropped at the ankle, and a fitted crimson T-shirt that caught the light like a signal flare. Crisp white tennis shoes grounded the look, deliberate in their defiance of the stage's formality. He looked less like a man about to give a keynote and more like someone unveiling a product that could bend the future, his presence runway-sharp and meticulously controlled.

"Good morning." His voice carried, steady, unhurried. "Yesterday was about energy. Today is about clarity."

The infinity glyph beat like a heart behind him.

"I started where most of you have been, grinding through a job that was burning me out. Sports betting was my escape. Then one night I saw it. Divergence across two books on the same game. I bet both sides. Guaranteed profit. Zero risk. And I couldn't stop thinking: *How many other variances existed?* That was the moment it clicked: arbitrage was the future."

A rare personal revelation from someone who usually curated his image with PR-firm precision.

"LineSniper was born. We've all come together around one simple idea: inefficiency can be measured. And when it can be measured, it can be used. The platform was built to exploit inefficiency. But without the books, there is no inefficiency to exploit."

A ripple moved through the room.

"That's the paradox. The house is the opponent we're built to outsmart, but it's also the reason we're in this room at all. Every profit. Every cash-out. Every story of a life changed by an edge. None of it happens without the house. We don't exist in spite of them. We exist because of them."

He slowed, leaning into the phrasing like it was scripture. "They are both our opponent and our oxygen. No books, no edges. No edges, no us."

Chase shifted in his seat. Oxygen? That wasn't how it had felt when LionBet froze him out last fall, limiting him to mere dollars a bet. To him, the books weren't air. They were a wall. He wondered how many in the room felt the same internal conflict but still nodded along, unwilling to break the spell Aaron was weaving.

Aaron drew a breath then shifted tone, softer, more diplomatic. "So where does that leave us? We can rage, we can chant, we can pound the table, and yesterday you showed the world how loud we can be. But volume doesn't change limits. Shouts don't create liquidity. Anger won't write the next chapter of this movement."

The crowd quieted, pulled forward in their seats.

"So today, instead of shouting about the house, we're going to talk with it. Not to capitulate but to map the future with the only people who can truly move it. If you care about promos, protections, products— if you care about the survival of the edge—then you care about this conversation."

The LED wall brightened. The infinity glyph sharpened. Beneath it, for the first time, a single word appeared: "CONVERGENCE."

Aaron gestured toward the screen. "Because this isn't about ending the fight. It's about recognizing what keeps the fight alive. And if we want this ecosystem to grow, if we want the edge to outlast us, then we need the house at the table."

Music swelled—cinematic strings, a steady kick. The house lights dimmed further, and the stage lights shifted into a cool indigo wash, aisles bathed in matching color as if the impending procession were a modern-day coronation.

"Please welcome the people who can answer what we've only guessed."

Murmurs bled into the music, a jagged counterpoint to the polished score. It felt sacrilegious: the man they'd spent two days deifying had invited the enemy to the altar. Nobody knew whether to clap, curse, or bolt. The walk-on track pressed forward, deafening and unrelenting.

Chase leaned toward Blaine, voice low. "Unexpected to say the least. This is either genius or the dumbest play I've ever seen."

Blaine didn't answer, eyes fixed on the stage.

As the crowd processed, the first logo lit the screen. Atlantis. Intentional, of course—the counter-book, the loophole turned legend.

Mason Rushmore emerged, tieless, grinning, a folk hero made flesh. The crowd erupted—applause, whistles, shouts. Social sportsbooks had been a lifeline, and Mason their swaggering patron saint. He basked in it, waving as he claimed the first chair.

Next: LionBet.

The ovation that had rattled the tiers for Mason collapsed into something far stranger. The walk-on music still played, steady and cinematic, but the crowd gave nothing back—no applause, no cheers, only the occasional boo slicing through the beat. A silver-haired executive emerged, suit immaculate, face set in corporate neutrality. He advanced like a man arriving for a quarterly earnings call, not a room full of arbers. By the time he took his seat, back rigid, jaw clenched, the message was clear. LionBet was not welcome here.

Then Dynasty.

The amphitheater turned sour. Boos rained harder, sharper. Someone shouted, "Lift your limits!" The line carried, echoed by others. The executive kept his eyes forward, marching to his chair under a chorus of resentment.

The boos still echoed as security made a subtle shift, moving a half-step closer to the crowd, additional black polos appearing at the base of the stairs. They didn't raise hands or bark orders, but the adjustment was clear: the temperature had risen, and they were bracing for worse.

Three seats filled. Two remained, one held for Aaron when the time came to join them.

The infinity glyph pulsed again. Beneath it, the word "CONVERGENCE" glowed brighter.

And then Faceoff.

The crowd fractured. Applause clashed with boos, colliding until neither won. Faceoff had long been the friendliest of the traditional books, the ally that wasn't an ally, but the house that still left a door unlocked. Their presence was both comfort and betrayal.

From the wing, Ainsley Caldwell walked on.

She moved with exactness, black pantsuit pressed sharp, hair pinned back. She shook Aaron's hand, nodded coolly down the row, and claimed her chair without ceremony.

The sensation was dissonance made physical. Aaron had led them into communion with the enemy, and the ground shifted beneath him. Part of Chase recoiled. Another part leaned forward, desperate to hear.

"He landed Faceoff?" Chase said aloud, looking to Blaine to see if he was as riveted.

Beside him, Blaine had frozen, blanched.

For two days he had drifted at the outskirts, dulled by drink, half-present. Now the fog burned away. His eyes locked on the woman onstage, rimmed in indigo light, a silhouette too familiar to mistake.

"Blaine? You good, man?" Chase pressed, a chill running through him as he saw recognition and disbelief spread across Blaine's face.

Blaine's lips parted. One word, fragile as glass.

"Mom."

27

THE STAGE

CHASE'S BRAIN STALLED, like someone had cut the power. "Mom." The word rattled in his skull, impossible, absurd, and yet Blaine had said it like a confession he hadn't meant to speak aloud.

He wanted to push, needed to understand, but the house lights dropped before he could speak. Darkness swept the amphitheater.

Blaine hadn't moved. He sat motionless, eyes locked forward, shoulders tense, sealed inside his own world, untouched by Chase scrutinizing him from a foot away.

Whatever Blaine had revealed—whatever that meant—wasn't getting unpacked now. The room belonged to Aaron, and there was no room for anything else.

While the panel settled into their seats, Aaron getting into position, Chase peered around the room, noticing for the first time the row of red lights winking from the back wall. Cameras, lenses glinting like extra eyes. Surrounding the eerie glow, logos staked above their zones, flags claiming enemy territory. Chase squinted, catching what he'd missed on the way in: The Athletic, Bloomberg, CNBC, even ESPN. Credentialed media, not just hobbyist bloggers.

Chase realized Aaron hadn't assembled these CEOs simply for the room. This was for the entire sports world.

Aaron settled into his chair, the last seat filled. His bomber jacket drank the indigo glow, crimson shirt bold as a matador's cape against the otherwise monochrome stage. He wasn't pacing like a founder hungry for applause; he was composed, settled into his role as moderator, the rational statesman.

"We're here for a conversation. Not fireworks," he said. "Yesterday proved there are disagreements with how our community interacts with the platforms overseen by those on this stage. But today, I ask for your respect."

The crowd sat up, still buzzing from the shock of seeing the logos onscreen, the respective leaders emerge.

Aaron turned first to Mason. It was, once again, a move rooted in controlling the energy of the room, feeding the crowd dessert before serving them vegetables.

"Mason, I would imagine you feel a bit like an interloper on this stage. Most everyone in the audience has used your platform. Tell us how you feel you differ from a traditional sportsbook."

Mason nodded, accepting the premise. "I was once one of you. Limits drove me insane. I'd claw my way up, only to get restricted as soon as I started to turn a meaningful profit. I hated it. It was fundamentally unfair. Rigged. I set out to build something else. A space where limits didn't strangle the player. Where you could grind and grow. Where you could win without fear of being clipped for being too sharp. Because in my house, the only limit is how far you're willing to go."

The applause wasn't polite. It exploded. Whistles pierced, hands slapped the rails. Several stood, an ovation after the very first question. Mason basked, nodding toward the audience zealously.

Aaron shifted next to LionBet. "Perspective from the traditional side. Do you see limiting as unfair?"

The silver-haired executive straightened, posture stiff. "Risk management isn't punishment. It's necessity. Casinos have managed volatility for decades. Sportsbooks are no different. Limits aren't personal. The goal is sustainability, keeping the lights on so the game continues, and—"

Boos rolled down from the back tiers. Not unanimous but sharp enough to fracture the room's temporary civility. He shifted in his seat, cleared his throat and droned on in jargon about liquidity pools and regulatory compliance.

Aaron let the moment pass without indulgence, pivoting to Dyntasy.

The Dynasty exec crossed one leg over the other, casual in a way that dripped arrogance. "I'll say what you don't want to hear. Limits exist because abuse exists. Arbitrage strains the system. Promos aren't free. Someone has to pay for it. At the end of the day, we're a business. We answer to investors, and I'd bet some of them are sitting in this room right now."

It was inflammatory, provoking by design.

"Lift your limits!" someone shouted. Others took it up, louder, angrier.

Chase's stomach tightened. The atmosphere felt combustible, a match looking for its strike.

Aaron's hand cut the air, steadying the stage. "Let's reframe. This isn't about recrimination. It's about recognition of our reality. Ainsley, how does Faceoff see the issue?" He turned to the poised exec.

Ainsley's presence commanded respect even before she spoke. "We know this community exists. Sincerely, congratulations, Aaron, on what you've accomplished here. The four of us wouldn't be on this stage if you hadn't built something that mattered, something that has gotten the attention of the market."

Aaron fought to keep his expression neutral, but the flattery landed.

She continued, "We know you're all sharp, disciplined, sophisticated. You're not casuals chasing parlays. And we don't see that as a threat—we see it as proof of what's possible. The challenge isn't silencing sharp play. It's scaling with it so the next generation sees a fair marketplace, not a game stacked against them."

She paused, eyes sweeping the tiers. "But passion has to coexist with scale. Faceoff has tried to strike that balance, modest limits while we work toward a model where coexistence becomes practice, not theory. Let me be clear. If sports betting is going to grow, if it's going to earn trust, we can't merely tolerate sharp play. We have to integrate it."

For the first time, the room didn't know how to respond. Was it appeasement? Performance? Or sincerity? Ainsley sounded like someone looking to invite people inside, not put locks on the door. The nuance might not have drawn an eruption like Mason, but it certainly didn't crater like LionBet's platitudes or Dynasty's provocation either.

Chase wanted to weigh what Ainsley had said, to form his own take, but he couldn't stop watching Blaine, eyes locked on her like he'd feared this moment his entire life. Years of throwaway lines came rushing back, but now they read like clues, all pointing to the same staggering truth. *Could it really have been this simple?*

He dragged his gaze back to the stage, even as the only answers he wanted sat a foot away.

Aaron shifted to the front of his seat, savoring how each member on the stage had played their role—unknowing actors, he the playwright. "We've heard the spectrum of voices. The community-built alternative. The legacy giants. The partner exploring adaptation. In light of Ainsley's words, the question that matters most is this…"

The room stilled.

"What does the path to coexistence look like from here? Will LineSniper—"

A shockwave slammed against Chase's ears, alien in its violence, too sudden to process. He flinched, eyes catching a white-hot trail slicing across his vision, too fast to follow, the air itself rippling in its wake.

A water glass on the table burst apart, crystal shrapnel scattering in all directions. Shards fanned to the ground, catching light like a flock of jagged prisms. Tiles on the LED wall snapped dark in ragged clusters, as if an invisible hand had cut their power. The sounds multiplied, a deafening, disorienting barrage. Each blast reverberated through bone, pressing him down like sound had turned solid. Fear raced to his throat, choking off breath before he could scream.

Security swarmed the stage, bodies attempting to shield the panelists, eyes raking the rafters.

Someone screamed, "Shooter!" and the noise had a name.

Chase's body moved before his brain did. Instinct hurled him down, cheek grinding against carpet, fingers clawing for the frame of the seat in front of him. His chest hammered, a single, ancient command directing him: *Run. Hide. Survive.*

There was nowhere to run, and so he hid, his mind tunneling to the single, all-consuming thought of Tara and the girls.

One final crack, and then only blackness.

28

AFTERMATH

HAD IT BEEN FIVE SECONDS or five minutes? He had no way of knowing. The concussive cracks had stopped, but darkness still clung to the room, heavy and unmoving. Then—light. A harsh white beam swept the aisles methodically, hands shielding eyes, faces pale and stunned. Sound followed: the stutter of radios, rubber soles scuffing carpet, and finally an authoritative voice cutting through the static.

"Police! Stay down! Hands where we can see them!" The order ricocheted across the chamber, barked again from the far side.

Then came the second line, steadier. "Stay calm. We've got you."

The house lights snapped back alive without warning, bleaching the amphitheater in sterile white, every row suddenly exposed. Chase squinted, eyes adjusting, the brightness cruel after the blackout. He looked around. People were rising, blinking, trembling. No blood pooled, no bodies slumped. Thank God.

Gloved hands gripped his shoulder, gently guiding him forward. "Let's move." The contact rattled him—evidence of his own helplessness—yet it carried a calm that told him the worst was over.

Chase forced his voice out, rough. "What happened? Was anyone—"

"We don't know yet." No room for follow-up. The officer was already on to the next person.

Blaine appeared at his shoulder, nudged forward by another uniform. His face was slack, eyes still shackled to the stage.

"You okay?" Chase asked, his throat dry.

Blaine blinked, like the question had come from underwater. "Yeah," he answered distractedly.

They moved in step with the others, a procession of dazed figures corralled toward the doors.

Disorientation gave way to fragments of clarity: no visible injuries, glass scattered only across the stage, panelists already gone. It wasn't carnage. It was aftermath. This hadn't been meant to mow them down. Not a massacre. It had been targeted.

*　*　*

They snaked through a back hallway into an adjacent ballroom, its glamour being stripped away in real time, reshaped into crisis command. Crystal chandeliers glittered above, incongruous against the folding tables being dragged across the carpet, laptops snapping open, cables spilling loose. Banquet chairs were shoved against the walls, gilt trim and burgundy fabric worn from a thousand conventions.

Now they held survivors of a shooting—close to two hundred badges dangling from lanyards, eyes vacant, waiting for whatever came next, never expecting they'd be the ones to learn what that was. Police tape bisected the room. Casino staff had vanished, replaced by tactical vests and the bitter smell of industrial coffee from carafes left behind by the banquet this room had once been set to host.

Chase and Blaine were directed to seats along the burgundy perimeter. They'd all heard the same steady refrain. "Stay seated. You'll each give a witness statement before release."

The room was muted, each person folding inward, replaying what had just happened. Chase was no exception. He wondered if the story had already broken through, or if it would dissolve into the country's daily tide of shootings. He pictured Tara, working at her desk, her phone lighting up—first the *Times,* then the *Post*. "Breaking: Shooting at Conference in Vegas." He ached at the thought.

All he wanted was to tell her he was alive, but no one had service.

The thick walls swallowed it, or maybe it had been blocked intentionally. Either way, the effect was the same: isolation. They were sealed in a bubble, no connection to the outside world.

Since their brief exchange in the amphitheater, Blaine hadn't spoken. His head leaned back against the wall, eyes unfocused, lost to a place he couldn't be followed. Chase thought he might have drifted off until he spoke, voice flat and unguarded.

"She hasn't changed," Blaine said.

Chase stared, unsure what to say or if a response was even expected.

"My mother." Blaine's eyes didn't leave the spot on the wall he'd selected. "She looked exactly the same."

Chase kept his voice low. "Your mom is…Ainsley Caldwell?"

"Yes," Blaine continued, still not looking at him. His knee bounced so hard the chair rattled, but his voice stayed flat. "She always chose work. The climb. Over me. And choices have consequences, so I made mine. On my eighteenth birthday, I told her I was done and left for James Madison. We haven't spoken since."

Chase wanted to fill the silence, but Blaine wasn't finished. It was like he'd been waiting to share this secret with someone for years.

"It's part of what drew me to arbing. The rush, the money—I love that. But mostly I wanted to stick it to her world. Every dollar I took from a book, I told myself it was her dollar. Like I was clawing at her bottom line, leaving scratches she'd never see. Stupid, right?"

Chase felt the instinct to nod, to agree it sounded childish, but he stopped himself. "Not at all," he said instead.

Finally Blaine turned his head, eyes glassy but sharp. "And now she's on a stage being introduced by the guy we followed here like he was Moses, and I'm supposed to what, text her? Tell her the weather's nice today? While bullets fly."

Two traumas at once. The mother Blaine had banished reappearing under blinding lights, and then bullets raining down on top of it. A double blow no one could prepare for. For once, Chase didn't feel envy or frustration toward his friend. What rose instead, against his will, was pity.

"I'm sorry," Chase muttered. It was all he could think to say.

"Ladies and gentlemen," a voice boomed from a portable PA at the front, snapping the room to attention. "I'm Captain Morales, Las Vegas Metropolitan Police. Hear this first. There are no reported injuries from the incident in the amphitheater."

Relief mixed with bewilderment, a rustle rippling through the chairs. No injuries. The glass, the LED wall—how had no one been hit? Chase pressed a hand to his chest, half-expecting to feel wet warmth. Nothing. He was fine. Alive. For a moment, he pictured what hadn't happened: crimson pooling into the carpet. The image wasn't real, but it still made his stomach lurch. Relief wasn't clean. It came spiked with guilt.

"The shooter is not in custody," Morales continued. "We are searching the property and nearby structures. The suspect facilitated the blackout to escape. We'll update as we can. For now, you'll remain here. Officers will conduct brief interviews and release sections as it becomes safe."

Hours passed. Officers rotated through the room, calling people one by one for questioning. Chase watched a woman two rows over blot her eyes with cocktail napkins, while a man nearby paced until an officer made him sit again. The air grew stale.

"Sir? You with us?"

His turn had come, a young agent in an FBI windbreaker approached with a tablet, adept at scanning for the small tells of shock. Chase managed a nod.

He looked no older than thirty, hair cropped short, voice professional. "Name?"

"Chase Dupree."

"Where were you sitting?"

"Center, about halfway down."

"Did you see the shooter? Anything unusual in your section?"

"No. Only the glass exploding."

The agent typed, nodding once. His face remained unchanged. "What about after the shots?"

"Everyone dropped to the ground. Security moved in."

"Anything else you can recall?"

Chase hesitated then shook his head. "No."

The agent studied him for a beat, scribbled something with his stylus, and moved to close the file. Ninety seconds, maybe less. Too easy. Too perfunctory. It was confirmation the shooter wasn't among them.

He was dismissed back to his chair. Blaine was taken next, questioned by a woman in a blazer with an FBI badge clipped at her hip. His answers came terse. The exchange stretched longer than Chase's, long enough that the agent flagged down a supervisor.

Chase didn't need to hear to know Blaine had given up the secret. Ainsley was his mother, estranged. Smart move, better to control the story than have it surface later. When he returned, he sat heavier, leaning forward with elbows braced on knees.

The clock crawled. They were brought water bottles, bags of pretzels—suite spreads replaced by rations barely fit for coach class.

By the time an officer finally approached, Chase's legs were stiff, back and head throbbing. He longed for an ibuprofen, cursed himself for not carrying his usual stash. "You're clear to go," the man said, voice neutral, already turning to release others.

By then it was late afternoon. Chairs scraped back as people collected what little they'd carried from the amphitheater and filed out with the slack weariness of parolees.

Chase stood, stretching sore muscles, and glanced at Blaine. His friend's face had reset to neutral, impenetrable. For hours they'd been caged. Now they were free. Only it didn't feel like freedom. It felt like being expelled into a world that hadn't changed but somehow never would look the same again.

* * *

They were funneled out of the ballroom in a controlled stream, officers posted at intervals along the hallway leading to the ARIA's vast lobby. The smell hit first—chlorine from fountains, undercut by the stale ghost of smoke that clung to every Vegas carpet—an aromatic reminder they were reentering civilization.

Then came the sound. A low drone at first, swelling with every step until it became a roar that filled the marble and glass cavern ahead.

The lobby had been transformed. Velvet ropes and yellow tape carved out a perimeter, giving the reception area a strange air of exclusivity. Beyond it the press surged forward—cameras hoisted high, boom mics thrust their direction, questions hurled with the desperation of people clawing for soundbites. They weren't within reach, but they felt too close all the same—red tally lights blinking, lenses pinning survivors like specimens under glass.

Above the bar, every mounted television blared the same feed, some iteration of a headline that made the moment feel all too real. **"BREAKING: SHOTS FIRED AT VEGAS SPORTS BETTING CONFERENCE."** The chyron scrolled beneath aerial footage of the Strip before cutting to the amphitheater stage, Aaron's photo filling the screen. Someone, somewhere, had pushed a press kit in record time. Chase felt the truth slam into him. This wasn't just news. It was the only news.

He reached instinctively for his pocket. For the first time since the blackout, signal bars returned. His phone convulsed—vibrating, chiming, erupting in violent succession. Texts, missed calls, voicemails cascaded across the screen. Tara. His parents. Colleagues. Numbers he barely recognized.

"Hold up," he muttered to Blaine, veering toward a recessed alcove by the concierge desk, away from the swarm of cameras. "I need to call Tara."

He dialed the number, hands shaking, and lifted the phone to his ear.

She answered on the first ring. "Chase? Chase?" The sound of her voice broke him open.

"I'm okay," he blurted, voice cracking. "I'm okay, I swear." The speed of the tears startled him. He pressed his sleeve to his face, turning from the cameras like it was shameful to be seen this raw.

"Oh my God. I saw—I saw it, Chase, the news—"

"I know. I'm sorry—I'm so sorry." The words tumbled out, useless but necessary. "We had no service. They held us in some room and just let us out. I don't know what they're saying on TV, but nobody got hit, Tara, nobody. I'll be back tomorrow. I had to hear your voice. I'm okay. I'm right here."

On the other end, her crying broke through, breath catching between words. "The girls... they asked where you were. I didn't know what to tell them. Just—just come home."

"I will," he whispered. "God, I miss you all so much." They stayed suspended in silence, breathing, neither willing to cut the line. Finally, he forced it. "I have to go. I love you."

He hung up and stared at the phone. The lock screen photo—his girls in an impromptu embrace outside a movie theater, heads tilted back in laughter—cut through him harder than anything else. Moments like this didn't ask what you valued; they told you. And everything else fell away.

Blaine stood where he'd left him, his expression hardened.

"Did you call Julia?" Chase asked carefully.

Blaine shook his head. "Sent a text. We're good. She'll see the news."

"That's it?"

"Yeah. No use making it a bigger thing than it is. Nobody died."

Chase studied him. The darkness was visible now, coiling tighter, pushing Julia out as he had his mother. Chase didn't press. Instead, he found Julia's contact and tapped out his own message:

CHASE: Sorry for the scare. We're fine. He's fine. I'm with him. Don't worry.

When he looked up, Blaine was already moving toward the elevators, talking to anyone in earshot—a trio from the arbitrage masterclass, two guys from the tax session, someone in a LineSniper hoodie. "Sky Suite tonight. Drinks. We're not ending the trip on that note." Others muttered their agreement. Word spread fast.

They reached the roped-off elevator banks, officers verifying room cards before allowing them to pass. The journalists' questions still barraged them from behind the tape. "Did you see the shooter? Was anyone hurt? Do police have a lead?" They stepped into the elevator, the racket mercifully extinguished as the doors slid closed.

Chase leaned against the mirrored wall, body still quaking. He remembered a technique his high school tennis coach had taught him, the physiological sigh. He inhaled deeply, lungs filling fully, then drew in a quick second breath before releasing it all in a slow stream through his mouth. It steadied him then, and it steadied him now.

He felt enough mental clarity to have his first processing thought: Mortality had brushed him close enough to smell its breath, and now the pull came fast and primal. Blaine needed to drink until the world blurred, until he forgot what had happened today. Chase needed something else. As the elevator ascended, the decision hardened. Tonight, he wouldn't resist. Tonight, he'd let himself feel alive.

29

BACCHANAL

STEAM SWALLOWED THE MIRROR within seconds of Chase turning the tap. He stepped under the torrent and let the heat work its way into him—skin first, then muscle, then the places fear had nested and gone rigid.

He leaned his forehead to the tile and let the spray drum. The day had split in two, before and after. The water couldn't stitch them back together, but it could make him clean enough to cross from one to the other.

He toweled off, pulled on dark jeans and a simple white tee, ran a hand through his hair, and again told his reflection the lie everyone told themselves after a scare. "I'm fine."

Outside the door, he heard a clatter of bottles. People were already there. He turned the corner to find Blaine standing behind the kitchen island with the hard focus of a bartender at peak rush, a row of shot glasses lined in recruit-like formation. He was pouring from two bottles at once, wrists turning in mirrored arcs. Tequila. Vodka. The backlit shelves threw honeyed light through crystal, the whole bar gleaming with the promise of a night to remember, or more likely forget.

"Immortals," Blaine called, and the clump nearest him answered like it was a toast to survival and victory at once.

Chase clocked familiar faces first—the handles he'd translated into flesh and voices over the last forty-eight hours. But there were new faces too. Guys in fitted black, women with club hair and glossy lips, a tall man hauling a road case by its handle.

"We brought a friend," someone said, patting the case like a pet. "Meet Slate, best DJ you've never heard of."

Ten minutes later, the suite's reading nook had morphed into a makeshift booth: controller and laptop stacked on the shelves, cables draped like ivy into a pair of portable speakers yanked from the media console. Slate, a skinny kid in a flat-brim hat, hunched over the gear, spun a dial, and a hypnotic beat thudded into the room. The suite, oversized as it was, suddenly felt too small—packed air, no exits, nowhere to go but deeper in.

Blaine pushed a shot into Chase's hand. "To not dying," he said.

"To not dying," Chase echoed, and they downed it. Tequila blazed a path, fire straight to his gut. A second glass appeared, hitting faster than the last. By the time someone pressed a craft beer into his hand, his head was already a quarter-step lighter than his body.

The early phase was all relief energy, a compulsion to prove you still existed by clinking glass to glass. The lights were low, the Strip a sheet of soldered stars beyond the windows.

Chase felt the tingle begin to center from his extremities, and he welcomed it. He let a stranger ramble about mispriced odds in some obscure tennis market, the words dissolving before they reached meaning. He watched Blaine pour with both hands again, the line at the island growing, his friend transforming an empty day into a full-blown function simply by deciding it would be one.

A cluster of women had drifted in—three, then five, then a dozen. At first, they could have passed as friends of friends. One perched on the arm of a sofa, balancing a flute of champagne. Another leaned into the booth to whisper to Slate, who kissed her cheek. The imbalance was immediate. The room's temperature ticked up without the thermostat moving.

Shots continued in waves. Someone started handing out lime wedges and salt, then gave up and passed the salt shaker. The kitchen island went slick, the floor sticky, a map of tiny spills charting the night's direction.

"This is living," someone shouted near Chase's ear, and for a moment he believed it—the bass hitting his sternum, the electric hum of being very much here.

Across the room, his gaze snagged on a figure that seemed to cut through the haze, the crowd parting around her. Blonde hair fell loose, deep blue eyes locking to his. Her dress revealed more than it concealed. She looked his age, late thirties, yet had the taut body of a cheer captain twenty years younger.

Chase's eyes snapped away, heat rising to his face. Almost against his will, they slipped back. She was still watching. This time, he held her gaze. A sly smile curved the corner of her mouth. His lips twitched in kind—the faintest betrayal, and he knew it.

Another woman touched her shoulder, and the thread between them snapped.

What came next arrived in a gesture so casual it almost didn't register: a small black case unzipped on the island, plastic baggies sliding out like folded secrets. The person who produced them did so with the smoothness of someone who'd done this before and would do it again. A metal straw. A credit card. Lines appeared as if conjured. Heads dipped. The hiss of a tidy inhale. The ritual of a wipe. Heads snapped back, nostrils flaring, pupils blown wide, as if their bodies had been plugged into a socket.

Cocaine changed the night's math. Conversations sped. Laughter outran jokes. A guy he'd never met hugged Chase like a brother. Another tipped his head back and yelled to no one, "Let's go!"

Chase had been around drugs. College house parties. A slow-motion bachelor party weekend where someone's cousin had cut lines on a Monopoly board.

This scene was disturbingly different. No wink, no pretense, no pretending it was naughty fun. It was open, brisk, unembarrassed. Exchange and consumption, as frictionless as tapping a card to pay. He watched Blaine lean down, thumb closing a nostril, a sharp practiced inhale. No hesitation. No glance around for judgment. When he came up, he licked his gums and grinned, like Chase had just caught him in his natural habitat.

"Sure you don't want in?" Blaine asked, all momentum, barely waiting for the answer.

"Yeah, I'm sure, man," Chase said, unconvincingly. He'd never once been tempted before—never. But with a few drinks in him, in this room, on this night, something darker stirred. He shook it off, but even through the blur he could see the suite devolving, everyone daring each other to go further.

He turned his attention away from the kitchen. The women weren't friends of friends. Someone had clearly texted a promoter—the kind of number that could turn a private suite into product on demand. They had kept arriving, dresses getting smaller with each knock.

Moral lines don't vanish all at once. They erode. First, a shirt came off, and then a skirt. More articles followed, each cheered with a whoop from men who clung to the thrill of being boys. If it was spectacle at first, it quickly evaporated into commerce. A woman—early twenties at best—straddled a man on the sectional, and the room adjusted around them the way pedestrians adjust around street construction: inconvenient, unsightly, but quickly folded into the landscape. Two more, stripped to near nothing, playfully wrestled on the carpet, surrounded by a ring of men throwing twenties like coins into a wishing well. It was a bacchanal that would have made Dionysus avert his eyes.

Chase was taken aback by how quickly things had spiraled. He angled toward the patio, hoping the night air might grant him a sliver of serenity. Through the door, he spotted a familiar jacket—one of the guys from breakfast—standing with his back to the room.

Relieved, Chase slid it open before the scene suddenly snapped into obscene focus, a woman on her knees, positioned between the man and the railing. Chase spun, yanked the door shut, and drifted back into the debauchery. Somehow, what waited inside felt less offensive than what he'd glimpsed outside. He moved through it, participant and witness, an anthropologist with a drink.

He wound his way back to the kitchen and drank two more shots, in quick succession. Not to forget but to cope. It didn't erase the day. It dulled and sharpened at once: the twin illusions alcohol is good at selling. He tipped from buzzed to drunk, but adrenaline still had its hooks in him, holding him upright, keeping his mind sharper than his body deserved.

An elbow jammed into Chase's back, someone maneuvering a bottle of champagne to the island. The person connected to it jumped on top, and with reckless flair, sabered the bottle with a chef's knife he had no business using. The cork clipped a pendant overhead before bouncing off a beam. Foam poured across the island, men bowed to it like a sacrament.

The room had crossed from living to something else. Living had limits. This was consumption for the sake of consumption, grief alchemized, then weaponized against the self.

Arms wrapped around his waist from behind, warm and certain, enclosing him before he could react. A soft cheek brushed against his, lips glancing skin. He turned slightly, and there she was—the blonde, up close now, eyes more vivid than they'd been across the room.

"You're cute," she murmured, breath hot in his ear. A hand slid lower, over his stomach, fingers making a promise they'd keep if he let them, pausing inside his waistband, centimeters from a touch he couldn't come back from. The graze forced his body to betray him, a shudder coursing through him as he thought about what could come next, blood quickening in ways he wished it wouldn't. "Come with me."

Alcohol stretched the moment, warped it. A sober mind would have been a simple no. Drunk, it came with a story. *Just this once. No one had to know. You almost died today.*

Logic took hold. He took her wrist, gentle. "I can't," he said.

She spun around to the front, hand unmoved, eye-to-eye, seduction incarnate. "Of course you can," she said, like she'd already factored in his protest and dismissed it. The hand at his waistband didn't move away. She wasn't selling. She was offering.

"I'm married," he said, and the word tasted like a boundary he was drawing for himself more than a piece of information for her. He placed his hands on her wrists and lifted them away gently, as if removing a necklace. "I can't."

She kissed his cheek again, lighter. "Suit yourself, handsome." Then she was gone, through the music, into the crowd.

Chase exhaled, palms braced on the stone of the island, waiting for the floor to stop tilting beneath him. DJ Slate sent the room into a strobe. In the flashes, everything looked like a crime scene and a painting at once. Every flash was glass exploding all over again. He wanted out, out of a party that had been nothing more than uninhibited vice all along.

He opened the fridge and grabbed a water, one of the few beverages that appeared untouched by the night, before heading to the hallway, intent on putting a door between himself and what the suite had become.

His own room was at the end. He could go in, lock it, shower again, sleep horizontal, and get the hell out of this forsaken city come sunrise. But just as his fingers encircled the door handle, he stopped, noticing the door to Blaine's room ajar. There was movement inside.

Keep walking, he told himself. But the curiosity pulled. He took two steps and looked in.

The sight inside stopped him cold. Blaine was behind a woman, satin dress bunched at her waist, headboard rattling in tune with thrusts. Sweat streaked down his face, coke dust still smudged at the edge of his nose. His hands gripped her with a desperate intensity—not passion, not connection, but a need to control something. Anything.

Crumpled bills littered the nightstand, a few fallen to the carpet near her discarded heels. The woman's hands clenched the duvet in habitual knots that had nothing to do with pleasure. Her voice rose in time, the sound of a performance given before.

For a split-second, Blaine's glazed eyes met Chase's. No shame, no apology, only an empty grin.

Chase recoiled, pulling the door shut behind him. His gut turned, not only at the scene but at the knowledge that Blaine was past the point of salvation. He had driven himself, full throttle, straight into ruin.

He stood in the hallway for a full minute, palms cold despite the heat in the suite, the shots sitting heavy in his stomach, head spinning above it. Then he turned to his room, closed the door, and fell back on the bed, staring at the ceiling. His eyes stung like they were full of salt.

He'd almost been shot at a conference. He'd watched a friend meet his past and choose a future that would keep hurting him. He'd said no when it would've been easy to say yes. He'd be home tomorrow. The thoughts swirled, circling faster and faster, never landing, never resolving, just motion without meaning.

One thing he knew for certain. What just happened in Vegas wasn't staying here. It was following them home.

30

FEAR PREMIUM

FOUR TELEVISIONS HUNG above the Thirsty Camel bar, each tuned to a different channel but all showing the same thing.

CNN ran a looping panel discussion—four experts boxed around shaky iPhone footage of the Vegas ballroom. The glass wall shattered behind the stage, shrieks rising, a conference attendee thinking they were capturing one moment, only to document what became a crime scene. Fox News had a retired FBI profiler talking about the "psychology of grievance-driven actors." ESPN was debating whether the incident would push leagues to rethink partnerships with betting companies. CNN showed a grainy freeze-frame of the chaos, "**SHOOTER STILL AT LARGE**," plastered in red at the bottom.

Marco watched it all from a lounge chair set deep in the Phoenician's desert-toned lobby, the ceiling fan blades cutting the still air above him in slow rhythm. The contrast jarred—the violence on-screen against the calm around him. He sat surrounded by terracotta tile, potted succulents, a trickling fountain designed to lower heart rates. A sanctuary selling serenity, except for the screens that wouldn't let go.

He let the noise bleed together from all four screens.

"The arbitrage community has always been fringe, but this looks like something darker."

"Sportsbooks are in the spotlight. How safe is this industry, really?"

"Shooter on the run. Was he spurned by his own?"

Marco had been in that ballroom two days earlier, close enough to smell the cordite. Now it was chewed up and reassembled into a cautionary tale. The longer he watched, the less it looked like what he remembered and the more it looked like the story everyone else wanted it to be.

A businessman in a golf polo leaned on the bar, phone to his ear, voice carrying. "Bet you it was a local," he was saying. "One of those guys tossed out when sports betting became legal. The whole Vegas industry shrank overnight. Some poor bastard loses his job, gets bitter enough to do something stupid. Happens every day." He shook his head and scribbled something on a cocktail napkin.

On the other side of the lobby, a family in resort wear shepherded their kids past the TVs. The mother's voice was tight, annoyed. "Why are they even showing this here? We're on vacation. Don't look, sweetie. Come on, let's go find the pool." The little boy craned his neck anyway until his father tugged him along.

Marco checked his watch. 6:56 a.m. Aaron had said he'd be here at seven sharp.

He shifted in the chair. It was the first time he and Aaron would see each other since the shooting. Aaron had texted him late Thursday night, after hours with law enforcement: concise and to the point.

AARON: Come to Phoenix. Need to regroup.

By the time Marco had a chance to respond, an email from Aaron's assistant dropped into his inbox with a Delta confirmation and a room at the Phoenician. No explanation. No back-and-forth. Just coordinates.

He'd called home from McCarran before boarding. His wife had been direct. "You were supposed to be coming back. Enough is enough."

But Marco had found himself saying the opposite—that this was work now, that Aaron needed him, that the community needed clarity. "This is part of it," he'd told her. "If I disappear now, it looks like capitulation. Even guilt." LineSniper had changed their lives. She'd come around.

A hand clasped his shoulder. "Morning."

Aaron stood over him in fitted black joggers and a sleek performance tee, the kind of athleisure that looked built for speed but polished enough to pass in a club. His sneakers were spotless, his hair neat. There was an ease about him, a charge in his step, like a man fresh off a win. No sign he'd been in a room full of federal agents forty-eight hours ago.

"You good?" Aaron asked.

Marco started to answer, but Aaron gestured toward the doors. "Walk with me. My place is ten minutes up the trail. Clears the head."

The desert took over quickly, the resort slipping away behind a screen of palo verde and red rock. The Scottsdale sun hadn't cleared the serrated line of Camelback Mountain above them, but the trail was already rinsed in a warm gold, climbing in gentle switchbacks. Warmth already hung in the air. Their shoes scuffed on the gravel.

At first there was only breath and crunch. Aaron set the pace, brisk but not punishing, the way of someone who hiked this loop often, not as recreation but regimen. Marco followed half a step behind, hands loose at his sides, the last two days dragging at him with every incline.

Finally, Marco said, "How are you holding up? After everything?"

Aaron didn't break stride. "Centered and dialed in."

"You sure? That was…" Marco searched for words. "…intense."

Aaron tilted his chin toward the horizon. "Perspective helps."

They climbed another minute in silence. A hummingbird shot past, a flash of green. Marco's shirt clung with sweat. He wanted to believe Aaron's composure, wanted to anchor himself in it.

"How's this impacting LineSniper?" he asked finally. "I've been worried."

That made Aaron slow his pace. He pulled his phone from his pocket and urged the screen awake, scrolling with quick, economical motions before handing it over. A custom dashboard app looked back at Marco.

"10x subscriber growth year-over-year since Thursday. Retention rock solid. We're far exceeding September numbers in July, historically our worst time of year."

Aaron pointed to a heat map at the bottom. "It's not only New Jersey, Pennsylvania, and Maryland anymore. Oklahoma, Colorado, Oregon—states that barely moved the needle last year are spiking. Even crazier? We're seeing sign-ups from places we don't serve. People in London, São Paulo, Seoul, paying for access they can't even use. Subscribing in solidarity. That's not growth. That's viral."

Marco blinked at the graph, the curve nearly vertical. "We...growing exponentially?"

Aaron's voice was steady, almost offhand. "Like I knew we would."

The sentence hit him broadside, staggering in its suddenness. Marco stopped. Dust rose around his shoes.

"You...knew?"

Aaron turned, face calm, expression unchanged. "Of course. Because I staged it."

For a moment Marco thought the desert glare had warped what he heard. "You...what?"

Aaron slipped the phone back into his pocket. "I hired a contractor. Ex-military. Paid through intermediaries, all in crypto. Eight to ten rounds. Fired into preselected spots—LED screen, podium edge, water glass on the stage table. Enough for chaos, never for casualties."

Marco's throat tightened. "You staged a shooting."

"I engineered optics," Aaron corrected. His tone was measured, almost gentle. "There's a difference."

"You brought live rounds into a packed room," Marco said. His voice was rising. "There were hundreds of people—"

"And none of them were in the line of fire," Aaron cut in. "Do you think I left that to chance? Every shot was mapped. The contractor was trained to hit a dime at fifty yards. He hit exactly what I told him to hit. I didn't hire a YouTuber."

Marco shook his head, heat prickling his scalp. "You risked lives."

"I priced the risk," Aaron said. "There was virtually none. All upside."

"Upside?" Marco was incredulous, unable to comprehend the words he was hearing from someone he revered. "What *upside* possibly justified what you did?"

"You saw the numbers, Marco. The return is here." He tapped his pocket where the phone rested. "We jumped from niche to mainstream in forty-eight hours. The books respected the product before Vegas. That's what got them to show in the first place. Now they fear the movement."

"That's supposed to help?"

"It's supposed to be the truth."

"And the guy they're looking for?"

Aaron's mouth twitched. "They won't find him. They'll find a story. Reddit threads of disgruntled arbers being iced out by their own. Screenshots of limits. A few leaked DMs. The media will do the rest. They always do."

A fury was rising into Marco's voice. "You made it look like one of us turned violent?"

"I made 'us' look like a movement with teeth," Aaron said. "The legend of the disaffected bettor predates me by centuries. I gave the press a pattern they already knew how to recognize."

"And we ride the outrage?" Marco asked. "Is that the plan?"

"We ride the attention," Aaron said. "Outrage is a gas pedal, not a steering wheel."

"You brought me here to tell me this," Marco said, glowering, a statement, not a question.

"I brought you here because I told you I would keep you in the inner ring," Aaron said. "I'm keeping that promise."

Marco laughed, short and humorless. "That's what this is? Keeping promises? You staged a shooting, Aaron, and now I'm party to that."

Aaron shook his head once. "I orchestrated a catalyst. Words matter."

Marco reeled. "Not to my son," he said. It came out sharper than anything he'd said so far. He saw Mateo's face in his mind, his son's eyes catching a glimpse of the coverage at breakfast. "He's five. He's going to see this. He's going to hear words like 'violent' and 'extremist' and think they mean me."

Aaron didn't look away. This was when people either left or leaned in.

"I know," he said. "I'm telling you because you deserve the truth. The decision now isn't about what happened Thursday. It's about what Thursday bought."

Marco stared. "Which is?"

"Thursday bought us leverage. Not because of what we did but because of what the world now thinks we are," Aaron said.

"And fear," Marco added.

"And fear," Aaron agreed. "Nothing frees capital like fear. Fear moves markets."

* * *

By the time they crested the trail and dropped toward the ridge where Aaron's condo stood, Marco felt unmoored. The building was glass and concrete set against desert scrub, minimalist lines pointing toward Camelback like compass needles.

The elevator was key-coded to open straight into the living room, a hidden seam in the wall. Inside, the temperature dropped, the silence absolute. Aaron slid his phone onto a low cedar table adorned with a bowl of blood oranges, their skins beading under the chill of the AC.

"Topo Chico?" Aaron offered.

Marco glanced at the oranges, everything deliberately placed to draw the eye. "Water's good."

"Topo Chico is water," Aaron said, smiling as he reached into the fridge. "Bubbles make people honest."

Marco didn't smile. He took the bottle but didn't drink.

"Sit," Aaron said. "Or stand. Whatever helps."

"So why did you really bring me here, Aaron? No spin. You must want something to have told me what you just did."

"You're here because none of this works without you," Aaron said. His tone softened. "You think I don't know that? Your voice gives the story its spine. People don't only sign up because of edges. They sign up because they believe in how their lives can change. You give them that belief."

FEAR PREMIUM

Aaron reached for a folder lying on the counter, slid it across the wood grain. Inside was an equity document, complete with summary terms. He offered people paper because it felt real—the opposite of a pitch deck, not projection and aspiration but numbers and binding language.

"I'm not asking you to be a contractor. I'm asking you to be a partner. Family, if you want the word. You've earned that."

Marco read. His eyes flicked once at the percentage.

"Two and a half percent of LineSniper?" he asked.

"Two and a half percent," Aaron confirmed. "Fully diluted, meaning that's your slice no matter what else I issue. And if we sell, it all vests at once. You'd get the full payout. We're pushing a one-hundred-fifty-million-dollar target."

Marco's eyes stayed on the line that mattered. 2.5% might as well have been written in gold leaf. "You're flattering me," he said.

"I'm compensating you," Aaron said. "Flattery is free. This isn't. You are the voice that makes this more than a tool. People don't upgrade because they see a decimal. They upgrade because they see a future that looks like yours."

Marco's jaw worked. "And if I say no?"

"Then you say no," Aaron said. He didn't blink. "You go home. You keep making your videos. And we'll still be friends, because that's not a lever I pull. But it will be harder. For you. For us. For the people who listen to you."

"That sounds like a lever."

"It's not meant to be," Aaron said. "It's meant to be honest. This makes your voice permanent inside the thing you've been building with me. It makes the upside you've created show up in your bank account at acquisition."

"Acquisition?" Marco questioned, still fixed on the number as if it might shift.

"The acquisition," Aaron repeated. "They'll call. It'll be Faceoff. They've got the stomach to move fast and the most to lose if this

227

becomes a movement they can't model. They won't only be buying the product and our data. They'll be buying a chance to put a lid on the narrative. They'll tell themselves they can neuter us, prevent more violence. That's fine. We name a number—and we finish this without lighting another match."

Marco lifted his head at that. "Say that again."

"We're done with theater," Aaron said. "We needed ignition. We have it. From here, it's math and timing, commas in the right places, a number that sounds obscene on first hearing and inevitable by the time we're done. No more stunts. No more chaos. We've already paid for the attention. Now we spend it."

Marco nodded once, as if committing the sentence to memory. "No more theater."

"No more theater," Aaron said again. "You have my word."

"So what do you need from me right now?"

"First, you sign. Then, a message," Aaron said. "Recorded here, today. Calm. Responsible. Not apologizing for existing. Emphasizing safety, community, and education. No taunts. No heat. Remind them we're people with kids and jobs and lives, not caricatures with handles. We win with our minds."

"You wrote it already," Marco said.

"I outlined," Aaron said. "It needs your voice to be true. Then you fly home and spend a few days off-grid with Mateo. Let the curve do what it's going to do. I'll take the calls."

"You make it sound so clean."

"It is clean," Aaron said. "Messy would be doing nothing and hoping we survive the attention without shaping it."

"Two and a half," he said again, quieter. "On a hundred and fifty."

"On a hundred and fifty," Aaron said. "And the delta if we push higher."

Marco nodded. "You ever wonder if this ends with us as the story that warns people what not to do?"

Aaron didn't hesitate. "There'd be no legends without the graves of the ones who fell short."

Marco turned. "I'm going to step outside," he said. "Give me two minutes."

"Balcony's to your right," Aaron said.

He slid the door open. Heat spilled in—dry, immediate. The desert shimmered below. He stepped out onto the balcony, palms on the rail. He couldn't tell if he was about to secure Mateo's future or sell it. *No legends without graves.*

When he came back in, the cool air greeted him, citrus faint in the room. He walked to the table and signed. His hand shook, but the line was clean.

The Topo Chico glistened on the counter, a ring of condensation spreading beneath. He finally twisted the cap off the bottle and drank. "I'd be lying if I said I wasn't terrified of what comes next," he said.

Bubbles really did bring out the truth.

31

WORKAROUND

"ARE YOU SERIOUS, CHASE? Here?"

The swing chains clanked behind her, that unmistakable metallic rattle of restless kids at play. They were at Garfield Park, Saturday morning, before DC's stifling August heat settled in, a bright jungle gym with mulch spread generously to soften the falls. Cece and Savannah darted between the slides and web of climbing ropes, faces bright with the easy joy of kids who didn't yet recognize tension between two adults.

Chase sat on a bench at the periphery of the playground, head down, phone in hand. Tara's voice cut through the hum of squeals and chatter, loud enough that a dad at the water fountain looked over before deciding he hadn't heard anything.

The question hit the usual nerve. His first instinct wasn't to answer but to decide if it deserved one.

He thought of the night he'd come home from Vegas three weeks earlier. He remembered the apartment door opening, Tara not saying anything at first, just folding herself into him tightly. Her face buried in his chest, the tiny sound she made that wasn't quite a sob and wasn't quite a laugh. The girls hugged his legs, oblivious to the torment their mother had endured during those long hours after the news of the shooting had reached her. Chase had stood there, emotion and gratitude overtaking him, never imagining he'd ever be that necessary to anyone.

Whatever softness Vegas bought him was gone. Her voice had a bite to it.

"Look at me."

He did. "What, Tara?"

"Jesus, Chase." Tara's eyes shot to the phone. "You're doing this while we're here? They asked you to push them on the swings, and you said, 'One second.' You've been 'one second' for twenty minutes."

He glanced toward the structure. Savannah shot down the slide feet-first, a whoop, hair electric, Cece waiting at the bottom to catch her and half-succeeding so they both tumbled and laughed. He should have been over there. He knew that.

"They're happy as can be. Plus, my mom's with them. She doesn't get the time we do. I'm giving her some space."

Louise sat at the top of the miniature slide, a grown-up who'd taken a wrong turn into recess, the girls shrieking as they tried to coax her down.

"You nearly died in Vegas because of this betting. How was that not a wake-up call?"

He let out air. "No one was close to dying. That was a freak outlier. A lunatic with a grudge. I still made **$7,411** in July. Vegas didn't change the math or the profitability." He paused. "Look, beyond the numbers, that morning—" He fumbled, glanced toward the swings. "If I quit now, all the sacrifice, all the fear in that room, it all evaporates, all becomes nothing. There's more purpose in it than ever before. So yes, I'll keep going."

"Got it," she said evenly. "You need to prove to yourself that almost dying had a point. And you're going to prove it by risking losing everything else."

The careful nuance Chase had created suddenly felt far less nuanced. But still, Blaine.

"*Blaine* let it devour him, not me. You didn't see him in Vegas, Tara. *That's* what it looks like to lose everything."

"Julia's been texting me. She doesn't know what to do. She cries every day. She's lost the husband she knew. Quinn's lost her dad. And that's the bar you're telling me you still clear? Convincing."

Hearing Julia's name made him bristle. He'd labored over what to say when her text came the day after he got back.

JULIA: He seems worse than ever before, Chase. What exactly happened in Vegas?

After long deliberation, he'd settled on brusque honesty.

CHASE: It wasn't good, Julia. I really did try to talk with him, but a lot happened. You need to ask him. I'm sorry.

The exchange left them both unsatisfied. She hadn't texted since.

A boy sprinted past in a cape and clipped his leg. "Sorry!" the kid blurted before veering away, fabric snapping behind him. A dad jogged after, mouth full of apology. The swing squeak continued with its consistent tempo. Somewhere a gate clanged shut.

"I don't want a scene," Chase said quietly. "Not here."

"I'm not making a scene," Tara said, same volume. "I'm telling you I don't recognize you when you hold that phone closer than you hold any of us."

"We agreed to this. I'm filling the buckets, building the savings, financing memories for this family for years to come. And on top of that, I'm doing everything I said I would—the dishes, the laundry, the drop-offs and pick-ups. What more do you want, Tara?"

"You keep calling it *we*. There's no 'we' if you're somewhere else every time I look up. Being present isn't the same as being *present*."

He looked toward the slide again. Cece waved, her face bright, waiting for him to wave back. He did, too late for her to see. She'd already turned to help Savannah climb the ladder.

Tara followed his gaze. "They want you on the ground with them, not making a market out of playground time."

"I'll go," he said. "In two minutes."

She laughed, soft and humorless. "You hear yourself?" Tara rubbed her palms on her jeans and stepped back. "I'm done having this conversation. You can either be with us for the next hour or with your phone."

She turned toward the play structure. He watched her go, watched Cece run to her, watched Savannah point up at the monkey bars, asking for a lift.

He stayed on the bench, stubbornness building. The slats were warm from the morning, the metal armrest cool against his forearm. Leaving now would be a concession to Tara's point, an admission of wrongdoing. The girls already had their mom and grandma, after all. He had money to make and an entire weekend to spend time with them.

A LineSniper alert flashed with a Faceoff/Atlantis arb. Thumbs came alive, locking in the Faceoff side of a Mariners pitcher strikeout prop. He flipped to Atlantis and placed the corresponding wager. In place of the familiar confirmation screen, a red message appeared.

"Sorry, you are not able to play in the Atlantis sweepstakes. Please contact Atlantis support if you need further assistance."

Fuck! Had he just been locked out of his own house, belongings still inside but inaccessible? Chase had diversified as much as he could, adding two social sportsbooks to his rotation—VigLess, a farmers' market for bets: no middleman, only you and some guy across the way haggling over tomatoes, and CrystalBall, the eBay for bets, where you posted your number and waited for someone to take the other side. But without Atlantis, everything collapsed. Profits would fall from thousands to mere hundreds a month.

He tried again. Same message. Again and again, willing a different outcome, begging for a glitch. None came. Frantically, he tapped out an email to Atlantis support.

The response came back three minutes later, stock and cold.

Hi Chase,

We hope this message finds you well.

Your account has been suspended in accordance with our Terms of Use, under our fair play rules in Section 12. Unfortunately, Atlantis does not permit customers to use the platform for the purposes of arbitrage or other means to exploit pricing inefficiencies.

You still have access to your Atlantis Cash balance to redeem cash, but you may only do so at a rate of $5,000 per week. You will not be able to place additional picks or make additional deposits on the platform.

Thank you for your loyalty and business.

Regards,

Terrance

Cold rippled through him, fast and total. His hearing tunneled, the playground thinning into distant noise. He had $45,000 in his Atlantis account—nine weeks of slow withdrawals ahead, assuming he could get the money out at all.

The old reflex kicked in—to fix, to find an angle, to tell himself this was a glitch in a system, not an irreversible ruling. He looked back at the screen, at the message that didn't change no matter how many times he blinked.

The phone buzzed before he could decide what to do next.

BLAINE: You seeing this shit?

BLAINE: Rushmore folded. Like full-on bent the knee.

The name looked foreign after weeks of silence. Blaine hadn't answered a text since they landed back at DCA and hailed separate Ubers.

CHASE: Yeah. Locked out ten minutes ago. Game over.

BLAINE: Devastating. I've got 32k in there!

Chase started to type that he was in for forty-five, but the texts kept coming—faster now, punctuation unraveling, Blaine's thumbs barely keeping up with his fury.

BLAINE: Rushmore's a coward&!! Guy built Atlantis on "player freedom" then caves the second the suits call. One of "us" my ass! What a bitch!! He's dead to me!

BLAINE: Too bad they didn't get what they deserved in Vegas! Crooks every one of them!

Chase's eyebrows lifted involuntarily, unsettled but not exactly surprised.

BLAINE: Can't silence a movement!!

Chase rubbed his temple. The panic in Blaine's messages wasn't only about money. It was about identity. The same sickness he'd seen in the hotel suite that night in Vegas—eyes red, voice high, conviction mistaken for clarity.

CHASE: Take a breath. We'll figure it out.

BLAINE: Don't patronize me. This is war, man. They started it.

The final message slammed like a door. Chase stared at the screen until it dimmed, wondering if the sound of madness was infectious.

* * *

The next day, Tara dropped the girls at summer camp—temporary peace, from eight to three. Louise was in the living room, insisting on folding a month's worth of laundry. The dryer thumped steadily, a low industrial note in the background.

Chase sat at his desk, an inane document open, cursor blinking. He'd stared at the same line for fifteen minutes. His thoughts kept sliding off the screen and back to Atlantis. Those red error messages burned behind his eyes like afterimages. Every few minutes he'd check his phone again, hoping for an email that changed the verdict. Nothing.

He flipped to Reddit instead, muscle memory guiding him to r/ArbMasters—the private board ArbOracle had built back when the movement still felt underground. He'd joined it months earlier but hadn't checked it since Vegas. The icon glowed gray, meaning he still had access. Most didn't.

Inside, a new sticky thread was at the top: "Beat the Suspensions—Protected Discussion (Invite Only)."

It had ArbOracle's signature under it, same timestamped precision he always used, down to the second. Chase clicked. The post opened with a threatening banner. "Access limited to verified members. Do not screenshot. Do not reference publicly. Violation = permanent ban."

Then the text read, "With Atlantis's crackdown, we've moved from scaling smarter to preserving profit. The methods still apply. Multi-accounting has always been possible. Now it's necessary. Rules are just the house's way of slowing you down. Don't slow down. Borrow trusted IDs. Compensate your counterparties—friends, relatives, whoever—with a percentage or flat retainer. Keep them uninvolved. Keep them ignorant. The best firewall is their innocence."

Chase read the last line twice.

Tentative hope reappeared. The question wasn't whether it would work. It was who.

He turned toward the living room, listening to the rhythm of the dryer. Louise hummed something under her breath, an old country song.

He already did her taxes every spring, knew her Social Security number by heart. All he needed was a driver's license image to pass Atlantis's onboarding verification. He could use a spare Gmail address and the Google Voice number he'd signed up for to get a DC area code. Any messages would route back to him. Louise would never see a thing.

He sat there another minute, letting the idea take hold. He should've felt guilt or at least hesitation. What he felt instead was the settling simplicity that always came when a problem finally solved itself.

Louise was pulling a pile of towels from the dryer when he walked in. "That thing runs hotter than it used to," she said, shaking one out.

"Good to know," he said.

She smiled at him. "You look like a man who's been inside his head all morning."

"Work stuff."

She folded another towel, smoothing the corners. "That's the curse of working from home. You never leave the office."

He hesitated. "I actually wanted to ask you something."

Her hands paused mid-fold. "That sounds serious."

"It's not. Just…a small favor."

She cocked her head, half-amused. "Oh boy. What'd you do?"

"Nothing," he said quickly. "It's about a side project I've been running. A business experiment of sorts."

She set the towel down. "All right. Hit me."

He kept his voice casual. "I can scale it further if I bring on one more account, but I need a separate ID to do it. Totally legal. I'd pay you five hundred bucks a month for letting me use yours."

She blinked. "My ID?"

"Driver's license. A picture. You don't have to do anything. I'd handle everything."

She laughed, waiting for the punch line. "You're joking, right?"

He smiled faintly but didn't answer.

"Chase," she said, searching his face. "You're not serious."

He let the silence sit, steady as he could. She'd always trusted him.

"What is this really for?" she asked finally. She folded her arms as meticulously as she had the towels.

He shrugged. "Five hundred a month. No risk, no involvement. It's a small way to help me keep this project going."

She looked at him another long moment. Something in his calm unsettled her, and yet Chase had never asked her for much. "You're lucky I trust you," she said at last.

"I know."

She sighed. "Five hundred a month, you keep doing my taxes, and an extra FaceTime call every week with the girls."

He grinned. "Deal."

She reached for her purse on the counter, pulled out her wallet, and slid her license free with a small, incredulous shake of her head.

"You're sure this isn't going to put me on some list? I'd like to be able to fly places in retirement, you know."

"Positive," he said. "It's only verification."

He lifted his phone, snapped the photo quickly, the flash glinting off the laminate, and handed it back. "All set."

Louise slid the license back into her wallet. "You and your projects," she said. "I never know what you're building, but you always sound like you believe in it."

"That's half the work," he said.

When she left the room, he exhaled for the first time since the conversation started. The picture was already uploading. He created the new account—*LouiseDupree01*—entered the spare email and burner number, and watched the familiar Atlantis interface load, blue and clean.

The green confirmation light blinked once, then steadied. Order restored. Back online, and further away than ever.

32

CONTAGION

TARA'S FEET STRUCK THE TREADMILL in steady cadence, the machine's whir joining in to fill the empty gym. Sweat gathered at the base of her neck, her ponytail clinging to it. She'd spent the last few hours performing the role of "working mom," packing lunches, firing off emails, taking the trash down the hall to the chute. Now, finally, a few minutes that were hers.

With the girls back in school, she relished the return of routine—for them and for herself. These evening runs had become ritual—predictable, almost meditative. She wasn't training for anything. She liked the motion, the treadmill pulling her forward from the instant she hit Quick Start. The sweat wasn't achievement so much as verification—her body's way of reminding her it still belonged to her.

These post-bedtime hours had once belonged to her and Chase. Lately, they belonged to his betting. A grunt when she said she'd be back was the only sign he'd heard her at all.

She ticked up the speed. Taylor Swift, a guilty pleasure, filled her ears—the soft synth and echo of "The Archer." It was one of those songs that sank beneath the skin, haunting, questioning, impossible to outrun.

The lyrics cut out, replaced by that emotionless, robotic voice in her AirPods.

"Call from Julia Wexford."

Tara frowned, glanced down at her wrist, dread forming. Julia rarely called, especially at this hour. The two usually texted—quick things, check-ins, kid photos. Not this. She swiped to answer, dialing down to a trot.

"Hey, hang on. I'm on the—" she started, breath catching.

"Tara." Julia's voice came sharp, then softened. "I'm leaving."

Tara blinked. "Leaving where?"

"I mean *leaving*. I'm taking Quinn and driving to my parents' tonight."

The treadmill belt hummed beneath her.

"Wait, Jules, what are you talking about?"

"I've been talking about it for months. You just didn't hear me." There was no anger, just exhaustion hardened to resolve. "He's not the same person anymore. It's all bets, all numbers, all day and night. The drinking. The disappearing. Hell, I'm almost certain he cheated on me in Vegas. I can't keep Quinn in this house, as if he's ever even in it."

Tara hit the red Stop button and grabbed the rails a split-second before her balance wobbled. The belt slowed beneath her, then stopped entirely, her feet stumbling once before she caught herself at the back edge.

"My God, where is he?"

"No idea. Probably in some dark parking lot where he can focus on his bets. Maybe drinking with these new friends of his I've never met. Doesn't matter. I'll be gone before he gets back."

No drama. No second-guessing. Tara could hear the sound of movement on the other end—car keys, the rustle of fabric, a child's small voice muffled in the background.

"Does he know?" Tara asked quietly.

"Not yet. I left a note. I'm not staying to see him read it."

The treadmill's console blinked red digits into the dark—Distance: 4.21 miles. Calories: 448. It now felt trivial.

Tara swallowed hard. "You sure you don't want to wait a day? Talk it through?"

"I already did that part. There's nothing to talk through, nothing left to save."

The call went quiet again, the faint rev of the car's ignition bleeding through.

"Promise me you'll text when you get there," Tara said.

"I will." A pause. "And Tara…don't let it get to this point with Chase."

One last warning, then the line clicked dead.

Tara stood still, phone in hand, her thoughts ricocheting from shock to panic. Through the gym's window, she watched the streets of Navy Yard—streetlights washing over Canal Park across the intersection.

For the first time, her anger at Chase didn't feel righteous. It felt dangerous.

She looked down at the stopped treadmill, its sweat-soaked black belt gleaming like a river at night, and felt a tremor move through her. Whatever had taken Blaine—and driven Julia to run—might not be confined to their marriage. It might be contagious.

Tara took the elevator up, breathing unevenly from more than the run. Her shirt clung to her ribs, and for a brief second she considered showering first, cooling off before she faced him. But she figured there was no good way to say it, so she might as well get it over with.

Chase was still lying on the couch, phone in hand, fixated on odds and edges. The rest of the apartment was dark. She flipped on pendant lights above the kitchen island.

He looked up. "Hey, you okay?"

She was surprised he had noticed her entrance, let alone her body language. "Julia called," she replied.

He frowned, setting his phone down on the ottoman. "This late?"

"She's leaving. She took Quinn and left Blaine."

That got his attention. He straightened, brows drawing together. "Are you serious? What happened?"

Tara's hand flew up, part disbelief, part surrender. "Everything, Chase. The betting. The drinking. She said he's never home, that she doesn't even know who he is anymore."

He let out a low exhale and sank back into the cushions, as if distance might dull the news.

"She sounded done, like she'd been planning it for weeks."

Chase nodded slowly. "I mean, I can't say I didn't see it coming. He's been off the rails for months. If she knew half of what went down in Vegas, she'd have left sooner."

Tara looked at him, waiting. "That's it?"

"What do you mean?"

"She left her husband, Chase. Their daughter's in the back seat of her car right now. You don't think maybe this has something to do with it?" She gestured vaguely toward his phone.

He followed her motion then gave a half-shrug. "Blaine's situation is…extreme. You know how he is always all or nothing. I'm not like that."

She stared at him. "I wonder if he'd say the exact same thing about himself."

He gave a small laugh, the kind meant to diffuse tension. "Come on. I'm not even close to that. Just because he lost control doesn't mean everyone who uses LineSniper will. We've talked about this, Tara."

She crossed her arms, the fabric of the damp shirt cooling against her skin.

Chase met her eyes, and for a second there was something genuine there—concern, guilt, maybe even fear—but it passed.

"I feel bad for her," he said finally, recognizing empathy mattered here. "For both of them. But this isn't the same thing."

Tara didn't respond. The quiet stretched, heavy and close.

He broke it first. "She'll be fine. Julia's tough."

"She shouldn't have to be."

That one landed. He didn't have a reply.

Tara turned toward the bedroom, pausing at the door. "Don't become Blaine, Chase."

Chase nodded, though his eyes were already back on the screen, odds blinking, endless and alive. As she closed the door, she heard him whisper to no one, "I'm not him."

33

THE COMFORT OF MAYBE

THE MORNING MOVED ON AUTOPILOT—cereal bowls clinking, back-pack zippers stuttering, Cece correcting Savannah's counting while Savannah ignored her entirely. Tara moved through it all with maternal reflexes—snapping helmet straps, lining up scooters, shepherding the girls toward the door.

As they were about to leave, Chase appeared from the bedroom—barefoot, shirtless, a red crease across his chest where he'd slept on a headphone cord, hair sticking up in an unruly cowlick, the look of someone still halfway inside the night.

"Morning," he murmured, voice rough from too little sleep and too much screen time.

"Morning," she said, fastening the Velcro on a tiny shoe. "You have pickup today, right?"

He nodded slowly, barely there, rubbing one eye with the heel of his hand, the other hand massaging his neck. "Yeah, I've got it."

Normally he'd be leading morning affirmations, pouring orange juice, making oats, and reciting his trademark line—"Make a great day for yourself!"—as they headed out, the small chaos feeling like a kind of teamwork. Instead, as had been the case most mornings lately, he leaned against the doorway, eyes unfocused—an observer in his own home.

Tara was deeply unsettled by it, especially after last night's call. It had become too easy for him to let the morning happen without him.

The girls scurried out. His "Love you, girls," came a beat too late—reflexive, automatic—heard only by Tara as the door clicked shut.

Outside, Cece and Savannah zipped ahead on their scooters. Tara trailed behind, backpacks slung over her shoulder, calling out, "Watch the curb!" and "Wait at the corner!"

The half-mile to Van Ness Elementary always unfolded the same way: sidewalks all their own for the first half, then gradually swelling with life—dogs straining at leashes, parents pushing strollers, scooters clattering on uneven brick. By the last crosswalk, the pavement teemed with overlapping hellos and snippets of conversation—field trip forms, weekend updates, playground gossip.

Cece lifted a hand in her trademark under-chin wave to the crossing guard—a move she insisted was their secret—and rolled across like a pro, ponytail swishing behind her. Savannah followed, legs pumping twice as hard to keep up.

Tara pictured Julia, back in Ohio—Quinn eventually walking into a new school, Julia standing among strangers who didn't yet know her name. New parents. New teachers. The awkward small talk of starting over.

It didn't feel impossible anymore, the idea of a life reset. It felt like something faintly visible on the horizon, an outcome that now had a greater chance than zero.

She kissed the girls goodbye, handing them off to their respective teachers. The plan had been to metro straight to the office, but caffeine and clarity beckoned. Instead, she retraced her steps back to I Street, ducking into Compass Coffee across the street from their apartment.

The bell over the door chimed as she stepped inside. The smell hit first—rich, roasted, impossible to mistake. The kind that kick-started the circulatory system before the first sip: espresso, baked sugar, a trace of burnt milk from a rushed cappuccino.

The place carried the hum of Washington mornings—ambition, exhaustion, everyone pretending to be late for something vital. A member of Congress stood near the counter, identifiable by the unmistakable gold lapel pin glinting on his blazer. Her staffer trailed close behind, voice low but rapid, trying to sound both informed and indispensable as he recited the day's schedule. An intern in heels navigated the crowd with a cardboard tray stacked high with lattes for the office. A lobbyist leaned against the counter, voice smooth, each word calculated—coaxing agreement from whoever was on the other end of the call while flashing a grin at the barista. A few parents she recognized from school hurried through their orders, eyes on watches, eager to get home, scrub off the morning, and reappear as their professional selves.

Tara ordered a cappuccino and found a corner table by the window. A few minutes later, the woman behind the counter called her name—cheerful, oblivious—and Tara smiled back instinctively.

Across New Jersey Avenue, the third-floor windows of their apartment building were just visible through the leafy canopy. She caught Chase's outline—head bent over his phone, already absorbed, unaware he was visible to anyone looking. Unaware she was.

She opened her laptop, intending to check email, but her mind refused to cooperate. The low jazz from the speakers, the clink of cups, the conversational chatter—it all felt too normal, as if the world hadn't gotten the memo that something in hers was coming apart. She stared at her reflection in the darkened screen.

Her birthday had been two days ago. Thirty-nine.

In theory, Chase had done everything right. He'd taken the girls out early and returned an hour later, bursting in with a store-bought cake balanced precariously in one hand, a bouquet of balloons in the other. The girls sang—off-key, enthusiastic—and she'd laughed, because that part was still real.

Then he handed her a card and a small envelope with a flourish. Inside: a short, boilerplate husbandly message, signed with his old nickname, "Duckling," their private joke—the only sign he'd given it any real thought. In the envelope was a gift certificate for a massage scheduled that afternoon.

"And two more gifts coming—shipping delays," he'd said, as if sensing her awareness of his lack of advance planning, though not doing much to help his cause.

Still, she'd kissed him on the cheek, thanked him, told herself she was being petty for noticing the frantic undertone, the way he'd rushed out that morning to make it happen.

At the time, she'd told herself not to make it bigger than it was. People forgot things. Life was busy. He was under pressure.

But now, sitting in the café, that rationalization felt as thin as the foam on her cooling cappuccino.

She logged into their shared credit card account. It wasn't impulse—it was self-destructive curiosity. She needed to see if he'd remembered her on his own, or if the celebration had been built in a panic that morning.

The list of recent charges loaded instantly.

Lululemon—Saturday, 8:03 a.m.

Anthropologie—Saturday, 8:09 a.m.

Kilwin's Cakes—Saturday, 9:12 a.m.

All from her birthday morning. Of course. He hadn't forgotten. He'd remembered just in time. That detail, the scramble, the performative sweetness of it stung more than she wanted to admit. It wasn't about the gifts. It was about what they revealed: the constant triage of attention, the way everything in their life now felt like an afterthought to something unseen to everyone but Chase.

She closed the tab and sat back. Julia's voice returned, as clear as if she were sitting across the table. "Don't let it get to this point with Chase."

Tara had barely slept after that call, imagining Julia driving through the night, Quinn asleep in the back seat, Blaine gone wherever he went when he disappeared into himself.

She'd thought about looking things up last night but couldn't bring herself to do it. Denial had felt like mercy, and she'd needed what little sleep she got more than researched answers.

Now, in the sober light of morning, the warning landed differently. Julia hadn't been scolding her; she'd been throwing a lifeline, calling out from the undertow, trying to keep her friend from being pulled under too.

Every instinct told Tara to close the laptop, to stay in the comfort of maybe. But the need for proof overpowered the fear of finding it. She opened a new tab and began to type.

"How do you help someone stop gambling when they don't think they have a problem?"

Search results stacked down the screen—links to treatment centers, Reddit forums, podcast episodes. Each with different titles. A single bolded word threading them all. "Addiction."

Among the results, one thumbnail stood out: "Huberman Lab – Understanding and Treating Addiction with Dr. Anna Lembke." She fitted her earbuds and clicked, curious what science might sound like when it tried to explain her husband.

The voice was calm, deliberate, almost soothing.

"Dopamine isn't just about pleasure," Dr. Lembke said. "It's about pursuit. The craving becomes stronger than the reward itself."

Tara nodded without realizing it. That part made sense—the chase, the constant scanning, the late nights spent trying to stay ahead. She'd seen that kind of restlessness before.

Then came the line that made her stop.

"Addiction is a progressive narrowing of the things that bring you pleasure."

Her mind caught on the words, the sentence feeling like a diagnosis.

Chase used to care about a dozen things—work, the girls, fitness, music, her. Now there was only one thing that lit him up. His world had narrowed to bets.

She took out one earbud, hoping the flood of coffee shop noise might undo the realization, but it was too late. The definition had already fit itself around him like a mold.

Tara scrolled again. Another headline caught her eye.

"Addiction can exist even when everything looks successful."

Her throat tightened. She read the line again.

For months she'd fed herself platitudes. "He's winning. He's not out drinking. He's saving for family memories. We're busy parents. He's working hard. It's a phase. We're fine." It had been a comforting story. But now, that felt like wallpaper over rot.

She kept scrolling until a new link drew her in: "Gamblers Anonymous: Twenty Questions."

She clicked. The page was bare—black text on white. No ads, no color, no noise. The first line read, "Answer honestly. The goal isn't blame—it's awareness." Then came the questions.

Have you ever lost time from work due to gambling?
Yes.

Has gambling made your home life unhappy?
Yes.

Do you ever gamble longer than you intended?
Yes.

Have you ever lied about gambling?
Yes.

After winning, do you have a strong urge to win more?
Yes.

Have you ever told someone you can quit at any time but been unable to do so?
Yes.

She remembered his line from last night. "I'm not him."

The conviction in it. The blind spot.

The questions weren't really questions; they were confirmations. At the bottom of the list, a single line waited in bold. "If you answered yes to four or more of these questions, you may have a gambling problem."

She had stopped counting after the first six.

The past arrived without warning. Beige walls. Fluorescent lights. She'd driven in silence late into the night to get there. Her mother sat beside her, fingertips massaging her forehead, wearing the weary expression of someone who's seen recovery turn into relapse too many times to flinch. The doctor had been deliberate, direct. "He was lucky this time," he'd said.

She'd been too inexperienced to do anything, too uncertain of what help even looked like. But staring at the tile floor, she'd made herself a vow that the next time she saw the signs, she'd intervene.

A hiss from the espresso machine pulled her back. She tracked the methodical progress bar on the podcast, the voice still droning about neurochemistry in her remaining earbud, and felt something inside her shift from confusion to certainty.

It wasn't just a side hustle. It wasn't just ambition. Chase was addicted. She could finally name it, and now that she had, there was no pretending she hadn't.

34

DISTANCE WITHOUT DANGER

THE AIR INSIDE AQUABUDDIES SWIM FACTORY was set to a constant seventy-nine degrees, calibrated for "optimal child comfort," according to a sign Chase had seen once and never forgotten. The same logic probably dictated the steel drum music, fake palm trees, and tropical color palette, a Jimmy Buffett fever dream in an Alexandria strip mall.

On the pool side of the floor-to-ceiling glass, humidity fogged its surface. On the other side, parents sat in uneven rows of pastel plastic chairs, sweating through weekend athleisure as they took grainy photos of their kids.

Chase never understood the enthusiasm. To him, it was a racket. Forty-five-minute lesson, five kids per instructor. Call it nine minutes of attention each—less if your kid was even mildly competent and not constantly on the verge of sinking. At $45 per lesson, that came out to... He stopped himself. Some things were better left uncalculated.

For Chase, the lessons were forty-five minutes of sanctioned reprieve. The failed paradise aesthetic notwithstanding, he'd stopped pretending he didn't relish the dull comfort of sitting still while someone else took over. He sat on his side of the glass, scrolling the app that had made him more in the last year than his job had, and he was perfectly fine with that.

Out of boredom, he opened the health dashboard linked to the wearable strapped snugly around his left bicep. It tracked everything— heart rate, HRV, respiratory rate—and let him log more than twenty lifestyle activities, all in the name of optimizing well-being.

His eyes caught halfway down the behavior impact analysis.

Engaged in sexual activity—Two entries in the last six months.

Masturbated—High double-digit entries.

An old, adolescent shame reflexively rose. He was embarrassed by what it said about his marriage of late and by the absurdity of watching loneliness show up as data.

Before it offered any other reminders of how measurable he'd become, he closed the app. A sudden, irrational fear flickered through him: that someone nearby might see the screen and know exactly what it said about him.

He sought solace in a quick toggle to PickTracker, an app that measured in far less personal terms. Here, the data rewarded him.

August: **$14,322**.

September: **$19,952**.

The numbers lined up cleanly, no judgment attached, confirmation that discipline still paid.

Satisfaction swelled. The return of football and Louise's Atlantis account meant a gold rush. He'd missed the predictable inefficiency—college Saturdays and NFL Sundays might as well have been days raiding the mint.

A sharp whistle cut through the glass, piercing even on the "dry side." Chase looked up. Savannah stood before a lifeguard, her face a perfect mix of guilt and defiance. Whatever she'd done—jumped before her turn, probably—she wasn't sorry. He grinned. Classic youngest child. His lovable troublemaker.

The phone buzzed in his hand. A text notification appeared. For a millisecond, he saw a "B" and thought *Blaine*. But it wasn't him. Chase had texted twice since Julia left, simple check-ins, nothing pushy. No response. Nobody else had heard from him either. He tried not to dwell on the fact that silence was rarely good.

Unable to think of another productive move, Chase opened the Notes app. Below the monthly profit ledger entry was a Note labeled

"Wants."He'd started it years ago, a repository for everything that caught his eye, an adult Christmas list no one would ever ask for.

Two entries had bubbled to the top. Omega Seamaster Diver 300M Watch and an Apple Vision Headset.

Both had been sitting there since July, their prices ebbing and flowing like stubborn stocks. He'd been watching the fluctuations, telling himself he'd wait for the perfect deal before buying. Patience was the trick in markets, and everything else.

Yesterday, he'd gotten an email that unnerved him in its personalization. "Early Black Friday Pricing – Pentagon City Mall." Both logos listed side by side. Omega. Apple. The watch had dipped $500 from the lowest price he'd seen, and the headset was finally under $2,500. This wasn't impulse. He'd waited months for this, and he never let value pass him by.

Another whistle—long, final. He looked up. The class was over. The pool erupted in small-scale chaos—splashes, laughter, dripping limbs hoisted from the water. The smell of wet hair and plastic goggles drifted through as parents filtered onto the pool deck. Chase stood, slung the girls' towels over one arm, and joined the migration.

He met them by the kid-sized showers, working through his list of bribes, wondering why they treated shower water like acid after nearly an hour in a pool full of it. The bickering began on cue.

"Daddy, I'm cold. I need the purple towel, not the pink one!" Cece demanded.

"You can both share—"

"No, the purple is warmer."

After promising himself to only buy like colors from now on, Chase followed the crowd toward the changing rooms, water pooling around feet.

"Daddy, I have to potty!" Savannah chirped.

Chase closed his eyes. Of course it was now. They ditched the line and headed toward the bathrooms, Savannah hop-stepping beside him in the urgent choreography every parent could recognize.

They made it in the nick of time, Chase crouching to peel off the wet suit seconds before it became even wetter. Cece narrated the entire ordeal from the doorway. "She has to go bad, Daddy! Hurry!"

Outside, fathers fumbled with hairdryers and hair ties while moms shared amused smirks. Chase was no exception. He'd watched YouTube tutorials, practiced on dolls, listened to Cece's coaching, but the logic of little-girl hair remained a mystery to him.

After getting it into what he considered a serviceable state, Chase glanced at the clock above the sun-bleached mural of a smiling dolphin. It was 12:36 p.m. The girls had a birthday party that started at two. He'd promised Tara he'd have them back by 1:30 p.m. at the latest.

The mall was fifteen minutes north. If they were in and out, he could make it. Quick stop, efficient and earned. He'd have his dream watch and a new VR toy, and Tara wouldn't question the schedule.

Cece was watching him in the mirror. "What are you thinking, Daddy?"

"Nothing."

"About football? Commanders gonna beat the Packers, right?"

He'd always imagined a son for this stuff, but the universe had given him Cece instead, equal parts sweetness and smack talk.

The air outside hit lighter. The girls skipped ahead, hand-in-hand, still damp and glowing with that post-pool energy. There were moments—small, mundane—that reminded him what all the noise was for.

He unlocked the Pilot, helped the girls climb in, and buckled them up, *click, click*. Cece demanded a snack. Savannah asked for music.

"KidzBop it is," he said, handing back granola bars, cueing up the XM station, and setting his phone in the dash mount. The pop beat filled the car, cheerful and bubbly, the way the girls liked it.

* * *

The mall on Sunday had the energy of an airport, people circling, buying time and things they didn't need.

Miraculously, or perhaps by destiny, he'd found a parking spot near the entrance, wedged between an Omega boutique and the Apple Store.

Walking next to him, the girls were on their best behavior, fueled by his promise that each could pick one keychain from the Lego Store before they left.

He paused outside the boutique, guilt creeping in as he remembered his December vow: experiences over things. It had felt noble at the time, and he'd kept to it thus far. Trips, memories, meals—nothing that gathered dust. But standing there, he'd allowed the definition to expand. *This isn't breaking the rule*, he thought. *It's bending it toward utility.*

The watch wasn't a thing—it was an instrument. A timekeeper. A reminder that the seconds of those experiences mattered, a tool to keep him accountable to them. And the headset—well, that was practically a portal. Whole worlds waiting. Infinite experiences by other means.

He decided his conscience could wait and stepped inside.

The sales associate hovered, velvet-gloved and practiced in the art of affirmation. The Seamaster gleamed under glass, its seconds hand gliding with that impossibly smooth motion he'd always loved. He tried it on—solid weight, not gaudy, professional. He looked at his reflection in the mirror, wrist held just high enough to catch the light.

"Perfect fit," the associate said.

Chase nodded, already convincing himself. *It's precision,* he thought. *Discipline you can wear.*

One swipe of the card, and it was his for $6,270.

Receipt in hand, he drifted next door to the Apple Store. A demo headset sat on a stand like a shrine under surgical light. A young employee in a pale blue shirt smiled and asked if he wanted to try it.

While the girls played a game next to him on a display iPad, he slid the goggles on. The world vanished. He stood inside a rendered mountain range—crisp peaks, rippling wind, the sensation of distance without danger.

"Pretty incredible, right?" the clerk said.

Chase barely heard him. He reached out, rotated the digital horizon with his hands. *Endless new worlds,* he thought. *Pure experience.*

Cece tugged his sleeve. "Daddy, can we go get Legos?"

He lifted his wrist, admiring the Seamaster's effortless sweep before the number sank in—1:18. Still had to check out, get to the Lego store, find the car, get across the bridge.

At the counter, the clerk boxed the headset. Card swipe again, the accompanying digital chime—$2,749, including tax. It was a lot, no denying that, but together the $9,019 was still less than half of what he'd made in September—a calculated indulgence.

Chase cursed himself for the promise he'd made about Legos. He should have known better. Never negotiate with children when you're on a timeline.

The girls beelined toward the yellow Lego block that marked the storefront. Inside, walls were stacked with plastic possibility. Cece and Savannah split off, orbiting separate displays.

"One keychain each," Chase said. "Keychains, remember? Not sets, keychains."

Neither looked up. Every box was the most amazing thing they'd ever seen. Cece clutched a Star Wars kit the size of a carry-on. Savannah pointed to an Eiffel Tower taller than she was.

"We don't have time," he said, scanning for the checkout, tapping his new watch like it might help. "Keychains or nothing."

They finally settled. Cece with a stormtrooper, Savannah with a puppy, and he hustled them to the register, foot tapping as he checked the time again, willing the line to move faster.

Back in the car, he tossed the bags in the passenger seat and buckled in fast. Google Maps estimated arrival at 1:58 p.m., twenty-eight minutes behind, two minutes before the party was set to begin.

Three missed texts from Tara glared on the lock screen.

TARA: Everything okay?

TARA: Need to be home soon—party at 2!

TARA: Chase??

He typed quickly:

CHASE: Sorry. Pit stop at mall for a treat for girls. Traffic bad. 1:58 ETA.

Not entirely a lie.

Merging into traffic, he let the girls' KidzBop chorus fill the car. The water beneath the bridge shimmered ahead. Mercifully, traffic was light. Still, Tara was going to be pissed. He could already see her standing in the doorway, keys in hand, ready to turn them right around for the next stop on their social calendars. He'd shrug apologetically, joke that the girls already had dad wrapped around their fingers, maybe buy himself a grin. Then they'd all pile in the car, drive off to the party, and the day would reset.

A buzz rattled against the console. Chase eyed a string of LineSniper alerts sliding down from the top of the screen, half a dozen edges at 8%+. Big ones.

Easily a couple hundred bucks if I move fast, he thought. *Make a dent in the mall damage. Cover today's tax at least.*

He snatched the phone from its mount. One tap opened the app.

Rams QB over/under 234.5 passing yards. Edge: +8.2%.

Broncos receiver anytime TD. Edge +9.5%.

Cowboys running back over/under 13.5 yards longest rush. Edge +8.3%.

He could place these blindfolded. Easy money.

A horn blared behind him, a Maryland plate darting across lanes like it was qualifying for Daytona. Typical.

He toggled between books, calculating the profit in his head as he confirmed each bet. One hundred seventy...

Something flashed out of the corner of his eye. His eyes snapped up. Brake lights. The airbag detonated before the metallic shriek reached his ears.

35

1:54

FOR A MOMENT, nothing made sense. His body sat still while his mind kept moving, bracing for an impact that had already happened. White powder drifted through the cabin like snow, settling on his arms, the dashboard, the glass. The airbag hung deflated against the steering wheel, like a collapsed lung exhaling the last of its dust. Chase blinked hard, coughed once, and realized he couldn't hear anything except the high ringing in his head.

"Girls!" he shouted, voice raw. "Are you okay?" He craned in his seat, vision blurred, fighting the locked belt. The back seat was a cloud of chalky residue and deflated nylon. His eyes scanned the blur of shapes.

Cece answered first, her small, startled voice coming from directly behind him. "Daddy? What happened?"

"It's okay, angel. It's okay." He fumbled for the seatbelt release. His fingers slipped once before the buckle finally gave. Pain flared through his wrist. He looked down. The Seamaster's glass spidered in a series of cracks, its once-perfect second hand frozen mid-sweep at 1:54. He must have slammed it against the wheel. A brief flex of the wrist sent a searing jolt through him, like a jellyfish had taken residence beneath the skin.

Pushing aside the pain, he scrambled between the seats, catching a glimpse of Cece—eyes wide, not fear but confusion—scanning him for answers he didn't have.

Relief hit and instantly vanished.

Savannah.

Her seat was behind the passenger side, rear-facing. He couldn't see her, only the edge of the plastic shell, the strap of the harness. He twisted further, pain spiking again.

"Savannah!" he shouted, louder this time. "Savannah, answer me!" he pleaded.

Then a cough. Her cry followed. Chase's body gave out, forehead dropping to the back seat vinyl, torso in the back, legs in the front, breath shaking as the adrenaline drained from him and her cry filled the car.

Outside, horns blared. The Pilot sat sideways across two lanes, front end destroyed, smoke curling from the hood. Someone yelled, running toward them. Chase's door creaked open as he pushed himself upright, dragging himself back into the seat.

"Hey! You all right, man? You got kids in there?" a voice shouted.

"We're okay," Chase said reflexively, trying to convince himself more than the bystander. "We're fine"—more wish than fact.

Sirens rose, faint at first, then near, then deafening.

Call Tara. The thought landed hard and practical, the first clear directive to cut through the static of shock. He scanned the floorboard until he spotted his phone near the pedals, face up, the Faceoff screen still open, the bet confirmation bright and obscene.

He reached for it, fingers trembling, but before he could grab it, a police officer appeared beside the open door.

"Sir, can you stand?"

Taken aback, Chase flinched then nodded. The officer slipped an arm under his shoulder, steadying him as he stumbled onto the pavement.

As the officer glanced back into the car, his eyes caught on the phone still glowing in the footwell. The look lingered—curious, then assessing, then something colder. Chase followed the gaze and felt his stomach drop. The screen was still lit, his fingerprints smudged across it, the truth of what he'd been doing seconds before the crash shining there in plain view.

He wanted to explain—to say it wasn't what it looked like, that it was numbers, not gambling; logic, not risk—but he couldn't bring himself to speak.

The ambulance arrived next, paramedics swarming. One approached him, voice firm but kind. "Sir, did you hit your head?"

"No, only my wrist," Chase said. "Please check the girls."

"We will," the medic said. "Let me look at that wr—"

"I'm fine," he repeated, smaller this time. "We're fine. Everyone's fine."

The officer from earlier had retrieved his phone from the car and pressed it into his palm. He called Tara. The conversation was brief, just enough to say they'd been in an accident, that they were headed to the hospital. Her voice broke, then the line went quiet.

The girls were lifted out one at a time, trained hands bracing their heads. One of the paramedics glanced at the wreckage and shook his head. "You're lucky," he said. "Those seats saved them."

Lucky. The word stung.

Down the road, Chase saw the Kia Telluride he'd hit—its rear bumper crushed, taillights hanging loose. A woman stood on the shoulder with two kids of her own, one holding her hand, the other clinging to her leg. Another officer took her statement. She looked shaken but stable.

He felt sick at what he'd done. Guilt hit hard, forcing his eyes away. In the other direction, his stomach knotted as he watched them carry Cece and Savannah toward the flashing lights.

Once inside the ambulance, everything vibrated—the gurney, the glass, even the space in between siren bursts. Savannah sat beside Chase on the bench, buckled under a thin blanket, still sniffling. Cece sat on his other side, eyes fixed on the ceiling lights like they were cartoons.

"Daddy?" Cece whispered. "Are we still going to the party?"

He smiled weakly and brushed the hair from her forehead.

Out the rear window, he watched as the ambulance threaded through traffic. The siren carved space between cars, DC blurring past in streaks of light. He'd watched this scene with the girls a hundred times before—sirens racing past, guessing where they were headed. Now they were inside it, and he'd put them there.

He stared down at his hands, trembling despite himself—the cracked watch, and beneath it all was an ache that had nothing to do with the crash.

Minutes later, they climbed out and were directed through a double set of sliding doors into the emergency department. The hospital was noise and fluorescence—orders called across corridors, wheels squeaking, monitors chirping unevenly. A nurse guided them to a curtained bay and asked Chase to sit on a gurney pressed against a plain white wall. The girls were ushered into an adjoining exam room. The whole process felt mechanical: clipboards, questions, vitals, signatures. Another family to check, clear, and move along.

Cece complained her shoulder hurt where the seatbelt caught her. Savannah winced as a nurse pressed on her collarbone. "Bruises only," the nurse said. "Car seats did their job."

Thank God for that.

Chase leaned his pounding head back as a nurse secured a splint around his wrist, her movements brisk and impersonal. He could still hear the crunch of metal, the split-second between distraction and disaster. The image looped, mercilessly.

A doctor appeared, a thin man with the neutral calm of someone who'd seen every kind of wreck. "You took a good jolt," he said. "Any head pain?"

"Just a nasty headache," Chase said. "I've had them for months. It's not new."

"Still," the doctor replied, jotting notes. "Better safe than sorry. Given the headache history, we'll do an MRI rather than a CT to rule out concussion." The doctor scribbled something on his clipboard, already moving on to the next chart. To him, Chase was another file number in a long shift.

Chase nodded, matching the doctor's indifference, barely listening. His mind was already drafting the version he'd tell Tara: an unfortunate collision, airbags deploying as intended, everyone fine. No reason to panic. He'd sound remorseful but contained.

The curtain drew back.

She stood there in her workout clothes, hair half-pulled into a bun that hadn't survived the rush. For a second, she just looked at him. No expression. Absorbing the scene.

"What happened, Chase?" she asked accusingly, drawing out her vowels, teeth clenched.

He straightened. "We're fine," he said quickly. "I'll get the car replaced. We've got plenty saved."

Her eyes snapped. "You think I care about the fucking car right now?"

A nurse looked over from the desk.

Chase lowered his voice. "It's not what you think. I only looked down for a second—"

She rounded on him. "Don't you dare minimize this. You looked down? That's what you're going with?"

"I was checking something. I—"

"What?" Her voice rose again. "A game? A score? Another one of your bets?"

"Tara, stop—"

"No," she erupted, fury spilling over. "You stop." She pointed at his wrist. "Look at you. You could've killed them, Chase. You don't even get that, do you?"

He swallowed hard. "It was one second."

"A second? You almost killed your kids in a second."

He opened his mouth to argue, but nothing came.

She shook her head. "You're addicted to betting."

He stared at her. "Addicted?" A short, incredulous laugh escaped him. "Come on, Tara, that's not—"

"You are," she said, voice low but shaking. "You jeopardized your daughters' lives, and now you're trying to rationalize it. That's addiction, Chase. You think because it's some foolproof system that it's different.

That the profit makes it all okay. But it's the same disease. You can't stop."

He looked down, unable to meet her eyes.

"I promised myself I'd never live like this again," she said, voice quieting. "You know how much my dad hurt me. I watched him drink himself into excuses. He said it was under control. I wanted to believe him, until I ended up right here in a hospital waiting room, wondering why I ever tried. I swore I'd never let another addict put me back here. And you just did."

Chase recoiled as though she'd hit him, the word *addict* landing like a punch he hadn't seen coming. "Tara, I'm not him...," but his voice broke.

She exhaled, the anger thinning to exhaustion. "I can't do this right now. I need to get the girls home."

The nurse returned with paperwork. "They're both cleared," she said, cautiously.

Tara nodded. "Thank you."

She gathered Cece and Savannah from the adjoining room. Cece was holding her Lego keychain. "Are you coming, Daddy?"

He forced a smile. "They want to do one more check on me, okay? I'll be home soon."

Tara adjusted Savannah's blanket, jaw tight. She didn't look back. As they passed the nurse's station, Cece turned once, confused about what was happening.

He watched them disappear down the hall, helpless ache spreading as their footsteps faded.

A technician appeared in the doorway. "Mr. Dupree? We're ready for your scan."

He nodded, still watching the corner where they'd turned. "Yeah," he said. "Okay."

They walked to the elevator and rode to a floor humming with vents. The air cooled as they approached the imaging ward, home to towering MRI machines.

In the prep room, he removed his shoes and unbuckled his belt—the metal buckle clinking loud as it hit the floor, echoing to no one but Chase.

He stripped down, traded fabric for paper—the kind of gown that never quite closes, no matter how you tie it. He set the fractured watch and his wedding ring in a small plastic tray—tokens of the worlds he'd thought he could balance, now proof that he couldn't.

The tech escorted him from the changing room to the foot of the cylindrical tube, the air frigid and tingling with invisible energy.

"You can lie back now," the tech said gently, handing him a pair of earplugs before fitting the padded cradle around his head. A firm click followed, locking him in. In an instant, he was pinned—body still, head fixed, nowhere to look but up.

The machine loomed above, a pale tunnel demanding stillness. He closed his eyes as the bed began to slide inside.

The ceiling disappeared, the enclosure swallowing him whole, walls pressing so close he could feel his own breath bounce back against his cheeks, hot and shallow. The sound grew rhythmic, mechanical—*thunk, thunk, thunk.*

He stared upward, nowhere else to look, motionless.

For the first time in months, his mind wasn't calculating, wasn't running odds or edges. Just silence and the hum of consequence.

He thought of the broken watch, of Tara's raw emotion, of Cece's question in the hallway. "Are you coming, Daddy?"

How had it come to this?

The machine droned on. Time, once stopped at 1:54, moved again without him.

36

PEACE

AS THEY PULLED FROM THE HOSPITAL CURB, the Uber driver said carefully, "Rough day?"

Chase responded curtly, ending the conversation before it began. The streetlights illuminated the car's cabin in intervals while the news rumbled low. A weatherman delivered the forecast, his baritone composure giving way to the giddy thrill of a storm finally worth naming.

"Tropical Storm Kendra continues to intensify off the Carolina coast. Models now bring it near the DMV within forty-eight hours. Expect sustained winds of forty to sixty miles an hour, heavier gusts east of I-95, and three to five inches of rain possible in the District."

Chase rubbed at the hospital wristband cinched around his arm, a fastened reminder of his carelessness. His splinted wrist sat awkwardly in his lap. Monuments to grandeur flashed by—the White House, the Washington Monument, the National Archives, the U.S. Capitol. Chase's day felt microscopic, unimportant against the backdrop of a nation's accomplishments.

When the car turned into his apartment's semicircle drive, he looked up at their third-floor windows. The lights were on, the television throwing color across the ceiling. If the girls were still up, Sesame Street was likely announcing the letter of the day. From the sidewalk, it almost looked like a normal Sunday night.

He opened the door with his good hand and sat with one foot on the curb, the other still in the car. He considered staying there long enough to pretend this was the hard part. But the truth waited upstairs, and pretending had already cost enough.

The elevator rose at its usual pace, unaware its lone passenger privately wished it would slow. Inside the apartment, toys were still scattered across the rug, cereal bowls still stacked in the sink, half-folded laundry still claiming the couch. Everything was exactly as it had been left that morning. Nothing had changed, but everything had.

Tara stepped out of the girls' room with a half-zipped duffel slung over her shoulder, the girls' clothes pushing at the seams. She froze when she saw him by the door, then kept moving—startled, not surprised.

"I didn't hear you come in," she said.

"I just got back." He lifted the splinted wrist slightly, feeling foolish for how unnecessary the gesture was.

She nodded once. "How's it feel?"

"A bad sprain, they think. Lucky it wasn't worse." Funny, the man who'd spent a year engineering his life to outrun luck was now clinging to it.

"Good," she said, though it didn't sound like praise. She set the bag on the kitchen island and began folding a small T-shirt, pressing it flat against the counter before placing it on top of the pile.

"My mom's already on the road," she said finally, still looking down at the clothes. "Left Indy this afternoon. She'll stop overnight and be here tomorrow morning."

He frowned. Only then did the duffel click into focus, his mind a step behind his eyes. "Why?" he asked, fearing he already knew the answer.

"Because I'm taking the girls home for a while."

It landed like a one-two combo: she was taking the girls, and *home* apparently wasn't here anymore. "You're serious?"

"I am." She refolded the shirt even though it didn't need it. "The girls need quiet, and I need space."

Chase rubbed at the hospital wristband still digging into his good wrist. "Is that really necessary?"

Her eyes met his. There wasn't anger anymore, only an exhausted kind of certainty. "It is for me." She hesitated, deciding how much needed to be explained. "We don't have a car, so my mom's bringing the Outback. Stacey lent her car seats. It's been handled."

He stared at the duffel, unsure if he was too tired to fight or simply knew she was right.

She took a breath. "It's what's best right now."

He wanted to say something, but the sentences tangled, too knotted to escape.

Tara zipped the bag. "Try to get some rest, Chase."

He nodded. "Okay."

"I'll finish packing tonight. If we leave mid-morning, we'll be well ahead of the storm."

* * *

Chase woke before dawn. Sleep had come in fragments—phantom sirens and headlights flashing behind his eyelids. By five, he gave up and went to the living room, flipping on the TV. The news had surrendered entirely to weather.

"Hurricane Kendra continues moving north-northeast...Outer bands now impacting the Carolinas. Landfall expected late tonight near Wilmington."

He watched until the looping radar became a kind of hypnosis—green, yellow, and red bands swirling over towns he'd never been to.

When a commercial broke the trance, he walked to the kitchen, cracking and whisking three eggs in a bowl. It wasn't breakfast he wanted, more something to do.

He whisked until the yolks blended into a single new color. By afternoon, the apartment would be half empty, the strengthening winds his only company. Tara hadn't shouted, hadn't begged. She'd just made plans and followed through. Somehow, that was worse.

As the eggs cooked in the pan, he watched them turn from liquid to something firm, the obvious coming to him as he stirred. He'd be useless at work today.

He wiped his hands on a dish towel, picked up his phone, and realized he hadn't placed a single bet since the crash. That wouldn't be changing now. He opened a new message instead and tapped out a text to his boss.

> **CHASE:** Hey Emily, everyone's okay, but I was in a car accident with the girls yesterday. Going to take the day off to deal with insurance and a few follow-ups.

The response came in less than a minute.

> **EMILY:** Oh no, Chase. I'm so sorry. Glad to hear you and the girls are alright. Please take whatever time you need. Don't think about work today.

> **CHASE:** Thanks, really appreciate it.

The empathy, however formulaic, felt warmer than anything that had waited for him last night. What Tara said had been fair—maybe deserved—but kindness hadn't made the cut.

He turned back to the pan and scraped the eggs once more, watching the steam rise and vaporize.

By late morning, Kat had arrived. Tara had taken the girls down to meet her when she pulled up, helped her park in the building's garage, then gone to a late breakfast down the street.

Chase heard the voices first, gauging whether it was laughter or tears—sometimes indistinguishable—before the front door burst open and the girls bounded in. "Daddy!" they yelled in unison.

He pushed his chair back from the kitchen table, where he'd been wrestling with the first of what would be many insurance forms.

"Hey, girls," he said, forcing a smile. "Fun time with Kitten?" The name had started as a joke—Chase making a play on Kat's name when she was deciding what her first grandchild should call her—but it stuck.

Cece held up a package of crayons and Savannah pointed proudly to her chocolate milk mustache. Their energy poured through the apartment like sunlight into a room he hadn't realized had gone dim.

Kat came in behind them, oversized travel mug dwarfing her already small frame. Usually, she'd greet him with a quip—ask if he'd finished the book she'd loaned, tease him about still owing her one— but today she only nodded, polite and a little sad, unsure how to bridge the space between them.

"Hi, honey," she said softly, "sorry to hear about your wrist."

"Thanks," he managed. "Good to see you."

She broke eye contact almost immediately, following the girls toward their room. "Alright, kiddos," she called. "Let's grab those bags!"

Tara came in last, to-go cup in hand, hair pulled back, wearing that calm efficiency that came from too little sleep and too much resolve.

The apartment filled with the overlapping chatter of three generations in a hurry. Chase stood near the table, feeling like furniture in his own life.

Bags gathered, Tara crouched to zip Cece's backpack and tie Savannah's shoe. "Say bye to Daddy."

Cece wrapped her arms around his waist. "Bye, Daddy. Love you!"

He knelt, hugged her tight, and kissed the side of her head. "Be good for Kitten and Mommy, okay?"

After a brief show of resistance, Savannah followed her sister's lead, tumbling backward into his arms. "Bye, Daddy," she said then spun to plant an exaggerated kiss on his cheek, laughing as she pulled away. Their scent—strawberry shampoo, syrup, crayon wax—lingered on his shirt.

Kat appeared by the door, purse strap across her chest—the steady authority of a woman who managed family and logistics without breaking stride. "We should get going if we want to hit Indy before bedtime," she said, ushering the girls into the hallway and giving her daughter and son-in-law the moment they needed.

For the first time all morning, Tara met his eyes. A thin mist glazed them before she spoke.

"You know I still love you," she said, "but you can't have us and the betting, Chase. This family deserves all of you. You have to decide which one you want."

He nodded once. "I know."

She studied him a moment longer then leaned in and kissed his cheek. It wasn't goodbye, not yet, but it carried the weight of one.

"Will you have them FaceTime each night?" he asked.

She nodded as she turned. "Of course."

The door closed behind her with what felt like finality.

For a moment, there was only the hum of the fridge. Then, from the direction of the elevator bay, Cece's voice carried back through the door—small, puzzled, heartbreakingly clear.

"Why isn't Daddy coming?"

The question hit as unexpectedly as a second crash. It didn't matter that she hadn't meant it that way; truth rarely cares about intent.

* * *

By dusk the next day, Kendra had found her full voice. Wind prowled between Navy Yard's soaring apartments. Rain had been at it for hours, storm drains overwhelmed, the streets turned to rapids.

Chase had taken Tuesday off too, spending most of it horizontal on the couch. His periphery registered the streetlights blinking to life out the window. He poured a second glass of bourbon from the bar cart he and Tara rarely touched anymore. There was no pleasure in the taste. The caramel-brown liquid promised escape that didn't come. He drank anyway. This, at least, he could measure. Three fingers. Controlled pour. Slow burn.

He'd picked up his phone more than once—habit, not desire—thumb hovering over the apps that used to own him. The betting icons were like childhood friends he no longer trusted. He still hadn't opened them since the crash.

The apartment suddenly felt stifling. He pushed himself off the couch, crossed the living room, and opened the door to the patio. The storm had felt like a movie through the glass of the perfectly sealed apartment. Now, it felt real. Wind swirled around his ankles. A metal sign stubbornly clanged against its pole. Even the comfortable strip of shelter he'd dubbed his "outside room" wasn't fully immune to the onslaught. Mist dampened his face. Beyond the overhang, the intensity was far greater, rain shearing past in slanted sheets.

He set the bourbon on the small wicker table, turned on the portable speaker, and paired it to his phone, letting Spotify choose the score.

Minutes passed—music mixing with nature's own soundtrack—until a familiar guitar line cut through the wind. Then the vocals, unmistakably O.A.R., the words clean, unadorned, pleading. The song was "Peace." He hadn't heard it in years, but he recognized it instantly.

The lyrics spoke of a man staring at the wreckage of a relationship, ready to call off the fight, trying to salvage what had grown fragile before it shattered altogether. He longed to rewind the clock, to show he could still be the man she had once adored. Before more precious time slipped away, he wanted peace.

The message settled in a place the bourbon couldn't reach. His mind replayed the uncertain seconds before Savannah coughed, Tara's fury in the hospital, her lips against his cheek, Cece's question echoing down the hall.

The chorus swelled. His eyes burned. Tears fell. A sob climbed into his throat. He made no effort to stop any of it.

Out on the street, a gust shoved the lights into a wild sway—and then abruptly everything stopped. Rain stilled. Wind withdrew. The city inhaled and held it. A grocery receipt kited across the road, slow and weightless, spinning once before dissolving in a puddle.

He knew what it was. The eye.

The air cooled by half a degree, or maybe he was imagining it. Across the street, the apartment building looked like an oversized dollhouse, each window home to a different domestic scene. Somewhere down the block a siren wound down as if it too, had to admit defeat. For the first time since the crash, the world had stopped shouting.

His phone buzzed in his lap. The lock screen read: "Washington Hospital: New message in patient portal."

He tapped through the email, pressed the hyperlink, confirmed his name and date of birth. The portal loaded in that clinical font that always looked like it knew something he didn't.

Radiology report. He scrolled to Findings, the words resolving into half-meanings as they formed:

"Well-circumscribed ovoid T2 FLAIR hyperintense lesion is present in the right dorsal medial thalamus measuring approximately 9 x 9 x 8 mm."

He scrolled.

"Differential considerations included but not limited to: Infectious / inflammatory process, demyelination, low-grade glioma, or hamartoma."

His vision narrowed to a pinpoint. Panic ripped through him before thought could catch it. Every cell screamed to run. His body tried to obey, muscles tightening, blood rushing, but there was nowhere to go. The threat was inside him.

He typed "glioma" into Google. The first result didn't bother with bedside manner. Tumor. Cancer. The words repeated down the page like paid ads.

What Tara said returned, the decision suddenly uncomplicated. "You have to decide which one you want."

He wanted his family.

He wanted Tara.

He wanted peace.

Below, the loose street sign continued its clanging. The storm wasn't done.

37

NOTHING LEFT TO REFRESH

THE ZOOM WAITING ROOM was as clinical as a doctor's office. "Please wait for the host to start this meeting." Below it, a white wheel kept turning, his own fortune spinning, waiting to land on its ordained mark.

Chase killed the time staring out the window at Kendra's aftermath. It had been only thirty-six hours since the email on the patio, since the storm had temporarily rearranged the neighborhood—branches snapped and scattered, curbs lined with debris, puddles shaped like continents. A stop sign a block away leaned precariously. The Anacostia ran high and brown. Over it all stretched a sky too blue to believe, as if it had nothing to do with any of it.

He'd taken the whole week off. The out-of-office reply was vague enough to pass corporate scrutiny—"family travel," and "limited access"—because what he'd really been doing was falling apart in long, private stretches. He hadn't told Tara about the MRI result that dropped into his portal during the storm. If she'd been home, she would have seen the swollen eyes, the way he wandered from room to room holding his head like he was keeping it attached. In Indiana, they were buffered by distance and routine: cousins, a spare bedroom, the comfort of being elsewhere. He hadn't wanted to send his panic across state lines.

A soft chime. The waiting room dissolved, and a man's face appeared: mid-forties, head shaved, eyes dark and dependable. The name under the window read, "Amin Ghalazi, MD."

"Mr. Dupree? Can you hear me?"

"I can," Chase responded.

"Good. I'm Dr. Ghalazi. I know the report you received must have been unnerving, since it arrived before we had a chance to talk." The doctor's tone was warm. "Why don't we start with what we're actually looking at?"

He shared his screen. The MRI images filled the window—grayscale geography, white matter and gray matter like layered sediment. The small cursor traced a spot Chase had come to know.

"This area here," Ghalazi said. "Small, well-circumscribed lesion. It doesn't enhance with contrast. There's no surrounding edema. No mass effect."

Chase's chest tightened at the word lesion.

"Those are all *good* signs," the doctor added, as if he could see the mental trapdoor opening. "In plain English, it's not behaving like something aggressive. It could be a benign developmental difference, something you were born with that we're only seeing because imaging is so sensitive now. It could be a small demyelinating focus, essentially a tiny scar from a minor event we may never identify."

Chase swallowed. "But it's…there."

"It is," Ghalazi said, unflinching. "And I don't want to minimize how that feels. But from a radiologic standpoint, the pattern is reassuring."

"What are the odds it's a tumor?" Odds were how he had survived a year of stress; odds were how he'd taught himself to feel safe.

The doctor gave a small exhale that registered as both empathy and boundary. "Medicine doesn't really deal in odds the way you're used to. We talk about likelihoods, ensembles of signs that lean one way or another." He gestured with the cursor once more. "In your case, the pattern looks benign."

"So you're saying the odds are low," Chase said, needing it translated into the only language his nerves would let him hear.

"I'm saying it's not the kind of thing that keeps me up at night," Ghalazi said with a faint smile. "But I know it will probably keep you up for a while."

Chase nodded then shook his head, as if both were true. He stared at the luminous dot on the screen and felt the clenching in his chest again. For days he'd been trapped inside future reels: Cece in a too-big soccer jersey holding a plastic trophy, Savannah squinting at a stage light while someone called her name, tassels swinging at a graduation. Two girls in white dresses, aisle awaiting, hands threaded through his arm. Tara with silver at her temples on some fancy tour bus winding up an Italian hill, both of them laughing at an audio guide. The possibility of what could be, and that he might not be a part of it, gutted him every time.

"Is this why I've had headaches?" he asked, voice thinner now. "Could this…spot be causing them?"

"No," Ghalazi said, decisive, "this was an incidental finding. Given its location and behavior, I'm confident it has nothing to do with your headaches."

"Then why—"

"The pattern you've described—the timing, the triggers, the way they respond to posture—sounds cervicogenic. Neck-origin headaches. The MRI doesn't show anything that would suggest a headache generator in the brain itself."

Chase pressed his tongue to his molars. Cervicogenic. He'd heard the word enough times for it to be annoying. It meant the pain had a source you could point to and still not solve. "So…not cancer," he said. He hated how childlike it sounded and said it anyway.

"If it were definitively something malignant, I would tell you," Ghalazi said. "I would. That's not what we're seeing right now."

"What happens next?"

"We repeat the MRI in six months to confirm stability," the doctor said. "That's standard. I have low suspicion we'll see any changes in the comparison. In the meantime, if anything changes on your end—new neurological signs, or anything that feels off—call me. We can move it up."

Six months. To Ghalazi, it was protocol; to Chase it was purgatory. How was he supposed to wait half a year without knowing if the thing in his head was sitting still or quietly multiplying?

"You'll get a summary of our discussion through the portal," Ghalazi said. "And Chase, I know this feels scary. Try to live your life. Don't let this take more than it has to."

"Okay," Chase said, staving off yet another episode of tears, unsure if they were tied to fear, relief, or both. "Can I ask one more question? If you had to put it in numbers—"

"I understand why you want it that way," Ghalazi said, not unkindly. "Numbers feel like control. What I can tell you is that everything about this points away from the thing you're most afraid of."

Chase stared at the tiny white point again, a bright, disobedient star. From the other room, he heard clothes tumbling in the dryer.

"Okay," he said again. "Thank you."

"Of course." Ghalazi's face softened a degree. "And if you find yourself spiraling, that's normal. There's no need to reread the report. Step away from the search bar. Spend time with your family. Focus on healing your neck and addressing the headaches. We'll see you in six months, and I expect we'll be talking about the same small, boring thing."

"Small and boring," Chase said. "I can live with that."

"That's the idea," the doctor said. "Take care of yourself."

The doctor's face disappeared. The shared images collapsed into the Zoom interface then into a black rectangle reflecting only his ghostly face. He didn't move for a long beat. The apartment made its ordinary noises. Like a reflex he couldn't stop, he unlocked his phone and opened the portal anyway.

The words were the same as the first time. They always were, but they felt different when spoken by a professional. "Small, well-circumscribed lesion. Non-enhancing. No surrounding edema. No mass effect." He scrolled past "differential considerations," past the notes that sounded like guesses to anyone not trained to hear them as fences, grateful for Dr. Ghalazi's calming demeanor.

He closed the app, set the phone down, and pushed it away with two fingers as if it were hot.

The ruined Seamaster sat on the windowsill. He turned it over—1:54, still frozen. He could get the crystal replaced. He could pretend time hadn't stopped. Or he could leave it as the most honest thing he owned. He decided to fix it. A new lease on life—for the watch and for Chase.

He turned back to his laptop, opened his calendar, clicked through to April. Six months away. Low suspicion of anything other than small and boring. He set a reminder to schedule the next MRI, a task that doubled as a breadcrumb to a future that suddenly existed again.

* * *

By midafternoon, the apartment felt too small for the size of his thoughts. Chase slipped on a light jacket and stepped outside. He headed toward Capitol Hill, turning onto Duddington, his favorite street in the city. The ginkgo trees arched overhead, flaring gold, the leaves so bright they looked backlit. They floated down like paper bullion, littering the sidewalks in a carpet of sunlight. It felt like walking the road to El Dorado—mythic, absurdly bright, a little too beautiful for belief.

His best ideas always came while he was walking. Something about motion tricked the noise in his head into pattern. Halfway down Duddington, he stopped beneath branches stretched into a cathedral nave.

Over the years, residents had added a dozen or so benches along the one-way street, and Chase accepted the standing invitation to sit. He watched a single leaf spiral down, unhurried, and for the first time since Sunday morning, his thoughts turned to odds.

It wasn't a craving so much as a revelation. He knew his arbitrage days were over, yet ending without ceremony after everything it had taken from him felt wrong. For all his talk of logic, he was like every other bettor, superstition hardwired deep inside him. Despite knowing how ridiculous it sounded, beneath the math, there was always that ancient belief that fortune noticed you.

If there were gods of chance, and he'd started to think there must be, they deserved a farewell offering. His own story deserved an ending more deliberate than a totaled car and splinted wrist.

One last bet, he decided. Absurd by design. A test disguised as tribute.

He'd face down one of his most steadfast superstitions: avoiding the number six. He couldn't trace its origin—something about the witching hour, demonic forces, and bad omens—but he'd treated the number as a plague for years. Now he'd lean into it, stack it, tempt it. Six after six after six. If the gods had a sense of humor, they'd take it as an offering. And if the bet hit, he'd take it as permission to walk away.

The crooked calculus hardened into resolve. He opened his phone, the familiar icons beckoning. He chose the most familiar of all—Faceoff. His eyes scanned the home page, searching for something close to a coin flip. No need to overthink it. And there it was: LA Kings (+110) vs. San Jose Sharks. A West Coast game, too late to watch, irrelevant to anything except its own outcome. Perfect.

He entered $666.66 on the Kings moneyline and tapped. Bet placed. No celestial sign followed, just the golden leaves twirling around him.

The doctor had said small and boring. This was neither.

That night, Chase lay in bed with the phone propped against his leg. The apartment was quiet in the way buildings get after everyone else has gone to sleep. He tracked the game on his ESPN app, a single line crisscrossing a virtual rink through the first two periods, like a video game he wasn't playing.

The Kings were down 2-1 as the final intermission got underway. He looked at the bet slip—$666.66 wagered to profit $733.33—one last time before he tossed the phone to the empty side of the mattress and rolled onto his side. "Idiot," he muttered. "Superstitious idiot."

Sleep came unevenly. In the fog of it, he dreamed of a scoreboard he couldn't decipher, gold leaves spinning, and the watch on the sill ticking again.

When he woke, he sat up slowly, the splint on his wrist pulling tight, and reached for the phone with the careful dread of a college student checking a final exam score.

He opened ESPN. NHL scores. One tap away from knowing.

Ducks 4, Kings 2.

Shit.

The pit formed instantly. So that was it. The gods had passed their judgment. No sign, no symmetry, no reason to feel anything but foolish for believing in one.

He exhaled, long and hollow. *So what now?* Did he still quit without the sign he'd asked for? Or did the absence of one mean something else entirely?

He frowned. *Ducks?* Wait. The Kings weren't even playing the Ducks.

The screen showed "WED" at the top—two nights old. He tapped again, found the right date, and waited for the page to refresh.

Kings 3, Sharks 2 (OT).

"All hail the Kings!" he shouted to an empty room, fist-pumping in elation. "Unbelievable!"

The sign had come after all.

He clicked on the game recap and saw the headline beneath the scoreline: "Game-winning goal—Riley Jones (OT, 3:42)."

No way. Riley Jones. A fellow Miami University RedHawk.

A giddy laugh escaped before he could stop it, his head falling back against the headboard, the phone resting on his chest. He didn't believe in fate. Not really. But this felt too deliberate to dismiss as coincidence. Some convergence of math and mercy that had chosen to land exactly where he needed it.

"Thank you," he said quietly, unsure whether it was meant for the gods of chance, the hockey gods, or the indifferent universe itself.

He swung his legs out of bed and walked to the patio door, barefoot, wearing only soccer shorts. The forty-five-degree air bit at his bare chest, a cold shock that seized his breath like the first second under an icy shower. He exhaled steam.

A deal was a deal.

He opened his phone, thumb hovering over the first app, Faceoff. Withdraw funds. Confirm. Balance: $0. The first zero he'd seen since the start. A full circle drawn in digits.

One book followed another, the same loop repeating. Withdrawal. Confirm. Delete. Each felt like a small act of amputation. His fingers kept trying to move in old patterns, muscle memory searching for vanished icons. He'd read once that recovery's hardest part wasn't giving up the substance but the ritual—the motion itself.

He imagined a long-time drinker pouring out good whiskey, watching the burnished gold swirl down the drain—the body rebelling even as the mind agreed. That was what this was—an unlearning of pleasure, habit, necessity.

When the last app was gone, the screen looked naked—empty rows where his vices had lived, the remaining icons rearranged in their absence. His home screen was distinctly and newly foreign.

PickTracker remained. He opened it one last time, pulling his final October number, **$5,706.**

He copied it to his running Note as he realized this would be the last entry. A number caught his eye. His very first month, back in September '25, he'd logged $5,707. A single dollar apart, symmetry bookending the entire run.

Whether it was the strangeness or the cold, something finally caught up—a full-body shiver overtaking him. He retreated inside, grabbed a hoodie from the bedroom, and pulled it on, the cotton still holding a trace of yesterday's warmth.

At the kitchen table, he reopened the Note that had documented his entire run. One year and change, reduced to fifteen rows, including the total that told the whole story.

SEPTEMBER '25: $5,707

OCTOBER '25: $11,321

NOVEMBER '25: $16,243

DECEMBER '25: $21,353

JANUARY '26:	$41,237
FEBRUARY '26:	$28,942
MARCH '26:	$33,714
APRIL '26:	$24,622
MAY '26:	$19,196
JUNE '26:	$16,940
JULY '26:	$7,411
AUGUST '26:	$14,322
SEPTEMBER '26:	$19,952
OCTOBER '26:	$5,706
TOTAL PROFIT:	**$266,666**

Yet another cosmic joke—the sixes staring back, no longer unlucky, but marking the most profitable stretch of his life.

He remembered the dopamine, the panic, the nights of perfect arbs and fraught one-sided near-debacles. It was all here. The whole story in numbers.

And they showed he'd accomplished exactly what he'd set out to do. After setting aside taxes, he'd carved it all up with intention. $20,000 to family savings. $20,000 to the girls' college fund. $20,000 to his "fundowment," the account that would now spin off nearly $1,000 a year forever. Another $40,000 to his "immediate fun" account. $15,000 for Italy. $15,000 for Disney. $10,000 for the tropical getaway. $10,000 for ski week. $7,500 for the birthday weekends. Enough to cover three years of the boat membership. Each plan accounted for, every dream fully funded, with over $20,000 still untouched, even after Milan and the massages.

Every bucket filled. Every promise, somehow, kept. Now he had to spend it the way he'd meant to, with his family.

He opened Messages and found Tara's name.

CHASE: The apps are gone. All of them.

CHASE: I'm done. I'm sorry.

CHASE: I have a lot to tell you. Please come home.

He hit send, then closed his eyes. For the first time in months, there was nothing left to refresh.

38

CONTAINMENT

THE SUV EASED TO THE CURB outside Faceoff's headquarters in the Flatiron district, the city caught between night and morning. Her driver's breakfast, a Tompkins Square everything bagel, perfumed the cabin, warm salt, dough, and cream cheese filling the car. He was a creature of habit, loyal to the same bagel stop every morning. Ainsley envied him for that, the permission to treat himself to something small, something ordinary.

Outside, New York was beginning to stir. Delivery trucks idled at red lights, the first rush of caffeine seekers clustering on corners. The street was nearly empty except for the black sedan that had arrived ten minutes earlier, part of her permanent security escort.

Will, her private security lead, stepped out of the already-waiting vehicle first—tall, broad-shouldered, a college linebacker turned Marine turned private contractor. He scanned the street with the reflex of someone who still measured distance in threat vectors, not feet. When he reached her door, he opened it with one hand and stayed there, back straight, eyes sweeping the block again. Only after he gave a small nod and an "All clear, ma'am," the Marine cadence still in his voice, did she follow—the scent of the bagel trailing after her, tempting in its simplicity.

Inside the glass vestibule, the new state-of-the-art metal detectors were a clear upgrade from the old security desk that had once felt more hotel than headquarters. Two guards stood at either side of the archway, earpieces in place.

After Vegas, Faceoff had expanded her personal detail, assigning a rotating team to shadow her day and night. The building itself had followed suit, investing in a new security contractor, upgraded scanners, and reinforced access points that benefited every tenant. Together, the measures had transformed One Madison Avenue from a workspace into a fortress with secure Wi-Fi.

She removed nothing as she passed through—no bag checks, no pauses. Her face was her credential now, her retinas the key. The scanner lit green. She walked past, coat falling cleanly at her sides. The elevator waited empty, the ride starting smooth.

Halfway up, the car jolted faintly—normal, she told herself—but her fingers still tightened on the rail. Elevators, crowds, confined rooms, the list of places she trusted had shortened.

It had been three months since the incident, and her world still operated as though the shooter might be hiding behind every door. No one said the word anymore, but its absence hung like a stubborn residue. Her security team called it a "temporary escalation of posture". She called it the new normal. The harder part wasn't even the security—it was the sympathy. Strangers still sent notes, some heartfelt, some opportunistic. In her industry, even survival could be commodified.

The executive gym sat one level below her office, its new biometric lock another controlled variable in an uncontrolled world. Her thumbprint released the latch with a soft click. The lights hummed awake, instantly brightening racks of dumbbells and spotless mirrors. The air was chilled enough to keep sweat from feeling human.

She stripped off her jacket, pulled her hair into a knot, and climbed onto the nearest Peloton. She used to start her days with a run in Central Park—five miles before sunrise, her morning rite of solitude—but her security team had *suggested* indoor workouts were "preferable." The word had carried all the force of an order.

The bike's screen at least greeted her by name—another algorithm pretending intimacy. She started the ride at level fifty resistance, pace steady. Ninety seconds in, she stopped hearing music. The instructor's voice—upbeat, unrelenting—became white noise behind the sound of her breath. She lived by numbers. Power output: 297 watts. Heart rate: 162 BPM.

At minute fifteen, a forty-five-pound plate slammed into the floor behind her, the crash cutting through her headphones, sharp enough to make her jerk. For an instant, her body betrayed her—shoulders locking, pulse spiking to 181.

She exhaled hard. "Jesus," she said to no one, shaking out her arms. The man who'd dropped it hadn't even noticed.

One of her oldest friends from Kellogg had insisted she see a trauma specialist after Vegas. She'd agreed, the same way she agreed to quarterly audits—efficient, data-driven, discreet.

The therapist had called it progress when she'd gone a week without replaying the sound. Ainsley viewed it as compartmentalization. No matter the word, so much for progress.

She reset her pace, pretending the tremor in her calves was fatigue. The body remembered what the mind wanted forgotten. She rode until the clock emptied to zero then swung a leg over and steadied herself, light-headed from effort and too little breakfast.

By seven-thirty, she was in her office. The corner window framed a slice of the skyline, cranes jutting above new construction, the city's eternal appetite for more. Her workspace was immaculate, her schedule color-coded down to the minute. Order had become its own sedative—each cell filled, each minute accounted for, the illusion of predictability restored.

She glanced at the omnipresent ticker on her desktop—AIRB, Airborne Entertainment, Faceoff's parent company. The markets had mostly stabilized after Vegas, but sentiment still hadn't—one senator's subcommittee request, one poorly worded headline, and it could all be in flux again.

At the center of her workspace, a red folder sat at the top of a neatly ordered stack of briefing materials—the unmistakable cue that it mattered. The label read, "CONFIDENTIAL–STRATEGIC OPPORTUNITY ASSESSMENT."

She slit it open with a pen.

Target: LineSniper

Founder/CEO: Aaron Ramsey

Vegas returned as visceral memory. The pride in the applause she'd elicited from a hostile crowd. A flash of red. Shattered glass. Burly arms rushing her offstage.

It wasn't until hours later, in a hotel suite ringed with security, that she realized she'd stopped believing she was untouchable.

She closed the folder then reopened it, as if the act itself could erase the flashback. The brief was thorough—valuation models, liquidity scenarios, sentiment analysis, risk profiles. It read like any acquisition proposal, but she intuited what it didn't say. This wasn't only about synergy. It was containment.

LineSniper had become more than a platform. It was ideology—math cult and populist rebellion combined. Inconceivably, the shooter in Vegas had yet to be identified, but smart money—something Ainsley understood better than most—was on a disgruntled arber.

It didn't matter that LineSniper hadn't pulled the trigger. The culture it bred had made the pull possible.

For weeks, her M&A and finance leads had been building the scaffolding—quiet outreach to Aaron's team, exploratory models, back-channel conversations to test price tolerance. Ainsley had deliberately kept herself out of it until now, though she tracked every conversation, every data pull, careful not to let her team see how much of herself was tied to the outcome. The groundwork was finished; all that remained was the final approach. She was the closer.

She flipped to the next page, the one marked "Recommendation."

"Proceed to acquisition to extract full monetization potential from the platform's behavioral data and to neutralize systemic contagion risk."

She smiled at the phrasing. Her team had started thinking like her.

The rest of the morning passed in the usual regimen—briefings, internal calls, the small theater of corporate leadership. She performed focus flawlessly, each meeting another exercise in posture. By mid-afternoon, she'd forgotten she hadn't eaten. Hunger had become indistinguishable from drive.

At 3:59 p.m., her assistant knocked once and cracked the door. "Aaron Ramsey's ready for you on line two, ma'am."

Ainsley nodded, waited for the door to close, then adjusted the angle of her chair so the skyline framed her peripheral vision. She wanted him to hear confidence even if he couldn't see it.

She pressed the line. "Aaron, I've been looking forward to this conversation for some time. I appreciate you taking the call."

"Of course," he said with that same composure she remembered from Vegas—a shade too casual. "Before we start, I want to say again how sorry I am for what happened in July. There hasn't been a day since that I haven't thought about how many people were endangered in that room."

Ainsley pursed her lips. "I understand," she said evenly. "You're not the only one who's replayed it."

"I'm sure," he said, "but the responsibility was mine."

The line held—that thin, charged quiet between formality and vulnerability.

Ainsley pivoted, her tone recalibrating to business. "My team tells me you've had productive conversations these past few weeks. I thought it was time we spoke directly."

Polite but assertive. She didn't do small talk, and he knew it.

"I've read through the details. Impressive numbers, remarkable growth. You've built something real," she continued.

"Appreciate that," he said. "Though some would call it a liability these days."

"Scale always looks like liability until it's properly managed."

A pause. "And is that what you're calling this? Management?"

"Opportunity," she countered. "The question isn't whether LineSniper matters. You've established beyond any doubt that it does. It's a disrupter in our industry. Now, it's about who's best positioned to shape what it becomes next."

"And you think that's Faceoff?" He sounded genuinely curious.

"I think it's inevitable," she replied. "If we stay competitors, I think you're smart enough to know you remain at the whim of something outside your control. As partners, Faceoff benefits from invaluable data, the industry better manages inefficiency, and you, frankly, are well-rewarded for what you've built."

"Sounds like you've rehearsed that," he joked in sidestep.

"I don't rehearse," she countered, no hint of humor in return. "I prepare."

She could almost hear him smile. "So what's next? How long will this vetting go on before I know Faceoff is serious and not intentionally preventing me from exploring other offers?"

"My board meets Friday," she said. "And I'd like to walk in with clarity."

Urgency was a tool. She'd learned that dragging the calm before tightening the deadline made even confident men misstep.

"That's in four days. I'm not sure we're that advanced yet."

"You're the one who asked about timing. The board won't meet again for another quarter after Friday. Market conditions change. I might have to explore alternatives by then," she said, "but I'd rather not."

He laughed again, genuine this time. "Still direct."

"Still pragmatic."

The air between them tightened, invisible wires pulled taut.

Aaron's tone shifted, inquisitive now. "Tell me something, Ainsley. After Vegas, what makes you so sure you still want to be in this fight?"

She let herself breathe once before answering. "Because I don't lose."

He didn't respond immediately. "Then let's see if we can both win this round," he said finally.

"There'll be a jet waiting at Scottsdale Airport tomorrow morning. Seven sharp, local time. My assistant will coordinate."

"You're sending a jet?"

"I prefer punctuality," she said.

He hesitated before committing. "Alright, I look forward to making this official."

The line clicked dead.

Ainsley sat for a moment, the office drone returning like sound after submersion. She studied her hands, perfectly still on the desk. The tremor stayed buried, a vibration she'd learned to hide even from herself.

She opened the folder again, drew a line through "Recommendation," and wrote, "Proceed immediately."

Outside the window, construction cranes pivoted over a tower rising along Park Avenue. The relentless clang of steel on steel pierced the glass.

She listened, steadying her breath to match it. The city was always evolving. So was she.

She closed the folder, stacked it beneath the next, and reached for her phone. There was still plenty of time to get ahead of tomorrow.

The hammer struck again—once, twice—reminding her the world would keep building, with or without her permission.

She straightened the papers on her desk. For now, control remained hers.

39

THE LONG GAME

FROM THE OVAL WINDOW of the Gulfstream G700, Aaron studied the canyons below—vast, unfinished, unconquered—shadowed distance reminding him that power was mostly a matter of altitude.

He'd flown private before, but never like this. The white-gloved attendant had greeted him by name. His espresso waited, poured to spec, still steaming when he took his seat. Cream leather, stitched with Faceoff emerald, contrasted the dark walnut trim that gleamed with polish. A single orchid in a crystal vase was anchored to the console. The Wi-Fi connected in under a second, the network name a quiet flex: FO-EXEC1.

Opposite him, a woman named Brynn lounged on the leather couch, oversized sunglasses covering half her face. Her dark hair was gathered into a loose twist—a stylist's idea of spontaneous. She wore an outfit engineered for both airport paparazzi and private cabins: a cropped white top beneath a denim jacket, soft leather joggers, and pristine white sneakers.

A soft gloss on her lips caught light each time the jet banked, while she scrolled through Instagram. They'd met there, in fact—her message sliding into his DMs months ago. She had millions of followers. For now, though, her feed was on pause. This trip didn't allow for geotags or stories. It required confidentiality, a word foreign to her. She'd pouted for a day, then signed an NDA, choosing luxury over influence.

Aaron didn't see her as a date. More like company. He kept his eyes trained on her, appreciative in the way a collector studies a well-chosen object, then turned back to the iPad in his lap.

LineSniper's live dashboards glowed back at him, still humming even as the company's future hung in transit thirty thousand feet above the ground.

It felt surreal. Less than a decade since he'd created the platform's first prototype, and now Faceoff wanted to pay a number he'd barely dared to imagine. He toggled to the valuation memo his counsel had prepared. A $175-million headline figure, all cash. It still looked like a typo. If that was where things settled, after payouts and taxes and shareholder equity, his personal cut would hover just above $100 million. Enough to never need another reason to get out of bed.

For an unexpected moment, a flicker of guilt hit like turbulence—sudden, uninvited, passing quickly. He told himself the Vegas stunt had been necessary, no real harm done. The media had subsequently done its work: fear, attention, narrative—all redirecting exactly where he wanted them. Overnight, LineSniper had become both notorious and unstoppable.

He exhaled through his nose, a slow four-count, forcing the thought down. History didn't remember purity; it remembered winners. Carnegie underpaid the men who built his empire. Rockefeller crushed unions. Jobs stole ideas. Musk moved markets with a tweet. Greatness wasn't clean—it was decisive. He wasn't the first man to trade morality for momentum.

Aaron sipped his espresso, its surface trembling faintly with the hum of the twin engines.

"You look stressed," Brynn said. The sound startled him, snapping the silence he'd been floating in.

"Just thinking," he said.

Now she was the one studying him, phone no longer in her hand but on the seat beside her. She'd slipped off her sunglasses, revealing eyes far more captivating at cruising altitude than he remembered on the ground. A small shift in posture, deliberate.

"About the deal?"

Before he could answer, she unbuckled and crossed the aisle with a feline ease. The privacy curtain whispered closed behind her, sealing them off from the attendant's discreet invisibility. When she leaned in, her perfume—expensive, sweetly synthetic—folded into the cabin's filtered air. Whatever guilt he'd felt a minute ago faded away.

Minutes later, Brynn slipped away toward the restroom.

To Aaron, it was another transaction, an exchange where both sides got what they wanted. His first deal of the trip, satisfying in its completeness.

The plane banked northeast, flying to meet the sun. Out the window, contrails scrawled the sky like signatures of people who'd already cashed out.

He envisioned the meeting ahead—the glass, the suits, Ainsley Caldwell herself. He hadn't seen her since that July morning. She'd been dazzling even then: sharp, gracious, and quietly ruthless.

The attendant reappeared to refill his espresso, and Aaron returned to the spreadsheet, reviewing his talking points: user retention, cross-platform integration, the data moat that kept competitors out. The numbers spoke for themselves. All he had to do was stay composed, concede nothing, and let inevitability do its job.

By the time the jet began its descent over New York, his nerves, with Brynn's assist, had reorganized into something useful. He leaned back, closed his eyes for a moment, and rehearsed the headline he wanted to read in next week's Wall Street Journal. "Faceoff Acquires LineSniper in $175 Million All-Cash Deal."

The wheels touched down at Teterboro just past 3 p.m. EST—a whisper rather than a landing. From the first moment, everything ran on script—jet door open, stairs lowered, black SUV idling at the edge of the tarmac.

The attendant handed him his coat, and he was on the move, Brynn trailing a few paces behind, her sunglasses back in place. He thought he recognized someone stepping off the neighboring Gulfstream—a cable-news pundit, maybe, or a hedge-fund partner he'd seen on CNBC—but the moment passed before he could be sure. The driver was opening the door before Aaron reached it, the rhythm unbroken.

He slid into the back seat, checked his watch, and smiled. Exactly on schedule. Punctuality was a language he respected.

The ride into Manhattan was seamless—minimal traffic, no chatter, the skyline sharpening through tinted glass as the car cut south along the Hudson. Brynn scrolled beside him, recording a quick clip of the city's reflection in the window before remembering she couldn't post it.

An hour later, the SUV pulled up to Faceoff's headquarters. A woman in a navy sheath dress and low heels met him at the door—Lydia Cho, head of corporate development. Brynn was whisked away to the Ritz-Carlton NoMad, their temporary home for the remainder of the week.

"Mr. Ramsey," Lydia said, shaking his hand. "Welcome. Please allow me to escort you up to the boardroom for our preliminary conversation."

Aaron nodded.

Inside, Lydia pressed the button for the top floor. "Mark Ingram, our chief legal officer, will join us," she said. "Ainsley's currently tied up on a call. She will join tomorrow's session."

"Of course," Aaron said evenly. He understood perfectly. Her absence was deliberate, the opening move in a game she'd already begun.

As the elevator ascended, he watched the floor numbers climb in intervals—each one a reminder of how frictionless everything had been since touchdown. No waiting, no small talk, no wasted motion.

He'd traveled alone—"fewer mouths, fewer leaks." It was part confidence, part control. This was his company's legacy moment, and he wanted to own it alone. But his general counsel and outside advisors were on standby in the virtual waiting room, ready to join when summoned. He didn't need them for introductions. He trusted no one else to read people the way he could.

Tonight was about posture, setting the stage, and making sure the machine across the table remembered he'd built one of his own.

The meeting had lasted exactly ninety minutes—cordial, calibrated, and vaguely disorienting. It had been a humbling recognition of scale.

Faceoff's operation moved with military efficiency. Every face around the table seemed to know the next slide before it appeared. Every question had already been rehearsed in some other room.

When it ended, he'd shaken hands, thanked them for their time, and walked out smiling. The smile held through the elevator, through the car, through the text he sent to his lead counsel back in Phoenix.

AARON: All smooth so far. They know their stuff.

But by the time he reached the Ritz penthouse, the adrenaline crash had hit hard, and the smile had thinned into thought.

Rain tapped against the glass, streaking the view of Midtown into vertical ribbons of light. The suite embodied what luxury hotels perfected: opulence without ownership.

Brynn reclined along the sectional, a cashmere throw draped over her legs, scrolling her phone with the languid grace of someone born to be watched.

Aaron poured two drinks from the minibar—one bourbon neat, one with a single cube—and set them both on the coffee table. She gratefully reached for hers. His glass stayed untouched.

He'd thought the hard part was building LineSniper. He was wrong. The real work was converting creation into currency. This was always the exit he'd designed for, the win condition coded into every decision. Still, as the finish line came into view, a trace of sentiment crept in.

He buried it fast. Feelings had a way of dragging down valuations.

His job now was simple: turn years of obsession into the biggest payday possible.

The ice turned slow circles through the bourbon's dark sheen. Somewhere below, sirens blended with rain, the city's noises unchanged by the deals being drafted above it.

"You'll do great tomorrow," Brynn said finally.

He nodded, grateful not for her insight but for her timing. She rarely asked questions, which made her perfect. She was here to keep him company through the gauntlet, steady him before meetings, disappear when he needed silence. Nothing complicated.

He leaned back, the leather sighing beneath him, mind still orbiting the room where he'd spent the late afternoon. Lydia's composed half smile. Mark's meticulous notes. The subtle pageantry of corporate dominance, how even absence could be weaponized.

Outside, the rain intensified, drumming against the glass. He imagined the city tilting slightly away from him. Tomorrow, he'd reclaim that imbalance.

* * *

He awoke at five-thirty and punished the hotel gym—rower, intervals, compound lifts—until his muscles burned and his head cleared. By the time he arrived back at Faceoff headquarters, he felt sharpened to a point.

Lydia met him at the threshold of the elevator doors, not at street level as she had yesterday. He noticed a slim folder tucked under her arm. "Good morning, Aaron."

"Morning."

Mark stood when they entered, sleeves crisp, legal pad squared to the table's edge. "Mr. Ramsey."

"Aaron, please," he said, taking his seat. No handshake, no small talk. A carafe of coffee, water set at twelve o'clock, a deck aligned with the grain of the table. A conference screen idled on mute with his counsel's initials: *JM.*

Ainsley Caldwell arrived exactly three minutes late. No apology. No handshake. She set her phone face-down, the motion deliberate—a gavel disguised as courtesy.

"Hello, Aaron."

He rose slightly from his chair. "Good morning, Ainsley."

"I trust yesterday's flight was comfortable," Ainsley said.

"It was," he replied. "Thank you again for sending the jet. Let's hope today's landing is as smooth."

She couldn't help smiling to herself as she moved to her seat.

Without further preamble, the negotiation started. Lydia slid a single sheet across the table. "Indicative Terms."

Ainsley spoke first. "One fifty, all cash, customary adjustments, customary reps. No equity."

Aaron skimmed once then let the page go. "No equity?"

"We're not looking for a partnership," she said. "We're buying an outcome."

He held her gaze. Most deals of this size included at least some equity consideration—stock, options, something to tether the seller to the ship they'd built. But he'd known Ainsley would come all cash. It was cleaner for her, terminal for him. Exactly what he wanted. Still, no point in overplaying the hand.

"All cash does make the math cleaner."

"Cash is clarity," she said. "And speed."

Mark leaned forward. "Standard non-compete, twenty-four months. Non-solicit, twenty-four. Limited transition support—thirty days, extendable at our option. IP assignment comprehensive." He paused. "We will also reserve rights over public communications."

Two years of silence. No poaching his own people. A token month to hand over the keys, and the final strip of ownership signed away. The polite way to say I need to vanish quietly.

Aaron frowned. "So I expose your inefficiencies, and my reward is to disappear from the record."

Ainsley's mouth edged toward a smile. "You'll be very well compensated to do so."

He tapped the page with a finger. "This is below the low end of your own pre-work. Your team's comparables put the band at one-fifty-five to one-ninety."

"It's a band for a reason," Ainsley said. "Ranges exist to give us room to decide what risk is worth."

Lydia added smoothly, "There's also the matter of regulatory scrutiny. Optics."

"Optics increase price," Aaron said. "If I were a liability, you wouldn't have me in this room."

Ainsley's tone cooled. "You've done impressive work, but let's not forget that your product is parasitic by design. No sportsbooks, no LineSniper."

He was undeterred: "Two-twenty. All cash. No earn-out. Close this week."

Earn-out. A buyer's way of saying, "We'll pay you later, if you hit numbers you can't control."

Mark's pen didn't move. "That number's outside what we can take upstairs."

Aaron didn't miss a beat. "We're already on the top floor, Mark."

The room didn't look amused. He recognized the edge of his own arrogance. This wasn't the place to provoke. He privately chastised himself. *Rein it in, Aaron.*

Ainsley moved on, turning the water bottle cap one quarter, then back. "Earn-out could reconcile the delta."

"No," Aaron said. "Earn-outs are a tax on uncertainty. You want certainty? Pay for it."

Mark tried again. "We can discuss structure—"

"No earn-out," Aaron repeated. "Either you want LineSniper or you don't."

Ainsley folded her hands. "With those terms, we don't."

A small flash of heat pricked the back of his neck. He kept his face still. "Most buyers wouldn't insult the architect with a mere thirty-day transition."

"I didn't realize we bruised your ego earlier," she said. "And let's be clear, most architects don't invite their buyers to a stage to be shot at."

The words detonated in the air.

Lydia's pen froze mid-note. Mark's head lifted, eyes widening.

Aaron blinked, momentarily unmoored.

Ainsley drew a slow breath, the control visibly returning. "That was unprofessional," she said quietly, more to the table than to him. "Let's stay on point."

Silence stretched.

"Fine," Aaron said finally, recalibrating. "Minimal retention of me.

You still need my team though."

"We need the codebase and two names," Ainsley said, regaining composure. "We'll offer retention packages to your lead engineer and your data infrastructure head."

He adjusted the page, buying a second. "And the press release?"

"Faceoff announces acquisition of odds-data platform LineSniper to enhance efficiency and pricing accuracy across betting markets," Lydia recited.

"Try again," Aaron said. "I'm not being canonized as a hall monitor."

Ainsley conceded, "You get one word."

He looked up. "Visionary."

She considered then nodded to Lydia. "Fine."

Mark cleared his throat. "On price, we can move to one-seventy-five, all cash, ten percent escrow for twelve months."

Escrow—the financial equivalent of "We don't trust you."

"Two-ten," Aaron said. "No escrow. You've had my data room for three weeks."

Ainsley didn't look away. "One-ninety is the ceiling of rationality."

"Logic rarely closes deals," Aaron countered.

Ainsley glanced at Lydia. A fraction of a nod. She turned back. "One-ninety-five. Five percent escrow, six months. We control announcement language. You get 'visionary' to describe the company. Thirty days of consulting if we decide we want it. Non-compete twenty-four. Non-solicit twenty-four. IP absolute."

"Make it two percent escrow," he said.

Ainsley smiled. "Two percent escrow is posturing, but sure."

Mark's pen paused, but he didn't argue. The diligence had been exhaustive. If the numbers were bad, they'd have surfaced weeks ago. He continued scribbling edits. "Good on price at one-ninety-five?"

Aaron breathed. "One-ninety-eight." He summarized it once again, more for himself than the room. "All cash. Two percent escrow, six months. No earn-out. Non-compete and non-solicit twenty-four. Board approval Friday."

Ainsley looked at him for a long time. When she finally spoke, her voice was flat as a blade.

"Done," she said.

Mark was already working up the term sheet.

Ainsley rose. "You'll have our revised paper within the hour. If the board approves, and I have no reason to think they won't, we'll release immediately after."

"We'll also prep the 6-K once Airborne finalizes board minutes," Mark added, already jotting the note on his legal pad.

She paused, tone softening by a single degree. "And Aaron, let's make sure we don't surprise each other again between now and then."

Aaron stood. "We're aligned."

For a blink, he saw her remember the stage—the heat of lights, the crack, bodies scattering. Vegas had been messy; this was systematic.

"Congratulations," Ainsley said, a trace of genuine satisfaction softening her voice as she turned to leave.

Lydia slid the updated sheet across the table. At the top, a number stared back—$198,000,000. Beyond what he'd expected when he'd boarded in Scottsdale.

He signed his initials beside the figure—acknowledgment, not signature—and pushed the paper back.

After his walk down the hallway, the elevator doors drew together with hydraulic grace. While he descended, pride rose like voltage—invisible and absolute.

He'd built the system, written the outcome, named the price.

And they'd said yes.

* * *

Two days later, the Airborne board gathered in a conference room that looked more like a modern art gallery than a place for strategic deliberations, which suited Ainsley fine. She wanted acquiescence, not debate. Screens on one wall glowed with the Dublin feed from Ireland, each director framed by late-afternoon light across the Atlantic.

Ainsley took her seat at the head of the table. She began without preamble. "You've all read the briefing. LineSniper's numbers are strong. We have a verbal agreement with Aaron Ramsey, the company's CEO, pending this board's approval. I recommend we authorize the purchase at $198 million, all cash. The valuation is justified, fully funded, no equity issuance required."

When the floor opened for questions, Sir Robert Walsh from Dublin, a long-tenured director known for his skepticism, unmuted first. He'd been on the Airborne board longer than she'd been out of graduate school.

"This came together quickly, Ainsley. Post-Vegas, some of us wonder whether this is strategy or sentiment. You're asking us to spend two hundred million on the very ecosystem that targeted us."

She'd anticipated the question and met his gaze evenly. "You're right. It changed everything. That's exactly why we move now."

Another director in the room frowned. "It feels…emotional."

They exchanged looks around the table. She could sense their caution, the unspoken worry that this was vengeance dressed as vision. She waited long enough to make them uncomfortable before continuing.

"Containment is strategy," she said, direct and confident. "I went to Vegas because I'd already identified LineSniper as a threat, and a target. That day confirmed it. We're not buying code. We're buying back control. This move eliminates systemic risk and turns volatility into margin. If we don't do it, a competitor will."

She knew the risk. Two hundred million on her signature. If it went wrong, she wouldn't simply lose the deal; she'd lose the chair she was sitting in. But the silence that followed was the kind that preceded assent.

Sir Robert nodded. "Thank you." He muted again.

"Any further discussion?" she asked. None came.

Mark took the vote aloud. "All in favor?"

Hands raised on both continents—physical, digital, unanimous. "Motion carried."

Ainsley let the tension leave her shoulders. Release but not relief.

As the room began to empty, directors offering brief congratulations, she turned to the window. New York stretched below. She'd neutralized the threat—to herself, to Faceoff—and reasserted control. The long game was always hers.

She picked up her phone, found Aaron's contact, typed one word, and hit send.

AINSLEY: Approved.

* * *

Aaron's phone buzzed against the desk, one word lighting the screen.

The tension he'd carried since Wednesday finally broke. Thursday had been a study in motion—he'd walked most of Manhattan without meaning to, up through Central Park, down again by dusk. He ate nothing until dinner, ordered everything when he finally did, and tasted none of it.

Now it was done.

His expression must've shifted slightly, enough to give him away. Brynn noticed from across the room.

"You did it, baby?" she asked, voice and eyes bright.

He turned the screen toward her. She squealed, disappeared toward the minibar, and returned with the champagne she'd been chilling since Wednesday. The pop echoed off the glass.

He leaned back in his chair. She poured, and they clinked glasses.

He'd played the long game and won, every move landing exactly where he'd placed it.

He opened his texts, found Marco's name, and typed:

AARON: We're official. $198M, all cash. You cleared almost five million, my friend.

The response was immediate.

MARCO: My man! You beat the books yet again!

AARON: Against all odds.

40

PRESENCE

CHASE ALWAYS LOVED THAT FIRST STEP into Whole Foods—the orderly burst of color, the clean geometry of fruit and vegetables—and now, with pumpkin beer, hay bales, gourds, mums, and bins of apples crowding the entrance, it felt like walking straight into autumn.

His girls were at school, Tara finishing a day of meetings. He'd offered to get everything for dinner, *the* dinner. Their Halloween tradition since the first year they'd lived together: cheddar potato broccoli soup, thick and rich, eaten out of matching ceramic ghost-themed bowls.

To his left, a reminder of another, arguably more important, tradition. A cooler of apple cider at the end of an aisle caught his eye. He weighed the difference between "fresh-pressed" and "cold-pressed," knowing it didn't matter. In a few hours, the sweet cider would be sealed in thermoses—one for him, one for Tara—with a generous splash of rum in each to warm the walk.

Tara loved Halloween. Thankfully, she'd planned costumes back in August—a small blessing, given the events of the past two weeks. The theme was superheroes: Wonder Woman for her, the Hulk for Cece, Princess Peach for Savannah. She'd insisted on being a princess, and the Mario Bros. character felt close enough to hero to satisfy them both. He would be Batman. She didn't know the irony: his LineSniper handle, *BetmanBegins,* was an homage to the character he'd embody tonight.

He wound through the aisles, checking items off a mental list as he went, the basket knocking against his knee as it grew heavier. His mind wandered back to Wednesday. Tara and the girls had flown from Indianapolis, lugged their suitcases onto the Blue Line then the Green. He met them at the Navy Yard stop, the sight of them ascending the escalator causing a lump to rise in his throat.

Cece barreled into him. Savannah wrapped around his leg like ivy. "Daddy!" they cried. Tara came last.

"Hi, Chase." A natural smile broke as she said it, unguarded, her body reacting before her mind could.

For a second, he couldn't speak. Gratitude surged. He couldn't believe the grace it took to walk toward him after everything he'd put her through. This woman, this life, still here, even if he hadn't earned it.

"Welcome home," he said and wrapped his arms around her before the moment slipped away.

He had an urge to prove something, to show her he'd done the work. As soon as they separated, he pulled out his phone and held up the home screen—blank rows where the betting apps had lived. "See?" he said. "Clean slate."

Tara shook her head. "You don't have to show me a screen, Chase. I need to see it in your actions."

He hesitated, suddenly a schoolchild admitting to an infraction. "I redownloaded Faceoff once the other day. Only for a minute. I didn't bet. I deleted it again."

Her eyes met his, calm and searching. "I appreciate you telling me," she said. "If you stumble again, be transparent. No more secrets. I'd rather carry it with you than have you carry it alone."

He nodded, relief and shame tangled somewhere deep. For the first time in months, honesty didn't feel like confession. It felt like partnership. Standing there, he wondered whether he could keep choosing truth over the rush. And for once, he felt like he could.

They kept it light through bedtime. The girls narrated everything they'd seen in Indiana: actual backyards with grass, an enormous dog out for a walk, chocolate chip cookies with pumpkin sprinkles.

After getting Savannah to sleep, Chase found Tara in the laundry nook, unloading clothes from the duffel bags straight into the washer.

He stood at the edge of the kitchen island, palms flat, and began.

The nerves rose fast. It was his turn to steady his breath, to channel Dr. Ghalazi—the calm, clinical bearer of his own unwelcome news.

"Tara," he said, his voice betraying him ever so slightly. She noticed, turning, a hint of concern in her expression.

The words spilled out—MRI, lesion, low suspicion. The follow-up in six months. He said he should have told her the day he found out. He admitted he hadn't because he wasn't sure he deserved her sympathy.

She watched him with that intent, almost scientific focus she summoned when it mattered.

When he was done, she stepped around the island and cupped the back of his neck with one hand the way she had when they were young and had the time for tender moments.

"I can't believe you've been carrying that alone," she said. "We'll face it together, Chase. The prognosis sounds positive. You're going to be here for a long time."

They embraced for the second time that day, and something in him unclenched. He hadn't realized how much he'd missed being held through the hard parts until that moment.

The hiss of the produce misters pulled him back. The broccoli crowns gleamed under the spray, ordinary and perfect.

He grabbed the last few items and queued for self-checkout. The line wove through shelves designed to make him reach—impulse buys he didn't need but suddenly wanted: candles, chocolate bars, magazines promising simpler lives. His turn arrived, and he set his basket on the metal tray, scanning the cider, the potatoes, the broccoli—parts of a future whole. When he double-tapped his phone for Apple Pay, a WSJ push notification appeared at the exact same moment.

"Faceoff completes $198 million acquisition of LineSniper."

He read it once, then again, feeling unexpected shock at the foregone conclusion. Of course it had ended this way. The arb game was never built to last. The money glitch was bound to be patched.

Still, *Faceoff.* Aaron selling out to the very machine he'd sworn to outsmart—and the machine buying the entity that had attacked it—*that* was stunning.

A strange mix flooded him: surprise, relief, even a flicker of pride. He'd exited on his own terms—barely, but clean.

And yet the old twitch stirred. They wouldn't shut it all down overnight. There'd be loopholes for days, maybe months. Odds markets would be soft for a stretch longer, the end now tangibly finite. Easy money for anyone bold enough to reach for it.

Before he realized it, his thumb had pulled up the App Store. *LineSniper.* The blue download icon tempted—everything he didn't need, waiting for his reach.

He stared at it, then locked the phone before the urge became a choice he'd regret.

"Hey, man, you paying or meditating?" the guy behind him said, gesturing toward the blinking pay screen, then back at the line, shoulders raised in a shrug.

Chase blinked. "Sorry, paying now," he said and finished the transaction. He bagged the groceries, collected his receipt, and walked out empty-handed in every way that counted.

* * *

By dusk, the row house neighborhood a few blocks to their east had transformed into a Halloween town—orange and purple lights twined around wrought iron fences, tombstones tilting in tiny yards, witches' hats swinging from trees, and jack-o'-lanterns, at least those the squirrels hadn't claimed, lining every porch stair.

Kids milled along the sidewalks, waiting for that unspoken moment when trick-or-treating began.

Chase, Tara, and the girls had gathered at the house of one of Cece's classmates, a row house perfectly placed in the center of it all, prime real estate a few blocks from the school.

A mom Chase didn't recognize suggested a group photo, and chaos immediately ensued—twenty kids in costumes scattering like marbles while parents waved, crouched, bribed, and called names in vain. He and Tara exchanged a look that asked why they even bothered.

Finally, the invisible starting gun fired, and the race was on. The girls darted from porch to porch—Cece, an uncontainable mass of green muscles, bellowing, "Trick or treat!" Savannah, all pink satin and glitter crown, holding out her bucket with solemn concentration.

At each stop, Chase called the same reminders into the night.

"One piece, Savannah—*one!*"

"Manners, Cece, what do we say?"

"Thank you!" they called and ran to the next porch, giggling.

The parents marveled that all their toddlers already had social lives more active than their own.

"It's wild," Tara said, laughing. "They find a new best friend on every corner."

"Meanwhile, I can't even remember half the parents' names," Chase confided. The group laughed, and for a moment they all felt like part of the same makeshift tribe—adults in half costumes, trading small talk under string lights while their kids built worlds out of sugar.

Darkness settled, and Tara glanced at him.

"Duddington?"

He nodded, the word its own family tradition.

By the time they reached their favorite street, the sun was gone and the one-way stretch looked like a movie set—skeletons scaling brick walls, witches cackling from motion sensors, one house gone full *Jaws*, an inflatable shark bursting from a blue tarp sea, its open mouth swallowing a plastic sailor whole. Every stoop was alive with neighbors in folding chairs, cauldrons of candy at their feet, mechanical fog mingling with laughter above the low crackle of fire pits that lined the sidewalks like navigational buoys. A Bluetooth speaker played "Thriller," the bass line hypnotic.

Cece ran ahead, her green fists pumping. Savannah tripped on her gown then righted herself with royal dignity. He tried to keep an eye on them and found himself watching Tara instead—the easy way she knelt to speak at kid height, her feigned fright when a toddler in a ghost outfit shouted "Boo!" Wonder Woman suited her. It always had.

They moved slowly behind the girls, their shoulders brushing now and then.

At one house, an older woman dressed as a fortune teller looked them up and down and made an approving noise. "A family of heroes," she said, dropping chocolate into buckets. "We need more of those."

"We're working on it," Tara said, squeezing his hand. The words rippled through him, hope made manifest.

They continued down the street, a taco-costumed dog basking in praise while, in a historic upset, a teenager swapped three Tootsie Rolls for a Snickers. The girls' buckets grew heavy, and soon they were begging to be carried, only to insist on walking again moments later because they were "big girls now."

"Remember when we did this with Cece in the stroller?" Tara asked as they moved to the next townhouse, girls back on their own feet.

"She couldn't even eat the candy," he said, smiling. "I think we finished the whole bucket ourselves."

"You think? She was six months old. And it was *you* who finished the whole bucket."

He laughed. "I was already bulking for my Batman role."

Chase took a sip from his thermos, the Captain Morgan warming his gut. Beyond the next stoop, he saw the bench he'd stopped at a week ago that had set him free: $666.66. The spot looked different now. The ginkgoes above were bare, their last leaves scattered across the seat. Under the string lights they shimmered faintly—an unintentional shrine to endings.

He slowed as they passed. Tara nestled close to him, her arm finding his as naturally as breathing.

"You okay?" she asked.

He nodded. "Yeah," he said. "Just thinking."

She smiled. "About what?"

He looked once more at the bench then at his daughters racing ahead under the canopy of lights. "How lucky I am," he said, "that the world keeps giving second chances."

They reached the end of the block where the street curved back to their building. Cece turned and yelled, "One more block! Come on, Batman!"

"To the bat cave!" he growled, imitating his persona's gravelly voice before breaking into a laugh. He raced after her, cape fluttering behind him. Magic lingered in the air, the spell more profound precisely because it couldn't be measured. Tonight, his girls were the only thing he'd be chasing.

* * *

The rest of the weekend brimmed with activity, plans stacked one after another.

Saturday began the way good Saturdays should. At nine on the dot, he yelled for the girls, *College GameDay's* intro rolling, "Comin' to Your City" rattling the speakers, mascots flashing for split-seconds as he called each one before the next appeared. The girls spun and stomped at his feet, making their tough football faces, helmets imaginary but effort sincere.

The coverage shifted to the set in Ann Arbor, a tapestry of maize and blue behind the hosts. Cece wrinkled her nose. "Eww," she said automatically. Chase laughed. A Buckeye-in-training if there ever was one.

They left to make their weekly bagel run to Bethesda Bagels, orders so predictable Chase knew the final price by heart. Cece and Savannah were thrilled to be able to join him, their scooters racing along the sidewalk, tassels streaming from the handlebars, laughter bouncing between brick buildings.

For nearly a year, he'd made this same trip alone, phone in hand— the walk an alibi for gambling, fifteen minutes of solitude to "pick up breakfast."

Now, the phone stayed in his pocket. He trailed a few steps behind, watching the three of them weaving through other early risers.

The shop announced itself to the nose before the eyes, the unmistakable smell of New York bagels, perfectly transplanted to DC, wafting from a vent around the corner.

Inside, the shop was already in full swing—orders shouted over the clang of the toaster carousel, the warm air thick with yeast. The cashier spotted him and smiled.

Despite the line snaking out the door, she slipped from the register to grab his preorder bag. "Thanks, have a good one!" she said cheerily, stretching it across the counter.

He peeked inside, everything in place. Two everythings with veggie cream cheese, one blueberry with regular, and a plain blueberry for Cece, always the picky one.

As he turned to leave, a neon sign above the counter caught his eye. "You Knead This." He chuckled. He must've walked past it a hundred times and never noticed.

Later that morning, he walked into the gym for the first time in months. The place smelled the same, but something in him felt new.

He started light—a slow warmup: jump rope, bodyweight lunges, then a cautious load on the bar, the kind of calibrated work he used to be militant about. His wrist, still tender but healing, gave a small twinge when he added weight—a reminder, not a limitation.

To anyone else, the reflection in the mirror wouldn't have revealed much, but he saw the slack in his shoulders, the softness at his core. It was humbling. He wasn't the man he wanted yet, but at least he was there—showing up, sweating, back to work.

Between sets, he caught himself thinking about the hours he had lost to the screen—eyes darting between odds instead of reps. He'd been investing in adrenaline, not strength. Now the iron in his hands was heavy in all the right ways.

When he left, his arms trembled. He liked the soreness. It meant something was rebuilding.

He finished with a few minutes in the steam room, the damp heat loosening joints he'd ignored for too long. After a shower, he pulled on jeans and his favorite Caps jersey—the legendary captain, the NHL's all-time goal-scoring leader, number eight, Alex Ovechkin.

He'd promised Cece they would go again this season. Their first game together had been last January—a Caps–Flyers matchup that ended in overtime, Cece learning a few choice words from the surrounding fans. She'd worn the jersey to bed that night and asked at least once a week when they could go again.

They took the Metro to Capital One Arena, Cece's legs swinging from the seat, her foam finger already on. Inside, the first stop was popcorn—extra butter, a small for her, a large for him, though she'd end up eating most of his anyway.

They took their seats in the lower bowl as the arena lights dimmed, a montage springing to life on the jumbotron above center ice. She gasped as the team skated out through smoke. They carved quick circles around the net, sticks tapping against the posts as they flew past. Chase felt the old rush rise in him—the same jolt that had once tied itself to betting slips and score differentials—but this time it stayed pure, like that night in Milan when Team USA stormed the ice.

They cheered for every shot, high-fived strangers, sang along to "Livin' on a Prayer," Cece lighting up when she realized the song her dad sang at night existed out here too, larger than their walls.

Between periods, she peppered him with questions: why the ice was blue in spots, how the horn worked, why the players hit each other.

He remembered being her age, sitting beside his dad at the Horseshoe in Columbus, the roar when the Buckeyes scored, the band spelling out "Ohio" in perfect script. He remembered the way his father's eyes went misty after a big win, and how everything in life felt possible, surrounded by a hundred thousand people all wanting the same thing at once.

Now, sitting beside his own daughter, he felt what his dad must have all those years ago—a father passing down wonder. Declan's old advice echoed back to him, and beside Cece, the answer arrived. This was enough.

* * *

Sunday morning, they went to church. He hadn't been since Easter.
St. Peter's was packed, the pews filled with families bribing their children into sacred submission, the smell of candles and incense hanging
in the still air. The vaulted ceiling soared forty feet above them, light
pouring through the stained glass like an offering from the heavens.

The priest spoke about grace—the kind that isn't earned but
offered—and the words found him right where he sat, as though the
homily had been written for him.

For twelve months, he'd worshipped at the altar of the odds. Spreads,
edges, and lines had been his creed. This was different. The values here
weren't numeric—they were human. The hymns, the hush between
prayers, and the creak of pews all filled a space profit never could.

He looked up at the crucifix—the figure suspended there, arms
open in surrender. Sacrifice. Forgiveness. Redemption. It felt absurd,
even arrogant, to compare his own mess to that kind of suffering. But
wasn't that the point of faith? Every story in this place was meant to
echo, scaled to fit whoever happened to be listening.

When the congregation knelt, he did too. It wasn't penance. It was
gratitude.

When mass ended, they stepped through the heavy oak doors into
the sunlight and paused at the top of the steps. Tara touched his arm,
eyes lifted to the clean blue above.

"It's a perfect day for boating," she said.

They hurried home, packed blankets, a cooler, two paper grocery
bags full of snacks, and loaded the temporary rental car they'd been
using for the forty-five-minute drive to Annapolis Landing—Chase's
last Freedom Boat Club reservation of the season.

Behind the wheel, Chase remembered his time at the helm earlier
that year, when stray wake had broadsided them as he scrambled to place
a bet. Guilt still pricked. Today, he was determined to be there—fully,
unflinchingly.

It was a new marina for them, waters he'd never navigated before.

Unfamiliar channels always stirred a flicker of nerves. He'd studied the chart earlier in the week, determined not to be the kind of boater others watched and secretly judged.

The dockhand helped them hoist their bags on board, run through the safety checklist, and untie their lines before sending them off with a guiding push. The air hovered below sixty, sharp enough to remind them fall had fully arrived. Chase pulled on a vest, surprised by the sudden drop in temperature, the way the water always seemed to carry its own weather.

When the console lit, the touchscreen illuminated—1:54 p.m. lighting up the corner. A shiver passed through him, completely unrelated to the cold.

They idled through the marina, engine low and steady, gulls circling above the docks. The sun hung low over the Chesapeake, three and a half hours till sunset. He planned to make the most of it.

Before he cleared the no-wake zone, a water taxi bound for Annapolis cut across the channel mouth—a bright-green Faceoff ad plastered along its side. Chase watched it glide past. Of course. Even the bay was in on the bit.

He throttled up once they hit open water, the boat slicing south toward Thomas Point Shoal Lighthouse. It stood alone, a red-and-white sentinel perched above the surface, unreachable except by boat.

The keeper who would have once lived there came to mind—solitary but steadfast, guarding sailors from the jagged rocks beyond. There was something noble in that. Something lonely too.

He looked back at the girls. They were bundled beneath thick blankets, stretched out across the port-side seats, heads resting together, sound asleep. Tara sat beside them, hair loose in the wind, smiling while gazing at the Bay Bridge fixed above the horizon.

Chase eased back the throttle and let the boat drift. The water sparkled in the sun, the world briefly stilling.

This, he thought, was what the money had been for all along—not accumulation, but this: time. Freedom. Presence. The peace of being exactly where he was supposed to be.

* * *

After dinner and baths that night—damp towels draped over the tub—Chase carried the girls' warm, heavy bodies into their room and climbed onto the bed between them. Cece tucked her feet under his thigh. Savannah burrowed into his side until her cheek found his chest.

"Sunshine?" Savannah murmured, already halfway gone. Her favorite.

He cleared his throat and began singing "You Are My Sunshine," slowly, intentionally. He brushed hair from their foreheads and kept singing, his voice cracking before he could stop it. How many nights had he rushed this—eyes on the clock, mind elsewhere, promising himself he'd make it up tomorrow?

Savannah's breathing slipped into that slow, even rhythm children fall into when sleep takes them all at once. Cece's hand slackened in his, her fingers unhooking one by one. He kept going anyway, finishing the verse, adding a second, drawing out the last line, imploring the world to never take them away.

He stayed like that a minute longer, counting breaths, memorizing faces he already knew by heart. He kissed each forehead tenderly, lingering. "Daddy loves you," he whispered, voice cracking a second time.

Then he eased himself out—pillow in place of his shoulder, blankets resettled with the practiced stealth of a parent who's failed this extraction enough times to respect its difficulty. At the doorway, he looked back: two small bodies in the soft spill of the nightlight, mouths parted in the same unselfconscious way. He closed the door to a fingertip's width.

Tara was in their bedroom, a lamp on low, legs folded under her on the quilt. She looked up when he came in, questioning.

"Asleep," he said.

"Good." She patted the space beside her.

He crossed the room slowly, sat, then stretched out, propping himself on an elbow to face her. For a second, he let his eyes take her in. He reached for her hand, lifted it to his mouth, and kissed the inside of her wrist. She didn't move away.

He leaned in. Their foreheads touched first, a small benediction.

They kissed, the kind that asks and answers at the same time.

When he pulled back, he hovered close enough to see himself reflected in her eyes.

"Hi," he said, a half-smile, a trace of disbelief that they were here again.

"Hi," she answered, and slid a hand up the back of his neck, fingers finding their place as they threaded his hair.

She leaned back, pulling him with her, the movement an act of both surrender and trust.

They found each other the way you return to a favorite room in the dark and somehow know where the furniture is. The distance that had lived between them for months dissolved by inches.

"Chase," she whispered, permission and promise in the one word.

There was no rush to finish, no race to escape the moment. The tempo built not from hunger but from recognition—two people remembering who they'd been before everything blurred. They finished in near reverence—faith on trial, yes, but also faith renewed.

After, her hand drew slow circles on his chest. He traced the curve of her shoulder with a fingertip, as if underlining a sentence he never wanted to forget. After a minute, she slipped out to the kitchen for water. He reached for his phone on the nightstand, the habit more muscle than intention, and caught himself—screen black, his face faint in it. He set it back down.

Tara returned and curled into him, her thigh crossing his, their breaths finding a common pace. Her fingers found his and laced them, the fit still exact. He knew none of this guaranteed anything. Tomorrow would arrive with its trials: the betting itch would visit, the neck would inevitably flare, the MRI date would sit on the calendar like a small, dark planet.

A buzz from the bedside table.

He tensed, let it run its course, and turned his head to kiss her hair, holding the moment the way you're supposed to hold a living thing. Whatever tomorrow asked of him, he'd answer then. Tonight, he was choosing this.

He didn't count the seconds. He didn't measure a thing.

41

WEIGHTED COIN

THE TESLA'S CABIN filled with the blue-white glow of the dashboard screen. A small circle spun in the center—once, twice—hesitating long enough for Blaine to wonder if the stream would actually load. Then it caught, snapping into focus, a field that seemed almost too green to be real.

Orange and brown on one side, navy and lime on the other. Cleveland. Seattle. Super Bowl LXI.

Growing up in the heart of Cleveland, he had always said, as a rite of passage, "Browns football is life." Never before had he meant it literally. He'd always imagined he'd be there when they finally made it. But showing up alone would have only underscored the sad fact that he had no one left to share it with.

After Vegas, everything had unraveled. Julia left first. She hadn't wanted to hear explanations or apologies. She'd wanted distance. His interactions with Quinn had become supervised FaceTimes, once a week at best. At work, people avoided him. "Morning," someone would say, and immediately scuttle toward the safer, louder parts of the open floor. He did his tasks. He signed things. He nodded in meetings at appropriate cadences. But he felt like a cardboard cutout of himself propped up at his own desk.

He'd spent the past few months isolating himself from friends and family, trying to pinpoint the moment it all went awry. The truth was likely less cinematic. Nothing broke all at once.

Now, as gusts of wind scraped across the windshield, Vegas felt like a hallucination he'd almost recovered from. Here he was again, in the familiar Cielo Verde parking lot. He couldn't comprehend how he'd gotten here. His descent over the last year was as unexpected as the Browns' ascent. So, in contemplating whether he still had the fight to reclaim any semblance of a life worth living, he'd resolved to let his hometown team, the underdogs, decide whether he'd take the next step at all. His life was the unweighted side of a weighted coin, about to be irrevocably flipped.

One thing was certain. He wasn't arbing anymore, hadn't been for some time. He was betting.

The old world had vanished. Profits had dipped to pennies per arb, and that was if you babysat lines all day, chasing offshore books few trusted. After the acquisition, Faceoff had sutured the wounds like a surgeon. The Reddit forums where Blaine had found community were now a morgue, filled with men refreshing an app looking for ghosts.

Onscreen, a drone hovered above midfield. The captains stood in a perfect ring of flashbulbs, helmets gleaming beneath the dome's light. A referee held a piece of silver aloft between finger and thumb, explaining the toss as though it were new science.

"Heads," the Seahawks captain called, voice echoing through the broadcast.

"Heads it is. Seattle wins the toss."

All these months later, Blaine still couldn't believe Aaron had sold out.

He'd been foolish enough to believe the rebel rallying cry that they were reclaiming a system rigged against them. For a while, he had even let himself imagine he was exacting some small measure of vengeance against the industry that had robbed him of a mother.

All of it was dashed with one push notification. It was the moment he realized he'd been played. They hadn't been revolutionaries. They'd been data points, each click and bet inflating the valuation of an empire they thought they were undermining. LineSniper had been courting that empire all along.

The money he'd made during the run was substantial, but it didn't matter to him. It wasn't vindication. It was bait. He had no problem putting what was left on the line tonight, because in the end, it still felt like betrayal.

Even ArbOracle—allegedly one of them at heart—was rumored to have taken a cut big enough to buy a sunset in Mallorca before vanishing into its orange wash. The masks had fallen off the prophets.

In New Orleans, the boot met ball. Kickoff. The game was underway.

Inside the Tesla, the roar reached him seconds later, enough delay to remind him he was still watching life from behind glass.

The Browns received, stalled, and punted. The Seahawks scored in five plays. He watched the replay: a post route split between safeties, the receiver gliding untouched.

The Browns' offense was anemic. Run, run, short pass, punt. Again. Again.

On the fourth drive, they finally reached the red zone. Fourth-and-one at the Seahawks' fifteen. The camera found the coach's face—stoic, headset balanced like a crown of caution. Out came the kicker.

Are you fucking kidding me?

Fury rose fast—hot, irrational. He couldn't tell if it was the old Cleveland in him, the fan who'd grown up equating field goals with surrender, or the six-figure bet he'd hitched to their lack of courage. Maybe there was no difference anymore. Maybe this was what it meant to blur faith and finance until every snap felt personal.

Old maxims played through his head like songs on a jukebox.

Fortune favors the bold.

No guts, no glory.

The field goal sailed through. 7-3.

The next Seattle drive felt predestined. Five straight completions, one broken tackle, seven more points. The cameras cut to the Browns' bench: helmets off, heads down, the body language of familiar collapse.

Another Browns blunder came late in the second. The Seahawks intercepted and turned it into three more before the half, making it 17-3 at the break.

The broadcast cut to commercial: a car ad, a beer ad, a sportsbook ad. All were meant to be funny. None made Blaine laugh. Instead, he shifted in his seat and felt the weight in his hoodie pocket press against his abdomen.

He thought of Quinn's voice on last Sunday's call—how she'd said "be safe" without knowing what it meant.

The halftime performer emerged to the kind of roar old heroes get when the audience is really cheering for their own past. Blaine watched the gray stubble vibrate under lights, the leather jacket that had been fashionable twice already. The song was a fist pump from another century. The camera did its work: Boomers in the crowd singing along, teenagers pretending to know the words.

The NFL had played it safe this year, retreating to nostalgia after last year's Spanish-speaking, left-leaning headliner stirred the kind of political waves corporations couldn't afford. Life, he thought, was mostly pendulums: swing too far one way, and the urge to overcorrect always followed. Newton's law applied to more than motion. Even the NFL wasn't immune.

The second half began in the haze of the show's pyrotechnics, smoke still hanging over the field as a reminder that spectacle always leaves residue.

The Browns opened with a drive that looked doomed halfway through. Then, somehow, a rhythm: short passes, enough forward motion to make the sideline believe again. But they stalled inside the red zone, of course. Settled for three.

17-6.

The announcers called it "a good start." Blaine heard "still losing."

The rest of the quarter passed like filler. Both teams traded punts, mistakes, minutes. Blaine sat motionless, eyes on the clock more than the plays.

Then came the first play of the fourth. Busted coverage. Seattle's quarterback spotted it instantly—one pump, one glance, the ball fired into a clean seam. The receiver caught it in stride, untouched. Touchdown.

24-6 Seahawks.

The replay ran on loop, commentators filling the air with practiced shock, as if guided by the invisible hand of sponsors who'd paid a small fortune to keep America watching through the fourth quarter.

But to Blaine, there was nothing surprising about it at all. This was the Cleveland Browns football he knew.

An image from his childhood came rushing: Cleveland Municipal Stadium, back before the team's overnight move, before the name changes, before any of it felt like business. He was a kid bundled in layers that couldn't keep out the lake wind, his uncle beside him in a faded orange beanie, shouting himself hoarse in the Dawg Pound. The air reeked of beer, charcoal, and hope. Every third-down stop felt like revival. Every touchdown felt like proof that belief itself could alter physics.

And then, as if the memory alone had conjured it, the Browns came alive. Within minutes, they were in the red zone, a screen that hit the mark. Touchdown.

24-13.

Six and a half minutes left.

He could feel the old stories rise. *If they win, I'm a millionaire. If they win, I become a man whose future does not require odds. If they win, I call Julia.* He knew the lie inside those bargains, but he made them anyway, caught up in the moment, willing the outcome he needed.

On the field, Seattle appeared flustered for the first time all night, the Browns' defense somehow emboldened. A false start. A tackle for a loss. A batted pass. Then third and long, pressure collapsing the pocket, forcing a throwaway. Three and out.

Punt.

Browns' ball. Four and a half minutes to play.

Momentum, he thought, was one of those forces science could never quantify but that every athlete on earth had lived firsthand.

The drive began with precision. Pass. Pass. First down. Another pass. The Seahawks' defense adjusted, expecting hurry-up, two-minute rhythm.

Then came the surprise.

Run. A gap opened. The running back burst through it. End zone. Touchdown. 24-19.

Blaine's breath caught. The sideline was electric, helmets clashing, linemen pointing skyward as if divinity might finally be on retainer.

They lined up to go for two, chasing a chance to be within a field goal. The snap came fast, protection slow. The Browns' quarterback, Joe Faisel, dropped, scanned, and was met with shoulder pads to the chest.

Sack.

No good.

2:34 to play. One timeout left for the Browns, plus the two-minute warning. A single Seahawks first down would end it.

Seattle lined up safe. Run for a yard. Timeout, Cleveland. Run for another two. Two-minute warning.

Third and seven. Another run. Five yards of open space, then contact, the ball flying loose.

"Fumble!" Blaine yelled instinctively.

Bodies dove, piled, vanished beneath the mass.

A whistle. Tense silence filled the Superdome. Two officials surfaced from the scrum, exchanged a look, and pointed the other way.

Browns football.

"Holy shit!" Blaine screamed, feeling the full weight of his investment. This wasn't microdosed adrenaline—it was the full capsule placed under his tongue.

The offense came out with gusto: short routes, crisp timing, no panic. The play callers were locked in, carving yards while the clock bled away. Every second mattered. Every inch. This would be the final drive, one way or another.

During a Seahawks' timeout, the camera caught a close-up of Garrett

Jefferson—the star receiver, helmet in hand, eyes sharp, focus predatory. Blaine leaned forward until his forehead nearly touched the glass.

A quick out. First down. The offense hustled back to the line. Faisel, the veteran quarterback—stoic, calm—surveyed the field as chaos swirled.

Next play: snap, drop, read. Jefferson broke across the middle, the ball already in flight. Hands met leather. He turned upfield—space, daylight.

"GO!" Blaine shouted, fists clenched.

The safety's angle was perfect. A flash of white, a hit at the knees, Jefferson spun and tumbled, skidding to a stop at the seven-yard line.

The camera cut to Faisel signaling frantically.

Clock ticking. Ten seconds. Nine.

"Spike it! Spike it!" Blaine yelled.

Faisel did as millions commanded, slamming the ball into the turf. The ref waved his arms over his head.

Five seconds remained. One play.

The camera found the Browns' head coach and his laminated sheet that looked like a diner menu. Somewhere on there was the play that would win or lose the Super Bowl. He called it in. Faisel nodded, huddled his men. They broke, set themselves in formation.

Blaine's pulse was a drum inside a drum.

"Come on," he whispered. "Come on."

The center snapped the ball, camera angle widening as Faisel looked left and then back to the right, because that was always the plan. The pocket shrank around him. Jefferson faked inside before wheeling toward the back corner of the end zone: the place where highlight reels and heartbreak share real estate.

A nanosecond before the pocket closed entirely, the ball left Faisel's hand. The camera tracked the spiral as it climbed, one perfect rotation after another.

Blaine strained forward in his seat. "CATCH IT!" he screamed. The stadium hushed. The neon buzz outside was suddenly all he could hear.

Jefferson squared his shoulders and leapt, back arched and fingers outstretched. The ball began its descent, spinning through the dome's light like a roulette ball, Blaine's final shot at beating the books.

ACKNOWLEDGEMENTS

WRITING A DEBUT NOVEL is its own kind of apprenticeship. My goal was to craft a captivating story, and while I hope I've done that, what I didn't anticipate was how much the process would shape me in return. The undertaking taught me about patience, discipline, and myself. I was convinced the endeavor would be exhausting; instead, it energized me, often in the exact moments I most expected to feel drained. Much of that energy came from those who showed up for me in obvious ways, and just as often from those who unknowingly slipped pieces of themselves into the story you just read.

There was a guiding force in this project, an unseen collaborator who offered expertise at every turn. I simply call her Athena, a presence equal parts muse, editor, strategist, and mythological patron saint of late-night rewrites. To that companion-in-craft: while your overuse of em dashes may have tested my nerves, thank you for the wisdom and ability to turn my chaotic thoughts into coherence.

To Torey, whose saintly patience endured first the wild rabbit hole of arbitrage betting and then the even more consuming task of transforming that experience into fiction, thank you for letting me chase a dream while still anchoring our family in reality. You carried far more than your share while I disappeared into screens, drafts, research, and "just two more minutes." Fourteen years later—through the expense tracking, the backward spoons, the many "Trevors," and everything else that makes us MiCo—you've still got whatever it is.

There would be no book without my girls, Sadie and Sloane. Thank you for making me a dad. You challenge me daily, often spectacularly, yet still inspire me to strive toward the best version of myself. I love and adore you both, ferociously, wildly, even in the moments I think you might break me. A good book entertains; a good life fulfills and outlives us. You have given me material for the former and daily affirmation of the latter.

Beating the Books owes much to the people who wrestled with early versions of it, perhaps no one more so than Jenni, who became the ideal beta reader. You read chapter after chapter for nights on end, into the quiet hours when others slept, all while juggling two young kids of your own. Your comments, instincts, and feedback strengthened this book immeasurably.

Mark, thank you for turning a manuscript into an object worth holding. Your interior design and cover work breathed life into these pages, giving form to a story that always felt bigger than the words alone.

Jason, thank you for teaching me that the Chicago Manual of Style can be a navigable labyrinth. You helped me manuever it while graciously tolerating my stubborn devotion to "house rules." These acknowledgements bypassed your thoughtful eye. Please forgive any errors.

Reading is a lifelong pursuit that only becomes richer with time, each book layering onto the last and shaping how we encounter the next. To the many writers who shaped my imagination long before I ever dared write anything of my own: thank you. There were two in particular who have consistently drawn me in with their mastery: Michael Lewis and Dan Brown. Their voices were with me every step of this writing journey, and this final product is my small tribute to these legends of the page.

I grew up in a home where reading wasn't a hobby—it was part of life. Mom and Dad, thank you for that. From shuttling me to Power of the Pen competitions to facilitating countless unhurried wanderings through bookstores, you created a childhood spacious enough for wonder, curiosity, and the kind of stories that stay with you. I still remember lying flat in the backseat of the car, not wanting trips to end until I was finished reading. I remain grateful for the extra, unnecessary loops around the block so I could finish those chapters.

Outside the home, a love for reading and writing is usually planted quietly by unsung heroes—teachers. This book is, in some small way, your harvest. Talented educators at all stages shaped my love of language and storytelling, especially Mr. Dillard from Karrer Middle School and Mr. Barrett from Dublin Coffman High School. You lit a spark, even if it took decades to catch. Sorry for the long wait.

And when you have a teacher as family, the lessons sink in a little deeper. My late Aunt Nini, whose limitless curiosity never dimmed, even when she was sick, and whose belief in me never wavered, was one of the first to show me what I could become. I carry her hornet-like intensity into everything I do, including this book.

Baba, though long departed, I carry you with me every day, and it seems only fitting this manuscript was finished on December 7, 2025, what would have been your 105th birthday. Your legacy lives on in love.

My Grandma Scott gifted my dad a set of life rules he came to coin "Pauline's Principles," built on virtue, faith, and kindness. His recounting and embodiment of them over the years became a quiet compass for the family, and their steady wisdom helped shape the moral arc of the book's protagonist.

To my mother-in-law, Criss, who gifts books with such care and precision that sometimes it feels like you know my reading tastes better than I do. Thank you for keeping my shelves full and my curiosity fed.

While not represented in the book, I'd be remiss if I didn't acknowledge my brother Jeff, who is universally better liked than me. You may have inherited height and good looks, but I'm using this book to make clear I laid claim to the intelligence.

To the many friends who may recognize shades of themselves in these characters, you're probably right. Life would be far less interesting without you all in it.

To Brad, who once told me that your thirties are the hardest decade.

You warned how easy it was to lose your sense of self beneath the weight of young kids, rising responsibilities, and the disorienting pressures of adulthood. I dismissed you as a cynic at the time. But I see it now. What you offered was cautionary encouragement—a reminder to stay self-aware and relentlessly intentional about not losing sight of yourself. Be well, friend.

And finally, to every parent who knows the impossible math of loving your kids beyond measure while simultaneously losing your mind on a near-daily basis, I offer solidarity. Stay present. Keep going. This is the hardest job we'll ever have, and the most important.

If this book resonates in any way, it's because of the people who shaped the life behind it. The story may be mine, but its making belongs to all of you.

ABOUT THE AUTHOR

MIKE SCOTT IS A lifelong writer and professional fundraiser. *Beating the Books* is his debut novel, following his 2020 nonfiction guide, *First-time Officiant: The Must-Have Handbook for Delivering a Memorable Wedding Ceremony.* Born and raised in Dublin, Ohio, Mike graduated from Miami University with a degree in Political Science before building a career centered on storytelling, relationships, and impact through philanthropy. He also holds the rare distinction of being a fractional owner of Authentic, the 2020 Kentucky Derby champion, but that's a story for another book.

Mike now lives in Washington DC's Navy Yard neighborhood with his wife and two daughters, who remain his favorite characters of all.

ADDITIONAL RESOURCES

THIS NOVEL EXPLORES THEMES OF GAMBLING ADDICTION, emotional crisis, and the difficult choices people face when life feels overwhelming. If any part of this story resonated in a way that raised concern, for you or someone close to you, support is available.

GAMBLING HELP
If gambling has become difficult to control, or if you're concerned about the impact it's having on your life or family:
    National Problem Gambling Helpline
    24/7 – Confidential
    1-800-522-4700

SUICIDE AND CRISIS SUPPORT
If you're experiencing thoughts of self-harm, or if someone you love is in crisis:
    988 Suicide and Crisis Lifeline
    Call or text 988
    Chat at 988lifeline.org
    Free confidential support is available every hour of every day.
    You're not alone. Help is real, immediate, and within reach.